LE
TIMES

A R DANCE

**ARUNDEL
BOOKS**

First published in Great Britain in 2011 by
Arundel Books, 2 Audon Avenue, Chilwell,
Nottingham, NG9 4AW
www.arundelbooks.co.uk

The right of A R Dance to be identified as the author of
this work has been asserted in accordance with the
Copyright, Designs and Patents Act 1988

This novel is entirely a work of fiction. All characters and events portrayed, other
than those clearly in the public domain, are fictitious and any resemblance to real
persons, living or dead, is purely coincidental.

ISBN 978-0-9558133-1-3

Typeset in Garamond 11pt

Printed and bound in Great Britain by
Cox & Wyman Ltd. Reading, Berkshire

In memory of John Brunton
1954 – 2009

A talented writer and a highly respected journalist.
But most of all a very good friend.

AUTHOR'S
HISTORICAL NOTE

Leen Times is the sequel to *Narrow Marsh* and many of the characters portrayed in that book will be found in the pages that follow. And like *Narrow Marsh, Leen Times* is also set mainly in and around Nottingham, during the 1820s and 1830s. These years saw the continuing expansion of Nottingham into an industrial town, still based primarily on its traditional hosiery industry.

But behind the outward appearance of increasing industrialisation and wealth, there remained a large underclass who were forced to endure appalling housing and poor working conditions, had few rights, and nobody to speak up for them in Parliament.

It is against this background that *Leen Times* is set, and keen historians will recognise some of those events which constituted much of Nottingham's tumultuous and turbulent history: the 'twist net fever' of 1823-25, when fortunes could be made or lost overnight; the banking crisis that followed, leaving many families penniless; and the prolonged struggle for parliamentary reform and the vote, culminating in increasingly violent agitation, riots and the burning of Nottingham Castle.

However, readers might wonder whether I have gone a little too far in mixing fact and fiction, and I should perhaps apologise for misleading anyone into believing that Nottingham's first railway reached the town earlier than the Midland Counties Railway, which opened in 1839. *The Nottingham and Leen Valley Railway*, as portrayed here, is entirely a figment of my imagination. There never was such a line, nor was such a line ever proposed. But I trust that you will accept this piece of dramatic licence as an integral and important part of the plot.

CHAPTER ONE

—

NOTTINGHAM 1825

'Charles, come away from the water's edge. How many times have I told you?' The lad, a blue-eyed, curly-headed boy of almost three years looked up at his mother and reluctantly ran back from the edge of the canal, following her towards the door of a house that stood some way back from the towing path. His mother could only be described as beautiful, with a fine slim figure, green-eyed and golden-haired; and she looked totally out of place amid the hustle and bustle of the canal wharves. The only women normally to be found here were the wives and daughters of the boatmen, some of whom took their families with them on their journeys simply because they had no home other than the boats. But they were generally dirty and poorly dressed, their heavily lined faces, dark skins and worn demeanour the result of long days of unremitting toil. Apart from them, ladies of a certain profession from the poorer parts of the town, particularly from nearby Narrow Marsh, were known to frequent this area and would sometimes appear at night, plying their trade and hoping to earn some money from the boatmen who did not have their womenfolk with them.

'Come along inside now, Charles. Supper is nearly ready and your father will be back soon, and then it's off to bed for you.'

He followed her into the house, and through a door leading from the hallway into a large sitting room, comfortably furnished and showing all the signs of being the abode of a well-to-do family. Beyond the door, next to an ornate fireplace, stood a cot in which slept a child, a girl not yet a year old. A cheerful fire burned in the hearth, for although it was early summer the day had been cool. The room had a large bay window in the form of a semicircle, consisting of a series of individual window frames, each composed of small, oblong panes, features which were duplicated in the bedroom above.

Within the bay, fitted against the wall, was a padded loveseat upholstered in burgundy velvet, and from here one could command a clear view of all the comings and goings of both people and boats. This was no mere chance arrangement, for the house had been built almost thirty years previously by a wealthy Nottingham hosiery manufacturer and merchant, along with the adjacent warehouse and wharf, the house being provided for the wharfinger and his family.

The canal had finally reached Nottingham and opened in 1796, and the merchant had immediately spotted an opportunity to widen his commercial activities. Not only would the cost of importing his raw materials be reduced, as would be the cost of transporting the finished articles throughout the kingdom, but he judged that there was money to be made from this new mode of transport. He reckoned that if he owned and operated his own warehouse and fleet of canal boats, he could prosper even more. His shrewd foresight did not let him down and for almost twenty-five years the undertaking prospered, until his sudden and untimely death, whereupon his widow declared she had no further interest in any of his businesses, and decided to sell them all and retire to spend her remaining years with a spinster sister at Buxton.

It was a sizeable enterprise with an entrance off Canal Street, wide enough for the biggest carts and wagons to come and go. The premises afforded a long frontage to the canal with a side cut leading to a dry dock where boat repairs could be carried out. Adjacent to the side cut stood a large warehouse for the storage of goods delivered or awaiting transhipment, stabling for the boat horses and an office where all the administrative and clerical work was dealt with. At the rear of the wharf stood the house, a substantial brick-built property with a large sitting room, dining room and kitchen on the ground floor, four large bedrooms on the first floor, and further rooms in the attic for the use of servants. At the back of the house was a washhouse, along with all the other usual outhouses one would expect to be provided for a residence of such proportions.

Such were the premises, by now rather run-down and neglected, which had been advertised for sale in the Nottingham Journal in November 1821, and which a young man by the name of William Daniels had subsequently purchased for the princely sum of four hundred and fifty guineas, much to the astonishment (and, it has to be said, a degree of chagrin) of some of the principal merchants and traders of the town, and which was the subject of much discussion, debate and comment amongst the devotees of the Assembly Rooms on Low Pavement. Because, as was pointed out, nobody amongst the commercial fraternity knew much about him, other than the fact that he had at one time been wanted by the law for arson.

He was certainly not counted amongst those who regarded themselves as the leading lights of the town, and at the time he was only twenty-one years of age. Not only that, but it had been confirmed that his father was a mere framework knitter living in Narrow Marsh, so the only explanation was that his four hundred and fifty guineas had been ill-gotten. As is often the case when rumours abound, some snippets of truth had been worked on imaginatively by the rumour-mongers, one of whom stated that Daniels had been living in France and that his wealth could only, therefore, have been acquired by some underhand dealings with the French Government. Which, as everyone knew, was not to be trusted, particularly following the revolution there and the subsequent wars, whereby so many Englishmen had lost their lives in defending the country against the advancing hordes of Boney's army.

The facts of the matter were, of course, somewhat different. It was true that William's father was a framework knitter living in Narrow Marsh, and that William had lived for some time in France, where, unbeknown to his detractors, he had extended his knowledge and learning of languages, mathematics, history and sciences to a degree rarely found in one so young and from such a humble background.

But more importantly, he had recently saved the life of Abigail, the daughter of a wealthy factory owner, Nicholas Brown, from the murderous attack of a spurned suitor, one Josiah Sidmouth, knight of the realm no less, who even now was serving out a prison term in His Majesty's convict colony of Van Diemen's Land. For when Josiah had finally realised that Abigail would not be his, he decided that she would be nobody else's. The whole episode had been extremely embarrassing and particularly painful for Nicholas to bear, for Josiah had been his friend and business partner for many years, and Nicholas had hoped that his daughter would one day agree to become Lady Sidmouth. But his hopes had been dashed when she had fallen hopelessly in love with a common labourer, an employee at one of his warehouses, the young William Daniels. And this was a liaison that Nicholas, his wife Mary and Abigail's brother Peter were adamant could never be allowed to flourish.

Any girl less headstrong than Abigail would have buckled under her parents' determination to forge the match with the suitor of their choosing, but Abigail was not of that mind. And when she and young William had eloped, it was Josiah and Peter who had been instrumental in tracking down the lovers before they could marry. Abigail was soon returned to the bosom of her family, but to the dismay of both Josiah and Peter (who had come to hate William as much as Josiah did), William had escaped. And even when Josiah, with Peter's help, had managed to arrange for William to become the subject of an arrest warrant for the arson of one of Nicholas Brown's warehouses, Abigail still refused to believe he was guilty, and steadfastly rebuffed Josiah's continued amorous advances. It was then, when all seemed lost for William, and only a matter of time until he would surely be arrested, tried and hanged, that he had made his escape to France.

Eventually, after several years of heartache and anguish for Abigail and William, the truth came to light. William was at last proved to be innocent of any misdeed, and the part played by Josiah in the whole affair was revealed in the ensuing court case. It was at this point that Nicholas, who until then had believed that William was as guilty as his enemies had alleged, accepted that he was entirely blameless and deserved his sympathy. Not least because of what he had suffered, but more so because he had saved Abigail from a violent and savage attack which, had he not acted as he did, would undoubtedly have resulted in her death.

Consequently, Nicholas had agreed, albeit with some reluctance and misgivings, to his daughter's marriage to William. But there was still the enormous divide between their respective backgrounds and upbringing. For this reason, Nicholas had now withdrawn almost entirely from public life. His various enterprises - his hosiery and lace factories and his coal mines - he still maintained, but he left the day-to-day management of these affairs in the hands of his trusted managers.

Nicholas was rarely to be seen now at the Assembly Rooms, but, had he attended more often, the truth of how William Daniels had come to purchase the canal business might have been explained sooner, and the wild rumour mill would never have been set in motion. Because the four hundred and fifty guineas William had paid came not from some dishonest dealings across the channel, but as a gift from a grateful father to the one who had saved his daughter's life.

The wedding had, perforce, been a modest affair, for it was not often that a match is made between the highest and lowest in society. The marriage was by licence, to avoid the reading of banns, and on a Wednesday in late January 1822, Abigail and William were married at St. Mary's Church in the presence of a congregation of close family and friends. Abigail's brother Peter, however, had not been present, and the fact that his regiment, in which he was a commissioned officer, had been in India was a convenience for which he was thankful. Nicholas had laid on a small celebration to follow at his house on High Pavement, after which those present had returned to their homes whilst the happy couple left for a short honeymoon in Newark, at the home of Abigail's Uncle George and Aunt Alice.

On their return to Nottingham, it was not to the grand house of Abigail's parents on High Pavement that they went, nor to the crowded tenement in Narrow Marsh where William's parents lived with their other two sons and four daughters, but to the wharfinger's house which William had purchased; for this was to be their new home.

Their first few months there were a hectic time. The house had been somewhat neglected and was much in need of repair. It was still suffering from damage caused some years before when a nearby wharf had been the scene of a terrible explosion which had killed several men and caused widespread devastation to surrounding property. Abigail, in particular, would never forget that incident, as it had happened the day after her eighteenth birthday, and her Uncle George, who with Alice had come to Nottingham for her birthday party, had gone to the canal side that day to visit a business colleague. For a desperate hour, the whole family feared that George might himself have been one of the victims, until he had arrived back at the house, safe and sound but awfully shaken and dishevelled and covered from head to foot in dust and dirt.

And now, here was Abigail, mistress of her own home and keen to make it as comfortable and welcoming as possible, and it soon became a scene of great activity with workmen carrying out renovation, and painters and decorators busy both inside and out.

Meanwhile, William had thrown himself into his new enterprise with enthusiastic vigour. Having acquired the wharf and warehouse, he needed to attract business, and much of his time was now devoted to this end. There were advertisements to be placed in the newspapers, advising the manufacturers and traders of the town of the services he could offer, not only for warehousing their goods but more importantly for transporting them. For one of the first transactions he had made was the purchase of four canal boats. He had acquired these, second-hand, with the help of Abigail's Uncle George, a long established river and canal carrier based at Newark, who knew everyone in the trade. William had worked for him for a while some years previously, and George was pleased to be able help his new in-law.

And then there were employees to be taken on; men to steer the boats, others to carry out repairs to them, labourers to work at the wharf loading and unloading the boats. There were horses to be purchased and men to look after them. And of course there was the paperwork to be dealt with. Orders to be received and acted on, delivery notes and invoices to be prepared, copied and despatched, enquiries to be answered, money to be collected and accounted for, bills to be paid and disputes with awkward customers to be settled. In short, all the myriad items of a clerical nature that the running of a business entails.

At first, William did all this himself, but as his enterprise began to expand, and he was having to spend more time away from the canal, visiting existing customers and seeking out new ones, it soon became apparent that he would need to employ someone he could trust to take charge of these affairs. He needed someone quickly, someone he could rely on and who had the appropriate knowledge and experience; and then he thought of John Collins. Good old John Collins. He was a neighbour of his parents, and William had known him since he was a child. He was honest and trustworthy, and William knew he would be the ideal man for the job.

For many years John had been employed as a clerk to a lawyer in the town, but when the lawyer had embezzled some clients' money, and been bankrupted and imprisoned, John found himself without a job. Using the contacts he had made during his time as the lawyer's clerk, he had managed to find employment with a contractor engaged in canal building and had travelled all over the country, dealing with his paperwork and correspondence. So, not only was he familiar with the canal system and its ways, but he was also well versed in bookkeeping and the efficient running of an office. But much more than that, William owed him a favour. For without John's invaluable help, William would never have been proved innocent of those charges brought against him. And like everyone who lived in Narrow Marsh he was not wealthy, and William reckoned he would welcome the income that such a position would provide.

John was delighted to be asked and readily agreed to become wharf manager, but on the strict understanding that William would also take on an assistant whom John could train and teach, eventually to replace him when his time came to retire. William could see the sense in this, and wanting to help his own family he offered the position to his brother Benjamin, some four years his junior. Benjamin was, by trade, a framework knitter, working at home alongside his father, James, to whom he had been apprenticed. But for many years the hosiery industry had been subjected to long periods of poor demand and low income with only occasional periods of prosperity, and James believed that the future would be one of gradual decline. And much as he did not want to lose his son, James realised that it would be a good move for him. And so, with his full blessing, Benjamin left to become the assistant wharf manager and went to live with William and Abigail.

Benjamin was a quick learner, much like William, and under the guidance of Mr Collins was soon learning all the tricks and trades of the business. This took a great weight off William's shoulders, giving him the time to attend to all those other tasks and problems which go along with running a thriving enterprise. And before long, William was able to offer a home and job to another of his siblings, his sister Millie, now seventeen. For his own household was about to increase in size.

Ten months after their wedding Abigail gave birth to their first child, a boy whom they named Charles. And when she became pregnant again, Abigail decided that she would need someone to help out with the household chores. At first, William was inclined to question the need. Servants were something he was not used to. He had grown up in a household with six brothers and sisters and not a servant in sight; his mother had managed to bring up all of them single-handedly. But Abigail had always been used to having servants around, and although she was quite capable and not afraid of hard work, William eventually gave way. They could afford to employ someone, and by taking on his sister he was again helping one of his own family.

In June 1824 Abigail gave birth to a daughter, who was christened Catherine, the same child who now lay asleep in her cot next to the fireplace, whilst her brother played quietly, waiting for his father to return home.

CHAPTER TWO
—
VAN DIEMEN'S LAND 1825

As the last dying rays of the sun gradually dipped behind the high mountain range to the west, a bedraggled group of twenty or so shabbily dressed convicts, some painfully barefooted, trudged slowly along the dusty track towards a tiny, remote settlement. Both in front and behind them, mounted on a motley collection of ragged-coated, dirt-encrusted horses and ponies, rode a small band of troopers, clad in threadbare scarlet tunics and carrying loaded muskets with bayonets fixed.

As it pressed on, ever so slowly, little sound came from this dejected assemblage of human and animal kind, other than the drag of hooves and feet on the uneven, rocky, road and the occasional order from the guards to 'move it on'.

At last they reached their destination, a cluster of weatherboard buildings, scattered haphazardly around a central compound, where a few horses were tethered to a post. The encampment was surrounded by a stout wooden fence, and a fading painted sign over the entrance gate declared this to be *Picton Convict Station*. At the sound of the approaching group, a large shaggy-haired dog raised itself lazily from the ground, looked round to investigate the source of the intrusion, then with an apparent look of disinterest sank once more to the ground and resumed its slumbers. A uniformed officer emerged from a door in one of the buildings and greeted the leading trooper. The two men exchanged a few words, and then on a command from the officer, the convicts filed slowly into one of the huts, where they each threw themselves onto narrow wooden bunk beds. A mattress of straw was their only comfort, and a horsehair blanket the only means of warmth for the long, cold nights.

They had dreamt of this respite from their labours since before six o'clock that morning when they had set out, as they had done every day for many months, on the five mile trek north to where they were engaged in the task of road building. The Lieutenant Governor of Van Diemen's Land, Colonel George Arthur, had decreed that a road was to be built from the island's capital Hobart, in the south, to Launceston in the north, and the thousands of convicts who had been sent to Van Diemen's Land afforded an available and free workforce.

This was just one of many gangs on the island, housed in convict stations, each presided over by armed military guards; and woe betide any man who dared to defy their orders or to step out of line. A guard's words were final and many a man had come to regret ignoring them. Since arriving on the island in 1824, Colonel Arthur had imposed a rigorous system of policing, and a combination of British soldiers and his own appointed police ruled the island with a rod of iron. Some of his appointed police were themselves convicts who had come to be trusted, and so zealous were they to retain their privileged position that they were amongst the most severe and hated members of the force.

Harsh indeed were the penalties for any infringement of the strict rules under which they survived (one could hardly describe it as living), and many a back bore a lasting and painful testimony to the result of disobeying, even slightly, those in authority. It was not uncommon for a man to receive a hundred lashes or more, until his back was almost devoid of flesh.

The ultimate penalty for continued law-breaking was hanging, but before that stage was reached there was always the dreaded Macquarie Harbour. Lying on the west side of Van Diemen's Land, this was where the worst offenders were sent. Here, men were kept in the most awful conditions and worked almost to death, cutting and felling timber, and many of those sent there would gladly have exchanged that hell-on-earth for a scaffold and rope round their necks. Those who did survive vowed they would never again do anything to earn a return to what many considered to be the worst place in the British Empire.

The Picton gang was relatively fortunate. They were not chained together, nor kept in solitary confinement. And in due course, each man might look forward to release from the road gang and assignment to a settler, although some of these could be as bad a master, regarding the convicts as little more than slaves.

The nearest township to Picton was Green Ponds, three miles to the south, and itself some thirty miles north of Hobart. Every week, a small band of convicts would be marched under armed guard to Green Ponds to fetch food and other supplies. Sometimes, depending on the harvest and the seasons, there could be a shortage of food, and rations would be strictly limited; and then it was always the convicts who were the last to be fed. As the road building moved slowly northwards, the men would have further to walk each day until eventually a new convict station would be constructed to house the captive labour force, along with barracks for the military.

The convicts consigned to Picton were a mixed bunch. Every one, to a man, had been sent here from the British Isles following his conviction. Most were English, but there was a smattering of Irish, Scots and Welsh. Many were poor working men, although a few were from a higher station in life and their crimes generally reflected their former standing in society. A schoolmaster from Wakefield had been sentenced to life for forging coins and had been lucky to avoid the gallows, whilst a lawyer from Devon was handed down a ten year sentence for defrauding some of his clients. His mistake was to have included, as one of his victims, a wealthy local landowner and Justice of the Peace.

A few murderers were numbered amongst them, having had their death sentences commuted to transportation for life, but most were here following convictions for theft, often committed out of necessity to feed their families. Some of the prisoners were innocent, the victims of a penal system which afforded the accused little opportunity for defence, and where judges and juries consisted of men of wealth and position who usually regarded crimes against property as being more serious than crimes against a fellow man. For the innocent, the daily work regime was hard to bear, for they did not even have the satisfaction of knowing that at least they had committed a crime.

And those unaccustomed to manual labour suffered more than most, the endless days of physical toil being too much for some to endure. It was not unusual for such men simply to sicken and ultimately die of fatigue, or to be found hanging from a tree or roof beam.

But of all the men now at Picton, there was one who stood out from the rest. If ever there was a man who really should have been unable to tolerate the harsh conditions, and whose change of circumstances was more extreme than any of the thousands sentenced to this convict life, it was a man known to those around him simply as 'Josh'. He was in his mid-forties and had a demeanour, bearing and language which singled him out from all the others, the inescapable and sure signs of good breeding and education. When he had first arrived in Van Diemen's Land he was still showing the outward signs of a lifetime spent in the pursuit of leisure, the consumption of the finest food and drink that money could buy, and of having experienced little physical exercise other than riding to hounds. Not even the three month passage from London had been sufficiently long or arduous to substantially reduce his girth.

And now, three years into his sentence, although he was somewhat lighter and thinner and his hands no longer so smooth-skinned, nothing could disguise the fact that he was from a totally different background to all the others around him. One would not have expected such a man to survive the rigours of the life he was now forced to suffer, but there was, within him, an overriding and burning desire that gave him the strength to endure the worst that life could throw at him - the desire for revenge against those whom he believed responsible for the circumstances in which he now found himself. And every night, when he returned to the convict station and threw himself on his bunk, he mentally crossed another day off his sentence, another day nearer to when he would receive his ticket of leave and once more become a free man. For he knew exactly what he intended to do once that day arrived. He had had many long days and nights to formulate his plans. All he must do now was to bide his time, remain patient and ensure he did nothing which might extend his sentence.

If ever any of the other convicts asked him his surname, he always said it was Smith, a common enough name. And his story was always the same, that he had been crossed in love and been sentenced for 'teaching the girl a lesson'. The guards knew, or cared to know, little more. As far as they were concerned he was just another convict to be guarded and kept at work for as long as he was under sentence. But the authorities, at least any who were inclined to examine the official documents, knew otherwise. They knew that his real name was Sir Josiah Sidmouth, an extremely wealthy owner of land and property in the north of Nottinghamshire, and that he had been sentenced at the Nottingham Quarter Sessions in November 1821 to seven years penal servitude for the crimes of being an accessory to an act of arson, but more seriously for the attempted murder of the daughter of his business partner.

There had been many in the court that day who believed he had been dealt with leniently. But Josiah could afford to employ a barrister to defend him, and he had spoken long and eloquently on his client's behalf. He had told the court of the extreme provocation that he had suffered at the hands of certain agitators who, if they had had their way, would have brought financial ruin to his businesses and threatened the established order of society, of which Sir Josiah Sidmouth was such a respected member.

The accused was, the barrister reminded the court, a great benefactor, a supporter of numerous charities and provider of capital for manufacturing enterprises, without which many of those who were now employed, including many of those same agitators, would be out of work and starving. And then, the barrister had argued, there was the shock and humiliation his client had felt when he had learned that his beloved Abigail, the daughter of his lifelong friend and business partner Nicholas Brown, and the object of his affections, had spurned him in favour of a common labourer, a man from the lowest class of society. It was little wonder, the barrister maintained, that such a revelation should, temporarily, cause his client to abandon his usual upright and moral stance and, in a brief moment of madness, behave in a way so out of character for one who had always led an unblemished life. Indeed, he continued, it could be said that his client was more a victim of circumstances than the perpetrator of the crimes of which he now stood accused.

The jury had listened diligently to the arguments put to them, but, notwithstanding the intense pleading made on his behalf, had quickly returned a verdict of guilty. The judge who presided in the court that day was well known for taking a hard line, and so it came as a surprise to some of those present when Josiah received a sentence of just seven years transportation to Van Diemen's Land, surely the minimum that the judge could have handed out. Many another man of humbler origins appearing before him had faced the rope for far lesser offences.

But there were others present who were not so surprised. The judge, in his summing up, had referred on several occasions to those arguments so eloquently proffered by the learned council on behalf of the accused. There were even some who claimed that the judge knew Josiah, and had enjoyed his hospitality on a number of occasions. Some of the more liberal newspapers, in reporting the trial and sentence, even hinted as much.

And so it was that Sir Josiah Sidmouth found himself at the Picton Convict Station, acting as an unpaid road builder.

Sometimes, he would be amongst the group of convicts sent under armed guard to Green Ponds to fetch rations and supplies. The flat countryside between Picton and Green Ponds was known as Cross Marsh. How ironic, thought Josiah. For back in England, apart from his ancestral home and extensive parklands in the north of Nottinghamshire, he owned a town house in Nottingham, where he would reside whenever he went there to conduct business. And no more than a brisk five minutes' walk from this fine Georgian house in Castle Gate was the notorious area of Narrow Marsh. Not a dry, dusty, wide-open area like Cross Marsh, but a nasty, narrow street, a foul-smelling, fetid, cramped and congested sprawl of tenements, criss-crossed by yards and alleys, devoid of sanitation and home to hundreds of the lowest of the low, a haunt of criminals and prostitutes.

And the home of one man in particular, William Daniels, the very man whom he blamed for his present circumstances. It was he who had stolen Abigail from him, and it was he who would one day pay dearly for what he had done. Whenever his name sprang to mind it only served to spur him on and make him even more determined to survive his sentence until he could return home.

At first it had been hard for him to stomach. Having soldiers and policemen, all of them his social inferiors, ordering him about and expecting immediate obedience, was something totally alien to one who, for the whole of his privileged life, had been used to handing out orders, not receiving them. But he was firm in his purpose. For he knew that, provided he was of good behaviour, after four of his seven year sentence he could apply for a ticket of leave, and that time was fast approaching. He had made sure that he kept an impeccable disciplinary record, for he had no wish to spend a day longer than necessary in this inhospitable land.

He knew and understood the system well and had every intention of exploiting it to his advantage. If he could obtain a ticket of leave he would be free to work for himself, no longer part of a work gang or assigned to a master. But he had to remain above reproach to retain this privilege. The danger was that if anyone should denounce him for any reason, or make any complaint against him, he might lose his new-found freedom. He was aware of this, but had an insurance policy against that happening, which he knew was invariably effective - money. He had access to far more of that than most of the free settlers, magistrates and colonial officials, and he was confident that he would have no difficulty getting his ticket renewed each year.

So long as he behaved himself he would become eligible for a conditional pardon, and eventually a free pardon, enabling him to return home. And that is exactly what he intended to do. Most men, on reaching this level, could not afford to go home even if they wanted to, and so remained and tried to make a better life for themselves. But he was not like most men. He did have money, and plenty of it. Not here of course, but safely stashed away and invested back in England. And he also had something else to look forward to, something on which he could not put a price - the sweet taste of revenge. And that, Josiah told himself yet again, would remain his driving force, his one and only goal.

CHAPTER THREE

—

NOTTINGHAM 1825

'William, is that you? It's almost eight o' clock. Where have you been?' Abigail was speaking as she came out of the kitchen into the hallway. Charles, keen to see his father before being packed off to bed, ran eagerly towards him. William stooped, picked him up and threw him up into the air, catching him as he came back down to earth, squealing with delight. He loved this little game.

'And how's my little soldier today?' asked William of his son, as he repeated the exercise.

'One of these days, William, you'll do that once too often and he'll suffer some mischief!'

But Charles was too young to understand his mother's reservations. 'Again, daddy, again,' and his eyes lit up with each subsequent launch towards the ceiling.

'That's enough now, you two. It's long past Charles's bed time. William, come and have your supper. Millie was ready to serve it up half an hour ago, but when you didn't turn up I told her to get off. She wanted to see her mother first and then she was going to meet some friends and I had no idea how long you'd be, so I let her go.'

'I think there might be somebody else she's really after seeing, if what Benjamin told me is true. He thinks she's been seeing a lad in Carter Gate.'

'Well, let's hope she behaves herself,' said Abigail, a little sternly.

'Whatever can you mean?' asked William with a twinkle in his eye. 'Anyone would think she was your own daughter. She is seventeen. I seem to remember when you were that age you weren't backward in coming forward with the lads, at least not with one lad! Now, if I remember rightly you weren't more than sixteen when you and I really got to know each other, and …'

'Yes, well maybe,' interrupted Abigail, 'I know she's your sister, but she's living under our roof now, so we do have some responsibility towards her. But she's a good girl at heart and hard working; I'll say that for her. Anyway, come and sit down and eat your supper and tell me all about your day.'

An hour later and supper over, William and Abigail sat comfortably by the fire, the light from the glowing coals and flickering candles casting long shadows across the room. 'So why were you late getting back, William? You've been out since six this morning and you know you usually try and take a few hours off on a Saturday. You do look tired. I think you've been working too hard lately. You really should rest a little more.'

There was no doubt that he did look somewhat worn out. He had been fully occupied for the past few weeks, ever since the 'twist net fever', which had hit the town two years earlier, had suddenly begun to decline, resulting in many bankruptcies and unpaid bills. William's business had profited greatly from the twist net fever, but now he was suffering from its demise, for many of those who owed him money had either gone out of business or were delaying payment for as long as they could.

It had all started in March 1823, when Mr Heathcoat's patent for his revolutionary 'bobbin-net' lace machine had expired. That meant that every enterprising chancer could set himself up in the lace trade using the new invention, which undoubtedly was a great leap forward, a machine capable of turning out lace infinitely more quickly than had been possible before on the older machines, which were little more than homemade adaptations of stocking frames. In fact, so successful was Heathcoat's machine that many men with no experience in the lace trade, but with a sharp eye for business, believed they could soon make their fortunes. There was no shortage of capital, and men with money were queuing up to finance new lace making enterprises; lawyers, bankers, clergymen, landowners and wealthy farmers, all desperate to make a quick profit. And neither was there a lack of men to provide the labour. To Nottingham they came in their hundreds; farm labourers abandoned the plough to try their hand at lace making; smiths and mechanics from Sheffield, Birmingham and Manchester arrived, whilst blacksmiths and farriers were recruited into the business of machine building, such was the shortage of skilled men. Many residents of the town abandoned their usual occupations or professions to jump on the bandwagon and join the rush for instant wealth.

But the demand for premises, both for houses and workshops, could not be met and soon greedy speculators paved the way with a vast building spree, not only on the outskirts of the town but on every available plot and garden within the town which they could persuade the owner to part with. Stables, garrets, kitchens and cellars were converted into workplaces or bobbin and carriage maker's shops, and many a back yard found itself home to a hastily erected two room lean-to shed, rented out as a home and workshop.

And new buildings meant raw materials had to be brought in; bricks, tiles and timber, slate, sand and lime. Then there were the machines to be built and they required metal. Cotton imports increased to feed the new lace machines, and the finished products had to be exported. For a while everyone prospered; the investors, the builders, the landlords, the suppliers of the raw materials, the many new lace manufacturers and of course the carriers, like William. For almost two years, the twist hands, as those working the machines came to be known, lived the life of kings, earning wages previously undreamt of. Some men, prepared to work long shifts, were earning as much as £5 a week, an unheard of amount. Instead of walking to work they now rode on fine horses, and would stop on their way home, not for a pint of ale, but for a quart of claret.

But it could not last. The bubble grew bigger and bigger, and as happens with all bubbles that become too big, it burst. With a resounding and deafening bang. Output had simply exceeded demand and prices plummeted. Wages were reduced and sales slumped. Only those who had been in business for many years, who were well established and were not saddled by debt to landlords, machine smiths and suppliers, were able to weather the storm. But for many who had gambled all on making a quick buck, disaster was the only reward. Hundreds of lace makers were thrown out of work; some lost everything and fell into hopeless poverty; some died of despair, others of starvation or suicide.

William gazed into the fire, as if deep in thought. 'I spent most of the morning chasing unpaid debts, and then went over to Eastwood to meet a man named Gilbert Wells, who's sinking a new pit there. With a bit of luck I should get the contract to shift his coal, but it'll be some months before they start mining.

'I'm afraid I didn't manage to collect many debts, though. There's a lot of people got their fingers burnt with this twist net business. Invested all their life savings and now they've nothing left. The word is that all the workhouses are full, and there are whole families living and sleeping on the streets. It's terrible, Abigail. We might be owed money that we'll never see again but that's always a risk in business, and at least we have other work and contracts unaffected by this madness. I'm glad that father didn't get sucked into it. But then, he always was steady and a bit unadventurous. He'll never make a fortune from his stocking frame, but at least things are a little more settled now than they were a few years ago. I'll never forget all those lean times after the war finished. I sometimes wonder how we survived.'

Abigail looked at William as he continued to gaze into the fire. He seemed to be miles away and she wondered what he was thinking of; perhaps about the hardship he and his family had suffered back in Narrow Marsh, when trade had been so poor and many families could barely feed themselves. 'I know things are bad at the moment, but I want you to make more time for yourself. I don't want you working yourself to death. You're right, William, we are luckier than most and we don't owe anyone a shilling. Anyway, if things did get worse I could always ask father to help us out.'

'Oh, no!' William said, categorically. 'I'll not go cap in hand to your father. He's already helped out enough and I won't be beholden to anyone. No, we'll manage. And just what do you think Peter would say if he found out? We both know well enough what he thinks about me, and he's not even spoken to you since we were married.'

'Well, he's been in India for most of the past three years with his regiment, so it would have been difficult for him to visit,' said Abigail, but not sounding at all convincing in the defence of her brother.

'Maybe. But he could have written to you. We know he was back in the country last year for a month and he never made any attempt to see you. I know he hates me, but surely he could have tried to make things up with you? Of course, I think we know what he was doing while he was back in England; making sure Josiah Sidmouth's business interests and affairs were all in good order. He clearly thinks more of him than he does of you!'

'Well, I would certainly hope not!' exclaimed Abigail, a little annoyed.

They were only too aware of the rift that had developed between Abigail and her brother. Peter had sided with Josiah over the matter of Abigail's rejection of him in favour of William. And while Abigail accepted that William and Peter were never likely to be on amicable terms, she always hoped that one day Peter would forget the past and come to terms with the choice she had made.

'William, do you think he will ever return to England?'

'Who, Josiah? I wouldn't be surprised. Most criminals don't; they can't afford it. I never heard of one that did. But him! He's certainly got the money and a lot of land and wealth over here, so I'll bet he tries to return. Anyway, I've read that conditions for convicts there can be horrendous, so let's hope he suffers. After what he did to us, he deserves to. I have nothing but loathing for the man and I never want to see him again. Personally, I hope he dies a painful death in Van Diemen's Land. But I'll tell you one thing, Abigail; if he ever does come back here causing trouble, or tries to see you again, I'll not be responsible for my actions. I'd swing for that man!'

And as he spoke these words, he spat into the fire. Abigail looked at William. She had not seen him so angry for a long time. He was normally easy-going, but she was thankful that he could always be relied on to protect her and face danger should it ever arise. She too hoped that Josiah was out of their life forever, but she dreaded the thought of William doing something in anger that he might regret. She could not bear the thought of losing him, even if it was the result of his springing to her defence.

It was getting late and all William wanted to do was sleep. Tomorrow was Sunday, the one day when he could normally be assured of some rest and relaxation. He always tried to keep Sundays free from work so he could spend more time with his family, and whilst there were occasional items of business he needed to see to, he was usually able to spend most of the day with Abigail and the children. The wharf and warehouse were closed on Sundays and no loading or unloading of boats took place. Most of the boatmen also tied up for the day, and since the lock keepers did not work and most of the lock gates were kept padlocked, there was little point in their attempting a journey of any distance.

It was normally their habit on Sunday mornings to go to church, and although they now lived in the Parish of St. Peter they continued to attend St. Mary's, where Abigail's parents were regular worshippers, and where William's mother and father would sometimes put in an appearance. In the afternoon, if the weather was fine, they might go out for a walk, perhaps down to the meadows. A favourite spot was by the river at Wilford, a place that held a special place in their hearts, for it was here that they had spent their first day together, almost ten years ago.

'You go on up to bed, William. I'll wait up for Millie. She shouldn't be long now. She promised not to be late and it's already gone eleven thirty, so I expect she'll be back soon.'

William took a candle from a cupboard, lit it with an ember from the fire and made his way up the stairs. He collapsed into bed, but no sooner had he drifted off into sleep when he was suddenly awoken by the sound of voices below. Although he could not hear what was being said, the tone of the voices indicated that all was not well. He was unsure what to make of it, but he knew it was Abigail and Millie talking; they both seemed alarmed and he could detect a hint of fear in Millie's voice. He got out of bed, wrapped a dressing gown round him, and without bothering to light the candle, quickly made his way down the stairs to see what the commotion was all about.

On entering the living room he found Millie sitting on a settee, sobbing quietly, whilst Abigail sat next to her, an arm around her shoulders in an effort to try and comfort her. Also in the room, standing next to the fireplace, was a young woman whom William vaguely recognised as one of Millie's friends.

'Whatever is the matter? What's happened?' asked William. His first thought was that some harm had come to Millie, but seeing that she appeared to be unhurt he then thought that perhaps what Benjamin had told him about the lad in Carter Gate was true, and that she had had a falling out with him. Millie was still sobbing, and it was Abigail who spoke first.

'Millie's just come back with this young woman, who was kind enough to accompany her, and she has some frightful news. I'll just go and fetch some drinks while Millie tells you all about it.'

Millie now spoke, having composed herself, and stopped crying sufficiently to be able to make herself understood. 'It's Thomas. He's been taken by the constable and locked up in the gaol. They say he's committed a murder!'

For a moment or two, William wasn't certain just who Millie was talking about. He knew a number of men named Thomas, but this must be someone known to the family.

'Thomas? Thomas who?'

'Thomas Dewhirst - our cousin Thomas!' cried Millie.

Then the penny dropped. William's mother had a younger sister, Sabina, recently widowed, and her eldest son was called Thomas. William didn't see him very often, although he lived in the town. He was a framework knitter, like so many of their family, and had rooms in a house in Sunny Hill, towards Sneinton, one of the areas recently developed to cater for the expanding population. William had always known Thomas to be a quiet, unassuming and harmless young man, the last person anyone would suspect of being capable of murder. He was about a year younger than William and was unmarried.

Abigail returned from the kitchen with a tray of drinks and handed Millie a cup of warm milk with some brandy in it. 'Here Millie, drink this, it'll help calm you down.'

Millie took a sip, and it seemed to help, then taking a deep breath she began. 'I went to visit mother and father, and then I went to see a friend over in Carter Gate,' and she hesitated at the word friend. 'Then we went to The Neptune Tavern in Brook Street to meet some other friends, including Lucy here. We were having such a fine time, drinking and chatting, and then Lucy said she had to go out for a short while to visit a friend of hers who lives nearby.' Millie was beginning to sob again and was finding it difficult to continue.

'It's all right Millie, take your time,' said William, despite the fact he was anxious to know what had caused so much distress. Millie took another deep breath and continued.

'I think it might be better if Lucy tells you. She was there and can tell it better than me.'

William turned to the girl, who was still standing by the fire. She was slender, about twenty years old, of average height with shoulder length chestnut brown hair; hazel eyes and pretty enough to attract the attention of most men.

'Thank you for bringing my sister back; I can see she is still very distressed. Please take a seat, Lucy, and perhaps you can let us know just what's been going on.'

'Thank you,' she said as she sat down, and began her account of the night's events.

'My name is Lucy Fallowell and Millie and I have been friends for a while. I work as a clipper at Mr Allen's new lace factory in Leen Side and one of my best friends there is a lady called Clara Ford. She's quite a bit older than me, about thirty, and is married with one little girl aged six. I've known Clara for a year or so, and have recently been in the habit of visiting her quite often, ever since her husband left her and went off to live with another woman in Leicester. That really upset Clara at first, but I think she's now come to terms with the situation.

'She rents two rooms in a house in Brook Street, over in the Sunny Hill area, the same house where Thomas also rents a room. I know Thomas a little through having met him occasionally when I've been visiting Clara, and he seems pleasant enough; very quiet and reserved, and also quite melancholy. I've heard people say he gets very depressed at times, but then he's your cousin so I suppose you might know that already. Ever since her husband ran off to Leicester, Clara seems to have turned to Thomas for comfort. Her room is just across the landing from his. The truth is, he and Clara have been spending a lot of time together. She admitted that much to me. In fact, she's confided in me that she's two months gone, although she hasn't told Thomas yet. Oh dear, I'm sorry to have to say these things about your cousin, but I don't know how else to tell the story unless I do.'

'It's all right, you must tell us everything,' said William. 'You won't embarrass us. These things happen. But please, Lucy, carry on.'

'Well, last week Clara had a real shock when her husband suddenly turned up. He was waiting for her outside the factory gates one evening when we came out. She hadn't seen him for months, and he came to ask if she would have him back. She told me all about it, how he wanted to come back home, but Clara was reluctant. She said she couldn't trust him anymore, not after he'd run off to live with that woman. He spent a lot of time trying to get her to change her mind, but she wouldn't. He found some lodgings in Narrow Marsh and stayed there until he set off back to Leicester this afternoon. I know that he went to see Clara several times, and I think Thomas must have seen them together. Perhaps he got a bit jealous.

'Then earlier tonight I went along to The Neptune Tavern on Brook Street, just down the road from Clara's. There were quite a lot of my friends there, including Millie. Clara was supposed to be joining us, but when she didn't turn up I thought I'd better go and see if she was all right. When I got there, I found her to be quite upset, and she told me she had had words with Thomas. He had been to her room, and had chided young Annie, that's Clara's daughter, over something and nothing, but Clara took exception to it and told Thomas it was not his place to chastise her daughter. I hadn't been there long, when Thomas came into the room again, and once more chided young Annie. Clara then told him to leave, adding that she had seen her husband that day and had high hopes of a reconciliation. I know she didn't mean it and I'm sure she only said it to get back at him. Anyway, on hearing it, Thomas left, but in a few minutes he returned, and went up to Clara and appeared to hit her with his fist on her left side, then went away again saying, "There then, that's it!".'

And as she spoke these words, tears began to trickle down her cheeks. But she quickly wiped them away and continued with her tale.

'Clara was sitting on a stool and seemed in great pain. I went to comfort her and told Annie to go and get a cup of water. But then she got worse and was slipping into unconsciousness. I was so concerned that I told Annie to go and fetch Millie from The Neptune. They were soon back, and as it was beginning to get dark we lit a candle, and it was then that we saw blood on her left side where Thomas had hit her. I went across to Thomas's room to tell him about Clara, but he simply said, "It's no use, she's a dead woman". Then he ran out of his room and down the stairs and we heard the front door slam.

'By this time, Clara was gasping for breath and it was obvious that Thomas hadn't just hit her, but must have stabbed her with a knife or something. We were both very worried by now, so Millie hurried round to fetch Clara's mother, who lives nearby, and also sent for a doctor. Her mother soon came, but within minutes Clara was dead. The doctor arrived shortly after, but there was nothing he could do for her, so he went away and said he would send for a constable. The constable arrived and asked if anyone knew where Thomas was, or whether we knew if he had any relatives where he might have gone. Millie told the constable where Thomas's mother lived, and we both went along with him to show him, and that's where he was found. He was arrested and taken to the gaol, leaving his mother utterly distraught. Millie here was so upset by everything, what with her own cousin arrested for murder and her aunt in a terrible state, that I offered to bring her back home. And now Clara is lying dead in her cold room, with only her poor mother and daughter there.'

For a short while nobody said a word. Nobody seemed to know what to say next but it was William who finally broke the silence. 'What a dreadful tragedy. I think I ought to go round and tell mother and father what's happened. I don't suppose they know yet. I'll get dressed and set off immediately. I know it's late but I'd rather tell them myself than let them find it out from a stranger. You can be sure the news will be all over the town in no time. And I expect mother will want to go and see Sabina straight away. I feel so sorry for her. It's not long since her husband died, and now this. And Lucy, thanks again for coming with Millie. If you like, I'll take you back home. You don't want to be walking through the town alone at this time of night.'

The two of them were soon on their way, and William took Lucy back to her home before going on to his parents' house in Narrow Marsh. All was quiet when he got there, and he had to knock several times to wake them. An hour later the story had been told. William could see that his mother and father were both deeply shocked. They had had many upsets to face in their lives, but nothing quite as serious as this.

'Would you like to go round to Aunt Sabina's?' William asked his mother. Margaret seemed in somewhat of a daze and it was a few seconds before she spoke.

'Yes. I think I'd better. God knows what she's going through right now. I'll just get a shawl and we'll be off.'

'I'll come with you,' said James.

'No, James, you must stay here. We can't leave Sarah and Elizabeth by themselves. William will come with me. I'll be all right, but it's almost two o'clock now, so don't be surprised if I'm not back till later this morning.'

William's two younger sisters were both asleep, and William didn't envy his parents' job in having to explain everything to them.

Aunt Sabina lived in a small cottage on the corner of Hollow Stone and Fisher Gate, a short walk away. As they hurried along Narrow Marsh towards Plumptre Square, late stragglers, clearly the worse for drink, were wandering about, presumably trying to find their way home. Others had decided to give up the attempt and were already sleeping off the effects of a Saturday night's boozing, some in doorways, one right in the middle of the road. Lucky for him that little traffic passed this way in the early hours of a Sunday morning.

As they approached the cottage, they could see a dim light shining through a window. 'Look, Aunt Sabina must still be up,' said William. His knock on the door was immediately met by the sound of footsteps scurrying towards them. As the door opened, a more distressed face could not be imagined. The poor woman was only three years younger than her sister, but looked by far the older of the two. Many years of hard graft had taken their toll, but Margaret, who had seen her sister only a week before, could barely believe just how much she seemed to have aged. The sudden and unexpected death of her husband two months previously had been a real shock, and the news she had received that night had clearly come as a hammer blow.

Margaret turned to her son. 'You'd better get off home now William; Abigail will be wondering where you've got to. I'll stay with Sabina. Perhaps you'll come and see us tomorrow.'

The outcome of this sad affair can be told briefly enough. Within less than a day or two everyone in Nottingham knew all about the murder of Clara Ford, and it was the main topic of conversation in the many pubs and inns of the town. Even before the trial, the local newspapers contained long and detailed accounts of the lives of the victim, her estranged husband and her lover. The newspaper hacks had been working overtime, eliciting the lurid details of that fateful night from those who were in the know, and many others who weren't but who were equally happy to put in their two pennyworth. The following Tuesday, Clara Ford was buried at St. Mary's, and thousands of spectators, in a display of morbid curiosity, turned out to witness the ceremony.

Three weeks later came the trial. The prisoner made a sorry sight, alone and frightened in the dock. Although he pleaded not guilty to murder, he admitted what he had done but claimed that he had not known what he was doing.

The key witness was Lucy, who was called to give her version of events, and to all those present in the courtroom her evidence seemed damning. The prisoner then entered his defence. He spoke of severe head pains from which he sometimes suffered, when he had no recollection of his actions. There were heartfelt pleas for clemency by his advocate, who called a number of witnesses to show that he was of good character, but not of sound mind. Witnesses who knew him well said that he was very much inclined to melancholy, and it was revealed that several times over the previous few years he had tried to kill himself whilst in a fit of depression. On one occasion, the prisoner had thrown himself into the Trent, and only the swift action of passers-by had saved him from a watery grave. A druggist then gave evidence, and explained that some months before he had been summoned to attend the prisoner after he had taken a large dose of laudanum, and managed to save his life only by administering a very strong emetic.

But all these pleas were to no avail. The trial had lasted just three hours, and it took the jury no longer than five minutes to find him guilty. The execution was set for two days hence, and whilst in the condemned cell he was visited one last time by his poor mother.

And so, in front of a crowd of thousands, Thomas Dewhirst met his final, ignominious, end. None of his immediate family was there. William and Sabina had attended the trial but neither could bring themselves to join the mob at the final reckoning. Sabina went to her sister's house where she stayed for some days. William got out of the town on the day of the execution, and went up to Eastwood to discuss the contract for carrying coal from the new pit. He was glad to get away, for he recalled witnessing a public execution when he was just eleven years old. And he had no desire to witness another.

It was many weeks before the family felt able to discuss the events of that summer. They could not deny the appalling crime that Thomas had committed, yet they truly believed it was more a result of his state of mind, not of any evil or murderous intent. His remorse at what he had done had demonstrated that. And they were not alone in having some sympathy for him, for there were others in Nottingham who regarded him not so much as a hardened criminal, but more as an otherwise law-abiding young man who, for just a brief second, had lost control of his senses and committed an act which would reap a terrible revenge. Such is the law.

But his relatives all felt a deep sense of shame that one of their kin should have been responsible for such an awful deed. Nottingham was a town where almost everyone seemed to know almost everyone else, and often there would be whispering and pointing in the streets whenever William, his parents, siblings or Aunt Sabina were espied by those who recognised them. And there was no doubt that their association with a now notorious murderer might be used by anyone with a grudge against them. William and Abigail, in particular, felt this 'guilt by association' more than most. He was trying to build a respectable business, but there were still some in the town who resented his rise from nothing. And Abigail, hopeful that she could be reconciled with her brother, knew only too well that this latest episode would only give him further justification for his hatred of William.

Nine months after the trial, a convict ship arrived in Hobart. Amongst those on board was a young man from Nottingham named Randal Wainer, and along with half a dozen others he was sent to the Picton Convict Station. The existing convicts there were always keen to meet new arrivals, especially if they were from their home town, and it wasn't long before one convict, who called himself Josh Smith, soon learned that a Nottingham man was amongst the newcomers.

They soon got to talking, and in the course of their discussion Wainer explained that his trial had followed immediately after that of Thomas Dewhirst, the murderer. But unlike him, Wainer had only been charged with stealing a horse from a public house in Basford, following a drunken spree, and later attempting to sell it to a horse dealer at nearby Bulwell. Wainer readily admitted to Smith this foolishness on his part, and regretted he hadn't taken the horse to Derby, or further afield, to sell, where the theft might not have been known about.

And that would probably have been the end of their discussion, had not Wainer happened to mention that Dewhirst was a cousin of an old friend of his, Samuel Daniels, with whom he had got into a spot of bother years before when they were both a lot younger. In fact, Wainer explained, Samuel's elder brother William had a canal carrying business, and he had worked for him for a short time at his warehouse.

On hearing this, a wry smile spread across Josh Smith's face. He showed no surprise and certainly didn't say anything about knowing the Daniels family. But the information was stored away carefully for future use.

CHAPTER FOUR

—

NOTTINGHAM 1826

In the year that followed William continued working hard to build up his business, and was delighted when he landed the contract for shifting the coal from the new mine at Eastwood.

He was also fortunate to have weathered a mighty storm that had hit the world of banking at the end of the previous year, for in December of 1825, following an explosion of speculative and risky investments, there had occurred a financial scare and a run on banks throughout the country. Many people had borrowed heavily to invest in schemes which had no chance of success, and the banks, expecting to profit themselves, were quite happy to lend the money. When the bubble inevitably burst everyone panicked, and many banks ran into difficulties as thousands of worried depositors queued to withdraw their savings. Of course, not all banks had the cash to pay out and some of the smaller ones simply went bust, their customers losing everything. In Nottingham, Mr Moore's bank was at serious risk, and managed to survive only because the owner had a wealthy landowning friend, Squire Charlton of Chilwell, who was able to lend sufficient cash to see the bank through the crisis.

And all this came only a couple of years after the twist net fever and its ultimate and ruinous collapse. But William did not keep large amounts on deposit, most of his money being invested in his business. The new mine at Eastwood was now fully in production, and that alone meant he needed extra boats and staff to move the coal, much of which was destined for the Leicester and London markets.

On a hot summer's day at the end of July in 1826, William saddled a horse and set off to Eastwood to meet up with Gilbert Wells, the mine owner, who wanted to discuss some aspect of their contract. The Eastwood mine was situated about a mile from the Nottingham

Canal, and Gilbert had constructed a railway, or tramroad as they were often known, down to the canal, where a basin had been provided for loading coal into the boats. The wagons were hauled by horses and the operation worked perfectly well. There were other similar tramroads in the area, linking various pits to the canal, most of them relatively short in length, and during their conversation it soon became clear to William that Gilbert seemed to know a great deal about this particular mode of transport.

Over a lazy and satisfying lunch at a local hostelry, a wider discussion took place about the current advances in the use of railways. Gilbert told William that he had recently returned from a visit to the north of England where he had gone to look at new developments in the mining industry, which had long been established in that part of the country. Whilst there, he had inspected the newly opened railway between Stockton and Darlington, where some of the trains of coal wagons were drawn not by horses, but by steam locomotives. William remembered reading something about this in the Nottingham newspapers at the time.

And, as Gilbert further explained, the use of railways as canal feeders was a common feature in this part of Nottinghamshire, and some fairly lengthy lines had recently been built in preference to canals. One, from Pinxton on the Cromford Canal to Mansfield, some eight miles distance, had opened about six years before, although this relied entirely on the use of horses. William already knew about this railway, as he had, on occasions, sent boatloads of coal to Pinxton for transfer to the railway and onward conveyance to Mansfield. But horses still reigned supreme, and so far there had been no experimenting with the new steam locomotives in this area.

'You know, William, I think that we will be seeing more of these railways as time goes on. Why, just last year an Act of Parliament was passed to build a railway of some thirty-three miles, linking the Cromford Canal with the Peak Forest Canal, and that affords a direct link to Manchester. A canal was considered at first, but the terrain is so hilly that numerous locks would have been needed, and maintaining a constant water supply would have been a real problem. I believe construction is to start very soon, and I've no doubt that you could benefit yourself. Just think of all those goods coming over the railway from the North West that will have to be transhipped to boats; I'm sure there'll be money in it for an enterprising young man like you.'

There then followed a lively debate on the relevant merits of horses and steam locomotives, of the various pros and cons and the economics of the two forms of haulage. Their general consensus was that for short lengths of line, horses were quite adequate, but for longer distances, and particularly where heavy loads were involved, there might be advantages in the use of locomotives, albeit that the initial costs were high.

And then Gilbert made a statement which William never forgot. 'I can foresee a time when the use of railways, with trains of wagons hauled by locomotives, might even rival the canals for the longer distance conveyance of goods. Imagine a railway from here to Leicester and even to London. Consider how much quicker my coal could be delivered, in much greater quantities and with no interruptions when the canals freeze in winter, or run short of water in dry summers.'

'Well, I can't deny that you've hit the nail on the head there,' replied William. 'We're having real difficulties at the moment with low water levels, particularly on the Trent.' And William proceeded to tell Gilbert about the problems he was currently experiencing.

That month had been exceedingly hot and there had been little rain for many weeks. The Trent was at its lowest depth in living memory and barge traffic was being severely disrupted. Levels had dropped in some places to a depth at which it was almost possible to walk across from bank to bank, and heavily loaded barges were unable to move. Abigail's Uncle George, who had a barge business at Newark and who used the river for almost all his trade, had been seriously affected, and even William, who mainly used the canals rather than the river, had not escaped the crisis. Many of the small rivers and streams feeding the canals had all but dried up, and some of the canal reservoirs were almost empty. The result was a critical shortage of water, with numerous boats being tied up for days on end, waiting for levels to be restored. Journeys to London were taking twice as long as normal and the boatmen, who were paid for each load delivered, were complaining bitterly at the loss of wages.

As William rode slowly back to Nottingham, approaching Trowell he gazed across the valley towards Ilkeston. The Nottingham Canal lay alongside the lane, winding along on the level, whilst in the valley below, the Erewash Canal rose steadily up the valley to meet with the Nottingham Canal at Langley Mill. Normally, he would have expected to see several boats on both canals, but today he saw only one, and that was moving at a snail's pace. Riding high in the water it was clearly empty; had it been fully laden it would have had the greatest difficulty in moving at all. And he remembered what Gilbert had said. And he wondered how long this scene would remain unchanged, and whether the canals ever would make way for railways with locomotives hauling trains of wagons, and travelling faster than boats ever could.

His immediate hope was that nothing would happen to threaten his livelihood; canals were his life and his means of supporting his family. But he knew that nothing ever stood still. Times change. He had seen this in the lace trade and the new machines which had increased output so extensively. He was in the business of moving goods and there would always be a demand for that. But if a better and more profitable way of doing it could be found, then it would be bound, eventually, to succeed. And he decided that if that was to come about, then he wanted to be a part of it.

William arrived back home in time for supper, during which he told Abigail all about his conversation with Gilbert, and how he thought that one day there might be a future for this new form of transport.

'Well,' said Abigail, as she topped up William's beer mug, 'talking about new forms of transport, I have arranged a little surprise for you. It's your birthday on Thursday, so don't go arranging any visits or meetings that morning.'

William looked inquisitively across the table at Abigail. 'And just what are you planning?'

'Oh, I can't tell you that, it would spoil the surprise. But I know you'll enjoy it.'

'Come on now Abigail', he said, pleadingly, 'you know I don't like you to keep secrets from me.'

But Abigail continued to tease him. 'Well, you'll just have to wait and see. All I will say is that come Thursday you'll have a completely different view of things!'

Thursday 3rd August 1826 was a bright and sunny day. William and Abigail were woken early as Charles came noisily into their bedroom and climbed up onto the bed, his sister following. Catherine was barely old enough to understand birthdays, but young Charles was anxious to give his father the present that Abigail had bought and wrapped in pretty blue paper and tied up with red ribbon.

'And what, I wonder, is this?' asked William.

'It's for you, daddy. It's from me and Catherine.'

'Well well, aren't I the lucky one! Let's unwrap it and see what it is.'

'I'll do it,' cried Charles excitedly, and grabbing the present back, began to tear off the paper. 'Here you are, daddy' he said in triumph and handed to his father a leather pocket book.

'Oh, thank you,' he replied, and he hugged his two children and kissed them both.

'Mummy said you need it to write things down and keep notes when you are on business and meeting people.'

'Mummy's right, it's exactly what I need, thank you,' And he kissed them again. 'Now, you two go downstairs while we get dressed, and then we'll have some breakfast. Today will be a holiday, and we're all going out together. I think mummy has a surprise in store!'

Breakfast was soon over, and, as Millie cleared up and Abigail got herself and the children ready for their day out, William went to the wharf office to have a few words with Benjamin. He wanted to make sure he knew about a boatload of cotton for a new and influential customer that had been delayed by the recent low water levels, but would hopefully arrive that day, and to ensure that the customer would be advised as soon as it arrived. But William needn't have worried; Benjamin was fully aware of the importance of the consignment and appeared to have everything under control. He had got along fine under John's stewardship, and had now learned all the tricks of the trade. William was confident that Benjamin would soon be able to take over the job of wharf manager, which was probably no bad thing. He had noticed in recent months that John looked to be ageing quite rapidly and would probably welcome the opportunity to take life a little easier. But then he was well into his seventies. And although he had said nothing specific, he had hinted to William that he was now beginning to find the job a little onerous for a man of his age.

William was still chatting to Benjamin when Abigail came out of the house with the children by her side, all nicely turned out in their Sunday best. 'Come along William, we're ready now.'

'You'd better get along,' said Benjamin, 'you don't want to keep them waiting. Especially as Abigail's got a surprise for you!'

'What has she got planned?' asked William.

'I've really no idea. I did ask her, but she wouldn't say. Just something about you going for a ride and going up in the world.'

'Oh well, I expect I'll find out soon enough.'

William picked up young Catherine and carried her, while Charles trotted along beside. 'You'd better lead the way Abigail. Only you know where we're going.'

'It's not far. Follow me,' she said, and out through the gate they went into Canal Street, turning left then across the road and up Greyfriars' Gate. To their left, high up on its sandstone rock stood the solid, stone-built grey edifice of Nottingham Castle, property of the wealthy Duke of Newcastle. More of a mansion, thought William. It was not like the medieval castles he had seen pictures of. There had been one here once, he knew, but that had been knocked down on Cromwell's orders following the civil war, and the present structure later built in its place. As for its owner, William had no respect for him. He was a staunch supporter of the Tory cause, a man vehemently opposed to liberal ideas and to parliamentary reform. A man who would always do his utmost to hinder any changes aimed at improving the lot of the poor. But the duke rarely visited the castle, choosing to live in one of his other grand houses, and it had stood virtually empty for many years. As they walked along, William seemed in a dream.

'A penny for them,' said Abigail 'you're miles away. What are you thinking about?'

'Oh, nothing of any importance,' he replied, but he wasn't sure she believed him. As they approached Lister Gate, William was becoming aware that an unusually large number of people were all heading in the same direction. They continued past St. Peter's Church, up Wheeler Gate and finally into the Market Place.

For a moment the sight that met William's eyes took him completely by surprise. He hadn't been into the Market Place for over a week, so busy had he been. He was used to seeing large crowds here, for the Market Place, the largest in all of England it was said, had always been the venue for any gathering in the town. Many was the time that a protest had taken place here; many a riot had started, or finished; and heads cracked open, or worse, as soldiers had been summoned to break up a threatening mob. He, himself, remembered the militia dispersing mobs back in 1812 when the so called Luddite riots began; those dark days when the framework knitters were starving and trying to improve their lot.

But the crowd here today was not threatening and there seemed to be an atmosphere of joy and anticipation. Laughter filled the air and the sun shone down on a crowd seemingly determined to enjoy itself.

In the centre of the Market Place, a large circular area had been sectioned off with wooden boards to a height of about four feet, sufficient to keep out the hordes of interested onlookers, but low enough to afford a good view of the activities within, wherein could be seen, hovering, a large balloon. Once before, as a boy of thirteen, he had seen a similar object, when a man had made an ascent from one of the wharves along the canal side, close to where he now had his own premises. But this one was altogether bigger and far more impressive. Abigail led them on through the crowd to an opening in the fence, where two men stood guard, and showing them a piece of paper, they were all let through.

The balloon was fastened to the ground by several short, stout ropes, and was moving slowly in the gentle breeze. It was made of silk and was most beautifully adorned with intricate patterns in the brightest of colours. William judged it to be almost fifty feet high, and below the balloon itself was suspended a wicker basket, about six feet square, inside which some men were busy attending to the balloon and its apparatus.

'So this is what you've brought me to see,' said William.

'Well, yes, but rather more than just see,' replied Abigail, and putting her hand into her purse she took out a piece of printed paper and handed it to William. He unfolded it and read it silently to himself. Then he smiled and glanced at his wife in disbelief.

'You mean I'm going for a ride in that?' The piece of paper was a ticket, a receipt for ten shillings and sixpence which Abigail had paid for William to make an ascent in the balloon.

Mr Green, the owner of the balloon, was standing by its side, talking to a number of ladies and gentlemen who, it transpired, had also availed themselves of the chance to view Nottingham from above, and to get a bird's eye view of the town. William recognised some of them as leading manufacturers and wealthy business people. Mr Green explained that he would take six people at a time, and that they would rise to a considerable height, about four hundred feet, this being the length of the rope which would prevent them being blown away to who knows where.

The balloon had been filled with coal gas, which, being lighter than air, caused the balloon to float upwards. A few years earlier the town had been supplied with coal gas, which provided lighting in some of the principal streets and wealthier houses. For this special event, pipes had been laid from the gas main on Long Row, courtesy of the gas company, which received a handsome fee for its co-operation. The previous day, Mr Green and his men had been busy setting up all the necessary equipment to store the gas, and had been in attendance from early morning, filling the balloon and making it ready for its ascent.

With mounting excitement, the first six passengers were helped into the basket. Then, to the accompaniment of a loud cheer from the crowd, the ropes holding the balloon were freed, and slowly it began to rise into the air. Upwards it went until the remaining rope became taut. There it hovered, slowly swaying to and fro in the wind. A flock of birds flew close to it, perhaps curious at the sight of this unexpectedly large intruder into their domain. The occupants of the basket could be seen leaning over the edge, gazing down at the scene below. Abigail looked up, and she felt her knees turn weak as she thought of being up there herself, with nothing but the power of gas to prevent her falling to her death. And then she realised that she had paid for William to make the ascent, and suddenly her birthday present to him did not seem such a good idea. But William had no such fears and couldn't wait for his turn.

'Look,' he said to Charles, pointing to the sky, 'Daddy's going up there soon. You must wave to me when I get there.'

It was to be another hour before it was William's turn. He climbed into the basket, and as he did so he could tell that Abigail was not happy. 'I'll be fine Abigail, don't fret. It's not every day we get the chance to fly! Keep an eye on the children.'

Soon they were ready and once more the ropes securing the balloon were untied. There was a sudden lurch and the basket leapt upwards. The long rope was slowly played out and up and up the balloon rose. William stood in one corner, staring down at the panorama gradually unfolding beneath him. He had once climbed to the top of the tower of St. Mary's Church, the highest point by far in the town, but they soon surpassed this, until suddenly they came to an abrupt stop. William gazed around in a state of wonderment at the sites so familiar to him, but from a completely new perspective. It was a clear, fine day and he could see for miles.

Immediately below, the crowd in the Market Place seemed more like an army of ants. To the south he could see the canal and the wharves and warehouses, nestling below the castle. Many times he had looked up at the castle and imagined the hated duke looking down and keeping an eye on him. But for once it was William who could do the looking down. To the west the canal formed a silver ribbon and he could easily trace its course to Lenton, where it turned sharply to the north, past Wollaton Hall, and he remembered the time, as a boy, when he and his cousin Hugh had climbed over the wall into the grounds, and had nearly received a beating from the gamekeeper, until Abigail had come to their rescue. How long ago that was, he thought, and how much had happened to him since that day. From Lenton, the Beeston Canal continued to the west until it reached the lock where it joined the River Trent. He had travelled along there many times by boat, but how different it all seemed from up here.

Nearer, he could see High Pavement where Abigail's parents lived, and the Shire Hall with its prison at the rear, and below the sandstone cliff at the back of the prison the sprawl of houses that made up Narrow Marsh and Leen Side. Seen from the air, it was apparent just how tightly packed were the tenements. So tight, in fact, that it was almost impossible to make out the narrow alleys that ran between the squalid blocks of houses. Further to the west, on the edge of the town, smoke rose lazily from the tanneries and pottery works, near to the new houses on Sunny Hill where poor Clara Ford had been murdered by William's own cousin. And beyond there, the village of Sneinton, where he had nearly died in the warehouse fire when Josiah Sidmouth had sought to get rid of him. Everywhere he looked brought memories flooding back, some good, some bad. To the north he could see Gallows Hill at the top of Mansfield Road, and the windmills overlooking the Forest racecourse, and he thought of the day when he and Abigail had passed by there when they had set off on their ill-fated elopement. To the south, beyond the canal were the meadows and the River Trent, where he had spent so many happy days as a child, and beyond there lay Clifton Grove where Abigail had taught him to ride.

This was an experience he would never forget, for in every direction there appeared to be something new. And yet there was nothing he had not seen before, but never from this viewpoint. There was so much to see but so little time, and then his concentration was suddenly broken as Mr Green announced to the party that they were about to descend. He opened a valve to allow some of the gas to escape, then leaned over the side and waved a large white flag, a signal to the men below to haul them back down. Gradually they descended, everything becoming nearer and larger as they went, until finally they came to an abrupt halt as the basket hit the ground with a bump.

As William climbed out he could see the sheer look of relief on Abigail's face as she ran towards him, throwing her arms around him as if he had been away for years. Charles and Catherine stood still, wide-eyed and open-mouthed and clearly unsure what to make of it. They all waited while the next eager balloonists took their places in the basket, then stared, still spellbound, as it rose once more, high into a cloudless sky.

After it had returned to the ground, and the occupants had disembarked, a single gentleman was helped on board. He appeared to be a man of some means, dressed in the finest clothes, and the rumour was that he had come especially from Leicester and had paid the enormous sum of twenty-five guineas to accompany Mr Green in a free flight. As soon as they were ready, the harnessing ropes were untied, and slowly and silently the balloon rose once more. But this time, there was nothing to inhibit its flight. It continued its ascent to an enormous height, so that eventually it appeared as a tiny coloured ball against the blue backcloth of the sky. And then, encountering a north westerly current, it began drifting eastwards, beyond Sneinton and over the wooded hills at Colwick until it was no longer visible. William later heard that it had finally come back down to earth somewhere beyond Edwalton; and how he wished that he could have been aboard. What an adventure that must have been, he thought.

The birthday treat was not quite over, for Abigail had prepared a picnic, and they walked down through the meadows to the river, where they sat and enjoyed a lazy afternoon. Later that evening, after the children had been put to bed, William and Abigail sat outside the house. It was still warm, and as the sun slowly dipped, shadows played across the canal and the last reflections of the day darkened until they vanished in the inky blackness of the still water.

'What a day!' said William. 'You know, Abigail, when I was up there, gazing down on all the old familiar places, I could scarcely believe it was real. I could see the mass of houses in Narrow Marsh where I grew up. If someone there had told me that one day I would fly overhead, I'd have said they were mad. Thank you, Abigail; I don't expect I'll ever experience anything quite like that again. The thing is, what can I dream up for your birthday that will match that?'

'Well, as long as it involves staying safely on *terra firma*, I don't mind!'

CHAPTER FIVE

—

VAN DIEMEN'S LAND 1827

On a bright January morning, a large East Indiaman, on licence to the Honourable East India Company, sailed under a stiff breeze into the harbour at Hobart, Van Diemen's Land. Aboard was a small platoon of soldiers from the South Gloucestershire Regiment under the command of Lieutenant Peter Brown, along with a large consignment of male convicts. The ship was under charter to the British Government and had set sail from Plymouth some four months earlier with about forty prisoners from the West Country, calling at London en route to pick up some ninety more. The journey had been long and tiresome for the troops, who would much rather have been anywhere than stuck on a stinking prison ship, where, despite their quarters being on the upper decks, they could not escape the disgusting stench emanating from the cargo space below, now a transient floating home to a ragbag band of criminals.

The Lieutenant, in particular, had not at first been happy with this assignment, for it was usual for convicts to be transported by privateers, who would bid for the job of conveying these miserable wretches to their new home across the seas, with only a minimum presence of military personnel. It was normally those who put in the lowest bid who won the contract, resulting in the most diabolical conditions and treatment meted out to their unfortunate and reluctant passengers.

But on this occasion, it had been deemed necessary to send a much larger troop of soldiers, as it coincided nicely with some pressing and important military requirements. Firstly, they were to drop off supplies at Colombo for the troops in Ceylon and then, after delivering the human cargo to Van Diemen's Land, make a detour on the return and call at Calcutta. Here, they were to pick up a small company of the regiment that had been stationed there for some time, but most importantly they were to collect a large shipment of gold. This was destined for the coffers of the East India Company, and there was little doubt that it was income from the opium trade, in which the British Government had a keen and vested interest. For whilst the Government was normally content to hand over to contractors the conveyance of convicts half way round the world, it was a different matter when its own soldiers, supplies and booty were concerned.

As the ship came alongside the harbour, Peter realised that the drudgery of the last four months might turn out to have been worth it, and could even prove to be a heaven-sent opportunity. For with a bit of luck he might be able to establish the whereabouts and wellbeing of an old friend from back home in Nottingham, one Josiah Sidmouth. The two had been firm friends for several years before Josiah had fallen foul of the law over a rather delicate matter concerning the young Lieutenant's sister, Abigail Brown, or rather Abigail Daniels, as she now was. Before Josiah had left Nottingham on his long journey to Van Diemen's Land, Peter had promised to keep an eye on his property and business interests back home, and he had done the best he could, bearing in mind his own frequent absences abroad on military duty. But of Josiah himself, Peter had heard nothing.

It was the plan for the vessel to spend a week or two in harbour before setting sail once more for London; time to fully restock the boat with supplies, to carry out minor repairs and thoroughly clean and fumigate the cargo hold. And, of course, the troops were eagerly looking forward to shore leave and the many pleasures it afforded.

But the first task was to disembark the prisoners and hand them over to the local militia. Once that had been done, their responsibilities were over. It didn't take long to evacuate the ship. Most of the convicts were able to walk, although one or two who were suffering from injury or illness had to be carried ashore; and a miserable, ragged and hungry-looking sight they made. There was little sympathy for them amongst the soldiers, and only the ship's doctor appeared to have any concern for their welfare. But there was nothing more he could do for any of them now. He had done all he could during the long journey to keep them as healthy as conditions allowed, although not all had survived and the ship had arrived with five fewer convicts than when it had left the Millbank.

At the first opportunity for shore leave it was not to the nearest tavern or brothel that Peter made his way, but to the office of Dudley Fereday, the Sheriff of Van Diemen's Land, the man who was directly answerable to Lieutenant Governor Sir George Arthur for policing the colony, and who had enormous power and responsibility over the fate of all prisoners.

Peter quickly located the sheriff's office and, presenting his papers to the clerk, asked to see the sheriff. The clerk went out, but soon returned and took Peter through to an inner room, where a stout man of some forty years sat behind a large desk. Peter introduced himself, and after the usual pleasantries, came to the point.

'I have a rather strange request. I am hoping you might be able to give me some information about a convict who was sent here in 1822. His name is Sir Josiah Sidmouth.' And Peter proceeded to explain his connection with the man, to give a brief account of how he came to have been convicted, and why he now wished to enquire as to his wellbeing. Fereday appeared somewhat uninterested, but Peter continued.

'I've been taking care of his property and affairs while he's been away from home. He is an extremely wealthy man, and it was always his intention, God willing, to return home once his sentence is completed, if not earlier.' And on hearing the words 'extremely wealthy' Fereday suddenly began to show an interest.

'I see. And exactly what do you mean by *extremely wealthy*?' he enquired.

'He has a very large estate in north Nottinghamshire and the rents from his farms and property are considerable. He also has many business interests elsewhere which pay handsome dividends, not to mention the wealth which has been in his family for generations. He is certainly one of the richest men in the county.'

'I can't say I've heard of him. I'm a Staffordshire man myself and never spent any time in Nottingham. And you say this man is here? You must forgive me Mr Brown, but I'm a fairly recent arrival myself and you understand that I do not make it my business to get to know every cutpurse and horse thief personally.' And Peter detected a distinct hint of sarcasm in Fereday's voice.

'However,' he continued, 'your revelations intrigue me. It does seem strange that such an eminent and wealthy person should not have been brought to my notice. Rest assured that I will make it my business to inquire into your Josiah Sidmouth. I understand you will be in port for a week or two. Might I suggest you call back in, shall we say, three days' time?'

For probably the first time since he had taken up his position in 1825, Dudley Fereday stirred himself into action. He didn't really care for the post, but it paid well enough. His patron, Lord Hatherton, had landed him the position at a generous £800 per annum, and had even managed to secure him a year's remuneration in advance; and the one thing he really liked above all else was money. As soon as Peter left, he called the clerk into his office and instructed him to prepare a detailed report, by the following morning, on Josiah Sidmouth. He wanted to know everything about him. Where he had been stationed since his arrival, what he had been doing, whether there had been any disciplinary action taken against him, etc. etc.

The following three days passed quickly enough. As the Lieutenant of the platoon, it was Peter's responsibility to maintain discipline amongst the men. He knew full well that they all intended to make the most of the time that their enforced stay in port provided, and so long as no serious misdemeanours occurred he was happy to give them free reign to indulge their pleasures. In fact, for most of the time they were too drunk to cause any serious mischief. Peter, of course, had to maintain the dignity that his rank demanded, and could not risk fraternising with them or being seen in the same taverns and whorehouses they frequented. But there are ways and means for a gentleman to enjoy his pleasures, and Peter was soon able to establish where appropriate entertainment for one in his position could be found.

The rest of his time he kept in touch with the ship's captain, who was arranging the cleaning of the vessel and for some minor repairs to be carried out, and a gang of convicts had been assigned to this work.

Three days later, as arranged, Peter went along to Fereday's office, and found him much more amenable than on his previous visit. In front of him on his desk lay several sheets of paper.

'Ah, Mr Brown, take a seat. You'll have a beer?' and without waiting for a reply began to fill two large tankards from a stone jar on a side table. 'And a smoke?' he added, taking a large cigar from a box on his desk and handing it to Peter. He shook the ash from the end of his own half-smoked cigar, and offered it to Peter to light his.

'Well, I seem to have everything here about your friend,' he said, picking up the papers and waving them in front of him. Glancing down the sheets, he read out the salient points: 'Sentenced at the Nottingham Quarter Sessions in November 1821 to seven years ... held at Nottingham gaol until early January then taken by coach to the Millbank prison along with five others ... kept there for a couple of months and sailed on the 22nd March on the *Prince of Orange*, arriving here on the 23rd July 1822 ... has been at the Picton Convict Station most of the time, mainly employed on road building duties etc. etc. but has recently been moved to Hobart to assist in the surveyor's office ... will be entitled to apply for a ticket of leave later this year ... has been of good character and has no disciplinary record ... will be eligible for final release in about two years.' Fereday threw the papers back on the desk and looked up.

'So, that's a potted history of Sir Josiah Sidmouth's last few years. By the way, you might be interested to know that he refers to himself as Josh Smith; that's the name everyone seems to know him by, even the guards. Maybe he wants to hide his real identity.'

Peter drew long and hard on his cigar, then picked up his tankard and took a swig of beer. 'You say he'll be eligible for final release in about two years?'

'That's correct. Seven years he got.'

'And he's been of good character, no ill-discipline?'

'That's right.'

For a little while there was silence, as if each was waiting for the other to say what both were thinking. And then Peter spoke. 'I have heard, Mr Fereday, that you have a system whereby a prisoner who has been of good character might petition for early release. I expect there are certain formalities to go through, and then somebody in authority, such as yourself, maybe, will ultimately have to make the decision. As you will appreciate, I am not familiar with the detailed procedures, but might a preferable outcome perhaps be hastened in return for ... a consideration?'

Fereday closed his eyes in deep thought for a second or two, then peered intently across the table at Peter. '*A consideration*, you say. Now exactly what might you mean by that?'

Peter leaned back in his chair and nonchalantly blew a large smoke ring towards the ceiling. 'I think you can probably guess what I mean. I did say that Josiah is very wealthy. I'm sure he would be more than happy to defray any costs that might be incurred in making the necessary arrangements. I've no doubt His Majesty's representatives here have many expenses to meet, so any little extra income would always be welcome. And knowing Josiah as I do, I am certain he would be extremely grateful to you personally should you be able to expedite his return home. I have known him to be most generous to those individuals who have been of assistance to him; if you follow my meaning. We set sail next week, and I can easily find room aboard for one more passenger.'

Fereday again sat in thought, his hands clasped in front of him resting on his ample stomach and his cigar gripped between his teeth, whilst he rocked back and forth on his chair, which creaked alarmingly under his weight. He then looked across at Peter and breathed deeply.

'That's an awful lot you're asking. And even supposing it were possible to make such an accommodation and to come to a suitable agreement over the costs involved, just how would he pay? He can't have very much money here.'

'He's an honourable man, I can assure you. And as soon as he arrived back home he would make arrangements for the debt to be settled with alacrity. You have my word on that.'

'No, no, Mr Brown, that wouldn't do, that wouldn't do at all. I have no doubt you are right and that he is a man who can be trusted. But, speaking hypothetically of course, it would be much better all round if the affair could be nicely settled before he left, payment up front, all done and dusted and preferably in cash. No offence, Mr Brown, but it's a long journey back to England and there are all sorts of dangers that might be encountered. There's many a ship been lost on such a journey, and then there's the threat of pirates. Imagine that something untoward occurred and your ship went down, all hands lost. Where would we stand then? He'd be in Davy Jones locker and you with him. Who would settle the debt then?'

Peter deliberated. If a deal could be struck, Josiah could return with him. 'I understand your reservations, Mr Fereday, but how much are we talking about? What's the going rate in these circumstances?'

'The circumstances are entirely new to me, Mr Brown. There are no *going rates*. And you really are asking an awful lot. Why, the fellow's only just completed half his sentence! You must understand the chances I might be taking in agreeing to such a request. I think it really is a question of how desperate your friend is to end his stay here. But, assuming I were able to agree, I would have thought that, shall we say, five hundred guineas would not be an unreasonable price to pay for his freedom?'

Peter sat in silence, mulling over in his mind what Fereday had said. Five hundred guineas was a lot of money and would take virtually all his resources. He had a small amount of cash of his own and also some more, issued by the army paymaster for contingency purposes. Altogether, he could just about muster the amount needed, and he'd have to pay it back as soon as they got home. He was not willing to commit himself until he had spoken to Josiah; after all, it was he who would ultimately have to pay. But the possibility of leaving now, with a guaranteed and fairly comfortable passage home might appeal to him. 'I really would like to speak to Josiah; the decision must be his. Can that be arranged?'

'I don't think that would be a problem. He's working here in Hobart. Come back this afternoon, say about three o'clock, and in the meantime I'll arrange to have him brought over.'

It was almost midday, so Peter went to have a quick word with the ship's captain regarding supplies, and then called at an inn for some lunch. The time passed quickly enough, and just before three o'clock he returned. As he entered the office, Fereday was standing looking out of a window. He turned to greet Peter.

'Ah, Mr Brown, do please take a seat. Well, let's not waste any time. I have your friend here, in the next room,' he said, pointing to a door in a corner of the office. 'I'll go and bring him in. I'll leave the two of you together so you can discuss matters and I'll return shortly.'

Fereday went through into the adjacent room. Peter heard muffled voices, and just as he rose from his chair the door opened and in walked

Josiah. The last time the two had spoken had been in Nottingham gaol shortly after the trial. For a moment or two both looked at each other without speaking. Peter was immediately struck by how much thinner Josiah had become, his skin darker than before, and he certainly seemed to have aged more than the five years which had passed since their last meeting. Peter walked over to Josiah, and taking his hand shook it firmly. 'Josiah, it's so good to see you again. How are you?'

It was a strange reunion. It took some time for them to feel comfortable in each other's presence. At first, both were a little embarrassed; the wealthy landowning aristocrat, now reduced to nothing but a common criminal, and the young up-and-coming army officer. But before long the old camaraderie which had once existed between them came flooding back. Peter explained in detail what he had been discussing with Fereday, who had already mentioned something of it to Josiah, but not that he wanted five hundred guineas, nor that Josiah could find himself homeward bound within a week if he were able to agree to the deal.

Josiah had listened intently to what Peter told him. Five hundred guineas. A great deal of money, he thought, even for him. But then he did a quick calculation. The estate would have earned double that during the time he had been away. And he had spent none of it. He could afford it, so why not? The prospect of being on a ship and homeward bound within a week was an opportunity too good to miss.

'I'll tell Feredey I accept his terms. You say he wants cash. Are you sure you can spare it, Peter?'

'Just about. I have some of my own, and then there's the regiment's contingency fund. I can use that but I'll have to repay it as soon as we get back, and I would prefer that the affair was kept as quiet as possible. I would hate to upset the Colonel.'

'Don't worry about that. Once we're back in England I can soon arrange to get the money to you.'

Fereday returned shortly and was given the news he was hoping to hear. 'I suggest you bring me the money the day before you sail. And you, sir,' said Fereday looking straight at Josiah, 'will then be free to go.'

The three men shook hands on the deal and Peter and Josiah left,

Peter back to the ship and Josiah to his lodgings. All three slept soundly that night, each of them, for their own reasons, well satisfied with the deal and all looking forward with anticipation to the following week when the transaction would be finalised.

The following Wednesday afternoon Peter went once more to see Fereday, this time carrying a leather case which he clasped tightly by his side. The money was handed over, and after twice counting it and placing it securely in a locked drawer in his desk, Fereday opened the door and spoke to his clerk. Moments later Josiah appeared. For a man of such wealth he made an odd sight. His clothes were shabby and in want of repair, and his few possessions were bundled together in a battered old carpetbag. Most men of wealth would be embarrassed to find themselves in such apparent need, but not this one. He was virtually a free man, and tomorrow he would begin his journey home. He could hardly wait.

That night he slept on the ship, but lay awake for most of the time, making plans for what he would do when he got back to England. The journey would take several months, but what was that, he asked himself, after the worst years of his life? And he was determined to make up for those lost years. There were many things he intended to do once he got back, and at the top of his list was the little matter of a reckoning; to seek out and ensure that those responsible for his suffering would themselves suffer, and rue the day they dared to cross swords with Sir Josiah Sidmouth.

Early the next morning, with the wind set fair, and just before sunrise, the ship sailed out of the harbour in Hobart and headed due west towards the Indian Ocean. At the stern stood a solitary figure, gazing back at the island that had been his prison for nearly five long years, and praying for a safe passage home. It was to be a lengthy first leg of the journey which would take them to Calcutta to pick up the soldiers, but more importantly to collect the shipment of gold. The ship spent two days there while rations were taken on board, before setting off again, with one more port of call at The Cape of Good Hope.

Eventually, after a passage of almost six months, they sailed into the East India Company's dockyard at Deptford on a fine summer's morning. This time, the solitary figure stood on the bow of the ship as it approached its mooring. And never did the nauseous odours of the docklands smell so sweet.

Within an hour, the entire contingent of soldiers had been disembarked and discharged on leave, with orders to report to regimental headquarters in two weeks time. Peter, however, needed to stay with the ship until the cargo of gold had been checked and safely removed by the representatives of the East India Company.

Once this had been dealt with, and before doing anything else, Peter and Josiah stumbled into the nearest tavern and slaked their thirsts with a quart of ale, the first to have passed their lips for a very long time. The next stop was Josiah's banker in Threadneedle Street, where he withdrew money to repay the loan Peter had made to secure his freedom.

'I intend to spend a little time here in London,' said Josiah. 'I need to recover from that wearisome journey and there are certain items of business I must attend to before heading home. And after five years in that antipodean hell I'm owed some pleasures. There's nothing in the way of entertainments that London can't offer a man with desires and the means to pay for them, and I've got plenty of both! Then I'll get a coach north. Why don't you join me, Peter? I expect you could do with a rest, and there are things I'd like to discuss with you.'

'That sounds an admirable proposition and I am due some leave. But first I must submit my account of the voyage. I know it's tiresome, but give me a day or two to sort out loose ends and then I'll join you. Where will you be staying?'

'Well, usually when I'm in London I stay at my club, Whites, a splendid institution. However, under the circumstances I might not be welcome there just yet. Some of the members can be a trifle stuffy about those who have had a brush with the law. In any case, with what I have in mind we might be better off staying in a nice little bolthole I know in Soho which I've used on occasions in the past; a small private hotel with a very accommodating and discerning proprietress. Runs a very discreet house she does, serves the best beef and oyster pie in London and has one of the finest cellars in the city. Better still, she will happily arrange for any diversion or recreation that a man-about-town could wish for. I'll show you where it is and I'll book a couple of rooms. I'm sure we can find plenty to amuse us for a while!'

Two days later, Peter, having concluded all the necessary formalities at the regiment's London headquarters, joined Josiah. A leisurely lunch followed, at which every tasty delicacy on offer was consumed, washed down with a choice of the most excellent wines to be found anywhere in London. Josiah had his sights firmly set on getting back to his estate, re-establishing himself in society and increasing his wealth, but most of all in seeking to avenge himself against the man whom he considered responsible for his enforced absence from these shores.

But all that could wait, at least for now. So, having enjoyed the gastronomic offerings of the establishment, the two men set off in search of entertainment, and indulged themselves in every manner of personal gratification that one could imagine; not to mention some which those of a more sensitive nature could never even conceive. And so, having exhausted all their pent up energies and frustrations, they at last departed London a little poorer, but left behind some of the young ladies of the city a little richer.

Josiah had found that a coach left The Black Swan in Holborn at five o'clock every morning bound for York, arriving at Newark at about nine at night, and had booked two inside seats. There was an irony in Josiah's choice of stagecoach. For unbeknown to him, his chief antagonist, the man he was now plotting to destroy, had himself made this same journey, possibly on this very same coach some six years earlier when he had been returning from exile in France.

After a lengthy, tiring and bumpy journey, the coach eventually entered Newark's large Market Square and turned into the yard of The Clinton Arms, where the two men spent the night. The next morning, after a hearty breakfast, Josiah hired a horse and trap to take them the final dozen or so miles to his family seat south of Retford.

As the trap turned off the road and into the long driveway, a strange feeling came over Josiah. Looking around him at the old familiar surroundings, little appeared to have changed. The lawns and hedges were as neat as ever, and as the stone mansion came into view it seemed as if he had only left the day before. And yet, at the same time, he felt that he had missed so much. He had been denied six years' enjoyment of his ancestral home, six years of his life wasted, stolen from him; and that made him bitter. As he stepped down from the trap, he was more determined than ever to regain his rightful place in society, and to begin planning the demise of the man for whom he now bore an increasing hatred.

As soon as he had landed back in England, Josiah had sent a message instructing his staff to have everything ready for his expected arrival in the next week or so. Within a couple of hours of their return, he and Peter had dined and were now seated on the terrace enjoying the afternoon sun, a half-empty bottle of port by their side. As they talked, there seemed only one thing on Josiah's mind and he wanted to seek Peter's views. He knew he would be returning to his regiment shortly and that it might be many months before they were able to talk again. The subject matter was clear to them both; how to destroy William Daniels.

'So what do you think, Peter? He is your brother-in-law. Any harm to him might equally hurt Abigail.'

'Oh, I wouldn't worry about Abigail' said Peter with an air of disdain. 'She's strong enough to deal with any situation that might arise. She always was headstrong and independent. We were never that close, even as children, and I haven't seen her for nearly two years now. Of course, I would never wish her any actual harm, but she chose to marry William against much opposition so she must accept the consequences. Marrying out of one's class inevitably results in problems, and to be honest I don't think mother or father would really lose any sleep if something happened to William. I know that father relented and agreed to Abigail's marriage, but deep down, I believe he would rather the match had never taken place. He tolerates him, but I think that's about as far as it goes. But what exactly do you have in mind? Circumstances have changed somewhat, and whether we like it or not, he is now a successful and fairly well-off entrepreneur. From what I hear, his business is growing steadily and he is gaining some influence and respect in the town. It won't be easy to ruin him.'

'I'm sure you're right, Peter. We'll just have to be a bit more resourceful, that's all. It could take some time and we will have to wait for the right opportunity to present itself. But anyone who has a hanged murderer for a cousin is bound to have more skeletons in his cupboard.

Trust me, I'll find some pretext to strike and when I do I'll be ready. Are you with me, Peter?'

'You know I am. I'm as keen as you are to teach the scum a lesson. But whatever happens, William is my brother-in-law, so I must insist that any involvement on my part is kept under wraps. And how on earth did you know about Thomas Dewhirst? That all happened while you were on the other side of the world.'

Josiah smiled sardonically. 'Well, that was a stroke of luck, I suppose. We had a convict arrive from Nottingham who had once worked for Daniels. It was he who told me all about Dewhirst. But as far as Daniels is concerned I intend to put some feelers out, talk to people I know and find out just what he's up to. Business is always a risk and it's easy to make enemies. And I have one particular contact in Nottingham who I reckon could be of real use to us, someone I wouldn't really want to admit to knowing. Tell me Peter, have you heard of a man called Bill Giles? No? I thought not. Not a pleasant chap, but if ever a man needs something underhand to be done, goods to be stolen or fenced, a person to go missing or a body to be disposed of, he's the man to arrange it. He's made a tidy sum over the years and he's far too clever to get caught. He never gets his own hands dirty. He has plenty of others to do his work for him.'

The two men talked late into the night. Peter stayed for another day then went to Nottingham to visit his parents, and spent three nights there before travelling back to join his regiment in Gloucester. Peter made no mention of Abigail, but his mother, Mary, insisted he see her. Mary was only too aware of the rift between William and Peter, and knew that he would rather not go down to the canal in case William was there, so she sent a message to Abigail to come up to the house on High Pavement.

She came with the children, and spent a pleasant enough afternoon there. But Nicholas and Mary could both detect a coolness between Abigail and Peter, and William was never mentioned. The talk was limited to polite chitchat, what Peter had been doing and where he had been. But in relating his adventures of the past two years, and how his duties had taken him to Van Diemen's Land, he never revealed to Abigail that he had brought Josiah back with him and that he was now ensconced once more in his ancestral home. In fact, Peter had not even told his father, who for so long had been both a friend and business colleague of Josiah, until they had fallen out over the incident which so nearly ended in Abigail's death.

He knew that, sooner or later, news of Josiah's return would leak out, but during their long discussion Josiah had accepted that Peter's part in his homecoming should never be acknowledged. That was one price he had agreed to in return for Peter's help.

Abigail left at about five o'clock, saying that she had to get the children some tea and put them to bed. She kissed Peter goodbye, wished him good luck and told him to take care, and that she looked forward to seeing him again soon. But as she walked home, she could not help feeling that all was not well. Because, for as long as she could remember, she had possessed the uncanny ability almost to read her brother's mind. And she was convinced that he was now keeping something important from her, something he didn't want to reveal. When he had told her he had been to Van Diemen's Land she had felt a spark of unease. She knew of only one person who was there, and she hoped dearly that he would never return. But she also knew that if it were humanly possible, he would try. And what was worse, he had the money, the contacts and the means to do just that. And at the thought of it, a cold shiver went down her spine.

CHAPTER SIX

—

NOTTINGHAM 1827

Abigail arrived home just after William had come in, and straight away told him where she had been and that she had seen Peter. For a short time William said nothing, and seemed lost in thought.

'How is he?' he asked at last.

'Oh, he seems well enough. He was telling me all about where he's been with the regiment. He'll be away again in a day or two. He thinks he'll be going back to India.' But Abigail could tell that William really didn't want to discuss Peter, so she quickly changed the subject. 'And what have you been up to today?'

'Well, I called to see ma and pa, but first I went up to Stoney Street to see a lace manufacturer who's just installed two new machines. He's increasing his output and is looking to send a lot of lace down to London. I've given him a decent price and he's promised to get back to me without delay. If I do win the contract, then I think you can have that new hat and those new shoes you were telling me about!'

William liked to tease her occasionally, but she could give as good as she got.

'Oh, really, my lad,' she said with a twinkle in her eye. 'Well, let me tell you, I intend to have those shoes and hat come what may. In fact I called in at Mr Farmer's on Timber Hill today and ordered them. I told him to put them on your account and he promised to deliver them on Saturday, so I'll be able to wear them when we go to dine with the Kents!'

William and Abigail had been invited to a dinner party with their solicitor, Robert Kent, and his wife. William had used Mr Kent's services ever since he bought the canal business, having been introduced to him by Abigail. She had known him for a long time, having first met him during the affair to prove William's innocence of the charges that had been made against him, and to secure his return from exile in France. Heavens above, thought Abigail, that was all of seven years ago. How time had flown! And she had recently become quite friendly with Robert's wife, Agnes. They had only been married for a few months, and Agnes was enjoying her new role as wife and mistress of her own home, and liked having friends come to visit.

'And what about your mother and father, William? How are they? It's been a while since I last saw them.'

'To tell the truth, Abigail, I'm worried about them. Pa will be fifty soon and I can tell he's not in the best of health. Ma's not too bad, but she's beginning to look tired. She brought eight of us into this world, and with everything that's happened over the years she really could do with a rest. I've been thinking. It would be good for them to get away from Narrow Marsh to somewhere a bit healthier. If we could find them a nice little cottage out of the town I bet they'd jump at the chance of moving. Not too far away, but somewhere with decent fresh air and a garden where they could grow fruit and vegetables. Pa's always said he'd like to try his hand at gardening, but he's never had the opportunity. And after all, it's not as if we can't afford to help them.'

'But what about your sisters? What would happen to them?'

'Well, there are only three of them left at home now. Maria's plenty old enough to look after herself, twenty-two and still not married. I think she might end up an old maid, but she seems happy. She's got a steady job as a lace trimmer and I know she has lots of friends. I expect one of them would find room for her. That just leaves Sarah and Elizabeth. Sarah will be sixteen in December. She's a real good looker, as you know, and she's been courting a young man for over a year now. He's apprenticed to a carpenter and he finishes his apprenticeship next year. Ma thinks that as soon as he has, he'll be walking Sarah up the aisle. That just leaves Elizabeth. She's only twelve so she'll have to go with them.'

'And Samuel? Where's he now? I haven't heard you mention him recently.'

'Ah, yes, Samuel. Now, where do I begin? I was asking pa about him. He usually calls in whenever he comes to Nottingham, but they haven't seen him for ages, and it's at least two years since I saw him.

The last time he called he was living in Manchester, but he does move around a lot. He never writes. It never was his strong point, so they never know where he is. His trouble is, he can't seem to settle to anything and he's easily led, although I think he's calmed down somewhat as he's got older. He'll be twenty-six soon, never married, but never seems to be without a girl on his arm. A real charmer is Samuel. I'm sure if he's still around at fifty he'll be no different. Still, it would be nice to see him again.'

'So what are you going to do about finding them a new place to live? And have you said anything to them?'

'No, I thought I'd wait to see if I could find somewhere suitable, then I'd broach it with them. There's no immediate rush, but I would like to do something for them before too long.'

As it turned out, things moved faster than William envisaged. At the Kent's dinner party, one of the other guests was a Mr Joseph Hallam, who was the estate manager for William Charlton, the squire over at Chilwell. During dinner, the subject of property and land prices came up, and Mr Hallam happened to mention that there was an estate cottage in the village standing empty and that he was still looking for a new tenant. He bemoaned the fact that, despite it having a little piece of land attached, sufficient to keep a few chickens and grow enough food to feed a small family, and that the rent was not excessive, it had stood empty for over two months. From the description, it seemed just what William had in mind.

'Could I come and have a look at it?' William asked, and explained why he might be interested in taking on the lease.

'Certainly. When would you like to come over?' replied Mr Hallam.

William turned to Abigail. 'How do you fancy a ride into the country tomorrow? It's some time since we had a day out anywhere. We could take the children and trot over to Chilwell and it would be good to give the new gig a run out. The weather's fine at the moment, and a day away from town would do us all a power of good.'

William had recently purchased a new gig which he intended to use when visiting clients, but had only made short journeys so far and was eager to try it out on a longer run. So it was all agreed.

'I suggest you meet me at The Chequers Inn at about midday,' said Mr Hallam. 'You'll find it just past Chilwell Hall kitchen gardens, next to the smithy and opposite the lane up to Bramcote. If I'm a bit late, don't worry. Ben Flewitt's the landlord, he'll look after you till I arrive. The cottage is just along the road from there.'

'I'm looking forward to tomorrow,' William said to Abigail enthusiastically as they walked back home later that evening. 'It's one place I've never been to, but I've heard it's nice and quiet. And the cottage sounds as if it could be just what we're looking for.'

'You may be right, William. But if it really is as quiet as you say, I think it might take your mother and father a bit of getting used to. It'll be a complete contrast to where they are now. I'll never forget that first time I ventured into Narrow Marsh, trying to find you. What a shock that was!'

'Ah well, they breed 'em tough there.'

'A good job, too. Otherwise you would never have survived. But I agree with you, William. If we can find them somewhere better to live, we should do so. There's plenty who will never be able to get out of Narrow Marsh, but we can afford to help them, so why don't we?'

The next morning dawned sunny and warm with just a gentle breeze, a perfect June day. The children were very excited when they heard they were going for a ride out into the country in their father's new gig. After breakfast, Abigail prepared a picnic lunch while William fetched a horse from the stables and put it into the shafts. Just before eleven they climbed aboard and off they set. Into Canal Street, then up Greyfriar's Gate, Lister Gate, Church Lane, past St. Peter's Church and into the Market Place. Despite it being a Sunday, it was busy with people, most, no doubt, attracted out of their homes by the fine summer weather. Small groups of men were lounging about outside the many inns and public houses, some, by their antics and behaviour, making it plain that they had already partaken generously of the liquid refreshments available within.

As they passed through Chapel Bar, William cracked the whip, urging the horse up the steadily rising gradient of Derby Road. But the animal was young and strong and had no difficulty hauling its light load to the top. Once past the barracks it was an easy trot downhill. The town had now been left behind, and, apart from the occasional cottage, fields and gardens lined the road down towards Lenton. Soon they were rattling over the canal bridge and past the ornate stone lodge gates to Wollaton Park and Hall, and the memories of youthful excursions along the canal to Langley Mill came flooding back into William's mind. One occasion, in particular, he would never forget as long as he lived. He turned to Abigail, and nodded towards the lodge gates and the park beyond.

'Do you remember the day you rescued Hugh and me from the gamekeeper, after we'd climbed over the wall into the park? I didn't know you then. I was just fourteen and I'd only ever seen you once before, but if you hadn't been out riding in the park that day and happened to come by, I don't know what would have become of me. I'd certainly have got a thrashing from him. Benner was his name. I wonder if he's still employed there?' Abigail smiled and looked back at William. 'Have you ever wondered, Abigail, how fate can affect our lives? If you hadn't been there that day, we would never have got to know each other. I'd probably still be living in Narrow Marsh, doing a miserable job for poverty wages, and you'd have married some rich gent. I could have endured any number of thrashings by Benner, but the thought of not having met you is unbearable.'

Abigail didn't reply. She didn't need to. He knew what she was thinking. She just squeezed his hand and looked lovingly into his eyes.

Although they were on the Derby Turnpike, they encountered few other vehicles that morning as they trotted along. To the left, the land swept gradually down towards the River Trent, about two miles distant, and beyond it they could see the hills of Clifton, and the trees marking Clifton Grove. And this time, it was Abigail who reminded William of the day they had spent there as she taught him to ride a horse. To their right, their view was obscured by the high brick wall that surrounded Wollaton Park, but as the road rose somewhat they were able to glimpse, in the distance, the four tall towers of the hall standing prominently at the top of the highest point of the park.

In a short distance they came to another, smaller, set of lodge gates, immediately opposite the lane to Beeston. This was the Ashby Turnpike, and, after stopping at the gate to pay the toll, they turned into the lane which wound its way between fields and gardens, past a number of large imposing houses and some scattered cottages. The road then took a sharp right turn, and, after crossing a little brook by a narrow bridge, soon brought them to the village of Beeston. William thought it a mean-looking place. There were a few dilapidated cottages and a couple of beer houses on the turnpike, but the centre of the village seemed to be over to their left.

On the corner of the crossroads, where a lane headed down towards the canal and river, there stood a tall dour-looking factory. William knew this to be Mr Lowe's silk mill, as he had carried the occasional consignment for him to London from the wharf on the Beeston Canal. It was silent today, but William knew that by six the following morning many of the inhabitants of the area would be trudging along here to spend another long day at the machines, no doubt for a pittance of pay. Mr Lowe was not renowned for his generosity, and was known to be a fierce opponent of those who were seeking parliamentary reform and better wages for the mill hands. In that respect Mr Lowe was not alone and many of the local gentry shared his views, including Mr William Charlton, the squire of Chilwell, who before long might be his own father's landlord.

Passing the Parish Church of St. John, Beeston was soon left behind and the road once more took on a rural atmosphere. But within a short distance they found themselves surrounded by numerous greenhouses. A tall brick building on their left carried a freshly painted sign, declaring this to be *Mr J. Pearson's Seed Warehouse*. All around, the land was laid out for the propagation of plants, flowers, bushes and fruit trees. Here, the road took a sharp dip down, and to the children's delight they splashed their way through a shallow ford where a small brook crossed the road, winding its way from the low hills on their right and along its meandering course towards the Trent.

Rising up on the other side of the brook, they were now approaching the outskirts of the village, and more buildings came into view. A narrow, tree-lined lane formed a crossroads, where a large rambling house occupied one corner, in contrast to the smaller cottages on the other three. These were mostly single-storeyed with tiny windows and thatched roofs, many in need of urgent repair. A small group of elderly people sat outside, chatting and enjoying the late morning sunshine, and they nodded a pleasant greeting to the strangers coming into their village.

More houses and cottages followed, and a range of farm buildings on their right immediately preceded a pair of tall, ornate, wrought-iron gates hung on solid stone pillars, guarding the main entrance to Chilwell Hall. To either side of these gates, a high wall of stone and brick marked the boundary of the squire's house and grounds. But so high was the wall, so thick were the bushes and so tall were the trees within the grounds, that the hall itself lay secluded and unseen from those passing by on the road below.

Opposite the hall gates, a narrow lane flanked by fields of cows and sheep led to a cluster of tiny cottages, across from which, and behind a small grassy area and duck pond, stood a substantial, ivy-covered house with twin gables and tall chimneys, nestling snugly behind low well-trimmed hedges.

William then reminded himself of the directions he had been given by Mr Hallam, and as they passed the entrance to the hall he observed, on the opposite side of the road, the squire's extensive kitchen gardens. Next to these, and fronting immediately onto the road was a row of old buildings, the first of which was The Chequers Inn. Facing it, another narrow lane rose steeply from the road and vanished round a sharp bend, the lane to Bramcote as described by Mr Hallam.

Next to the inn was a blacksmith's forge and cottage, and beyond that a tiny chapel, which, from its humble appearance and simplicity, William took to be of the nonconformist persuasion. The inn appeared to be by far the most ancient of the three. The two end walls each consisted almost entirely of solid stone chimney stacks, but the rest of the building was timber framed with whitewashed walls of wattle and plaster, and a thatched roof.

It was a long, low building of two storeys, the tiny windows of the three upper rooms being almost hidden under the overhanging thatch of the dipping roof. A single door in the centre of the inn marked the entrance, over which hung a square wooden sign depicting a chequers board, badly in need of repainting.

Voices could be heard from within. William stepped out of the gig, and was just lifting the children down when the door opened and a man came out. He was tall, about sixty years old, but well built, with a ruddy face and long white side whiskers.

'Good day, sir,' he said with a smile. 'That's a fine gig you have there. Have you come far?'

'Nottingham,' replied William. 'I'm here to see a Mr Joseph Hallam. He told me to meet him at The Chequers Inn. Do you know him?'

'Oh, aye, we all know Joe. The Squire's steward. He's not here at the moment but I expect he'll be along shortly. He usually calls in for a couple of pints on a Sunday. You can wait for him inside, or there's a nice garden round the back. You might prefer that. Your children can play there while you're waiting.'

'Thank you, I think we will.' The man said goodbye and set off, but almost immediately he turned into the cottage next to the forge. 'He must be the blacksmith,' William said to Abigail as she stepped down from the gig, the picnic basket in one hand. William carried Catherine while young Charles skipped alongside.

'Look, we can get to the garden down the side here,' said William, leading the way, and they were soon seated on a bench at the back of the inn. The garden was given up mainly to a large grassy area, bordered by pretty flower beds alongside the hedges on each side. A few apple and pear trees grew at the bottom of the garden, whilst the rear wall of the inn was almost completely covered by huge climbing roses, festooned with pink, red and yellow flowers, the thick branches signifying their considerable age. 'I'll go and get us something to drink and we can have our picnic out here. I don't suppose the landlord will mind.'

William entered the inn through the back door and as he did so the babble of conversation from those within suddenly ceased, the sure sign of a stranger's intrusion. He found himself in a small oblong room, thick with the smell of tobacco. It was simply furnished with wooden settles along the walls, and some tables and chairs in the middle on the flagstone floor. The only natural light came from four tiny windows, two looking out into the garden and one either side of the door to the village street. The right-hand wall was taken up by a large stone fireplace, whilst at the other end of the room was a tiny bar in one corner, behind which a door led to a small kitchen. Inside the kitchen, William could see a low wooden trestle on which stood two barrels. A man was filling a stoneware pitcher from one of these, and once it was full he came through and placed it on the bar.

'Good day,' said William, and, having broken the silence, the murmurs of conversation gradually started up again. 'I'd like a pint of ale please, and do you have something less strong? My wife and two youngsters are outside in your garden.'

'I've some lemonade, nice and fresh. The wife made it just this morning.'

'That'll do fine,' said William. The landlord poked his head round the kitchen door and shouted.

'Rose, bring some of that lemonade through.' Shortly, a woman appeared carrying a jug. She smiled and nodded silently at William as she handed the jug to her husband, who began to fill three mugs he had taken from a shelf. Both she and her husband were small and stocky. She was older than him, and William reckoned she must be getting on for fifty.

'I assume you're the landlord. Mr Flewitt, is it?' continued William.

'That's me. Ben's the name. My fame has obviously spread,' he quipped. 'But I've not seen you in here before.'

'No, it's my first visit to Chilwell. I've come to see Mr Joseph Hallam and he said to meet him here. It was he who gave me your name. I spoke to a man who came out the front door just as we arrived. He said he thought Mr Hallam would be along soon.'

'Oh, that would be Tom Keetley, the blacksmith. Lives next door. Yes, Joe will be along in a bit. When he comes in I'll tell him you're in the garden. What name is it?'

'William Daniels, from Nottingham.'

William took the drinks into the garden and they set about eating the picnic they had brought. They had almost finished when Mr Hallam emerged from the back door, a tankard of ale in his hand.

'William, and Abigail, how are you both? It's so good to see you again. And what about you two young rascals?' he said, looking down at the children who were staring up at this stranger. 'How do you like it out here in the country?'

Catherine stared silently at Joseph for a few seconds before burying her face, shyly, in her mother's skirts. Charles was bolder.

'We came in daddy's new gig. It was a bit bumpy. Have you got a gig?'

'I have, but I bet it's not as grand as yours.'

'No, I expect not.' replied Charles, with all the innocence of childhood.

'You found us all right then, William?'

'Yes, quite easily. Thank you for meeting us. We've just about finished our picnic, so whenever you're ready we can go and look at the cottage.'

'Well, there's no hurry on my part. My wife's been to church over at Attenborough and then she's calling to see an old lady she knows there, so she won't be home just yet.'

They sat in the warm midday sun, chatting and finishing their drinks. Joseph was able to answer all William's questions about the village. He wanted to find out everything he could about it and satisfy himself that it was the right place to offer his parents a new home. Soon they were ready to go.

'Come along then,' said Joseph. 'It's not far. Just down the road.'

They followed him down the side of the inn then turned left and on through the village. On the opposite side of the road, behind a long garden, stood another public house, The Red Lion.

'Two pubs. You'll not go thirsty here!' said William.

'Three actually. We also have The Bull's Head a bit further on.'

They ambled slowly along the road. With the exception of one very large and imposing house, all the other buildings were modest, either simple labourers' cottages or small houses. Some had the familiar long row of windows in the upper storey, indicating their use by stocking makers. In a couple of minutes they reached the cottage.

'Here we are,' said Joseph. The cottage was on the left, a few yards back from the road, behind a small patch of garden. He opened the simple wooden gate in the low fence surrounding the property and they followed him up a cinder path. On either side was a fine display of flowers, but the many weeds suggested recent neglect. Joseph took a key from his pocket and unlocked the door. Before going in, William stepped back to take a good look. It was small, two-storeyed and built of brick, rendered and whitewashed. The roof was tiled, and four windows, two up and two down, indicated the rooms. At each end was a chimney stack. The front door opened into a small entrance hall, and directly ahead a narrow flight of stairs led to the upper floor. On each side of the hall, doors led to the two downstairs rooms. They followed Joseph through the right-hand door into a small square room with a simple fireplace. Then back to the other room which was clearly the main living room, bigger than the first, with a much larger fireplace and deep mantelpiece. From this room another door led into a small kitchen-cum-scullery. This contained an iron cooking range and next to it a big stone sink with a waste pipe leading to the outside. On one wall were two cupboards; but apart from these few items of furniture, all the rooms were bare. From the kitchen a door led out to the rear of the cottage.

Upstairs there were two rooms, each of a similar size to those below. The upstairs rooms had wooden floorboards, whilst those downstairs were all stone-flagged. They retraced their steps and followed Joseph out into the garden. This faced south, and was bathed in the full sunlight of early afternoon. On the left was a small brick outhouse which doubled up as both privy and wash house. 'A privy, just for one cottage!' exclaimed William, who remembered his own childhood in Narrow Marsh where one privy was shared by dozens of households. To the right was a wooden shed with one very wide window facing down the garden. William looked in and was surprised to see a stocking frame.

'That'll be taken away soon,' said Joseph. 'It belongs to a hosier in Beeston. The former tenant rented it, but he and his family have moved away to Loughborough.'

The garden was quite long. William judged it perhaps a hundred feet. A path led down the middle to a low hedge, beyond which were fields containing cattle. Each side of the path was taken up by vegetable plots, fruit trees and bushes, all overgrown and unattended for some time. There was a gap in the hedge, behind which was a well and a pathway leading to the cottages on either side.

'There's plenty of fresh water from the well there; it's shared with the adjacent cottages,' explained Joseph.

'And didn't you say it's been empty for about two months?' asked William.

'That's right. It's a nice little cottage, simple but well built. Put up about fifty years ago. It'll be cosy enough, once it's cleaned up a bit and furnished.'

'And how much is the rent?'

'Five pounds a year, payable each quarter day.'

William took Abigail on one side. 'What do you reckon? It seems fine to me. The rent's not excessive. A little more than what they're currently paying, but think how much better this would be for them. Their own garden, water on hand and their own privy! They could get the cottage cleaned up. Even have the inside whitewashed. And the air. Just breathe in that fresh air!' After a short discussion their minds were made up.

'We'll take it,' said William, extending his hand to shake on the deal. 'At least, providing my mother and father want to move. But I don't think they'll say no. I'd like to bring them over here to have a look at it first if you don't mind, and then I'll get back to you, if that's all right.'

'That's fine,' said Joseph. 'You'd better take the key, then you can show them round whenever it suits you. When you've been, come and let me know and bring the key back. I live in the house opposite The Bull's Head.'

'Oh, just one more thing,' said William. 'That stocking frame. Do you think it could still be available?'

'Well, as I said, it belongs to a Beeston hosier. I know he was intending to remove it shortly, but I don't know if he has a use for it. Why, do you want it left here?'

'It just occurred to me that father might like to keep his hand in. It could bring in a bit of extra money, provided the rent for it isn't too high.'

'Leave it with me. I'll find out and let you know.'

William and Abigail had one more look round the cottage, then thanked Joseph, who locked the door, handed over the key and accompanied them back to the inn. They said their goodbyes, then climbed into the gig and set off for home.

'I'll go round and see ma and pa tomorrow and tell them all about it,' said William as they trotted along the road towards Beeston. 'But you'd better come with me. Ma's bound to want a female opinion. And I guess they'll want to have a look at it, so I could bring them over here one day next week.'

The following day, William and Abigail walked over to Narrow Marsh and told William's parents all about the cottage. At first they were somewhat stunned, but after the idea had sunk in they became quite excited. William said he could take them to have a look at it the following weekend. So, on the Saturday afternoon James and Margaret, along with the two youngest girls, Sarah and Elizabeth, came down to the boatyard. William had the gig ready, but it was a bit of a squeeze this time, with five of them aboard. Apart from the steep climb up Derby Road, where the two girls had to get out and walk, the journey went smoothly, and within the hour they had arrived and were busy inspecting the cottage. It didn't take them long to make up their minds. James had only ever lived in a town, but Margaret had been born and brought up in a Derbyshire village, so moving here would be a bit like returning to her roots.

The arrangements were soon made. William let Joseph know that they would take the cottage. James gave notice to his landlord that they were to quit their tenement in Narrow Marsh and the eldest daughter, Maria, found lodgings with some friends. A month later, one of William's large four wheel delivery carts was loaded with the family's possessions for the short journey to their new home. Despite looking forward to the move, they did have a few regrets at leaving the area that had been their home for so many years. And so, after saying goodbye to all their near neighbours and friends, and giving them an open invitation to come and visit them at any time, they climbed into William's gig and followed their belongings to their new life in the country.

It didn't take them long to settle in and Margaret soon had the cottage furnished to her liking. James had been allowed to keep the stocking frame, which gave him a small but steady income, and he also set to with a vengeance clearing the garden of weeds and preparing it for planting, and although it was now late summer, he still had time to put in some winter vegetables. They quickly got to know their neighbours, and before long had settled down and were becoming accustomed to their new surroundings.

William had been very busy since the move, but after a few months he found the time to take Abigail and the children to visit his parents and see how they were getting on. He could tell that they both seemed much better, and there was no doubt in his mind that the move had been a good one for them. This was a far healthier place to live and William felt pleased that he had been able to help them. He had a feeling that all seemed well with the world; his business was thriving and his parents were happily settled in their new home. But, as is sometimes the case, just when everything seems to be in harmony, things can happen to shatter the illusion.

And so it proved to be, for in late November there came the news that his maternal grandfather, Abraham, had died, leaving his grandmother Matilda, to fend for herself. Abraham had been ill for a considerable time and it was clear that his long years of toil in the ironworks at Butterley had worn him out. All the family went to the funeral at Pentrich, and Margaret was particularly sad to have to leave her mother all alone. On their way back, William heard her mention to James that she would like her mother to come and live with them in their new home.

Although he had never managed to see him very often, William had always been fond of his grandfather. And just as he was getting over the sadness he felt at his death, there soon began a series of disturbing incidents which made him believe that he had become the target of a deliberate campaign to discredit him and cause harm to him, his family and his business.

CHAPTER SEVEN

—

NOTTINGHAM 1828

As 1827 drew to a close, William was able to look back with some satisfaction over what had been a hard, but ultimately rewarding twelve months. On Christmas Day, William and Abigail, along with the children, joined Abigail's parents at St. Mary's Church for the morning service. Afterwards, they called in at their house on High Pavement for a festive glass of mulled wine, before returning home, where William's parents and most of his brothers and sisters were to join them for a big family gathering, the first for many a year. A rare old time was had by all, and after their dinner, as William and his father sat contentedly by the fire enjoying a drink and a smoke, William couldn't help but consider just how different things were from when he was a child. He now had a fine house and his own business and never, in his wildest dreams, could he have believed that he would achieve such a position in life. And he remembered a previous Christmas Day, when he had passed by that grand house on High Pavement and spotted coming out the door the girl who was now his wife. What luck that he had passed by the house just at that moment. Had he been a few minutes earlier or later, the whole course of his life might have taken a different path. He might still be toiling long hours, a slave to the stocking frame, instead of the owner of a promising and growing enterprise.

The eating, drinking and talking went on until late, so late in fact that the visitors all stayed for the night. The next morning they set off back home, and in the afternoon William and Abigail went again to Abigail's parents, where her Uncle George and Aunt Alice had just arrived from Newark. Abigail was as pleased to see them, the first time since Catherine had been born, as they were to see their new great-niece. After dinner, George and William went into the library, and over a brandy spent some time discussing their shared interest in canal transport. George was fascinated to hear what William had to say about how he viewed the future, and how he thought that railways might one day take over from canals.

'I don't know about that,' said George, 'but if it should ever happen, I doubt that I'll be getting involved. I'm too old. I've been in the river trade for over forty years now. Boats, rivers and canals, that's been my life and I think they'll do me till my time comes. But I'm not one to oppose progress, not like some people I could name. I'll never forget the controversy that erupted when the idea of building the canal to Nottingham was first mooted. I realised straight away what a great benefit it would be to everyone, not least to those of us already involved in the river trade. I knew that it would open up new markets and increase my business. And with other canal schemes that were being promoted, before long I'd be able to send goods more quickly and easily from Newark down to London by river and canal. Much safer than sending them out via Boston and then by sea. But a lot of people were dead against it. Said it would put them out of business, ruin the countryside and reduce the value of their property. And they reckoned not a wife or daughter would be safe from the evil intentions of passing boatmen! What tommyrot!

'I particularly remember one chap by the name of Phillips who lived at Lenton, next to where the canal was to be built. He had some land and a workshop there making furniture, and he did everything he could to try and stop it. Silly man! He could have used the canal to bring in the timber he needed and then to transport his furniture to new markets, but he couldn't see it. Once the canal opened he sold his land to an enterprising young fellow who wanted to open a boat building yard, then retired and moved out to Wilford. It didn't do him any good though. With no trade to occupy his time, but plenty of money in his pocket, he turned to drink. A couple of months later he was returning from Nottingham one dark night, three sheets to the wind, and got run over by a cart near Trent Bridge. They took him home and put him to bed but he never recovered and died the following week.

'But that's all in the past. You have a long time ahead of you William. You must grasp every opportunity that comes your way. Mind you, I can imagine if ever these railways do get built, especially with their smoky, snorting fire-breathing engines, there'll be a lot more like Phillips and his kind to contend with!'

Their discussion was suddenly interrupted as Abigail came into the library. 'Now then you two, that's enough talking shop. Come on through to the drawing room. We're all going to have a game of blind man's bluff and the children insist on everyone taking part.'

But all too soon, the short Christmas holiday was over, and everyone returned to their normal day-to-day working routine. The tragedy of cousin Thomas had almost faded from their memories, but early in the new year a fresh scandal was about to erupt which would grip the townsfolk for many months. Some of those with a warped sense of humour found it amusing. Most considered it at the very least shocking, and a few found it quite frightening. But William was more worried that the episode might give his business a bad name.

It all started one day towards the end of January when William arrived home one afternoon to find Abigail in a state of some distress. She was seated at the kitchen table drinking a cup of tea, Benjamin by her side.

'Oh, you're back at last William, thank goodness. You've no idea what's been happening.' William sat down beside her and put his arms round her shoulders.

'Now then, whatever's the matter?'

'I'll let Benjamin explain. He got involved. He'll be able to tell you all about it.'

'Well,' said Benjamin, 'I was in the office going through some delivery notes when I heard a cart come into the yard. I went out, just as the man was lowering the tail board. There was a big wicker hamper on the back, bound with thick leather straps, and it seemed rather heavy so I offered to give him a hand. He kept looking round, and I sensed that he was a bit agitated. He said he wanted the hamper sent to London as quickly as possible, and I noticed that it was already labelled to a Mr Rogers at an address in Paddington. I helped him carry it into the warehouse, and asked him what it contained. He muttered something about that not being important, and said he was under strict instructions from his boss to make sure it got despatched by the next available fly boat; that it was essential that it was not delayed and that Mr Rogers was urgently awaiting its arrival. There was something about the man that made me suspicious. He was smallish, about forty years old with grey thinning hair and pockmarks on his right cheek. He wore an old pair of moleskin trousers, a filthy white shirt, dark blue muffler and an even dirtier blue jacket with holes in both sleeves. He looked much the worse for wear and smelt even worse than he looked. Goodness knows where he'd been! Anyway, I asked him his name and told him I needed to know what was in the hamper so I could work out the right charge. He said his name was Jones and that he didn't rightly know what was in the hamper. So I told him he'd better open it up so we could have a look. At this, he turned pale and said he couldn't possibly do that, or his boss would kill him. I told him he had a choice: either open it, or take it away. He hesitated for a moment, then said he'd go straight back to his boss to check what was in it, and that he'd be back in no time.

'Without saying another word, he got into the cart, took the reins and was off like a shot. Well, that only made me even more suspicious, I can tell you, so I told one of the men to keep an eye on the office and I followed him. I got out into the road just in time to see him in the distance rattling along Leen Side. I ran after him as fast as I could go, but he was really giving the horse some whip and I was having difficulty keeping him in sight. He turned into Crossland Street, but by the time I got there, there was no sign of him. I asked two lads who were loafing around if they'd seen him, but they were of no help until I tossed them a couple of pennies, when they pointed to the alley that cuts through into Crossland Court. But there was no sign of him there either, so I took the only other exit, which takes you through into Leen Court and had a good scout round there. Anyway, to cut a long story short, I eventually found the cart in a yard at the back of The King's Head, but there was no sign of Mr Jones. So I went in the back door of the pub and through to the front bar, where there were some men drinking, and asked if anyone knew where the man was that had the cart, a Mr Jones. The landlord said he didn't know anyone called Jones, but when I described him he said that sounded like old Bullivant, who did odd jobs for a man called Bill Giles. At the mention of this name, everyone went quiet, and a voice piped up saying it was best not to tangle with him. Then someone else said that, as he was coming into the bar a few minutes back, Bullivant had gone out into Narrow Marsh. And just as he spoke I saw Bullivant through the window with another man, getting into a spring cart. He was an evil-looking sod, the other one. I'll not forget his face in a hurry. So I ran out into Narrow Marsh, just as they were making off, and shouted at them to stop, but they were away too fast and turned down London Road towards Trent Bridge. It was pointless trying to follow them, so I set off back here. I was very suspicious by now, so I called in on the way to see Jeffries, the constable. He came back with me and when we got here we opened the hamper. You'll never guess what was in it!'

'Well?' said William, who had been hanging on to Benjamin's every word, 'what was in it?'

'Bodies! Two of them. An old woman's and a young lad's. Fresh they were, too. Didn't really smell much so I don't reckon they'd been dead long. They'd clearly been dug up recently, though. There was earth and mud still on them but they were well wrapped up in woollen sheets.'

'Where are they now?' asked William.

'Jeffries took them away to the Guard House.'

'Resurrection men!' exclaimed William.

'That's what Jeffries thought. He said there'd been reports of funny goings-on at night in St. Mary's burial ground, lights seen and noises heard, but this was the first proof they've had that any bodies had been dug up. I expect they'll have to find out who the Mr Rogers is in London, and they're trying to find the two culprits up here, but my guess is they'll be well away by now.'

'It was awful,' said Abigail. 'I was there when they opened the hamper. That poor old woman and that little boy. He couldn't have been more than four years old; nearly the same age as our Catherine. At least, they won't have known anything about what's happened to them.'

Word soon spread round the town and hundreds of curious onlookers visited the Guard House the next day to view and try and identify the bodies. The boy was soon recognised and his mother, terribly distraught, took the body away to be re-interred. The poor lad had only been buried the previous week. The old woman was also identified by her sons. She had been buried just three days before, having died a pauper, living in a wretched one room hovel where her body had been found covered in filth and vermin. But the most astonishing thing was that when her two sons removed her meagre possessions, they found over £100 hidden away in the room.

Over the next few days, resurrection fever swept through the town. The relatives and friends of anyone recently interred were anxious to check that their loved ones had not suffered the same fate, and many of them took to digging up the coffins to make sure they were still there. It came as a shock when it was found that over thirty bodies had gone; all, no doubt, sold to hospitals where the medical students were in desperate need of corpses for dissection. The events were extensively reported in the various newspapers, not only in Nottingham but much further afield. As for the resurrection men, they seemed to have vanished without trace and were never apprehended.

But what concerned William most was that his name was mentioned in all the newspapers as the chosen carrier of the cadavers to London. It was clear that all the other bodies that had been taken had been disposed of quietly and secretly without anyone knowing, but on this occasion it was almost as if the perpetrators wanted their exploits to be discovered. Perhaps their main aim had been to tarnish William's good name and reputation. And when, following enquiries, it transpired that the Mr Rogers at Paddington, to whom the hamper had been addressed, simply didn't exist, William became even more convinced that the whole sordid episode had been designed to cause him and his business the maximum damage and embarrassment.

From then on, William made it clear that no suspicious packages were to be accepted for carriage, and there was no repetition. But mud sticks, and in the following months, on more than one occasion, William got the feeling that some of his customers were not so friendly and forthcoming as before, and not quite so willing to trust him with the safe transport of their goods.

And then, later that year, there occurred another disturbing incident. In the middle of July, Nottingham suffered the most horrendous thunderstorm it had experienced for years; a day of continuous and unremitting torrents of rain. Streams overflowed and the Trent was close to bursting its banks. Such sewers that had been laid were unable to cope with the vast volume of water and many of the lower lying parts of the town were flooded, including much of the Narrow Marsh area, where ground floor tenements were awash with filthy water and sewage. Viewing the devastation for himself was heartbreaking, and William was thankful that his parents had moved and had avoided this catastrophe. The only benefit for William was that water levels were fully restored to the canals, and the overflow weirs ensured that his boatyard and premises escaped any risk of flooding.

The rain ceased late at night. Then early the next morning one of William's boats with a consignment of coal was dropping down through Castle Lock, just above the wharf. As the paddles were opened and the water level dropped, a body suddenly floated to the surface. The boatmen pulled it out and laid it below the lock at the coal wharf. William was summoned, and he sent Benjamin to inform the constable. But even before they returned, a crowd had gathered and the body was soon recognised as that of Walter Blundy, an elderly inhabitant of the town and a well-known eccentric character. Jeffries, the constable, arrived and ordered that the body be taken to The Navigation Inn, which stood alongside.

The next day the coroner attended and swore in a jury. There was nothing to indicate why or how the man had come to be in the canal, and there were no signs of violence against the body. A witness, who knew the deceased, said that he had seen him the previous afternoon walking through the Market Place in the pouring rain, without coat or hat, and had urged the old man to return home or seek shelter. He had replied that, as it was July, there was no need for a coat or hat, and that he would return home when he had concluded his business and when it suited him, and that furthermore he was not going to allow a little rain to dictate his movements. The coroner speculated as to whether the floods might have had anything to do with the incident, but after a short discussion the jury declared a verdict of 'found drowned' but with no explanation as to the cause.

Again, the local newspapers reported the incident. It was not uncommon for bodies to be found in the canal, most assumed to be suicides, and such incidents merited little coverage on the part of the press. But this was different. The man was well known in the town and many column inches were devoted to him. 'Old Walt', as he was affectionately known was best remembered, amongst his various whims, for having provided himself with a coffin which, he being a staunch supporter of the Tory cause, was painted blue inside. For over twenty years he had used the coffin as a cupboard, pending the day when it would fulfil its true purpose, and he was in the habit, each year on his birthday, of donning his best suit and trying out the coffin for size. He would then get several of his friends to parade the coffin through the town whilst he himself followed on behind as chief mourner.

A few days later the coffin was at last put to its proper and intended use. His funeral at St. Mary's Church attracted hundreds of mourners, after which he was laid to rest in accordance with his final wishes; not in the churchyard, but in the garden of his house near Canning Circus. The coffin, followed by the mourners, was carried there by those same friends who had performed the ceremony each year on his birthday. But this time Old Walt was not following on behind.

That would have been the end of the matter, except that, once again, some of the newspapers made clear mention of whose employees it was who had discovered the body in the canal. And then the Nottingham Journal, the principal Tory paper of the town, published a letter from a reader signing himself Joshua Smith which William read with growing anger and dismay:

Sir

It was with the most profound sorrow and distress that I read in your columns of the sad demise of Mr Walter Blundy, that most worthy resident of Nottingham, who for the most part of his 78 years has never flinched in his unswerving support of the Tory cause, a cause which your own pages have long espoused. I note, with interest, that the decision of the coroner's jury was that he was 'found drowned' but that is merely a statement of the facts. Am I alone in wondering what exactly caused him to be drowned? I do not, for one moment, believe that it was in Mr Blundy's nature to have been the instrument of his own death, and any suggestion of an accident whilst under the influence of strong drink would be offensive in the extreme, such was his devotion to the state of abstinence.

One could, therefore, question whether a third party might be involved in this tragedy. Knowing of Mr Blundy's political leanings, nobody could be criticised for thinking that perhaps some of those persons of a more revolutionary nature might see fit to rid the town of a man who has never refrained from declaring his support for our cause, and who, by his continued notoriety and existence, has for long been a thorn in the side of those who currently strive to bring about parliamentary reform and radical change. I note that the body was discovered by boatmen belonging to a carrier whose own views are well known in this town to be diametrically opposed to those of Mr Blundy. One must speculate, therefore, to what extent was it coincidental that it was his employees who found the deceased.

Yours faithfully

Joshua Smith

On first reading the letter, William's natural inclination was to seek legal advice with a view to bringing an action both against the newspaper and Mr Joshua Smith, for defamation. But, having thought the matter through and after discussing it with Abigail, they both considered that it would be better to ignore it and let sleeping dogs lie. The matter would soon be forgotten, they thought, and pursuing it would only lead to more publicity.

But it did not alter the fact that, so it seemed, somebody was determined to harm William. His support for those who sought change was no secret, and he was a firm supporter of the move for parliamentary reform and giving more men the vote. But many other respected members of the community agreed with him. So why, he wondered, should this Joshua Smith single out him for criticism, almost to the point of suggesting that he might be behind Mr Blundy's death? He had never heard of Joshua Smith, who had not given an address, as was customary. Most correspondents to the newspapers were well known amongst the town's business fraternity, so William made some enquiries; but nobody seemed to know who he was. William also wrote to the newspaper's proprietors, asking if they would confirm the writer's identity, but was curtly told that this was not their policy and that they would always maintain a correspondent's confidentiality, should he request it.

In his large country house in the north of the County, Josiah Sidmouth opened his copy of the Nottingham Journal and reread the letter, aloud, for the benefit of his guest. Placing it back on a table, he turned to the man sitting opposite him.

'Well, Peter, it seems our Mr Daniels has been having problems with bodies this year, what with consignments of them to London, and now his workmen fishing one out of the canal. He does seem to be awfully unlucky, if one believes in luck, that is. Personally, I'm no great believer in luck. I'm more inclined to the theory that for every effect there is a cause. Sometimes, though, it is necessary to manipulate things a little, to oil the wheels, so to speak, and make things happen. As I said the last time you were here, Peter, I know we might have to be patient but if that's what it takes, so be it. Business is always a risk and it's easy to make enemies. But we've made a start! Now, have another glass of port and tell me what you've been up to. And how was India?'

CHAPTER EIGHT

—

NOTTINGHAM 1829

Towards the end of April one of William's boatmen brought him a message from Gilbert Wells that he wanted to see him as soon as possible to discuss a business matter. The output at his Eastwood mine had been increasing substantially and William was finding it difficult at times to provide enough boats to move all the coal. And then there had been some unfortunate delays when two of his boats had been found holed below the water line and had to be taken out of service for a few days whilst they were repaired. William never did find out how the damage had occurred, but he was convinced that it was not accidental and suspected that someone had sabotaged them.

He was worried that these recent problems could have caused Gilbert to look for another carrier and that he might lose the contract, so he sent a message back saying he would come up to Eastwood in two days time.

William breakfasted early that morning, said goodbye to Abigail and the children and joined the boatmen as they headed north. He rarely got out on the boats, so busy was he with other aspects of the business, and he enjoyed what for him was a rare treat. An empty boat was making the short journey up the Nottingham Canal to collect another load of coal, and riding high in the water, progress was swift. Once they had passed the top lock at Wollaton it was level all the way, but now the canal twisted and turned, hugging the contours as it made its way north along the side of the Erewash valley. On they went, through Trowell, Cossall and Awsworth, until before long they could see in the distance the wharf to where horses brought the coal wagons down the tramroad from the mine.

It was very near here, William recalled, that the ill-fated uprising of 1817 had come to an abrupt and violent end when the waiting cavalry had easily routed the marchers making their way from Pentrich to Nottingham. His own Uncle Edward had been amongst the men taking part in this attempt to overthrow what they considered a corrupt Government. He had been fortunate to escape being captured by the soldiers and had had to flee for his life. The whole sorry episode had been a hopeless and unwise affair, thought William, but one born out of desperation amongst men trying to support their families on starvation wages; men who had no vote and nothing to lose, except their lives. And some did. Others were gaoled, others transported, and some, like Edward, managed to escape. He had gone to France and was still there, fearful of returning until times changed.

As they approached the wharf, a pair of horses was just arriving with a train of four wagons, to join another four already waiting to have their contents transhipped into the boats. The wharf and tramroad had been built by Gilbert when he had opened his colliery. The canal had been widened sufficiently to allow the boats to turn, and a stone platform built for the boats to moor alongside whilst they were loaded. Adjacent to this platform there were sidings to store loaded and empty wagons. Two brick buildings stood nearby. One was a small office furnished with a desk and a chair, a cupboard and a stove, where a colliery clerk recorded details of the wagons handled and the weight of coal despatched, and issued the delivery notes to the boatmen. The other was a store room for various tools, shovels, ropes, lamps and oil, along with a supply of coal for the office stove and hay for the horses.

The boat turned and moored up by the platform. William stepped ashore and within seconds a gang of men was busy shovelling coal from the wagons into the boat.

'Hello there, William.' William looked up as a man came out of the office.

'Gilbert, how are you?' The two men shook hands, and spent a little while chatting before they got down to business.

'I've got the horse and trap here. I thought we'd go up into Eastwood for some lunch. There are two good friends of mine I'd like you to meet, and a proposition we want to put to you.' William climbed into the trap beside Gilbert, intrigued to know what the proposition might be.

'It's not anything to do with the problems I've had recently shifting your coal, is it?' enquired William, with a slightly worried look on his face. 'I know there've been some delays, but it's been mainly down to a shortage of boats. I had a couple that were damaged and I'm convinced it was sabotage, although I can't prove it. Several things have happened lately which have made me suspect that someone is out to harm the business. And then there have been difficulties with low water from time to time.'

'Well, I'm sorry to hear about your boat problems, but rest assured, that's not what I wanted to see you about, and I'm more than satisfied with the job you've been doing for me. Although, indirectly, some of the delays you mention do have a bearing on what we're going to talk about.'

It was only a short distance into the town, and soon they had left the country lane and were trotting up the hill towards the town square, past rows of newly erected terraced houses, a sure sign of the growing importance of mining in the area. At the top of the hill, next to a set of crossroads, Gilbert steered the trap into the rear courtyard of the town's largest hostelry, The Sun Inn, a fine Georgian building. They left the horse and trap in the care of a stable lad, and William followed Gilbert through a back door of the inn. As they entered, a buxom, rosy-faced woman emerged from a room on their left, from which emanated the most tempting and appetising aromas.

'Ah, Mr Wells, there you are,' she said, with a broad smile on her chubby face. 'Your friends have just arrived and I've taken them through to the parlour and given them a drink. Would you like me to serve your lunch now?'

'Give us about ten minutes if that's all right, Mrs Chambers, but perhaps you could bring us a couple more tankards and a jug of ale and we can all help ourselves.' The landlady showed them to the parlour which had been reserved for their meeting, and very soon returned with the beer.

'Gentlemen,' said Gilbert, addressing the two men seated at a table, 'I'd like to introduce to you Mr William Daniels, whom I've already told you about. William has a thriving canal business based in Nottingham and he's responsible for moving all my coal. And William, please meet Mr Christopher Aldridge and Mr Richard Cheadle.'

The two men stood up and shook William warmly by the hand. Both were older than William, by a good twenty years he judged. Mr Aldridge was a tall, thin man with receding hair and seemed rather quiet and studious. From his appearance, William would have guessed him to be a bank clerk or perhaps a solicitor, and was completely taken aback when he learned what his business was. Mr Cheadle, on the other hand, was of medium height and built like an ox, with a full beard and jovial face. His worn hands and weather-beaten features indicated that he was a man who had done his fair share of manual labour.

Once the introductions had been completed they all sat down at the table, and Gilbert had just begun to pour them some beer when the landlady knocked on the door and entered, carrying an enormous steak and kidney suet pudding. A servant girl followed behind with a tray loaded with dishes of vegetables, a large jug of gravy and a plate of freshly baked bread. The young girl, who was only a slip of a thing, seemed scarcely able to carry it, and looked distinctly relieved when she had placed it on the table.

'I hope that will keep you going, gentlemen, and I've a lovely fruit pie for your pudding. Just give me a shout when you're ready for it.'

'Thank you, Mrs Chambers. This looks delicious,' said Gilbert, and all four of them gazed down at the table with mouthwatering anticipation. None of them had eaten for several hours, and for William the boat journey and fresh air had only added to his appetite. He was ravenous, and the sight before him was enough to set his taste buds alight. There was a clattering of serving spoons as the men helped themselves, and for the next few minutes little was said as they each attacked the food set out in front of them. Once everyone had satisfied their initial hunger pangs, their discussion continued, interrupted only by the occasional sound of spoon on dish as someone took another helping.

'Well, William,' Gilbert said, 'I expect you're wondering what this is all about, so let's make a start. You remember earlier today when we talked about the delays that have occurred moving the coal, and I said how that does have a bearing on what we want to talk about? And do you recall about three years ago, when we had a long chat about the use of railways?' William nodded in agreement. 'Well, that's why we're here today. Christopher and Richard are old friends of mine, and we've all been doing business together for many years. Christopher owns an iron foundry just north of Hucknall which his father established almost forty years ago. He's grown up with the business and has run it very successfully ever since his father died suddenly when he was only sixteen. Richard, on the other hand, is a self-made man, a bit like you, William. He started as a pit lad at the age of ten, but by his own hard graft he's made his mark and now owns various enterprises including a wire works and a tile and brick kiln near Linby, a couple of miles north of Hucknall up the Leen Valley. I supply them both with the coal they need, which of course has to be taken over there by horse and cart. And that's the problem. It's difficult and expensive, what with the roads being so bad, and it's hampering the expansion of their businesses. They're both looking to increase their output. Bricks and tiles are in great demand for all the house building that's taking place and it's the same with iron. Everywhere you look, factories are springing up, and that means a need for more raw materials. But the lack of decent transport is holding things up.

'At first, we considered promoting a branch canal from Langley Mill across to Hucknall to supply coal and bring the goods back this way and down the canal, and there's no doubt it could be done. But we now think the best solution is a railway. What finally convinced us is that there's also the possibility of sinking a new pit over near Hucknall. It's been known for some time that there's coal in the Leen Valley, but it's always been too deep to be got easily until now. You probably also remember, William, that I told you I'd been up to the North East looking at mining developments. Well, there are some fine new pumping engines now available which make it practical to sink deeper pits. That would make a new deep mine feasible, but it would be no good without efficient transport.

'To put it in a nutshell, William, what we have in mind is to promote a railway from Linby in the north, down the Leen Valley into Nottingham, to supply the town with coal, iron, bricks and all the other commodities from the mills, factories and workshops along the way. There are lots of them that would benefit from a railway. At the moment all they've got are the roads and at times they're impassable. We're all of the opinion that there's great potential there, but business is being held up by lack of decent transport. We would also need a wharf in Nottingham where goods could be transferred from the railway to the canal for onward conveyance. That would be vital to the profitability of the project. We have the knowledge and experience with the mines and the mills, but we need someone to take care of the transport side of things. That's where you come in, William. We need someone we can trust to be able to move the goods further south, and also to get involved with the management of the railway itself; and we believe you're the man for the job.'

William did not reply immediately, but carried on eating his meal, whilst thinking carefully about what Gilbert had said. At last he spoke. 'I think you may be right and I can see the benefits of a railway. You might think that strange, coming from someone whose business is moving goods by boat, and I know that a lot of canal companies and carriers are opposing railway schemes in other parts of the country. But I agree we can't stand still. If a railway were to bring me more business, so much the better. And if I can make money from carrying goods by water, why not by using rail as well!'

'That's the spirit!' said Richard, raising his tankard. 'It's good to meet someone who thinks like us.'

'But it would be a massive project,' continued William. 'Have you done any surveys, spoken to the landowners and considered all the implications? And I believe you would need an Act of Parliament. I'm flattered that you should invite me to get involved in the running of the railway, but I have to say I know nothing about them. I have no expertise or experience in that direction.'

It was Christopher who spoke next, and as he did so he confirmed William's initial impression, that he was the man with the brains, the knowledge, the contacts and the wherewithal to bring such an idea to fruition. While Richard was clearly a 'hands-on man', Christopher was the one who took care of the paperwork.

'I can see, William, that you have an intuitive mind and shrewd understanding of all the issues and possible difficulties, and that's no bad thing. None of us has ever been involved in the promotion of a railway, but over the years I myself have had some experience in organising and helping to finance other large enterprises, acting as an agent and broker, arranging suppliers, contractors and the like. We've already had some preliminary surveys done and we've spoken informally to the landowners. There are only six of them and they haven't voiced any great objections, provided the financial inducements are satisfactory to them. You are right that we would need to get a Bill through Parliament, but hopefully we can convince enough members of the benefits of the line, and, provided there aren't too many objections, we are confident of the Act being granted. There are no real engineering obstacles, no tunnels required and the gradients are relatively easy. There'd be quite a few bridges and culverts needed and some cuttings and embankments, but nothing to cause serious problems.'

'But what about money?' asked William. 'Where would that come from? It won't be cheap.'

'True enough,' replied Gilbert, 'these projects never are. The three of us have some capital available and we can always borrow more using our businesses as collateral, but that alone wouldn't suffice. We would certainly need much more, but between us we have many contacts and potential investors, not only locally but elsewhere, particularly in the north of England. There are always people prepared to put money into a project provided they're confident of getting a decent return. Eventually, we can foresee the railway being extended further south, to Leicester and even London, but if we can prove its effectiveness with a relatively short line, that would give the impetus for further extensions and prove the doubters wrong. There are plenty of them around, but if we can make this work, people will be flocking to have a slice of the cake. And talking about cake, I think, gentlemen, it's time for our pudding! I'll just go and let Mrs Chambers know we're ready and I'll bring another jug of this excellent ale.'

Gilbert was soon back with the beer and their discussion resumed, but it was interrupted again when Mrs Chambers entered, carrying a large steaming pie, the juices from within running down the sides of the golden pastry crust which topped the mound of apples and rhubarb within. The servant girl followed with a jug of piping hot custard. Mrs Chambers and the girl left them to help themselves and they proceeded to devour the pudding, until not a morsel of fruit, a crumb of pastry or a drop of custard was left.

'What a splendid meal!' declared Gilbert, as he pushed away his bowl and leaned back in his chair. 'And one more thing, William, we are hoping that you might take a financial stake in the project yourself.'

'I have to say you make it sound an inviting prospect,' replied William, 'but I would need to consider the matter in more detail before I committed myself financially. And I would need to talk to Abigail. I've not been in business all that long, and whilst I'm doing quite well now I know things can sometimes turn sour. Just look at what happened a while back with the twist net fiasco and all those people who got their fingers burnt. I've known what it's like to survive on next to nothing and I wouldn't want to risk being in that position again. I might seem a bit cautious, but I've witnessed poverty at first hand and I don't want to take my family down that road.'

'You're right to be cautious,' said Richard, who so far had said very little. 'I, too, started out with nothing, but a young man with his head screwed on right, who's sensible and willing to work hard won't go far wrong. And you seem to me to fit that bill. All I would say is, we're convinced this will be a winner. But you take your time, talk to your wife and let us know what you decide. Even if you don't want to invest any money, we'd still like you to take charge of the actual transport side of things. Do we all concur on that, gentlemen?' The others nodded in agreement.

'So what happens now?' asked William.

'The first thing we must do,' replied Christopher, 'is to form the company so we can publish the prospectus, issue shares and start to raise capital. I've already briefed my solicitor who's willing to act for the company and he's ready to start preparing a Bill to put to Parliament. We'll need a comprehensive survey and costings to be arranged, as they form an important part of the Bill. Provided we get it through Parliament we can then draw up the detailed plans for construction, get the contracts agreed and building can start.

'There's much to be done. I'm going to concentrate on the administrative side and Richard is going to talk to some of his many associates in the building trade, as there'll be a lot of work we could put their way. Gilbert is going to take another trip up to Newcastle to visit some of the contacts he's already made there, men who have experience in railway surveying and construction, and the building of locomotives and pumping engines for the mine. In fact, William, we'd like you to accompany him if you can spare the time. We think it might be useful for you to take a look at just how railways work, especially if you do eventually get involved in day-to-day operations. I therefore suggest that we all meet here again in say, a month's time, and report back on how things are going. Is that to everyone's satisfaction?'

And so it was agreed. The meeting ended and each of the men returned to their respective homes. Gilbert gave William a lift back to the wharf, as he had asked the boatmen to wait for him once they had loaded the coal.

'When will you be going to Newcastle?' William asked as they turned off the lane into the wharf.

'I'm not sure yet, but in about a week. Are you going to join me?'

'Yes, I think I will. If I am going to be involved with the railway, I'd better come and have a look at how things are done. How long would we be away?'

'A week. Ten days maybe. It all depends on how quickly we get round to seeing everything we need to. Plus a couple of days travelling each way.'

'I'll talk to Abigail and let you know. I'll send a note up with one of the boatmen and I promise not to keep you waiting.'

William and Gilbert shook hands and William climbed aboard the boat. It was now fully laden, and lay low down in the water. One of the boatmen untied the mooring ropes, and at a signal it had heard a thousand times, and a sharp crack with the whip to its hindquarters, the horse took the strain and soon the boat began to move.

This was a journey William had often made and he knew and loved the countryside well. But there was no time to admire his surroundings today. Instead, he sat below in the tiny cabin, deep in thought, and he found it hard not to think that the day's events had just been a dream. He had been invited to join three other men in forming a company to build a railway, to help operate it and, if he desired, to invest in it. Throughout the journey he weighed up all the pros and cons, the risks and the chances he might be taking, and the possible gains to be made. And as the boat dropped down through Castle Lock and pulled into the wharf, William left the cabin and emerged into the approaching dusk. He had made up his mind, and he knew exactly what he wanted to do.

After their supper William and Abigail sat by the fire and talked late into the night. He explained to her all about his meeting and everything that had been discussed, the plans for the railway and how he had been asked to become a part of them, and the proposed visit to Newcastle. He then told her that he had given the matter much thought and had come to a decision, but promised that he would only take that decision if she was in complete agreement.

Abigail sat for a while, staring into the dying embers of the fire, turning over in her mind all she had been told. At last she looked up at William and said, 'I think it's time we went to bed. You've had a long day and you must be very tired. In any case, you'll need to be up early tomorrow. You'll be heading off to Newcastle next week and there must be an awful lot of business you'll have to sort out first, so I suggest you go and get some sleep.'

CHAPTER NINE

—

TYNESIDE 1829

The following Thursday evening Gilbert arrived in Nottingham, having hitched a ride on one of the coal boats. Everything was arranged for the visit to the North East and two tickets had been purchased for the coach to York. Gilbert stayed overnight, and at six the next morning he and William walked up to The Milton's Head Inn on Tollhouse Hill, from where the coach left.

It was a fine spring morning, and although William was looking forward to their journey, it was with mixed feelings that he kissed Abigail goodbye. On the one hand, he was excited, for he had never been that far north before and loved to explore new places. On the other hand, he was reluctant to leave, for this would be the first time since they were married that he had been away from her for a single night. He was also a little concerned because she had seemed off colour recently and had been complaining of feeling unwell. He had spent the past week clearing up urgent items of business, and before he left he asked Benjamin and Millie to take good care of Abigail and the children while he was away. And he told Abigail to rest up, and that if she felt any worse, she should call the doctor.

As they made their way northwards out of the town along the Mansfield Road, his mind was taken back all those years to when he and Abigail had set off early one Sunday morning on foot along this same road with the intention of eloping. As the coach passed through Worksop, William noticed a signpost indicating the road to Retford, and he was painfully reminded of Josiah Sidmouth whose large country estate lay nearby. He had never been there but Abigail had, once, after their ill-fated elopement when the search parties led by Josiah and Peter had finally caught up with them. William had managed to make his escape from Peter, who was hell-bent on his destruction, while Abigail had been forcibly returned to her parents in Nottingham, spending a night en route at Josiah's residence.

The coach made its first stop at Mansfield, where the horses were changed, and there were similar stops at Tickhill, Doncaster and Tadcaster. A refreshment stop was made at Doncaster, before York was reached at about six o'clock. William and Gilbert stayed there overnight and the evening was spent exploring this ancient town. William was hugely impressed by the minster, the old castle walls and the quaint medieval streets with their overhanging half-timbered buildings. And he promised himself that one day he would return with Abigail and the children and show them this fascinating place. He would have liked to have spent more time there, but just now they had pressing business in the North East, and so early the next morning they were on their way again, joining another coach for the journey to Newcastle.

It was evening before they finally arrived. Their journey had been long and tiring, but not without interest. Throughout the day William had gazed almost continuously at the surrounding scenery, observing with his usual curiosity the variety and changing nature of the towns, the villages and the landscape through which they passed, so different from what he was used to back home. Shortly before Darlington they crossed the boundary from the North Riding of Yorkshire to County Durham, and the importance of the coal trade to the area quickly became apparent. Increasingly, they noticed the telltale signs that men toiled underground; spoil tips and horse gins, headstocks and smoking chimneys; engine houses with rocking beams. Once, as they approached the outskirts of Newcastle, the coach had to stop where a set of rails crossed the road, and a horse trotted over, leading a short train of loaded coal waggons downhill towards the River Tyne.

'They call them waggonways up here,' said Gilbert. 'There are lots of them dotted all around serving the mines up in the hills. Most of them are worked by horses and some still have wooden rails, but we're here to look at the latest developments, the newest lines with iron rails and steam locomotives. Nearly all the coal mined in these parts goes down to staiths for loading into boats, most of them bound for London.'

Gilbert had arranged for lodgings at one of the town's principal inns. He had already been in contact with an old acquaintance of his, Ralph Armstrong, who was much involved with mining in the area. Ralph had a lifetime's experience of the trade, having started as a pit lad at the age of eight and worked his way up to become a viewer, as the mine managers were known here. He was now highly respected as an authority on all aspects of the industry and he was to be their guide for the duration of their stay. As Gilbert said to William, 'If Ralph doesn't know the answer, he'll know a man who does.'

Soon the coach entered the bustling town centre, rattling over the cobbles, and came to rest in the yard of The Black Boy Inn. In no time at all the two men had left their bags in their rooms and headed, hungrily, for the dining room, where they ordered food and drink. They had not been there long when a man entered and approached them. He was about fifty years of age, tall and stocky, with greying hair; clean-shaven but with long side whiskers. His calloused hands and weathered complexion showed him to be a man who had spent most of his life in the open.

'Here's Ralph,' said Gilbert, getting up to greet him. He introduced him to William and invited him to join them, and the three men soon got down to business. Ralph was a native of the area, and for most of their conversation William had the greatest difficulty in understanding him. He had met a few men from Tyneside before and knew the accent to be very different from his own, but Ralph's was so broad that at times he appeared to be speaking in a foreign language. Not only was his accent so strange, but his whole vocabulary seemed to consist of dialect words which were completely alien to William.

'Don't worry', said Gilbert after Ralph had left. 'I figured out most of what he was saying. The accent up here takes a bit of getting used to, it's true, but you'll soon get to understand what's being said.'

It had been agreed that Ralph would pick them up early the following morning to begin their exploration of the area. At eight o'clock sharp he arrived in a pony and trap, and the three men set off. He did likewise every morning for the next eight days and each day they visited a different area, looking at coal mines big and small, old and new. All over the area they roamed, to Shield Row and Gibside, Coalburns and Risemoor. During one of their trips, after they had been to examine a recently sunk pit, complete with the latest mine pumping equipment and headstock gear, Ralph took them on a short detour to view a local curiosity, which he said was the oldest railway bridge in the world. They stood and gazed in awe at the Causey Arch, a massive stone viaduct spanning a deep ravine and towering eighty feet above the burn below. Ralph explained that it had been built over a hundred years previously and that at one time it had carried nearly a thousand waggons a day from a colliery on Tanfield Moor down to the Redheugh and Dunston staiths. But that colliery was now worked out, so the waggonway and bridge were rarely used.

They followed the course of some of the waggonways, sometimes in the pony and trap, but mainly on foot. Several times they travelled down to the riverside on one of the trains, riding on a loaded waggon, and back again with the empties. They spent time observing the operations at the staiths and inspecting the equipment which tipped the coal directly into the boats.

Much of what they saw had been common practice for many years, but it was the latest developments they were keen to view, and three whole days were spent examining the recently opened Stockton and Darlington line. William was amazed at what he saw here. Most of the trains were hauled not by horses, but by steam engines. This was the first time William had ever seen one of these machines in action. He had heard about them and read about them, but seeing one of them working made a deep and lasting impression on him.

They had stopped at a point where the lane they were on passed close to a sharp curve on the line. First there came the noise, a rhythmical clattering of iron wheels on iron rails, and to accompany it a steady *whoosh, whoosh,* not dissimilar to the noise made by the pumping engine at Gilbert's mine. A thin rising trail of smoke and steam indicated its approach, then round the curve it appeared, lumbering towards them like some fire-breathing dragon from ancient myth, a hissing, clanking, iron monster. A large, barrel-shaped iron boiler was mounted on sturdy frames, towering above the four wheels which guided the engine along the rails. Steam and smoke poured from its tall chimney at the front, while a veritable spider's web of pistons and rods, levers and cranks, all ingeniously linked together, moved in unison, up and down, back and forth, turning the wheels and driving the engine forward. The speed was not excessive, perhaps no faster than a horse would trot when drawing a single waggon, but behind the engine stretched a train of twenty or more waggons, each fully laden with coal. The engine trundled onward with such ease as to belie the huge weight it drew along behind it.

On an open platform at the rear of the engine stood two men. One was feeding coal into the furnace, shovelling it from a small truck behind the engine, whilst the other was busy at the controls. Each wore a dark peaked cap, pulled forward to protect their eyes from the smoke which blew back from the chimney and swirled around them. Their faces were as black as the coal which, by its very existence, provided for their employment, and around their necks, as if to add a splash of colour to the scene, each sported a brightly coloured spotted neckerchief, which from time to time they would use to wipe the grime and sweat from their brows.

William stood transfixed as the lumbering procession passed by and slowly vanished round the curve. But even after it had disappeared from view its presence was still felt in sound, smell and the telltale wisps of smoke and steam drifting across the fields in the gentle breeze. He considered that whereas a single horse, with a man leading it, might haul just one or two waggons, one of these locomotives with two men in charge could easily haul a train of some twenty or more. It was not hard for him to understand why so much money and effort was being expended in developing this new mode of traction. Over the next few days they saw a number of them in action. At first sight they could be quite frightening to behold, but it seemed that in the areas where they were in use, everyone had become so accustomed to them that barely a head was turned when one passed by. Even the horses, cattle and sheep were unmoved, and never even looked up from their grazing nor gave them so much as a glance.

On the final day before they returned home, Ralph took them along to an address in Forth Street, the premises of *Robert Stephenson and Hawthorn Limited*. Robert was the son of George, the man who had surveyed and built the Stockton to Darlington Railway, and who was now busy constructing a line to link Liverpool with Manchester. And now his son was following in his footsteps as an engineer of some repute. It was here, in this recently opened factory, that the locomotives they had seen in action had been built. One of the foremen had been appointed as their guide, and, after briefly explaining the different stages of the process, their tour began.

The premises consisted of a number of separate workshops, each with its own specific function. But it was when they were taken into the main erecting shop, where the engines were actually assembled, that William really appreciated the scale of the operation. He had, many times, been inside lace and hosiery factories in Nottingham, where the noise and activity could be overwhelming, but never had he witnessed anything quite like this. In every respect these works were bigger and noisier, and utterly awe-inspiring. The factories in Nottingham were staffed mainly by women and children, working to produce the most delicate of fabrics, but here there were no women and children; just an army of brawny men, toiling and sweating, hammering and riveting. Smiths worked at their furnaces turning out the myriad parts that went together to form the engines; iron plates and boiler parts, pistons and cylinders, wheels and cogs, rods and tubes. Along one side of the erecting shop stood a row of engines in varying stages of construction, each awaiting the arrival of another vital piece of its anatomy. At the far end, a large door allowed the finished engines to be hauled out, to await delivery to their new homes.

The foreman was a man who clearly had the profoundest knowledge of every aspect of the manufacturing process, and who displayed an almost childlike enthusiasm for his responsibilities. William was completely spellbound, but what with the din of all this activity, and the foreman's broad Geordie accent, he was barely able to understand a word he was being told. Gilbert realised the problems he was having and tried to interpret as best he could.

After a while, they left through the large doors at the rear, and standing outside was a newly completed engine which two men were attending to. A fire had already been lit and smoke was slowly drifting from its chimney. The pressure in the boiler was rising rapidly and hot water and steam were beginning to leak from some of the pipes and joints, sizzling and hissing as they escaped into the atmosphere. William stood alongside, engrossed by the preparations taking place.

Nearby, Gilbert was deep in conversation with Ralph, who then went and spoke to the foreman. A few words were exchanged and Gilbert came over and spoke to William. 'How would you like a ride on it?' he asked, nodding towards the engine. 'This one was finished yesterday. The fitters are making some final checks, then they're going to take it for a test run up and down the yard. The foreman says we can travel with them if we want to. They'll be ready shortly. What do you say?'

William could barely contain his excitement. He was like a child being offered a new toy to play with, and he wasn't going to let anyone take it away from him. 'What do I say? Why, yes of course!' William went over to the foreman and grabbed his hand, shaking it vigorously. 'Thank you so much. You've been most helpful, but to be allowed to travel on one of your engines just tops everything!'

They didn't have much longer to wait and soon the pressure had built up and it was ready for its trial run. The foreman had some last minute instructions for the fitters, who then helped William and Gilbert up onto the small footplate. In front of them was the firebox and the various levers, valves and other controls, and beyond it the boiler, the heart of the engine where the steam was produced. Behind them was a truck containing a supply of coal and a barrel of water from which a pipe led into the boiler. One of the fitters took a shovelful of the coal, opened the small door to the firebox and threw the coal in. As he did so, a waft of radiant heat could be felt. The driver then reached out and took hold of one of the levers. He pulled this towards him, and after a second or two there was a hiss of steam and a shudder as the engine sprang into life. On each side of the boiler was an inclined cylinder, and at the same time the pistons began to move, one down and one up. These were attached by a series of rods and links to the wheels, and, as they began to turn, the engine suddenly lurched forward. The speed slowly increased and the shuddering and vibration lessened as the engine got into its stride.

The firebox door was open, the glare from within illuminating the area around their feet. With each stroke of the pistons the fire turned a lighter shade of orange as the exhaust of steam from the cylinders drew air through the red-hot coals. Just like the bellows in a blacksmith's forge, thought William. The engine was now moving along effortlessly, rocking slightly from side-to-side as the wheels went over the joints in the iron rails. But they were now approaching the end of the line, and the driver, manipulating two of the controls, soon brought them to a halt. Another lever was moved, then another and suddenly they were travelling back again in the opposite direction. Three times they did the return run, after which the fitters announced to the foreman their complete satisfaction with its performance.

It was with great reluctance that William left the works, so fascinated had he been with everything he had seen and experienced there. But the next day they were to return home, and Gilbert had arranged to meet another old friend of his that evening.

Abel Reynolds was a Yorkshireman by birth but had spent most of his adult life in the North East, where for many years he had been involved with the building and maintenance of many of the colliery waggonways. He was well respected as being reliable and diligent, and in recent years had been contracted to build some of the new railways designed for use with locomotives. Gilbert was convinced he was the ideal man to oversee the construction of their proposed line down the Leen Valley. Over dinner, Gilbert told Abel of their plans for the new line, and was most grateful when he agreed to come to Nottingham as soon as they were ready to move forward with their plans.

William and Gilbert both slept soundly that night. They had achieved much since their arrival in Newcastle, and, as the coach rumbled south the next day, they spent many hours discussing everything they had seen and learned. After another overnight stop at York they were on the last leg of their long journey, but William was getting restless. He would not have missed this trip for the world and considered it had been worth every hour he had spent away from home; and he was now convinced that he stood to gain much from his involvement in this new mode of transport. Gilbert left the coach at Mansfield, to go and visit a business colleague, but for William, all he wanted to do was get back and see Abigail and the children.

It was shortly after eight when the coach came rattling down the Mansfield Road into the town, and finally drew up in the yard of The Milton's Head Inn. Ten minutes later William was opening the front door of his home. 'I'm back,' he shouted, and immediately he heard a scurrying of feet from above. Abigail came running down the stairs to greet him, and throwing her arms around him, welcomed him home with a hug and a kiss.

She had just put the children to bed, but, on hearing the noise and the voice of their father, they soon appeared too, running to greet him with squeals of delight. An hour later the children had been put back to bed, and William and Abigail sat down to eat the supper Millie had prepared for them. Over supper, William related everything that had transpired since he had left, almost a fortnight before; where he had been and what he had seen. But so wrapped up was he in his own exploits that he failed to notice that Abigail seemed anxious and a little quieter than usual. But eventually he realised something was amiss.

'What's the matter, Abigail? You look worried. Has something happened while I've been away?'

'It was just something I overheard yesterday when I took the children with me and walked up to see mother and father. Charles and Catherine had been playing in the garden, and I went to bring them in for their tea. When I came back inside the house I heard mother and father talking, but they didn't know I was outside in the hall. Father was telling mother that Josiah Sidmouth is back in the country. He said he had been talking to a colleague in the town who claimed he'd been back for almost two years. As soon as I entered the room they stopped talking. I don't think they wanted me to hear, so I didn't let on I'd heard them.'

'What! Two years? Surely that can't be right. He was sentenced to seven years. How could he possibly have been back that long?'

'I really don't know, but that's what father said, and he seemed quite definite.'

'To be honest, Abigail, nothing about that man should surprise us. He's got plenty of money, so he could easily afford to return. If he did manage to come back so early, then I bet he had to grease some palms, and I wouldn't put that past him. But he must have been lying low. I wonder where he's been hiding? Up at Retford I suppose. He can't have been back to Nottingham much or I'm sure we'd have heard before now.'

'Well, there's one person who I'm sure will know. And when I next see my brother I'll have a few questions to put to him. And heaven help him if he tries to pull the wool over my eyes!'

For a while William sat, lost in thought.

'A penny for them, William?'

'Oh, sorry Abigail. I was just thinking; If Josiah really did return a couple of years ago, that would have been several months before the affair with the body snatchers, and the drowning of Walter Blundy. And then there was the damage to two of the boats. I'm still convinced that was sabotage. Do you think he might have had anything to do with all that? None of those incidents did us any good. Or am I just letting my imagination run wild? Still, it's no use worrying. I'll keep my eyes and ears open and see what I can find out. But enough of him. Tell me, how have you all been keeping while I've been away?'

'Well, the children are fine and Benjamin has coped admirably by himself. If you do get involved with this railway business, at least you'll have someone reliable you can depend on to take care of things here. And I'm so pleased Millie's around to help me, even more so now, under the circumstances.'

'Circumstances?' said William with a slightly troubled look on his face. 'What do you mean, Abigail? What circumstances?' And suddenly, he remembered that before he had left for the north, she had not been feeling very well. 'You're not ill, are you, Abigail?'

'Oh, no, I'm not ill. But you're going to be a father again.'

William was overjoyed at hearing this news. It was over five years since Catherine had been born, and he was beginning to wonder whether they would ever be blessed with any more children.

But it came as a big surprise for them both the following January, when Abigail gave birth to twins, a boy and a girl, whom they christened Simon and Sophia.

CHAPTER TEN

—

NOTTINGHAM 1830

It was on a Saturday evening in August, at about seven o'clock, when a knock came on the door. William was deeply engrossed in the weekly newspapers. He enjoyed his Saturday nights, when he could sit and relax after the long working week, and liked to keep up-to-date with all the latest news. He got up from his chair and went to the door, and, on opening it, was confronted by two men, each carrying a large pack on their backs. At first glance William assumed they were pedlars, come to sell their wares.

'Hello William, good to see you again,' said one of the men. The other, slightly older man stepped forward and grabbed William by the hand, shaking it firmly.

'Likewise,' he said. For a brief second William was somewhat puzzled, for at first he did not recognise them. And then, suddenly, the penny dropped.

'Samuel! Whatever are you doing here? And Edward! I've not seen you since I was in France – that must be ten years ago. Well, don't just stand there, come on in.' The two men followed William into the sitting room, just as Abigail was coming down the stairs. She had heard the voices and was curious to see who had come visiting. 'Abigail, look who's here. Can you believe it?'

'Ah, the lovely Abigail, my favourite sister-in-law,' said Samuel, as he put his arms round her, hugged her tightly and kissed her firmly on the lips. She had only met him briefly on a few occasions, the last one being at her wedding, when he got hopelessly drunk, but his greeting did not surprise her. She knew he could be the most outgoing and friendly chap when he wanted to be and never backward in coming forward, especially where the ladies were concerned.

'Your *only* sister-in-law, Samuel,' said William, 'and Abigail, this is my Uncle Edward, ma's youngest brother. I know you've never met him but I've told you all about him. Only two years older than me but my uncle just the same. He's been in France for the last twelve years or so. You remember I told you he had to leave the country in a hurry after the Pentrich uprising, when he was in danger of being arrested by the authorities. Well, what brings you both here? There's such a lot to talk about. Where do we start? Sit yourselves down and I'll get some drinks. Is beer all right?'

'I'll fetch it,' said Abigail. 'I was about to go and get a bit of supper. Have you two eaten recently?'

'Not for a while,' replied Edward. 'Something to eat and drink is just what we could do with. We've travelled a long way today and only got to Nottingham about an hour ago. We haven't had much since this morning.'

Soon Abigail returned with food and drink, and the four of them settled down to their supper and a long chat. Edward explained that he and Samuel had come over from France about a week before and had been slowly making their way north. They'd stayed at Leicester the previous night and had walked all the way to Nottingham, having run out of money for the coach fare.

'So you've both come from France then?' said William. 'But Samuel, what were you doing there? The last I heard, you were in Manchester.'

'Ah, Manchester. Yes, I was there for a time, but had to leave in a hurry.'

'Don't tell me,' said William. 'I bet there was a woman involved. Or the law; or probably both.'

'How did you guess?'

'Not hard, Samuel. I remember you of old. Go on then, tell us all about it.'

'Well, I was getting along fine in Manchester, doing a bit of business here and there, wheeling and dealing and making ends meet quite nicely. There's always money to be made in a big town, especially a growing one like Manchester. The cotton trade's taking off in a big way so there's stuff coming and going all the time, people passing through, and it's a poor man who can't turn a situation like that to his advantage. I'd got a nice little number going, dealing in imported cotton, buying it in and selling it on to factory owners. One of my customers was a chap called Cooper who had a little factory off Deansgate. Nice chap, but he had an even nicer wife, name of Dinah. Trouble was, he was nearly fifty and she was less than half his age. And what's more she'd been forced into the marriage by her father. It turns out he owed Mr Cooper a whole load of money, and Cooper said he'd write off the debt as long as Dinah married him. She was only sixteen at the time and didn't have much say in the matter, and she soon got to loathe him. But me and Dinah, well, we got on like a house on fire and whenever she could sneak away she'd come round to my lodgings. Sometimes, when he was away on business she'd stay for days on end.

'It was while he was away one time that Dinah had a bright idea. She loved fancy things, new hats, dresses and shoes and the like, but her old man was a bit tight and wouldn't buy her much. Now, he had a big store room at his works where he kept bales of cotton, most of which I'd sold him. Dinah had a key to this room, so one night we went round there and took a load of the cotton and hid it in a lockup I used. When he got back, I sold his own cotton back to him. He never twigged for ages.

'Then one day he did find out; and about me and Dinah too. I never knew how, but I did have my suspicions. There was a guy who worked for him who'd been looking for an excuse to put one over me ever since he caught me with his daughter, but that's another story, and I think it was him who tipped Cooper off. Anyway, he came round to my lodgings in a real rage. He came rushing up the stairs, ranting and raving and I just had time to lock the door and prop a chair under the handle. That gave me long enough to climb out the window before he forced his way in. I lay low for a day or two, and then I managed to see Dinah. He'd knocked her about a bit but fortunately nothing too serious. But she told me he was out to get me and had paid a gang of heavies to rough me up. I'd seen what those chaps can do and I didn't intend to hang around. So I decided it was time to move on.

'There was a pal of mine by the name of Toby who worked on the barges bringing cotton over from Liverpool and he owed me a favour, so I went to see him. He was about to set off for the docks at Hull with a cargo of cotton goods, so I hitched a ride with him and five days later we arrived. It was hard work mind. I lost count of the number of locks we went through, climbing over the top of the Pennines and across Yorkshire. Toby had a brother in Hull who was also in the barge business, so we stayed with him for a week or so while he tried to find us another load to take back. But nothing was on offer, and Toby was about to return empty to Manchester when his brother was offered a contract to take a shipment of goods down to the port of London on a coaster, and they asked me whether I wanted to join them as they needed another pair of hands. Well, why not I thought? I didn't want to go back to Manchester, and though I don't know much about boats, Toby said it'd be all right and just to help out and do what he told me.'

As Samuel was telling his story, William and Abigail sat quietly, hanging on his every word, and Edward, who of course had heard the tale before, could see that they were thoroughly enjoying it. Abigail took the jug of beer and topped up Samuel's mug. He took another swig and continued.

'We got down to London all right and dropped the goods off at Limehouse. We were due to go back to Hull a few days later with a cargo of tobacco and spices, but the stuff wasn't ready so we decided to have a bit of fun while we waited. I'd been to London a couple of times before, but never down to the docks. My God, it's rough down there. You think Narrow Marsh is bad, but you should see that place on a Saturday night! It's awash with sailors from all four corners of the globe. Turks, Spaniards, Yankees, Chinese; you name 'em, they're all there. And it only takes one of 'em to say the wrong thing and all hell breaks loose. And the locals can be just as bad too. The law don't exist there. It's every man for himself when the tables and chairs start flying!

'Now, you asked how I came to be in France. I'll tell you. The third night we were in London should have been the last. We'd got the cargo nicely loaded that afternoon and were due to sail on the tide first thing the next morning, so we decided to have one last fling. We settled down in a pub in Stepney and a right dive it was, too. We were having a nice time when a chap came in with a couple of girls in tow, and soon we all got to talking. He was a Frenchy who told us he'd come over from Calais with a cargo of wine. He spoke quite good English, but the two girls could only manage the odd word, just enough to get by. I never did find out who they were or why they were there, but that didn't bother me at all, and where the rest of his crew was I had no idea. One of the girls in particular was a pretty little thing, all dark hair and fluttering eyelashes and I think she took a shine to me.

'Well, come midnight we were all fairly tipsy, and Toby and his brother decided to go back to the boat as they'd had enough and had to be up early the next morning. I said I'd be along shortly so off they went. The rest of us had another drink, then the Frenchy suggested we all go back to his boat, where he'd got a stash of the wine hidden away. It didn't take long to get there and soon we were stuck into a bottle of red. I'd been eyeing up the little dark-haired one all night, and I knew she was up for it, so I had a little whisper in her ear and off we went. After that, I didn't remember a thing until I woke up with an almighty thumping head. I heard a knocking sound and guessed it was the boat banging against the dock side, and found myself alone in a small cabin, lying on a straw mattress. I made my way up onto the deck and had a good look round but there was no sign of the Frenchy or the girls. The boat was deserted. Sure enough we were tied up at the dock, just as I thought. I was still a bit queasy, but not so much that I couldn't tell something was wrong. It had been dark when we'd got on the boat, but I could swear this wasn't the same dock. It just didn't seem the same. The buildings looked different, and it smelled different too.

'Then I heard voices and looked over the side, and there was a gang of men all talking in a foreign language, which I didn't understand, but thought sounded like French. Now, in London the dockers are all English. They're the only ones allowed to do the job. Then it dawned on me. I looked at the buildings alongside, some of which had name boards on them, and they weren't in English, but I did recognise the odd word. We were in France! Calais as it turned out. I never did see the Frenchy again, or the girls, but it was clear what had happened. I don't know whether I'd been spark out for one day, or two, but the boat had set sail from London and returned to Calais with me still on it!

'I climbed over the side and went ashore. I wasn't sure what to do. I had no money, no food, and only the clothes I stood up in. I'd taken all my belongings with me when I'd left Manchester in a hurry, and they didn't amount to much; a few clothes and a bit of money, but they were all in a bag back in Limehouse on Toby's coaster! So here I was, stuck in a foreign land, poor as a church mouse, hungry, no friends and nowhere to go. And then I remembered Uncle Edward. I knew he had gone to France when I was about fifteen, and that he was living with Aunt Hetty in Calais, and that you, William, had also lived with them for a time. Of course, I didn't know them all that well, as I'd only met them a few times when I was a kid. But, as they say, "any port in a storm" so off I set to try and find them.

'It didn't take me all that long. I asked the men on the dockside if they knew where there were any English people, and although none of them spoke English, one of them evidently understood what I was asking. "Les Anglais, les Anglais" he kept saying, then pointed along a road, saying "carry, carry". I wasn't sure what he meant by "carry" so I walked along the road and soon came to a little café. It was full of people so I went and asked in there. One of them knew a bit of English and he told me to go to an area near the canal called the *Carré*, as that was where most of the English people lived. That's what the man on the dockside must have meant. It was plain sailing then. I found the area and started asking around and I soon found some English people. I even recognised their accents and you'd never believe it - they were from Sneinton! It turns out most of the English living in Calais were from around Nottingham, so it wasn't all that strange, but the good thing was they knew where Edward and Hetty lived.

'They were astonished to see me, I can tell you. At first, neither of them recognised me, but it was over twelve years since we'd last met. Anyway, they made me very welcome, gave me some food and found me a bed for the night.'

From time to time, as Samuel was telling his tale, a smile spread over William's face, but none of his escapades surprised him. This was typical of his brother. If there was trouble to be found, he was always the one who'd find it; a scrape to get into, he'd get into it; a girl to charm or a quick buck to be made and he'd be there. But at heart, he was genuine. A bit of a rogue, and no denying it, but one you could depend on if help were needed. William was certain of that, and Abigail, who could judge people quickly and accurately, also realised it. This was the first occasion that she had spent any time in his company, and, whilst he was obviously a rough diamond, she liked him.

'And how long ago did all this happen?' asked William. 'How long were you in France?'

It was Edward who now took up the story. 'Samuel stayed with us for about two months. He didn't want to go straight back to England; said he liked the area and asked if he could stop for a while. I think the truth is that he just wanted to keep away until all the fuss in Manchester had died down! And we had the room, so he stayed. Hetty and I were still living in the same house we were in when you came over. We even found him a bit of work, doing odd jobs and so on.'

'So were you still working for the Leake brothers? They were very good to me when I worked for them. And Hetty, how is she?'

'Yes, I was. And I'm a skilled framesmith now. I know lace machines inside out, so there's plenty of work to keep me busy. But I've always missed home. A few of the Nottingham folk got homesick and went back, but Hetty is happy enough and I don't think she'll ever return.

'After Samuel had been over for a week or two we got to talking and I had a yearning to come back. I always intended to, but you know that I had to lie low for a while. I didn't dare risk returning too soon in case I got arrested, but then I began to think that it might be safe now and that after twelve years the authorities had probably given up trying to catch anyone else who'd been involved in the uprising. But I've got two trades now: framesmith and my old job of ironworker, and I reckoned I'd always be able to find work. So I gave it a lot of thought and decided to give it a go. And if things don't work out I can always go back to Calais. Matthew and Miles Leake were sorry to see me leave and said there'd always be a job for me anytime, if I ever wanted to go back.

'So that was that. We got a package over to Dover and made our way up here. I'd saved a bit of money, so we took the coach to London, spent a couple of nights there then travelled north, stopping overnight at Towcester and Leicester. We finally reached here this evening and went straight to your parents' house in Narrow Marsh but found they don't live there anymore. A neighbour said they'd moved to Chilwell, but they told us where you live, so here we are. And to tell the truth, William,

I'm glad I'm back. You know I've always had an interest in politics and I think now's the time to get involved in the cause again. It looks like reform might become a reality at long last, so maybe everything we fought for in 1817 wasn't in vain after all. And what a time to be back in England! The old king dead, a new one on the throne, and here we are in the middle of an election. Reform will be the main issue for the next Parliament and the Whigs are in favour, so let's hope they win. But it won't be easy. The Tories are dead against any changes and they have a big majority in the House of Lords, where those old reactionaries, like The Duke of Newcastle, will go to any lengths to keep things as they are.'

Edward had touched on a subject which William himself had been following closely, for it was a time of much turmoil in the world of politics. In June that year, George the Fourth had died and had been replaced by his brother, William the Fourth. At the same time the Government, under the leadership of the Duke of Wellington, a high Tory and fierce opponent of reform, had collapsed, and the country was in the throes of a general election.

'I must look up some of my old friends and get myself up-to-date with exactly how things are going in this election,' continued Edward.

'Still the same old campaigning Edward, then,' said William.

'And why not? If men don't stand up for what they believe in, the likes of his lordship in his castle up there, will keep us down-trodden forever.'

'I agree with you Edward, and so does most of Nottingham. Mind you, the duke himself rarely comes here now. The castle has stood almost empty for years. I think he spends most of his time in London, or at one of his other mansions.'

'Must be nice to have a choice of houses to live in and not have to pay rent on any of them! But even if he doesn't come here much, he still wields great influence. One way or another, we have to rid the world of him and his sort. He's nothing but an unrepentant interfering borough-monger of the worst kind. He selects the Tory candidate himself, then instructs his tenants to vote for him - those that are lucky enough to have a vote - and if they don't, he simply threatens them with eviction. I understand that's what happened to over thirty of them last year at the Newark by-election when they refused to vote for Sadler, the duke's candidate.'

'Well, Edward, as long as you go about it by peaceful means. We don't want a repetition of last time, what with men being executed, imprisoned and transported. And we don't want to have to smuggle you out of the country again.'

'Oh, don't worry about me, William. I'm older and wiser now, and there's more than one way to skin a cat. But I reckon reform's almost within our grasp now, and I intend to get involved as much as I can; peacefully and legally of course! But something has to be done. It's bad enough that most men still don't have a vote, but we also have Members of Parliament representing almost nonexistent places, while large towns have no representation at all. Take Manchester, for instance. Samuel can tell you all about what a growing town that is, one of the biggest in the north, with thousands of inhabitants but not a single MP! Yet the almost deserted village of Old Sarum in Wiltshire, which only has a dozen voters, returns two MPs, both in the gift of Lord Caledon. Tell me, where's the justice in that?'

'You're right, of course, Edward,' agreed William. 'I'm lucky. As a property owner I do get a vote and I've cast it for the Whigs. Still, that wasn't too difficult a decision as the Tories haven't even bothered to put up any candidates! Nottingham is a Whig town, and there's a great deal of support for reform. But as you said, Edward, it's not the same everywhere and there are lots of other places, mainly rural areas, where the Tories can virtually guarantee to get elected, especially since they own most of the land and property and can decide on a whim who keeps their job and who doesn't. It's a brave man - or a foolish one - who defies his lord and master and votes the wrong way.'

'And that's another bone of contention. Everyone knows who you've voted for. If we had secret ballots things would be easier. Still, we won't have long to wait for the result. I understand voting's being going on for most of the month so we should know soon what the chances are of getting things changed. But that's enough of politics. Now tell me, William, how are your parents?'

William explained all about their move to Chilwell, and that Benjamin and Millie now both worked for him and lived with them.

'They're both out at the moment, somewhere in the town. You know what young folk are like on a Saturday night! Anyway, you two, what are your immediate plans, apart from putting the world to rights?'

'Well, the first thing I must do,' replied Edward, 'is go up to Pentrich and visit mother. I've not seen her for over twelve years and she's all alone now that father's died.'

'Yes, you must,' said William. 'I've not seen her since your father's funeral. There was talk of her coming to live in Chilwell with ma and pa now they've settled in there. Why don't you go over to Chilwell first to see them, then you could take ma with you up to Pentrich. I'm sure she'd love to go with you. And what about you, Samuel? What have you got in mind? If you're staying for a while I'd better put the word out for all fathers to lock up their daughters and the wealthy to lock up their silver!'

'William! I'm sure he's not that bad!' exclaimed Abigail, coming to her brother-in-law's defence.

'I know, I was only joking.'

'That's all right,' said Samuel, 'I'm used to it. I think I'll tag along with Edward. I want to go and see ma and pa, and I might even go up to Pentrich too. But I want to hang around Nottingham for a while and look up a few old pals.'

'Well, you want to be careful which old pals you look up. You've had some dubious ones in the past that you'd do well to avoid, like that Baggy Holmes who got you into all that trouble. Then there's Randal Wainer. Mind you, that's two you'll not be seeing again.'

'Oh, why's that?' asked Samuel.

'Transported. The pair of them. Holmes was sent to Bermuda for housebreaking, then Wainer shortly after to Van Diemen's Land for horse stealing. In fact Wainer worked for me for a week or two. He came along and gave me a sob story and as I knew him slightly I gave him a chance. But I had to sack him. Totally unreliable he was, and I reckon he was nicking stuff, too. Actually, his trial was straight after Thomas's. You probably don't know about that.' And William began to relate the sad account of cousin Thomas.

It was now getting late and they were all tired. 'Would you like to stay here for the night?' asked Abigail. 'We've a spare room up in the attic and I can soon find you some blankets. It won't take me long, and in any case I shall stay up until Millie and Benjamin get back.'

'Thanks, that would be a great help,' replied Edward. 'But we'll not impose on you after tonight. We'll both get off tomorrow over to Chilwell, then up to Pentrich, and when we get back to Nottingham we'll find ourselves some lodgings.'

The next morning nearly everyone was late getting up. Sunday was the one day of the week when William didn't work. Benjamin and Millie were sleeping off the excesses of their night on the town, while Samuel and Edward took the opportunity to recover from their tiring journey from France. Abigail alone had risen at a respectable hour, but only because the children were up and playing noisily and needed feeding. After breakfast Samuel and Edward got ready to leave.

'Hold on a minute,' said William. 'No need to walk. I'll give you a ride in the gig. I've not seen ma and pa myself for a while and I fancy a trip out. Abigail's going over to see her parents today and taking the children, so there's no need for me to rush back. And there are three pubs in Chilwell that I think you'll like!'

William got back home at about five o'clock, shortly after Abigail. Over supper, William told Abigail about his trip to see his parents and that Samuel and Edward were staying there for the night, then taking Margaret over to Pentrich the next day.

'It'll be a long walk for them,' said Abigail.

'Well, it would have been, but pa's made a friend of a chap in the village who's got a horse and trap. We saw him in The Red Lion, and he offered to lend it to them for the day, so they're all going up, pa, Sarah and Elizabeth too, a real family outing.'

'I expect Matilda will be surprised when they all turn up.'

'Yes, but thrilled too, I guess. Poor old gran. She's got some good neighbours who keep an eye out for her but she must miss Abraham. They were married for nearly fifty years, you know.'

'Do you think she'll go and live with them at Chilwell?'

'Well, I hope so. I know ma wants her to and I think she'd be much happier, having family around her all the time. And she's getting on. She's over seventy now. But enough of my lot. How's Mary and Nicholas? Have they heard from Peter recently?'

'Oh, they're fine and they enjoyed having all their grandchildren to see them. They haven't seen Peter for a long time, but mother said she'd received a letter from him last month. He was in Canada for over a year, then he came back to England for a short time, then straight over to Ireland. But he told her he expects to be back in England by Christmas for a spell of leave and has promised to come and stay with them. And when he does, he can expect a grilling from me. I'll soon find out whether Josiah really is back home. Peter might be a Lieutenant and order his men about, but I'm not one of the troops and he holds no authority over me. Oh, Peter, if only you knew what awaits you when I get you alone!'

It was about a week later that Samuel and Edward called to see William and Abigail. They told them about their visit to Pentrich and that Margaret's mother had now decided to go and live with her daughter at Chilwell. They also explained that they had taken lodgings in a house on Kid Street, and that Edward had already found work in a nearby lace factory. His skill as a framesmith, along with the continuing expansion of the lace trade, meant that he was never likely to be out of work for long. Samuel, on the other hand, had no particular skills but didn't seem too worried. He said he had always managed to make ends meet, which was true, but William felt a little uneasy that he might soon land himself in trouble again, unless he found regular employment.

'You really ought to find yourself a steady job, Samuel. You can't just keep drifting along for the rest of your life.'

'I think you must be getting old, William. You're beginning to sound like father,' replied Samuel. 'He gave me the same lecture last week. Said I should stop messing about and settle down.'

'Well, he's right. And if you think I'm getting old, don't forget you're only two years behind me! You need a job to keep yourself out of mischief. If you can't find anything I might be able to help you. There's a railway going to start being built shortly and a lot of men will be needed. It'd only be labouring, but there's plenty of money to be earned if you're not afraid of hard work.' And William told Samuel about the plans for the new line.

'Thanks, I'll bear that in mind,' said Samuel, 'but I've got one or two ideas of my own. And don't worry, I'll not starve.'

A couple of days later, news of the election result reached the town, but it was not the news that most of Nottingham wanted to hear. The Tories had retained power and the Duke of Wellington remained Prime Minister. William expected that Edward would take the news badly, but over a few drinks one night in The Salutation, Edward was far from depressed at the state of affairs.

'I've been meeting some old friends recently, men who have been following closely just what's going on in Parliament. One of them has a contact at the heart of Government and he reckons that things might soon change for the better. Although the Tories won the election, there's a lot of division in their ranks. Many of them are aware of the strong tide of support across the country for reform and are fearful that outright opposition could rebound on their party. There seems to be a big split developing between them and the old diehards, like Wellington. We live in interesting times, William, and nothing would surprise me.'

And before the year was out, Edward's predictions had come true. At the end of October, a Whig MP announced his intended reform motion in the House of Commons. Wellington declared himself wholly against, but within a fortnight he lost a vote on the issue of the Civil List payments to the new king, and immediately resigned. The king, who was known to favour the Whigs over the Tories, called on Earl Grey, leader of the Whigs, to form a Government. Grey's absolute priority was to bring in a Reform Bill.

And so, as the year drew to a close, the scene was set for a battle royal.

CHAPTER ELEVEN

—

NOTTINGHAM 1830

William was pleased that his Uncle Edward had at last returned home from his enforced exile in France, and was equally happy that Samuel was where he could keep an eye on him, for he was always fearful that he might return to his bad old ways again. Samuel had, in his youth, served a couple of stretches in the House of Correction, mainly under the influence of his old accomplice, Baggy Holmes. And even when William had been living with his parents in Narrow Marsh, he had always felt that it was his responsibility, as the eldest son, to try and keep his brother on the straight and narrow, even if he didn't always succeed. Now it seemed more important than ever.

But William had other pressing matters on his mind. It was now well over a year since he and Gilbert had gone up to Tyneside to view the latest railway developments taking place there, and things had been progressing rapidly with the proposed Leen Valley line. Abel Reynolds had been as good as his word and had come down from Newcastle to undertake the necessary surveys. The company had been formed and a Board of Directors appointed, of which William was one, and the prospectus issued. The Bill had been prepared to put to Parliament and shares offered for sale to the public. The scheme had been well received in the area, with support coming from most of the business fraternity, the town council and the newspapers, which carried regular items detailing the progress of the plans and editorial comment urging residents of the town not to oppose the proposal which, as the Nottingham Review stated: ... *will surely bring enhanced wealth and prosperity to the town and ensure that Nottingham maintains its position as the principal manufacturing and trading centre for the midland counties.*

Nevertheless, there were, as is always the case with anything new and unfamiliar, some who were bitterly opposed: a handful of landowners living near to the route, but not sufficiently close to receive compensation for any land that might be required; some local carriers fearful that the railway would result in the demise of their businesses, notwithstanding that the additional trade would increase the demand for the services of those same carriers; and the usual collection of cranks and self-appointed experts, whose various pronouncements assured anyone prepared to listen that the very sight and sound of a passing locomotive and train would be enough to cause cattle in the fields to drop dead of fright, and pregnant women to abort their unborn children; that anyone foolish enough to ride on such a monstrosity would likely find that their brains would explode at speeds greater than twelve miles per hour, and that within a few years horses would become extinct!

Fortunately, most members of the House of Commons, along with their illustrious lordships in the Upper House, were of a somewhat sounder mind and were neither impressed nor convinced by these doom-laden warnings. In November the Bill completed its passage through Parliament, the king gave it the Royal Assent and *The Nottingham and Leen Valley Railway* was added to the growing number of such schemes now authorised by Act of Parliament to commence construction.

There had been much interest in the scheme and most of the available shares had been purchased, not only by local men with a direct interest in the project but also by investors from elsewhere who hoped to realise a good return for their money. In particular there were investors from the north, who, having already witnessed the success of similar enterprises there, were keen to extend their financial tentacles. William himself had invested, purchasing shares to the value of £1,000, using some of the profits he had made from the canal business. He had considered investing more and obtaining the balance by mortgaging the wharf and house, but Abigail had been insistent that they should not risk their home and only source of income. William continued to attend the regular board meetings, and once construction had started, more of his time was taken up with matters relating to the railway. Luckily, he had Benjamin to rely on, and his brother was now so competent in all the affairs of the canal haulage business that William was confident to leave him in charge, knowing that it was in safe hands.

As soon as the Bill became law, the contractors were ready to move in. The company, in anticipation of a favourable response from Parliament, had already put out to tender the various contracts for construction of the line, so that once all the legal formalities had been finalised construction could begin. In no time at all, what had formerly been a peaceful and tranquil ribbon of countryside from the town northwards through the villages of Basford, Bulwell, Hucknall and beyond, became the temporary home to hundreds of navvies, many from Ireland and Scotland, who set up camps in hastily erected shacks. Horses, men, machinery and materials occupied almost every patch of ground alongside the route, now pegged out by the surveyors.

At first, there was a noticeable degree of hostility between the resident population and the newcomers. Whilst the extra trade that the navvies brought to the local shops and pubs was to be welcomed, there were inevitable clashes with some of the inhabitants of the area, and on a number of occasions troops had to be sent from the barracks to quell potential riots, particularly on Friday nights after the men had been paid and seemed intent on spending their wages as fast as possible in the nearby hostelries. Many of these fights were the result of arguments between navvies and natives; and the subject of these arguments was invariably the local women. Some of the navvies had their wives and families with them, but most were single men, and flush with money they were determined to seek out the company of any available woman, single or otherwise. This did not go down too well with the local men, who for the most part were less well paid than the navvies, and it did not help that many of the women were more than happy to allow these strangers with money aplenty to treat them, much to the disgust of those who regarded them as *their* women.

Early in December, Abigail's mother received a letter from Peter saying that he intended to come and stay with them over Christmas and hoped to arrive in Nottingham about the twentieth of the month. Despite what had happened in the past, Abigail liked to see her brother whenever he returned home. But his visits always made things somewhat awkward for her, as William had no desire to see him, and Abigail knew the feeling was mutual. Peter and William had not spoken, nor even been in each other's company for many years, and such was William's antagonism to his brother-in-law that whenever a family gathering took place where Peter would be present, William would manage to find an excuse to absent himself.

And that is exactly what happened when Abigail and the children went up to High Pavement on the Wednesday afternoon before Christmas. William took them in the gig, but then set off immediately as he had some urgent railway business to see to and did not expect to be home until late. Nicholas and Mary expressed their regrets that he could not join them but they both, inwardly, breathed a sigh of relief, not out of any dislike for William but in the knowledge that his absence would avoid any acrimonious exchanges between son and son-in-law.

'Where is Peter?' asked Abigail as she sat down on a comfortable sofa in front of a roaring fire in the drawing room, the twins one on either side of her, whilst Charles and Catherine played noisily on the floor. 'I thought he would be here by now.'

'He is,' said Nicholas. 'He arrived last night but he went out this morning to visit someone in the town. He'll be back shortly, though.'

'And who's he gone to see?' enquired Abigail. But before Nicholas could reply she continued, 'It's not Josiah is it? I do believe he's back in England.'

For a moment, Nicholas was stunned into silence by his daughter's bold statement. 'And where did you hear that?'

'Oh, father, you know how news gets around the town. I'm sure it must be true, and if it is, he could hardly hide himself away for ever, now could he? And if he is back, then I'll wager Peter will know.'

'Well, that's as maybe, Abigail, but there's no need for you to concern yourself. Everything that happened between you and Josiah is in the past, and I think it better if that's where it stays. So far as I'm concerned though, I have no wish to have anything more to do with him, not after what he did to you.'

'And I would also hope,' joined in Mary, 'that Peter would think the same too. I would be most upset if I found out that it was Josiah he had been to see.'

'Well, Mother, there's an easy way to find out,' said Abigail. 'I'll ask him!'

'Oh dear, Abigail, you haven't changed have you? You never were one to skulk into the background, even as a little girl. But do you think it wise to raise that subject? We don't want any disagreements or falling out, not at Christmas.'

'I've no desire to fall out with Peter. I just want to know if these rumours are true.'

'Well, I'd much rather you didn't say anything. Like your father says, it's best if we forget all about it.' Just at that moment they heard the front door open, then close. 'I expect that's Peter now.'

A few seconds later the drawing room door opened and in strode Peter, looking very dapper in cream trousers and blue frock coat over a high-collared white shirt and matching crimson waistcoat and cravat. He strode over and gave his sister a hug and a kiss. 'How are you, Abigail?' he asked. 'It's good to see you again. I must say you're looking well; motherhood definitely becomes you. And these must be my new niece and nephew,' he continued, kneeling down by the sofa where the twins lay, quietly slumbering.

The greetings over, they left the twins sleeping soundly and went through to the dining room, where the cook had laid out a spread of cold meats and preserves, cheeses, cakes and sweet pastries and pots of coffee and tea. Over their meal, Peter proceeded to tell them all about his periods of duty in India, Gibraltar and Ireland, and young Charles sat enthralled as his uncle regaled them with accounts of daring raids and heroic deeds performed. But even such stories as these can become tiresome to children, and soon Charles and Catherine grew restless to go and play elsewhere.

'Come along children,' said Mary, 'let's go back to the drawing room. We'll check on the twins and see if we can find a game for you.' As soon as they left, Nicholas brought out a brandy bottle and poured a glass for himself and one for Peter.

'So what are your plans now, Peter?' asked Abigail.

'I shall stay here until after Christmas, then I'll have to head back to barracks. I need to be there by the 10th January.'

'That's quite a decent period of leave.'

'Yes, but the first for over a year.'

'And where will you be posted next? Do you know yet?'

'I'm not sure. I expect it will be one of the colonies again; there's always trouble brewing somewhere in the Empire that has to be sorted out. You know what these foreigners are like, devious and disloyal, and most of them completely untrustworthy; more like a bunch of common criminals.'

'A bit like the criminals we ship out from this country to Van Diemen's Land, then,' said Abigail nonchalantly, 'although they're not all common, are they? In fact some of them are positively well connected and wealthy, I believe.' There was no reply from Peter. Abigail looked across the table at him, and she knew she had touched a raw nerve. Just for a brief second she noticed that look she had seen before, one of irritation and annoyance.

Nicholas coughed loudly. 'More brandy, Peter?'

'No thank you, father. If you'll excuse me I think I'll go to my room. I have some paperwork I need to look at.'

'But Peter, surely that can wait. It's so long since we saw you. Can't you do that later?' pleaded Abigail in her most persuasive and endearing manner. 'Life can get so tedious here in Nottingham at times. I'd love to hear more of your exploits, where you've been and who you've seen. Do you ever come across any of your old friends during your travels?'

'I would expect that to be most unlikely,' suggested Nicholas. 'The odds of a chance encounter with an acquaintance in foreign parts must be exceedingly slim.'

'Oh, I wasn't thinking of a chance encounter, more of an arranged one. After all, it would be rather churlish to have travelled half way round the world, and not try to meet up with an old friend whom you knew to be in the vicinity, someone who might have been away for a long time and would love the opportunity to hear all the news from back home.' Abigail could tell that Peter was now becoming somewhat annoyed at her subtle hints and innuendos, but was trying hard not to show it.

'Father's right. Apart from colonial officials and other British exiles, most of those we meet are foreigners. Just whom do you think I might know who resides abroad?'

'Well, I can think of one who left for Van Diemen's Land about eight years ago, and I know you were there a few years back. You might have come across him.'

Peter could contain his anger no longer, for he knew only too well to whom Abigail was referring. 'Why don't you just come out with it and say what you mean, Abigail? I suppose you're thinking of Josiah. Well, I didn't see him. Why should I? I was there on regimental business, not looking up a former friend. And that's all he is, a former friend. The past is the past and I don't wish to discuss him any further, so I'd be obliged if you didn't mention him again.'

'But you see Peter, I have heard on good authority that he is back in England. In fact, I understand he has been seen in Nottingham recently.'

'Well, I wouldn't know anything about that. I only arrived here last night. Now, if you'll excuse me, I must go and deal with that paperwork.'

Peter rose from the table and walked towards the door. But no sooner had he done so than Abigail followed him into the hallway. He was about to start up the staircase when Abigail reached out and gently took his arm. He stopped and turned, and as he did so Abigail looked him straight in the eye. 'Look at me Peter. I do not want to fall out with you, but if I find out that you have renewed your acquaintance with that despicable rogue, you will have me to reckon with. If Josiah had had his way he would have destroyed William, and me too. I know he's not one to let matters drop. I am quite sure he is back here, so take heed and stay away from him for your own sake. If you get embroiled with that man again you will live to regret it. Do you understand?'

Peter glared at Abigail with a look of exasperation on his face. 'I've said all I intend to, and have nothing more to say on the matter.' And he brusquely removed Abigail's hand from his arm and carried on walking up the stairs.

Abigail went into the drawing room, where Mary was busy reading Charles and Catherine a story. 'Come along you two, it's time we went home. Your father should be back by now. Put your scarves and coats on while I see to the twins. Mother, you will come and join us on Christmas Day, won't you? William brought home a big plump goose he was given by one of his customers and Millie is so looking forward to cooking it.'

'Yes, of course. But don't expect Peter. He did say he's been invited to spend the day with some friends. He hasn't said who and I don't want to interrogate him. Oh, Abigail, I do wish things weren't so awkward between him and William.'

'Well, if he will get himself mixed up with certain people, what can we do? Father came round to accepting William and it's a pity Peter can't. I think he's too easily led and allows himself to be influenced by the opinions of others. And we both know who I'm talking about!'

It was after seven o'clock and a dark, moonless night, as Abigail and the children left and made their way home. Nicholas insisted on accompanying them, and carried one of the twins. No sooner had they shut the front door behind them, when the back door opened and Peter quietly slipped out, down the garden path and along the narrow entrance at the rear of the property. He made his way down Malin Hill to Plumptre Square, and into The Town Arms. He soon found the landlord, who was busy sweeping up some broken bottles from the stone-flagged floor in one of the tiny bars.

'Oh, it's you again is it?' he said, 'I suppose you've come to see Mr Smith have you? He's in his room right now. Follow me.' The landlord put down his brush, and picking up a candle went out of the bar, along a dark corridor and up half a dozen steps to a back room, where he knocked loudly on the door.

'Mr Smith, your gentleman friend's here to see you again,' he shouted, then turning to Peter, 'He's in there.' The landlord turned round and returned to his chores. The door opened.

'Come on in Peter, and shut the door behind you.'

Peter entered the room. It was tiny and shabby with bare floorboards, a meagre fire in the hearth and just one small window, over which hung a filthy threadbare curtain. The furniture consisted merely of a single bed, a chair and a table. On the table stood a glass and a bottle of wine, a book, some paper and pens and a flickering candle. 'Good God, Josiah, do you really have to put up with staying in a place like this, with all the money you have at your disposal? It reminds me of the prison cells at the barracks.'

'I've lived in a lot worse. This is a palace compared with what I had to endure down under. Anyway, it suits me to go unrecognised at the moment, and it won't be for long. As I told you this morning, I've had some business to attend to and people to see, and the sort of people I'm talking about feel more at home here than they would in my house in Castle Gate. When the time's right I'll go back there under my own name, but for the time being I prefer to remain incognito. Anyway, how was Abigail? I assume you've seen her.'

'Yes, and she's heard something. She's sure you're back.'

'And what did you tell her?'

'Nothing much. But she as good as asked me outright if I'd seen you in Van Diemen's Land and I had to lie to her. I told her I'd not seen you, but I don't think she believed me. I know I promised to help you get back at William, but I don't want my name mentioning if anything untoward should happen to him.'

'You know what we agreed. You just keep me informed of what he's up to. Find out what you can, especially about his business dealings, and leave the rest to me. I hear he's involved with this new railway company.'

'I really wouldn't know about that. It wasn't discussed but I'll let you know should I hear anything. I have to go back to Gloucester in a couple of weeks and I'm not certain how long I'll be away. I haven't even heard yet where my next posting will be.'

'Well, if you ever need to get any information to me, you can always enquire in the bar for Bill Giles, he's often in here. He can be relied on, rough as he is, and he'll always ensure any messages reach me. I'm returning to Retford the day after tomorrow and I don't think I'll be back in town again before you leave. But Peter, don't you let me down. You know what has to be done and I'm depending on you to help me.'

'Don't worry, Josiah, you know you can trust me. But I must get home before I'm missed. I'll let you know where I'm being posted and when I next expect to be in Nottingham.'

Peter left the room and returned the way he came. He was soon home, but could not rid himself of a gnawing sense of anxiety. Josiah appeared to have hardened and become even more embittered. His desire for revenge seemed to be taking over his life. Why else, he wondered, should a man with untold wealth be staying under an assumed name in a miserable backstreet pub in one of the poorest parts of the town?

CHAPTER TWELVE

—

NOTTINGHAM 1831

Christmas came and went. Peter returned to his regiment and was shortly posted back to Ireland. Samuel found himself a job at a new brewery, delivering barrels of beer to some of the pubs in the town and William was having to spend more time dealing with the affairs of the railway, where construction of the line was now well under way.

Edward, meanwhile, continued working in the lace factory but nearly all his spare time was now being spent with his new-found friends, campaigning for reform. Most nights they met in a back room at The Durham Ox on Pelham Street, for many years a haunt of those of a reforming, or as their opponents would accuse them, revolutionary, disposition. These meetings did, occasionally, attract some of the more extreme agitators who would willingly have joined in a violent confrontation with the forces of conservatism, and taken up arms just as the French had done some forty years earlier. But most of these self-professed fanatics were nothing more than taproom revolutionaries who loved a fight for its own sake, and would attach themselves to any cause which they thought might give them an excuse for a punch-up.

Nevertheless, sporadic outbreaks of violence had broken out against the Duke of Newcastle, who was regarded as the bête noir of the anti-reformers. Over Christmas someone tried to burn down a barn on one of his farms, and then in January there was a serious attempt on his life. News got out that he was to attend a ball at Lincoln and he was threatened with death if he attended. Undeterred, he decided to ignore these threats and travelled to Lincoln by coach. En route he was stopped by a horseman who warned him that a mob lay in wait ahead, stopping all coaches in search of him. But still he pressed on. On his arrival at Lincoln a hostile reception party of about fifty men was waiting for him, and despite being jostled and made the target of various missiles, the duke's servants and some local constables managed to get him safely into the venue.

But the majority who were present at these nightly gatherings in The Durham Ox were level-headed enough to realise that any serious outbreaks of violence would be swiftly, fiercely and almost certainly bloodily suppressed, and could put back their cause for another generation. They were more concerned that the victory of parliamentary reform, which they believed was now within their grasp, should not be lost due to the reckless acts of a few hotheads. Some of the regulars at The Durham Ox were amongst the first to join *The Nottingham Political Union*, an organisation devoted to canvassing for reform. Early in March it held its first public meeting at the Exchange, and so popular was it that hundreds struggled to gain admission. The mayor himself presided, accompanied by various aldermen and other influential citizens, and an address to the king and petition to the House of Commons were prepared, expressing support for the Reform Bill which had just been presented to Parliament by Lord John Russell, the leading reformist in the Whig Government.

A strong and irresistible wave of support for the Bill was now sweeping through the country, and there was euphoria when, on the 23rd March, it received its second reading in the House of Commons, albeit by only one vote. The Tory opposition now sought to dilute the effects of the Bill at the committee stages by pushing forward amendments, and a month later their tactics succeeded when the Government was defeated on the issue of whether the number of MPs should be reduced, this being one of the proposals in the Bill. Cynics were not surprised that MPs did not vote for a reduction in their numbers, and the end result was that Parliament was again dissolved. Yet another general election was hurriedly arranged, but unlike that of the previous year, this one was all done and dusted in just four days, and on the 1st June the Whigs were returned with a majority of 136.

Once more the tide had turned and there was a great deal of rejoicing in The Durham Ox when the result of the election arrived from London. News of such events was conveyed either by one of the stage coaches, or sometimes on a Pickford's van. The men at The Durham Ox would send someone along to The Maypole on Long Row or The White Lion on Clumber Street, the principal coaching inns of the town, to await the arrival of the London coach. The journey could often take ten hours or more, so that, depending on the actual time of day when events were unfolding in London, it might be the following day before news was received. But invariably, whatever time the news did arrive, in less than an hour it would be all over the town.

Following the election, the Reform Bill was reintroduced to the Commons and soon became the main topic of discussion in the town, and not only amongst the politically minded. Apart from a flurry of excitement at the end of August, when two young men were publicly hanged at the House of Correction for the particularly nasty rape of a young woman behind The Rancliffe Arms in Sussex Street, reform was the topic of the day. Those who would normally pass the time gossiping with their neighbours about the weather, or what her-down-the-alley's daughter had been getting up to, or the outrageous price of bread, found themselves catching up with the latest rumours of the goings-on in Parliament.

Throughout the summer this one issue took over the lives of MPs to the exclusion of almost every other matter, and the Nottingham newspapers carried lengthy reports of the debates in Parliament, the Review declaring its agreement, whilst the Tory supporting Journal was less enthusiastic about the seemingly inevitable changes. Many inhabitants of the town could neither read nor write, and this was especially so in the poorer areas. A number of pub landlords spotted an opportunity here to boost their takings, and provided 'readers' who would nightly read the papers to all and sundry, who, naturally, would have a drink or two whilst listening to the latest news from London.

Eventually, after lengthy debates both in the Chamber and the Committee Rooms, the Bill was passed on the 22nd September by a margin of well over a hundred. This was the news that thousands had waited for, but it didn't reach Nottingham until the following day, and that evening became a time for celebration. Edward went along to The Durham Ox accompanied by Samuel, who was now beginning to take an interest himself.

'Go on through to the back bar and I'll get us a couple of pints,' said Edward as they entered the pub. Although it was only just after seven, the front parlour was already busy; most of the seats were occupied and groups of men stood around at the bar. Samuel went to the room at the rear as instructed. There were already a dozen or so men there, but he managed to find an empty table in the corner, and was soon joined by Edward carrying two pots of ale, a couple of clay pipes and a plug of tobacco. 'Here you are, and I've got us a smoke.'

'Thanks, Edward,' said Samuel, and, taking a small knife from his pocket he cut a piece of the hard black tobacco, rubbed it between his fingers and carefully filled the bowl. He went over to the fireplace and lit a taper, put it to the pipe and drew strongly until the tobacco sprung into life, then handed it to Edward. 'I wonder if Uncle Isaac still makes these?' he said, examining the pipe. For many years, Samuel's uncle had been a clay pipe maker, and had a profitable sideline supplying public houses with cheap 'bar pipes' which the landlords handed out free when tobacco was purchased.

'Not anymore,' replied Edward. 'William was telling me about it the other week. He's knocking on a bit now, is Isaac, so he gave up a couple of years ago and his lad Hugh is carrying on the business. But he's running it down and William doesn't think he'll keep it going much longer; he's got other interests has Hugh. William says he's got in with a crowd at the St. Mary's Gate Theatre; does a bit of acting occasionally, but his main talent seems to be in writing plays and comic songs. Mind you, I can't see how that's ever going to make him any money.'

As they sat talking and drinking, the room gradually filled up and before long it was standing room only. Edward knew most of the men there and nodded a greeting to them as they entered. And it was men only. With the exception of a couple of serving girls who came in now and then to clear away tankards and glasses, this was a male dominated enclave. Some of the men joined them and Edward introduced his nephew. Soon the conversation switched to the inevitable subject, and the news that had been received was debated with joy and enthusiasm.

'Here's to reform and the vote,' said one of the assembled group, raising his tankard.

'To reform and the vote,' the others responded.

'Mind you,' said a dour, pale, ill-looking little man who sported thinning hair and an apology for a moustache, 'it ain't the law yet. The Lords have to vote on it.'

'Trust old Jeremiah here to put a damper on things,' muttered a red-faced, stoutly built man.

'But what he says is true,' observed Edward. 'It can't become law until the Lords vote it through and we all know what most of them think about it. We know exactly how the Duke of Newcastle will vote, and if they all act like him they could easily put a stop to it.'

'They wouldn't bloody dare,' insisted the stout man, angrily. 'Not now. Even those self-serving, sherry-swilling old reactionaries must realise the mood of the country. And if they did dare, there'd be mayhem. I wouldn't like to be in their shoes if they had the nerve to stop things. That spot of bother back in 1817 would be nothing compared with what would happen now. And not just round here. The whole country's crying out for change. There'd be a bloody revolution!'

'And another thing,' added the dour little man, 'even if the Bill is passed it won't make any difference for most of us. It might get rid of the rotten boroughs and provide some MPs in those big towns that don't have any, but men will still have to own a certain amount of property or pay so much rent to get the vote. I doubt if half of us in here will qualify.'

Samuel had said very little so far. He had never been one for politics. His interests had always lain elsewhere and at heart he was a ladies' man. As long he had a girl on his arm and enough money for a few drinks, he was happy. But now he was finding himself drawn more and more towards the cause. The subtlety of the arguments he found rather tedious, but he understood exactly what was at stake, and to him it seemed clear that if you wanted something badly, you simply went out and fought for it.

'Well, if that's true, maybe we all need to be bolder,' declared Samuel. 'I'm up for a bit of action and I tell you what: if we really want to show we mean business, let's demonstrate it. We could start by burning down the duke's castle. He might not use it much, but at least it would make him sit up and think.'

'Here, here, well said, lad,' agreed the stout man. 'That's what we want, fighting talk.'

'Never! That's where you're wrong. I know it might give us all a bit of satisfaction, but we've come too far now to spoil everything by a madcap drunken riot.' The speaker was an elderly white-haired gentleman. 'I've waited all my life for this, and I don't want to see it ruined by the actions of a bunch of hotheads.'

The debate continued into the night. Most agreed that victory for the reform movement was now in sight, and, whilst the Bill might not be as far-reaching as many had hoped for, most of them accepted that any sort of violent reaction would not help the cause. In any case, the Bill had now passed through the Commons and there was just one hurdle left. It was expected that the vote in the Lords would take place within a couple of weeks, so all they could do was to wait and hope. And as they walked back home, Edward had a few strong words to say to Samuel.

'I'm pleased you're taking an interest, Samuel, but you need to be careful what you say in public, threatening arson and the like. There are plenty of people who will use any excuse to try and stop things changing and it wouldn't surprise me if there were still some spies knocking about, working for the opposition. Not everybody in the pub shares our views. I know most of the regulars there, but I have noticed the odd stranger coming in now and again. Any excuse to discredit us, and they'll use it. Don't forget what happened back in 1817, the last time we tried to change things. Scores arrested, three men executed, a dozen or more transported and others gaoled. Even I had to get out of the country. We don't want all that again. I know it might have been the beer talking tonight, Samuel, but sometimes you need to be discreet. Some people have long memories.'

It was exactly two weeks later, a Friday morning, when their lordships began their long debate on the Reform Bill. Passionate speeches were made on both sides, and opinions tended to fall on party lines, Whigs for the Bill, Tories against, and it was evident that there was a groundswell of opposition. The Tories had a large majority and they represented the wealthy landowning families who had, for centuries, regarded themselves as natural leaders with the right to decide how the country should be run. And they had no intention of forfeiting easily what they considered theirs by birth, no matter what most of the population might want. To many of them, the very concept that common working men, most of whom could neither read nor write, should actually have a say in who should represent them, was absurd in the extreme. The debate went on all day. So long in fact that it was the early hours of the next morning before the vote was finally taken.

Meanwhile, in Nottingham, there was plenty to keep the townsfolk occupied and entertained, for it was the week of the annual fair, the most important and eagerly anticipated week in the town's calendar, a time not only to stock up on provisions not normally available, but to have some fun too. For over five hundred years there had been an autumn fair in Nottingham and geese, fattened up in readiness, had been driven from as far away as Norfolk, giving it the name by which it was known far and wide - Goose Fair.

Preparations for the fair had begun almost two weeks before, as travellers began to pour into the town from near and far; country folk with their seasonal produce to sell and tradesmen from further afield. Shoe makers arrived from Northampton and hatters from Luton, linen weavers from Barnsley and cloth merchants from Leeds and Halifax, cutlers from Sheffield with knives and scissors, and potters from Staffordshire. Apart from the numerous well-stocked stalls, all kinds of showmen and entertainers headed into town, and for a week the population was spoilt for choice. Wombwells came, as usual, with their Wild Beast Show. There were Punch and Judy men, freak shows and merry-go-rounds, actors and comedians, strollers and singers, dancers, jugglers and magicians - all vying for the townsfolk's money and attention.

But the fair also offered the prospect of easy money for the less honest, both inhabitants and visitors alike, and many an innocent citizen would become the victim of a pickpocket, cutpurse or confidence trickster. And for those who revelled in drunken debauchery, or who sought an excuse for a fight or worse, the Goose Fair provided an unrivalled opportunity. Gangs of youths would come over from neighbouring towns and villages, and the natural rivalry which already existed between them and the town's young men would often explode into a full-blown riot.

But this time there was another factor, which would make the year of 1831 a year to be remembered. This year would see riots not only to equal, but to exceed anything which had gone before. And for once, the opposing gangs would drop all pretence of rivalry, and join together in an outpouring of hatred towards a common enemy.

The fair had opened on Monday, but Saturday, the final day, was the busiest, a day when many either did not work or finished work early. The afternoon and evening saw exceptionally large crowds gathering as people flocked in from outlying areas, determined to enjoy a night out in the knowledge that the morrow would give them a full day to recover from their excesses. The public houses were particularly busy serving food and drink to the hundreds milling around the town centre. The Market Place was the main area for the various attractions, whilst all the side streets leading into it were lined with stalls of all kinds.

In The Durham Ox, Edward and Samuel were seated around a large table in a corner of the bar, enjoying a pint of ale with some of their friends, when William and Benjamin came in.

'William, Benjamin, over here', shouted Samuel across the crowded room, 'and bring some more ale with you.' Benjamin joined them while William went to the bar, and he soon arrived carrying a large jug of the foaming brown liquid. 'Here, William, room for another one,' said Samuel moving along the bench.

William placed the jug on the table and invited them all to help themselves. He didn't make a habit of drinking in the Nottingham pubs. Not that he didn't enjoy a few pints in congenial company, but what with the canal business and now the railway, he rarely found time for social gatherings. But it was ages since he had had a night out with his brothers and friends, and Abigail had insisted he join them. William knew many of those around the table, and Edward introduced him to the rest. Most of them had been there for a few hours, and some had been in the town for much of the day. The public houses and inns had been open since early morning, and William could tell that one or two of those present had been drinking steadily since then. Before long, talk turned to the Reform Bill.

'So, Edward,' said William, 'you seem to be in the know. What's the latest position?'

'Well, the Bill's gone to the Lords. We reckon they started debating it yesterday, but there's no word yet of any decision.'

'They daren't throw it out, surely, not after the Commons passed it. And everyone knows the mood of the country.'

'You'd think not, but nothing would surprise me,' replied Edward. 'They can be obstinate when they have a mind to be. Can you really see the Duke of Newcastle voting to pass the Bill, whatever the people want? I can't. And if most of the other Tories think like him, they might just put a stop to it.'

'There'll be a bloody riot if they do,' came a voice from somewhere behind a pint pot.

'Anyway,' continued Edward, 'a couple of the lads have gone to meet the Pickford's van. It's due in just after eight, and they usually bring the latest news with them. If any decision's been made, I'm sure we won't have to wait long for it.'

It was at about a quarter to nine when the two lads entered the bar. Most of those present knew who they were, where they had been and the purpose of their errand, and within a few seconds the noise and hubbub in the room, the chatter and laughter and clinking of glasses and tankards ceased, and an eerie silence pervaded. All eyes were on the two lads. For a second they said nothing, but from the looks on their faces it was easy to see that they were not best pleased.

'The bastards. They've thrown it out!' For another second the silence survived but then, in an instance, all was noise and clamour. Men were shouting, asking questions, demanding answers. Above the din a voice rang out loudly from behind the bar as the landlord called for order.

'Quiet, quiet,' he yelled, 'let them speak.' Gradually the noise subsided. 'Just what was the news. Tell us what you've heard, lads.'

'All they could say was that the Lords have thrown out the Bill. That's all. Nothing more, no details, just that they've thrown it out.'

The news spread like wildfire. The town was still full of revellers at the fair, and within minutes of the Pickford van's arrival, it seemed, everyone, whether out in the streets or in the pubs and inns, had heard the news.

'So, what now, Edward?' asked Samuel. 'Is it time to start banging a few heads?'

'None of that talk, Samuel. Some might resort to violence, but I've said it won't get us anywhere, satisfying as it might be. No, we have to be smarter than that. We need to get the corporation to act. They're on our side in any case. I think we need to press the mayor to do something - call a meeting of the corporation, petition the Government and the king. Let them know how damaging this decision of the Lords is.'

Edward was not alone in his judgement of the situation and what needed to be done, for across the town other groups were thinking on similar lines. Within less than an hour, several petitions had been written and presented to the mayor, requesting that a public meeting be held as soon as possible. The mayor, ever mindful of the possible repercussions should the hotheads and troublemakers have their way, swiftly gave his reply, and by eleven o'clock that night had responded by announcing that he had called a meeting of the burgesses and inhabitants of the town to take place on the following Monday morning at eleven o'clock in the Market Place. Again, this news spread rapidly. Overnight, printers were busy, and on the Sunday, posters were hastily distributed throughout the town and surrounding area, so that by the appointed hour on Monday morning the Market Place was even busier than it had been during the previous week's fair.

But before Monday came, there were to be further developments. Everyone was desperate for more news, so by the time the mail coach was due from London on the Sunday morning hundreds had already congregated outside The White Lion Inn on Clumber Street, eagerly awaiting its arrival. As it drew up, one of the passengers announced that in London the reformers were 'beating to arms', an announcement which was received by certain sections of the crowd with loud cheers. This was all the excuse that some of those present needed, a signal to start venting their anger. Within minutes, a small mob was seeking out the premises of those they knew, or believed, to be opposed to reform. The first to be attacked was the shop of a druggist on Clumber Street, immediately opposite The White Lion.

Throughout the day sporadic outbreaks of violence continued and others suffered a similar fate: a bookseller on Long Row, a doctor on Stoney Street and a hosier on Pilcher Gate. Windows were smashed and items stolen, and as evening drew on the excitement of the mob continued unabated. The mayor attempted to dissuade them from further violence, and although he was sympathetic to their cause he was himself the subject of an attack which left him injured. The Riot Act was read, but there was little the authorities could do. Such few constables as were available found themselves hopelessly outnumbered and the outrages continued into the night. All those prominent citizens who had voiced opposition to the Reform Bill now had cause to fear for their safety. The offices of the Nottingham Journal, the fiercely anti-reform newspaper, was amongst many to suffer when it was paid a visit by the mob.

Eventually, as the night wore on and tiredness took its course, the crowds gradually dispersed. But the following morning a huge throng of people began to gather in the Market Place to hear the mayor speak. At eleven o'clock he appeared, along with other speakers, on the balcony of a house on the south side of the Market Place, where matters were conducted peacefully enough. Resolutions were drawn up, moved and seconded, and it was agreed that these would be sent to ministers of the Government and to the king, urging them to do everything within their power to ensure the Reform Bill became law. At last the meeting came to an end, and the majority, being satisfied with what had been agreed, returned to their homes or went quietly about their business.

But the proceedings had little effect on a sizeable minority whose intentions were far from peaceful. Some of them were passionately committed to the cause of reform, but had been so offended by the action of the House of Lords that they were prepared to take the law into their own hands and vent their feelings by violent means. The rest were there, not out of any feelings of frustration, but merely because they saw the opportunity for riot, destruction and rich pickings. Many of them were petty criminals, pickpockets and thieves both from the town itself and neighbouring villages, and were there to take full advantage of the fair, then the races, due to take place that week. As the crowd dispersed, the mob made its way firstly to Mr Sharpe's windmill on the edge of the Forest, where they destroyed the sails and smashed the machinery. Had it not been for the arrival of a small troop of hussars, the windmill would certainly have been completely demolished. The authorities, fearing further disturbances, had called for the assistance of the cavalry but they were limited in number, as some had already gone over to Derby to deal with disturbances there. As the rioters made their way back into the town, they attacked more premises belonging to anti-reformers, and the hussars were hard pressed to attend each incident. The small number available had been split into separate detachments, each led by a magistrate, and for several hours these small bands of cavalry were galloping hither and thither around the town, trying in vain to prevent further outrages.

As the day wore on, the mob became bigger and bolder, and, fortified by drink, headed out towards Colwick Hall, two miles outside the town and the home of John Musters, a prominent Tory magistrate. They stopped only once, in Sneinton, to tear down some iron railings with which to arm themselves. Rain was falling as, bent on destruction, they approached the hall. Mr Musters was away, and Mrs Musters had been confined to her bed. But on being warned of the approaching menace, she, her daughter and a visitor hurriedly made their escape and, despite the weather, hid in some bushes. The rioters soon gained admittance to the hall and an orgy of theft and vandalism began. Furniture, paintings and ornaments, some of extreme value were destroyed. Ale, wine and food were consumed, and plate, silver and clothes carried away. Before leaving, some of them attempted to burn down the hall by starting a fire in one of the rooms. Someone, hoping to accelerate the fire, added a feather bed to the conflagration but this only succeeded in dampening the flames and thus saving the hall from being razed to the ground.

Fired with success, and fuelled with the contents of the hall's wine cellar, the mob now headed back to the town and made for the House of Correction. Their attempt to tear down the gates and free the inmates was thwarted by a small detachment of hussars, and whilst they dealt with the rioters, another group, about six hundred strong, headed off along Wheeler Gate.

Suddenly, a cry of 'to the castle' was heard, and the mob turned up Friar Lane and Park Street. Although almost empty, for the Duke of Newcastle had not resided here for many years, the castle represented everything and everyone who opposed the reform movement. After some difficulty, three of them managed to make a hole in the sturdy wooden gate of the Castle Lodge, and once inside the grounds, were soon able to open the gates. About thirty or so went in, and headed up the hill towards the main building. Breaking a window, they gained access and began a systematic destruction of anything they could lay their hands on. Chandeliers were torn down to be used as weapons and tapestries were ripped from the walls, some of which were retained and later cut up and sold as souvenirs.

Some of the men now set about preparing to set fire to the building. Holes were made in the floors of the upper rooms to help quicken the blaze, and broken furniture was set alight. Others went down into the basement kitchens and started fires there. Soon the blaze took hold, and the mob, by now a hundred and fifty strong, quit the burning edifice, loudly proclaiming their triumph. A small band of hussars had arrived but there was nothing they could do, and the rioters soon dispersed to escape arrest. Despite the continuing rain, the fire had taken a firm hold, and by ten o'clock it had reached its height. Flames leapt from every window, and clouds of black smoke swept across the town. Streams of molten lead ran down from the burning roof, and the strong smell of cedar wood, of which much of the castle's ornate panelling was made, filled the night air with its distinctive aroma.

The castle stood on a high sandstone cliff, and the inferno could be seen for miles around. Thousands flocked into the town to get a closer look, and filled every road, street and space in the vicinity. Its lofty elevation meant there was little chance of putting out the fire, as water would have to be carried by hand from down below. There was no chance of saving it, and the authorities had no choice but to let it burn.

By midnight, helped by persistent squally showers of rain, the raging fire had begun to die down and by daylight the next morning the damage was clear for all to see. The building was now nothing more than a smoking, roofless shell and everything but the soot-stained walls had been totally consumed. Inquisitive visitors came to examine the smouldering remains, and the saddest discovery of all was the blackened and mutilated corpses of two young children, no doubt drawn to the scene out of curiosity. Even sadder was the fact that their identities were never discovered, and nobody ever came to claim the bodies.

The events of the last two days had been closely followed by Edward and Samuel, along with their friends at The Durham Ox, and, for a short time, William had joined them, keen to find out the latest news. But they made sure they did not get involved with any of the actions of the mob, whose exploits they deplored.

The Tuesday morning passed off peacefully enough, but towards midday the rioters began to gather again. Having recovered from their excesses of the previous day, they were now looking for further excitement. Edward and Samuel walked over to The Durham Ox at midday, and on their way noticed small groups congregating in the Market Place, most of whom, they reckoned, were not local men but strangers from outlying districts. Some had been in the town since the previous week's fair; others no doubt had been attracted by the burning of the castle.

In The Durham Ox there was but one topic of discussion amongst the regulars. The events of the last few days were hotly debated, and what they thought the outcome might be; whether the violence and destruction meted out would make it harder for the Government to reintroduce the Reform Bill, or whether such actions would demonstrate just how strong support was in favour of it. About two o'clock they were joined by another of their friends who said a rumour was going round that some of the rioters had set off towards Beeston, where they intended to target Lowe's silk mill and then Chilwell Hall, the seat of William Charlton, a former High Sherriff of Nottingham. Both Mr Lowe and Mr Charlton were prominent Tories and known to be strongly against reform. On hearing that Chilwell was likely to be the scene of further disturbances, Edward immediately grabbed Samuel by the arm.

'Come on, Samuel, drink up. Mother's living at Chilwell now with your ma and pa and sisters, and their cottage is just along the road from the hall. I know it's not them they'll be targeting, but we all know what can happen when a drunken rabble gets out of hand. We'll see if William's around. He can take us in his gig.'

They hurriedly finished their drinks and got up to leave. But as they did so, Samuel accidentally brushed against a stranger sitting nearby, almost knocking over his beer in the process.

'Oi, watch what you're doing!'

'Sorry pal,' said Samuel, apologetically.

'You will be if you do that again,' replied the stranger in a threatening tone. He was a rough-looking individual, smelly, with dirty, ragged clothes and pockmarks on his face. Samuel was generally amiable and easy-going, and his mother always said he could charm the birds from the trees. But when roused, or provoked, he was not one to turn the other cheek. Samuel stopped, turned round and met the stranger face to face.

'I said sorry, what more do you want? It was an accident and you've not lost any beer.' The stranger kept silent and looked a bit sheepish. He realised he had said the wrong thing to the wrong man. But before the incident could get out of hand, Edward stepped in.

'Come on Samuel, just leave it. He's not worth it, and we have to get over to Chilwell.' Samuel gave the man one last look. He didn't need to say anything more. He knew the stranger had got the message. They hurried across the town to the canal, and, as they passed through the Market Place, sure enough, there was now no sign of the mob. They arrived at the wharf and were relieved to find William there. Quickly they explained what they had heard.

'Benjamin, you'd better come along too,' said William as he harnessed one of the horses. 'If there's going to be any trouble, the more hands we have the better.' Within five minutes they were on their way.

'Do be careful, all of you,' cried Abigail, as they pulled out of the yard and into the street.

'Don't worry, Abigail. We can take care of ourselves. Just have some supper ready for when we get back.'

The rain was still falling as they trotted up Derby Road, and, passing the barracks, they noticed a number of cavalrymen, mounted as if ready to set off. William urged the horse on, and they galloped briskly down the hill towards Lenton, and soon turned off the Derby Road and into Beeston Lane. There were now clear signs that the rioters had passed this way, for they could see recent damage to the fences and gates of some of the large houses which stood back from the lane. At the entrance to one of them, they stopped to question a group of workmen who were inspecting some such damage. They explained that a drunken mob had done it and had threatened to break into the house, under the mistaken belief that it belonged to William Lowe, the silk mill owner. It was only after they had managed to convince them that this was actually the residence of Mr Alfred Lowe, who was neither a mill owner nor a Tory, that they had gone on their way, but not before they had demanded some food and liquor, which Mr Alfred Lowe had granted them, considering it a small price to pay for being left in comparative safety. As they stood talking to the men, Benjamin suddenly interrupted them.

'Look, over there', he exclaimed. 'Smoke!' A large pall of black smoke was rising into the air, and flames too became visible.

'Seems like the rumour was true, then. That'll be the silk mill,' said Edward.

Their assumption soon proved to be correct; for shortly afterwards, as they trotted into Beeston, the damage was only too clear to see. The mill, a large four-storeyed brick building, stood in the centre of the village on one corner of a crossroads. The streets were thronged with people and the whole population must have turned out to witness the scene. Flames leapt from every window and thick black acrid smoke billowed skywards. There was a constant noise of crashing and banging as timbers gave way and machinery fell from the upper floors, destroying more of the structure during its descent. William observed the onlookers with sadness, for their dismay at the sight before them was plain to see. He reckoned that most of them were strong supporters for reform, but many of them relied on the silk mill for their livelihoods, and the fire would surely bring unemployment, poverty and despair. Who was to know what Mr Lowe would do? He might rebuild the mill, but that could take months or years, and in the meantime there would be no wages for his workers. Or he could decide to move elsewhere, somewhere where he considered the inhabitants to be less hostile. Whatever happened, there would be many a family going hungry that winter.

There was no sign of those responsible for starting the fire, so William asked one of the bystanders if he knew where they had gone. The man nodded in the direction of Chilwell. 'About half an hour ago. I think they were heading for Chilwell Hall. Most of 'em were the worse for drink, and I heard one say they needed to teach old Charlton a lesson.'

With some difficulty William managed to steer a path through the crowd, which was almost blocking the road. As they slowly made their way forward, Benjamin became aware of a chap standing a little way off from the rest of the crowd, and noticed that he seemed to be taking a particular interest in them, staring at them as they approached. He seemed vaguely familiar and Benjamin thought he half-recognised him, but couldn't immediately place him. He was sure he had seen him before, but couldn't remember exactly when and where. He was of middling age with thinning hair; he looked rough and his clothes were dirty and torn. As they trotted by in the gig, the man turned as if to keep them in view, and that was when Benjamin noticed the pockmarks on his right cheek.

'What's up Benjamin? What are you staring at?' asked Samuel.

'That man over there; he seems mightily interested in us and I'm certain I've seen him before.' Samuel followed his brother's gaze.

'I recognise him. That's the man I nearly came to blows with this morning. I wonder what he's doing here?' And Samuel told Benjamin about the incident in The Durham Ox.

In less than five minutes they had reached Chilwell, and, passing the entrance gates to the hall, were relieved to find no sign of the mob or evidence of any disturbance. They were soon at the cottage, and as they pulled up outside, the door opened and Margaret came out.

'Good gracious, this is a surprise! All my sons, and my brother too! To what do we owe the pleasure? I hope there's nothing wrong.'

'Well, we hope not, too,' said William, giving his mother a hug. 'We were concerned for you, though. We'd heard that rioters were heading over to Chilwell and we wanted to come and see that you were all safe. But there doesn't seem to be any sign of them. They burned the castle last night, and now the silk mill at Beeston's gone the same way, but you probably know that already.' James had now joined his wife on the doorstep.

'Yes, we've heard all about that; bad news travels fast. You'd better come inside. Mr Hallam's just called by and he's been telling us about events up at the hall; he'll be able to tell you what's been going on.' They all trooped inside and went into the living room.

'William, it's good to see you again. How are you?' said Joseph, shaking him firmly by the hand.

'Very well, Joseph, and you too, I trust, despite these troubled times. Now let me do the introductions: these are my brothers Samuel and Benjamin, and this is my Uncle Edward. This is Joseph Hallam, the squire's estate manager, the man who was good enough to offer ma and pa the cottage. Well, Joseph, what's been happening? We came over as soon as we heard the mob was setting out this way, but they seem to have disappeared.'

'I have to say, gentleman, the last few days have been the most eventful since I came here over thirty years ago. I doubt there's ever been anything like it in Chilwell before. The last bit of excitement we had was a couple of years back when the pedlar went missing, and everyone reckoned that old Baguley up at the Ash Flat House had murdered him, but that's another story.

'We've had a real tragedy here, but it could so easily have been worse. I don't suppose the news has reached Nottingham yet, but the squire died on Saturday morning and his body is still lying up at the hall. There was only his daughter Caroline in the house at the time, and she's only seventeen, poor girl, along with Martha the housekeeper. He'd been ill for a while, what with gout and a heart complaint, and it was becoming clear that he didn't have long left to live. So his two sons, who are at school at Eton, were sent for, but they arrived too late.

'They travelled up on the coach from London yesterday and it must have been an anxious journey for them. Even before they got to Trent Bridge they could see the castle in flames, and when the coach arrived in the town they found it virtually in the hands of a violent mob. It was out of the question to send the squire's carriage to fetch them; the livery might have been recognised and they would certainly have been attacked. But Mrs Ward, the landlady at The George The Fourth Hotel, she looked after them and sent them over here this morning in one of the hotel carriages, using the byroads. They got here safely, only to find that their father was dead and that his body had been carried into the barn to conceal it from the rioters, who it was feared might attack the house. We'd had a warning from one of the hussars who rode over here. He told us the mob was threatening to burn down all the houses of known anti-reformers. I asked him if they could send some more men to protect us, but he said they hardly had enough men to keep the peace in Nottingham, and that all available cavalry had been sent to Wollaton to protect the hall there, as they expected that would be the main target for the rioters.

'So one of our gardeners, a strapping lad with a very persuasive tongue, and not someone you'd want to argue with, volunteered to go and try and stop them. He met them, about half way between here and Beeston and he managed to put them off. He told them that the squire was lying dead at the hall and that there was nobody there but his three young orphan children, and surely they wouldn't want to harm them. Much better, he suggested, to go to Wollaton, knowing that the yeomanry were there. He even went with them so far, just to make sure they didn't change their minds. He got back here about an hour ago, so what's happened at Wollaton I couldn't say. In the meantime, Martha had packed away all the silver plate and other valuables and took them, along with the three children, to one of the estate farms, about a mile away on the Stapleford Road, a lonely spot. They'll be safe enough there if the rioters should return. Mind you, Martha has insisted that she remain in the house. She says she's not afraid of them and she'll face up to them if needs be.'

'Well, I'm relieved to hear that no harm has been done,' said William. 'Things can so easily get out of hand and there's nothing worse than a drunken mob on the rampage. And the great pity is, most people are in favour of reform; but this lot, with their antics, could wreck any chance of it happening. I think some of them don't really care one way or the other; for them it's just an excuse for a fight and the opportunity for a spot of looting. All of us here are in favour of the Reform Bill. I know the squire was against, and your job depends on him. It's just a shame that such an important matter should end in violence.'

'It's true I have to be careful what I say,' replied Joseph. 'I have my opinions and I'll keep them. But whatever one thinks of the old squire, he was always good to me. As far as this reform business goes, I only hope it gets sorted out soon without any more trouble.'

Having satisfied themselves that their family was safe, the four men set off back to Nottingham. They later learned that about seventeen of the rioters had been arrested when they attempted to break through the gates to Wollaton Hall, by the soldiers who were waiting for them. Over the next few days there were a few more sporadic outbreaks of fighting, looting and damage to property, but the cavalry was gradually getting the upper hand and its constant presence in the town was proving effective in restoring order. And soon, large numbers of weary revellers were seen to be leaving and heading back to their own towns and villages.

But the events of the past week were to have repercussions. The Duke of Newcastle, whose property in Nottingham had now been reduced to an empty shell, had returned from London to his country seat of Clumber Hall, fearful that it, too, might become a target for the mob. Fortunately for him, it had already been occupied by soldiers who had anticipated that it might be at risk, and no harm had come to it. The duke, however, now turned his attention to the magistrates, whom he condemned for their failure to deal with the situation, and loudly warned that England was on the brink of revolution. He called for arrests to be made and reparations against those responsible for the violence. By December, a number of men had been arrested and awaited trial for their part in the riots.

But before then, William himself received an unexpected visit from two of the town's constables, who insisted that he accompany them to the magistrates. The men had arrived at the wharf one morning shortly after breakfast. Abigail was busy about the house when a loud knock came at the door. William, who was about to leave on business connected with the railway, answered it.

'Mr William Daniels?' enquired one of the constables.

'Yes, I'm William Daniels.'

'I have a warrant here for your arrest in connection with the firing of Mr Lowe's silk mill at Beeston. You will accompany us to the Magistrates' Office at the Town Hall immediately.'

For a moment William was speechless. What was the man talking about? There must be some mistake, he thought. Before he could reply, Abigail came to the door and she could sense that something was wrong.

'What's going on?' she asked, a worried look on her face.

'These men have come to arrest me in connection with the fire at the silk mill. It's obviously a mistake, but I'll have to go with them. Don't worry, Abigail. I'm sure I can soon get things sorted out. But send Benjamin along to tell Robert Kent what's happened, and ask him to come to the Town Hall, if he can.'

William left with the constables, and straightaway Abigail sent Benjamin with a message for Mr Kent, their solicitor on Friar Lane.

On arrival at the Town Hall William was locked in a secure cell with barred windows, but within the hour was taken to a panelled room and brought before the magistrates. There were three of them sitting at a long bench. The one in the middle spoke. He was an elderly, thin-faced severe-looking man, unsmiling and precise in his speech.

'Mr Daniels,' he said, peering over the spectacles perched on the end of his nose, 'we have received information that you, along with three other men, were seen at Beeston on the 11th October when the silk mill was destroyed by fire, and that you had a part in its destruction. And that afterwards you proceeded to Chilwell with a view to further misdemeanours. We also have information that two of the other men with you had, that very morning, been heard discussing radical ideas in The Durham Ox on Pelham Street, and stated that they intended to go to Beeston and Chilwell. What have you to say?'

William didn't need long to understand the reference to the two men in The Durham Ox. These were Edward and Samuel. It was no secret that The Durham Ox was a regular meeting place for those with an interest in radical politics and William knew that they had been there that morning. That was where they had heard about the threats to property at Beeston and Chilwell. He kept the magistrates waiting for a few seconds before replying, and was about to speak when a man entered the room. He went over to the magistrates and whispered something which William could not hear. 'Oh, very well then,' said thin face, and the man left.

'It seems you have an advocate here who has insisted he be allowed to join you. In view of the seriousness of the matter we have agreed that he may observe the proceedings.' The door opened again and Robert Kent entered, a little breathless. 'Sit over there, Mr Kent,' continued thin face, pointing to an empty chair. 'You may listen but not speak. Is that clear?'

'Perfectly,' replied Robert.

'Now, Mr Daniels, you will answer my questions.'

'What I have to say, gentlemen, is firstly that I had nothing whatsoever to do with the crime you seek to charge me with. Secondly, the two other men you allude to are my brother Samuel and my Uncle Edward. It is true that they had been at The Durham Ox that morning. They both hold the same views as myself, that the House of Lords was wrong to throw out the Reform Bill, a view held by the majority of respected persons in this town, by both our MPs, by the mayor and virtually all the corporation, as no doubt you are aware. It is of no surprise that they were discussing radical ideas. Everyone in the town knows that that is what happens at The Durham Ox. That is where men who hold such opinions go. Had I been with them, I would undoubtedly have joined in their discussions.'

'But they were heard to say that they were going to set off for Chilwell; to which place the mob had already gone. Is that not true?'

'Well, gentlemen, I am not a spokesman for the mob, but subsequent events would certainly support your supposition. On leaving The Durham Ox, my brother and uncle came to see me first. Another brother joined us and we all set off for Chilwell in my gig. It was quicker than walking and we needed to get there without delay.' William's confident manner seemed to have unnerved the magistrates a little, and he began to detect a look of unease on their faces.

'But you haven't explained why you needed to get there so quickly. Unless it was to join in the threatened activities of the rioters, what other explanation can you give?'

William stared intensely at each of the three magistrates in turn before replying, savouring their nervous disposition. He was beginning to enjoy the interview and was determined to exploit his increasing advantage to the full.

'Gentlemen,' he replied at last, 'you said that you received information about my whereabouts that day. Was your informant not able to tell you why he thought we might be going to Chilwell? If not, then he cannot be a very efficient informant, and I fear he may be guilty of having wasted an awful amount of your valuable time. I have no doubt that you are all busy men. I know I am, and if you value your time as highly as I value mine then you will want to take issue with your informant, who as far as I can see is out to cause mischief to me, and is using you as his tool to do so. Perhaps you would care to tell me who your informant is so that I can take issue with him myself.'

There was a wry smile on William's face as he spoke, but not on those of the magistrates. Two of them sat open-mouthed, apparently dumbstruck at William's confident replies to their questions. But the thin-faced man in the middle seemed apoplectic with rage. The veins on his large white forehead were visibly protruding and his equally pale face had turned a bright shade of red. Unable to contain himself any longer, he brought his fist down violently on the bench, causing the three tumblers and glass decanter of water to rattle noisily.

'I will not tolerate this disrespect,' he thundered. 'You are not here to ask us questions. You are here to answer our questions, and by God, I will make sure you do,' he spluttered, pointing a bony and shaking finger at William. 'One more word of insolence from you and I will have you taken to the House of Correction forthwith. Now, Mr Daniels, you still haven't explained why you needed to get to Chilwell so quickly. It is our contention that you wanted to join the mob, is that not correct?'

'No, it isn't,' replied William nonchalantly. The three magistrates waited, expecting more.

'Well?' demanded thin face, furiously. 'Give us your explanation, damn you.'

'Of course,' replied William, calmly. 'You see, my aged parents reside at Chilwell, in a cottage just along the lane beyond Chilwell Hall. The cottage is one of the squire's. My grandmother also lives with them, as do two younger sisters of mine. When my brother and uncle heard that a drunken gang of rioters was heading towards Chilwell you can readily appreciate their concern. We are all too aware of how such riots can get out of hand, and the harm and damage that can be done to innocent individuals. Just imagine, gentlemen, how you would have felt had it been *your* defenceless relatives in such potential danger. What were we supposed to do? One old man and four women, at the mercy of a mob! We did what any law-abiding citizens and concerned relatives would have done, and the four of us set off as quickly as we could. We reached Beeston, only to find that the mill had been set alight. The rioters were no longer there but we were informed they had marched off towards Chilwell. When we got there, we were relieved to find that they had been persuaded to leave well alone.'

For a few moments the three magistrates sat in silence, then got their heads together and whispered uneasily amongst themselves.

'That's as it may be,' said thin face, 'but what evidence do you have to support your statement?'

'I suppose you could go along and talk to the workmen who were inspecting the damage done by the mob to the property of Mr Alfred Lowe on Beeston Lane. It seems they mistook his house for that of William Lowe, the silk mill owner. We were actually talking to them when we saw smoke rising up from the fire. And if their word isn't good enough, I am sure Mr Joseph Hallam can vouch for us. We met him as soon as we arrived in Chilwell and it was he who explained how they had managed to persuade the rioters to go away. I assume you know Mr Hallam. He's been the estate manager at Chilwell Hall for about thirty years. His employer for most of that time was Mr William Charlton, the former High Sheriff. Mr Hallam is a good friend of both myself and Mr Kent here,' said William turning round and nodding towards Robert.

William had to try hard to prevent an expression of victory spreading across his face. The three men again whispered amongst themselves at some length before delivering their verdict. But this time it was one of the other two who spoke, his voice barely able to conceal a distinct tone of irritation.

'Very well, Mr Daniels. You may go. We are satisfied with your explanation.'

The three magistrates immediately rose from their chairs and quit the room by a back door, as if embarrassed to remain in William's presence any longer, leaving him to be shown out by a clerk. Once outside, William turned to Robert.

'Thank you for coming, Robert, I appreciate it. But right now, I need a drink. Will you join me?'

'Gladly, but listening to you in there, I don't think you needed me. You were sailing close to the wind though, I hope you realise that. Old

Stringer can be a real tyrant. He was the one doing all the talking. I've come across him once or twice before. He has a bit of a reputation and he won't like what happened.'

'Well, I'm not going to worry about him. But I thought it might be useful to have you there. When the constables came for me I really didn't know what to expect. I had no idea what I might be charged with or what evidence they had. But once things got going I knew I had no case to answer, and that I could prove it.'

It was almost midday, so the two men headed for The White Lion in Clumber Street. 'Come on Robert, I'll treat you to some dinner. The beef steaks there are second to none. But first, I ought to let Abigail know what's happened. She'll be worried stiff.'

They found a table and William ordered the food and some drinks, then scribbled a quick note to Abigail. This he handed to one of the potboys, asking him to run along as fast as he could and take it to the wharf, and promising him sixpence when he returned.

'What I'd like to know is, who's out to cause trouble? Somebody's been making false accusations about me. They must have known I'd been over to Chilwell that day, but why should they go to such lengths to try and implicate me? This is not the first time I've been targeted.'

And William proceeded to tell Robert about the other incidents: the damaged boats, the bad publicity he had received over the episode of the resurrectionists, and the body his men had pulled out of the canal.

'Those other events were annoying, but nothing as bad as this. If I hadn't have been able to prove my innocence I could have been charged with arson and we all know the penalty for that. That's the second time someone has tried to implicate me for starting a fire. We all know who was responsible last time. I wonder who it was this time? I can tell you, Robert, I intend to find out. And when I do, God help whoever it is!'

CHAPTER THIRTEEN

—

NOTTINGHAM 1832

The consequences of the riots were that a number of men were arrested and tried at a special assizes in early January. Only two were actually charged with setting fire to the castle, and they were found not guilty due to lack of evidence. But five were sentenced to hang, and four to transportation for life, all in connection with the firing of the silk mill at Beeston. Yet such was the outrage amongst the residents of the town against the death sentences, that in no time at all a petition of over twenty-five thousand signatures was presented to the king, urging clemency. Day after day went by with no sign of mercy, until, on the day before the executions, two of the men had their sentences commuted to transportation for life. But for the remaining three there was to be no reprieve, and on the morning of Wednesday 1st February George Beck, John Harrison and George Hearson had their young lives prematurely brought to an end on the gallows outside the County Gaol, in front of a huge and mainly sympathetic crowd.

Edward and Samuel were amongst the spectators, but not William. He had once been present at a hanging as a boy, and had no desire ever to attend such a spectacle again. But later that day, he and Benjamin joined Samuel and Edward in The Durham Ox, where a crowd had gathered to have a drink in memory of the three men.

'They didn't deserve that,' insisted Edward, 'even if they were guilty; and I for one ain't convinced of it. Somebody had to be made to pay though. And what's worse, they didn't even live to see the Reform Bill get passed. Still, they reckon the Government's going to try again soon. Let's hope it gets through next time.'

'But just think,' said William thoughtfully, 'it could so easily have been me up there on the gallows with them. If we hadn't stopped to talk to those men on Beeston Lane, and if Joseph Hallam hadn't been at father's that afternoon, I would have had problems convincing the magistrates not to send me for trial. And you can be sure that you three would have been implicated too.'

'Makes you shudder to think of it,' added Samuel, 'and we still don't know who tried to set you up. I've been thinking about it and I'm convinced that the man with the pockmarks on his face might know something. You remember him, Edward, he was in here that day, and me and him had words as we were leaving.'

'Well, you did try and knock his beer over!' joked Edward, trying to lighten the atmosphere.

'Then later on we saw him at Beeston and he seemed to be watching us, but I've not seen him in here since,' continued Samuel. 'I bet he's been keeping his distance. If he knows we come in here he'll stay clear, I expect. In fact, I've been keeping my eyes open to try and spot him. I thought I might have seen him the other day when I was walking down Narrow Marsh. A chap came out of The King's Head just before I got there and from behind it looked like him, but I couldn't be certain. I followed him but soon lost him in the crowd.'

'That's it,' exclaimed Benjamin suddenly. 'Now I remember where I saw him - The King's Head! When we saw him at Beeston I said I'd seen him before but couldn't recall where. Well, now I do. Do you remember the day, about four years ago, when that chap brought a crate down to the wharf to send up to London, the one with the dead bodies in, and I followed him? That's where he went, The King's Head. He told me his name was Jones, but the landlord said he knew him as Bullivant. That's him, I'll swear to it. He had pockmarks on his face and he smelt something dreadful! I nearly caught up with him, but he and another bloke shot off down London Road in a horse and trap. When he came to the wharf with the crate, and I asked what was in it, he got all confused and agitated and wouldn't say. Kept talking about his boss and how angry he'd get if it wasn't sent off that day. I knew he was working for someone else; the man who was in the trap with him, perhaps.'

'Maybe I should pay a visit to The King's Head and see if I can find him,' suggested Samuel. 'I bet I could get him to talk!'

'You want to be careful,' cautioned William. 'I know that pub of old; there's a lot of rum folk go in there, I wouldn't like to get on the wrong side of some of them.'

'Don't worry. I can take care of myself. I deliver beer to some other pubs down there, so I might just call in and have a word with the landlord next time I'm passing. See what I can find out.'

A few days later, Samuel came home from work one evening just as Edward was going out. 'I'm going down to The Durham Ox, are you coming?'

'I'll be along in a bit. I've got to call somewhere else first but I'll tell you all about it when I join you.'

Intrigued, Edward set off, but he didn't have to wait all that long, and within the hour Samuel arrived. 'Well, what's the secret?' asked Edward as Samuel sat down.

'I've found our man, the pockmarked one, the body snatcher.'

'Really? Tell me more.'

Samuel half drained his pint pot before speaking. 'I was down Narrow Marsh this morning delivering a couple of barrels to The Loggerheads, so I decided to call in at The King's Head. I tried to get the landlord to take some beer but he gets his supplies from elsewhere. Of course, I already knew that, but it was an excuse to get on his right side and pick his brains. I had a pint and stood him one. Told him I used to live nearby as a lad, and we had quite a chat about some of the locals who still go in there.

'Then I asked him if he knew a chap with a pockmarked face. I told him a pal up at the brewery was an old friend of this chap, and hadn't seen him for ages, but understood he drank there, and I'd promised to try and find out. As soon as I described him, I could tell by the landlord's face that he knew who I was talking about. Benjamin was right, his name is Bullivant. Amos Bullivant. The landlord said he's in there almost every night and usually ends up staggering out at closing time. Turns out he's single and lodges just down the road in Leather Alley. So, on the way here I did a detour and called in The King's Head. I didn't stop, just went in the back door, down the corridor, through the bar and out the front; kept my head down and my eyes open, but he was there all right, in the smoke room with a couple of other blokes; but he didn't see me. I think we should go and have a word with him, see if we can't get him to loosen his tongue. What do you say, Edward?'

'We might have to hang around a bit. He could be in there for hours. I suppose what you have in mind is waiting till he leaves then "having a word" with him when there's nobody else around.'

'Yes, something like that. If we stay in the front bar we can keep an eye out and we'll see him when he leaves. And if he's had a few pints he probably won't remember us anyway. We've plenty of time though, it's only half past nine,' said Samuel, pointing to a large clock on the wall. 'I'll get us each another pint first, then we'll get along.'

It was approaching ten when they left the pub and made their way along Fletcher Gate, past the Weekday Cross and down Garners Hill to Narrow Marsh. A cold, biting wind was blowing and occasional flurries of snow swirled around. It was like old times for Samuel. Nothing seemed to have changed since the days of his youth, much of it spent getting up to mischief in and around the maze of courts and alleys that led off in all directions. A stranger could easily get lost here, and some did, much to their regret. But Samuel knew the area like the back of his hand; every court, every square, all the little yards and the alleys that linked them. He could get from one end to the other by a variety of routes and could soon lose himself, if need be, from any pursuer. Edward, however, was not so familiar with the area and was happy to follow his nephew.

After a few minutes they emerged from an alley into a small courtyard, surrounded by tall grim-looking houses. There was no light, save for the occasional glimmer from the moon as clouds scudded across the night sky. Down a narrow passage in one corner of the court they went, through a gate and into the back yard of The King's Head. A dim light shone from a window next to the back door, just enough to illuminate their way up the path.

'That's where he was earlier,' whispered Samuel, as they passed the door to the smoke room, and a quick glance confirmed he was still in there. They went through to the large front bar which looked out onto Narrow Marsh. The room was cosy and warm with a welcoming fire burning brightly in the hearth. The bar was busy but not full, and they were able to find an empty table by a window, with a good view both of the street outside and of the passage leading to the front door.

'This'll do fine,' said Edward. 'You sit down and I'll get us some beer.' An hour and two pints later and the pub was beginning to empty. Samuel had his back to the door, but Edward had a good view of those heading for home. 'Aye, aye, drink up Samuel, I think he's on his way.' Samuel put his face close to the window and wiped the condensation from the glass. A single lamp hung above the door providing a meagre glow, but enough to see the faces of those leaving the pub.

'That's him! He's just gone past.' The two men hastily finished their beer, and, putting on their coats, they scurried out into the street and turned left to follow their prey. He was about thirty yards ahead and was alone, swaying slightly as he went. He turned off Narrow Marsh just where Samuel expected. 'Leather Alley, that's where the landlord said he lives. Come on, quickly, he could vanish into any of the houses there and we'd never find him.'

Turning off the road, they immediately entered a narrow dark tunnel, running between and under the row of tenements lining the street. The tunnel soon opened out into a small courtyard surrounded by other properties, some of them dwellings, some of them workshops. Just for a moment, Samuel feared they had lost their man, but suddenly he reappeared from the shadows in the corner where he had stopped to relieve himself of some of the ale he had consumed that night. There was no one else around and Samuel took his chance. Walking boldly up behind the man, he gently tapped him on the shoulder.

'Hello, squire. Amos isn't it?' The man stopped and turned round, peering into the gloom, trying to focus on the stranger who stood not a foot away from him.

'Who are you? What do you want?' he said aggressively. 'I don't know you, do I?'

'Well, not really, but we have crossed paths a couple of times, which is what I'd like to have a word with you about.' Amos was quite clearly much the worse for drink, and seemed to be having difficulty working out what was going on. Had he been sober, he might have been more alarmed to have been accosted by two strangers in a dark alley late at night. Most such encounters invariably resulted in robbery or violence.

'I've got no money on me, spent it all on ale. You're wasting your time if you think you can get owt from me.'

'Oh, don't worry. It's not your money we're after, it's information.'

'Information? What information? What are you talking about?'

'Well, to start with, you might like to tell me all about the crate you took to Mr Daniel's wharf for despatch to London. Remember? About four years ago it was. The crate contained corpses, work of the body snatchers. When you realised you'd been rumbled you made an excuse and left very sharpish.'

'No, not me, I don't know anything about that. You've got the wrong man there.' Amos was sounding more confident now, cocky almost, and Samuel was beginning to think that it might take some time to get him to talk, and that he might need to be more forceful. It was cold, and he had no desire to spend all night politely trying to persuade Amos to tell the truth. He decided that he would have to use different tactics. Next to where they were standing was a gate, the entrance to a builder's yard. Samuel knew it well; he and a mate had once nearly been caught trying to pinch some lead from there, back in the days of his misspent youth. Grabbing Amos by the scruff of the neck, he manhandled him along, pushed open the gate, and forced him into the yard. Edward followed and shut the gate behind them.

'That's better, a bit of privacy. Now, think again. Four years ago, a crate, corpses, sending them to London by canal; is it coming back to you yet?' But still Amos stuck to his guns.

'I've told you, I don't know anything about it; it's nowt to do with me. Go and find some other bugger to worry.'

'Well, perhaps I need to refresh your memory. Maybe I need to knock some sense into that thick skull of yours,' and bending down, Samuel picked up a rusty iron bar that was lying on the ground. Holding the bar in his right hand, he grabbed Amos's skinny neck in his left and pushed him up hard against a wall, lifting him slightly as he did so, causing him to gasp for breath.

'Jones, that's the name you gave to the lad at the wharf wasn't it? But that's not your real name is it? When he became suspicious you made an excuse and left in a hurry. But he followed you, although you perhaps didn't know that. You went to The King's Head and the landlord there told him your real name, Bullivant. But then you did a runner along with another man. Bill Giles was it? You know him don't you?'

Whether it was the iron bar which Samuel was now holding in a most threatening manner, or mention of the name Bill Giles, Samuel couldn't be sure, but Amos's resolve suddenly evaporated. Samuel released his grip on Amos's neck, and after a few seconds he recovered enough to speak.

'All right, now you mention it I do seem to remember something about it, but I had nothing to do with body snatching, I was just doing a job, just delivering the crate to the wharf.'

'Who for? Bill Giles?'

'Yes.'

'So, what was he up to then? And why did you choose that particular wharf? There are other carriers. And the name and address on the crate turned out to be false. There never was a Mr Rogers at Paddington.'

'I don't know anything about any Mr Rogers. All I do know is, Giles was most particular about which wharf I took the crate to. He said I was to keep watch and let him know once the boat had left with the crate on. Then I was to go straight to Leicester and alert the constables so they'd search the boat when it passed through there and find the bodies. That's all. Don't ask me why.'

'You do a lot of jobs for Giles, do you?'

'Now and again.'

'Pays well, does he?'

'He keeps me in beer money.'

'And what other jobs do you do for him? How about spying?'

'Spying?'

'Yes, you heard, spying. Keeping an eye on people, feeding him information and the like.'

'He sometimes asks me to find out things for him.'

'What sort of things?'

'Oh, all sorts.'

'How about people setting fire to silk mills?'

'Silk mills? What silk mills?'

'You know exactly what I'm talking about. Don't try and make a fool out of me.' And as he spoke, Samuel tossed the iron bar into the air, catching it as it dropped. He leaned close to Amos, so that their noses were almost touching. 'Now, Mr Bullivant, you'd better start talking, and make sure you tell me everything. I don't take kindly to my family being messed about and done wrong by. See this iron bar here? It could do an awful lot of damage to a skull, even a thick one like yours. There's a canal just down the road with a big deep lock. Yours wouldn't be the first body found in there. I bet they'd think you just fell over on your way home from the pub, banged your head on the gates and drowned.

'I'm talking about the silk mill at Beeston. You were there the day it got burned down, last October. You were also in The Durham Ox earlier the same day. I know that, because I nearly knocked your beer over as we were leaving. You don't normally go in there, do you? But you were there that day. I reckon you were spying on us and overheard us saying we were going over that way, and then you followed us. I also had my two brothers with me, the lad who was at the wharf when you took the bodies there, and William, who owns the wharf. He later got arrested and taken before the magistrates. They told him they had information that he'd been seen with the mob setting fire to the silk mill. Fortunately he was able to prove he had nothing to do with it, otherwise he could have been dangling on a rope with the other three; and the rest of us as well.'

Amos had now completely lost all his bravado and a look of fear had spread across his face. 'All right, I'll tell you what I know; but God help me if Giles ever finds out. Nothing you could do would be as bad as what he's capable of. I once saw what happened to someone who crossed him.' Until now, Edward had remained silent, content to let Samuel do the talking, but now he spoke up.

'You've no need to be scared of us, so long as you tell us what we want. We've never even met the man, but you can rest assured he'll never find out from us that we've even spoken to you.'

'You don't know him then. I suggest you keep it that way. He's a vicious and powerful man with some even more powerful friends. Nobody ever crosses him and gets away with it. Anyhow, he told me to keep an eye on you all and see what you were up to. He knew you two were involved with the reformers in The Durham Ox. He said there'd be a bonus for me if I could implicate you. All I did was follow you to Beeston. I told him you'd been there, that's all. I never said you'd started the fire or even been part of the mob that did.'

'But I bet you would have said that, and on oath if necessary, if the money had been right.'

Amos made no answer. Samuel dropped the iron bar back on the ground. 'You can go now. Like we said, we'll not be saying anything to Giles, but if ever we come across you interfering in our lives again, you'll regret it. My advice to you is to leave town and get as far away as possible.'

Samuel and Edward left the yard and headed for home, leaving Bullivant to his own devices.

'Poor bugger,' said Edward. 'You really put the frighteners on him. I wonder if he will leave town?'

'I doubt it. He won't want to upset Giles, but he knows what to expect if he crosses our path again.'

'But Bullivant's only the errand boy in all this. Giles is dishing out the orders, but who's he working for, I wonder? We don't know much about him, but from what Bullivant said it seems he's mixed up in all sorts of underhand dealings.'

'Then I think I'll make it my business to find out a bit more about our Mr Giles. I've still got a few contacts from the old days. I'll have to renew a few acquaintances and see what I can discover.'

'Well, be careful how you go. But from what we've found out tonight, someone is targeting William. It's him they're really after, not us, and I've a shrewd idea who might be behind it. Giles himself might be a nasty character, but I guess he's just a fixer who'll do anything for money.'

'I agree. And if you're thinking the same as me then we'd better have a word with William, and the sooner the better.'

The next evening Edward dropped in at the wharf after work to tell William about their 'discussion' with Amos Bullivant. He was just about to knock on the door when Abigail opened it.

'Oh, hello Edward. If it's William you've come to see, I'm afraid he's out at the moment, but come on in. I don't think he'll be long. In fact I thought that was him now. He's been up at the works all day. Some sort of problem with one of the contractors, but he'll be able to tell you all about it when he gets back.'

Edward sat by the kitchen fire while Millie prepared supper. Abigail was upstairs putting the twins to bed and Edward entertained Charles and Catherine with stories about his time living in France.

'Come along, you two,' said Abigail as she came into the kitchen. 'Your turn now, off you go to bed.'

'But I want to see father first,' said Charles, and just at that moment the front door opened and William came in.

'You're late!' said Abigail, a little sharply. 'Edward's here to see you and your supper's ready. Say goodnight to Charles and Catherine, they're just off to bed. Edward, will you stay for some supper? I'm sure there's enough to go round.' A few minutes later Benjamin joined them, and soon they were all seated around the large kitchen table enjoying a delicious rabbit stew Millie had cooked.

'So, what brings you here, Edward?' asked William.

'I've got some news for you,' replied Edward. 'Your young brother, not this one,' he said, nodding towards Benjamin, 'the other one; he had a very interesting chat last night with a man called Amos Bullivant.'

'Bullivant? Isn't that the chap who Benjamin followed, the one who brought the crate down with the bodies in and said his name was Jones?'

'That's the man. And it really was him. Although he denied it at first; made out he knew nothing about it. Until Samuel persuaded him that it might be in his best interests to come clean. Along with a bit of help from an iron bar and a threat to feed him to the rats in the canal.'

'And where did all this happen? How did you find him?'

Edward proceeded to tell William in detail the events of the night before. 'So there we have it. He's working for Bill Giles, doing his dirty work for him. Giles must have been the man who fed the information about you to the magistrates.'

'But from what Bullivant told you, Giles himself is just a fixer. There must have been someone else pulling the strings. It's a right little spider's web of intrigue.'

'Well, Samuel has said he's going to do a bit of digging; speak to a few of his old mates and see what he can find out about Giles. I told him to take care, but I think he can look after himself. But what about you, William? Abigail tells me you've been having a spot of bother up at the railway.'

'That's right; things aren't going as smoothly as we'd hoped. I suppose these projects often run into difficulties, but suddenly everything seems to be going wrong. A lot of the navvies have left to find better paid work elsewhere. There's a number of new lines being built up north and they all need labour, and word has it there's a major line being planned to link London to Birmingham. Labour seems to be in short supply generally, so any skilled navvies can command better wages. The contractors here have an agreed price to stick to, so they're finding it difficult to pay higher wages. And with fewer men, they're running behind schedule.'

Edward smiled as he heard this. 'So for once the working man has the upper hand. We're used to wages being depressed when it suits the bosses, but now the boot's on the other foot!'

'True enough, I can't argue with that,' agreed William. 'That's the law of supply and demand! But on top of all that, they've hit some unexpected construction problems near the top end of the line. The terrain's fairly straightforward for most of the route with no real obstacles, at least that's what the surveyors thought. But now they've hit a patch of boggy ground. They're trying to devise a method of stabilising the formation but it's taking a lot longer than anticipated. And, of course, the contractor hadn't reckoned with the expense of it all. It's a bit worrying, but I'm sure things will work out in the end.'

Abigail had been listening quietly to what William was saying, and the anxious look on her face did not go unnoticed by those around the table, particularly by William.

CHAPTER FOURTEEN

—

NOTTINGHAM 1832

The next few months were a worrying time for the railway company and its contractors. A shortage of navvies combined with further construction problems meant that the work was slipping behind schedule, and the more the works were delayed, the longer it would be until the company could begin to earn money. News of these difficulties was well reported in the newspapers and the shareholders were not happy. But for one man, at least, the information was like manna from heaven.

Seated in the morning room of his country house one sunny day in late June, Josiah Sidmouth read the article in the Nottingham Journal with increasing interest. He was delighted to be reading something that pleased him. Especially after the news which the papers had been full of for the past few weeks and which certainly did not please him; for the Reform Bill had at last become law. On the 4th June, the House of Lords had finally succumbed to pressure, and after the king had threatened to create sufficient Whig peers to ensure its safe passage through the Lords, the Tories had finally climbed down and the Bill was voted through. The king gave the Royal Assent, and so the long years of agitation by the liberal fraternity at last proved fruitful. There was much rejoicing throughout the kingdom and in every town the air rang to the joyous pealing of church bells.

But not everyone was happy. The Dukes of Wellington and Newcastle, along with other diehard Tories, viewed the changes with utter dismay and foreboding. The Act swept away the many rotten boroughs, reduced the number of MPs in small towns, but created MPs for the large and growing industrial towns such as Birmingham, Manchester, Leeds and Sheffield, which until then had few, and in some cases, no representatives in Parliament. Many more men would be entitled to vote and the powers of the landed gentry were slowly, but surely, being eroded. Not good news for the likes of Josiah Sidmouth. But at least the reports about the railway and its troubles lifted his spirits that fine morning.

He sat back in his comfortable armchair and read the article for a second time. Then, with eyes closed and arms folded, for several minutes he concentrated deeply as an idea slowly evolved in his mind. A wry smile crept across his face as, rising from his chair, he went into the library and sat down at his desk. Taking out paper and pens he spent the next half hour or so writing, and having carefully folded, addressed and sealed the two letters, he summoned his butler and instructed him to have them despatched forthwith.

The first was addressed to Lieutenant Peter Brown, care of the Regimental Headquarters of the South Gloucestershire Regiment, in which he asked Peter to let him know when he would next be coming home on leave, explaining that something fortuitous had 'come up' which he considered required their joint and urgent attention. The second was addressed to the Proprietors of the Town and County Bank in Nottingham, and having introduced himself and briefly explained his financial position, he concluded by stating: *I have a proposal to present to you which I believe you would be foolish not to give your utmost consideration to; and consequently, unless I hear to the contrary I will wait upon you at your premises in Bridlesmith Gate at eleven o' clock in the forenoon next Friday.*

On the following Wednesday, Josiah travelled to his town house in Nottingham, and having rested and refreshed himself after the hot and dusty journey, decided to dine out. The Spread Eagle on Long Row was his choice, an establishment whose proprietor was an old acquaintance of his and where he knew he could expect good food, polite service and a degree of privacy; and it was only a short stroll from Castle Gate. He was soon shown to a table in a corner of the dining room, and having ordered a bottle of claret, poured himself a large glass whilst awaiting his grilled lamb chops. The room was not yet busy, it being only late afternoon, and the only other diners were four men seated a little distance from him. Nevertheless, he could not fail to hear snatches of their conversation, most of which concerned the state of the hosiery trade and was of no particular interest to him. Then his ears pricked up when he heard mention of the new railway.

'According to the Review, they're having serious problems at the moment,' said one of the men. 'Hit some difficult ground, and they're short of navvies. It seems a lot of them have gone up north where they can get better wages.'

'And if this cholera was to spread to them, there'd soon be none left at all,' added another. 'You know what squalor they live in, those navvies. They reckon there have been more confirmed cases this week and more deaths, most of them down in Narrow Marsh.'

Josiah continued to listen intently to what was being said. He remembered that there had been mention in the papers a few weeks previously of a suspected case of cholera, but he had taken no real notice of it, and not having been in the town for a while was a little out of touch with the local gossip. And so, when he arrived back at his house he immediately summoned his housekeeper, Mrs Barton, a middle-aged widow, sound and reliable in her work and a veritable mine of information on all the local tittle-tattle, and asked what she knew of the cholera outbreak.

There was very little that went on in the town that she did not know about, and if there was she soon made it her business to find out. If anything of note was rumoured to be going off, or the slightest whiff of scandal began to circulate, you could be sure that Mrs Barton would be hot-footing it to the appropriate location, neck craned, eyes peeled and ears finely tuned. She explained to Josiah that there had been a number of suspected cases of cholera since early in the year, and now it seemed to be turning into an epidemic. The first confirmed case had been established in Narrow Marsh, and that was where the first deaths had occurred.

'I blame it on the Irish,' said Mrs Barton, emphatically. 'The filthy pigs! Narrow Marsh is full of 'em these days; they come over here to find work and all congregate there, and you wouldn't believe the way they live. My sister's husband has to go there sometimes delivering skins to a tannery, and you should hear the tales he tells about how they carry on; disgusting it is! Now I know there's a lot of our own sort living down there who aren't too fussy, but the Irish! Do you know sir …' and before continuing she looked round as if to make sure nobody else was listening, despite their being alone, and lowering her voice, continued, 'Do you know sir, they don't even bother using the privies, and they all sleep together in the same beds along with their dogs and cats. One family even kept a couple of pigs in the house! Can you believe it? There's no wonder the cholera's taken hold. They should clear them out, the lot of 'em, I say, and send 'em packing. Goodness knows what will happen to the rest of us if it spreads! You mark my words, sir, no good will come of it, no good at all. And I should stay clear of that dreadful area if I were you!'

'Never fear Mrs Barton, you can rest assured on that score,' said Josiah, as he thanked her and sent her off to go about her business. But unbeknown to her, she had just handed Josiah a piece of information which he believed would be invaluable to him. Although he had long been aware of the dreadful insanitary conditions that prevailed in Narrow Marsh, he hadn't known of the large Irish population which now resided there; but he made a mental note of the fact.

Two days later, at ten minutes to eleven in the morning, Josiah picked up his briefcase, stepped out of his front door and took the short walk to Bridlesmith Gate and the premises of the Town and County Bank. The building was narrow, three storeys high with small leaded windows, a steep gable to the roof, timber-built and very ancient-looking. It was nowhere near as large and imposing as most of the other banks of the town, but then Josiah already knew that. He entered the building through the single iron-studded oak door, then into an outer office, where he made himself known to a clerk seated behind a desk.

'Yes sir, you are expected. Please follow me,' said the clerk, and Josiah was soon shown into an inner room, wood-panelled from floor to ceiling and tastefully furnished with a large mahogany table and six plush, red leather chairs, a fine oak sideboard, and, in one corner, a tall grandfather clock. On the wall above a fireplace hung two large portraits mounted in ornate, gilded frames of men dressed in the style of the mid-eighteenth century, which Josiah could not help but admire. Three men were seated at the table, but all rose to their feet as Josiah was shown in.

'Good morning, sir,' they said in unison.

'And a good morning to you, gentlemen,' replied Josiah.

'Please be seated,' said the man in the middle. He was clearly the eldest of the three, a dapper little man dressed in a dark green jacket, cream shirt and yellow waistcoat and cravat, clean-shaven but with a surprisingly thick head of white hair for a man so old, a man Josiah judged to be about seventy.

'Allow me to introduce myself. I am Bernard Bennett and these are my two younger brothers, Bartholomew and Benedict; we do like the Bs in our family, and what with us being bankers into the bargain,' he said with a smile. 'We are the joint proprietors of the bank, and this is our inner sanctum. But I couldn't help noticing that you were admiring the portraits.'

'I certainly was,' replied Josiah, keen to demonstrate his affability and to win the trust and confidence of the brothers as best he could. 'Fine-looking gentlemen to be sure; ancestors, I presume?'

'Indeed,' declared Bernard with mounting enthusiasm, 'that's our grandfather on the left, also named Bernard, and the other is his son, our father, another Bartholomew. We were an old and well-established Newark family, but our grandfather left there when he was a very young man to seek his luck in the West Indies. He did very well for himself and made a small fortune in the sugar trade, but in 1740 he came back, and with the money he had made he founded the bank in Nottingham, married, and settled down. Family tradition has it that he had to leave the Indies in a hurry after a scandal involving the wife of a slave trader, but that's something we prefer not to talk about. Then after grandfather died in 1775, his eldest son, our dear father Bartholomew, took over the running of the bank. And now here we are, sadly the last of the line. As you can see, sir, we are all quite elderly and none of us ever married, so there are no sons or heirs to pass the business on to. But enough of our situation. Now, sir, we are all curious to hear what you have to say, but first let me offer you some sherry and a piece of Madeira cake; we partake at eleven thirty every morning on business days.'

Bernard poured each of them a small glass of sherry and passed round a plate on which lay exactly four very thin slices of cake. Josiah was already beginning to detect that frugality and prudence were the watchwords in this establishment, or perhaps the fortune made by their grandfather had not survived the passing of two generations.

'Thank you, gentlemen,' Josiah began. 'I will try and be as brief as possible. I'm not a man to beat about the bush, and I always think that in matters of business it's best to get straight to the point. I would like to buy your bank.'

For a few seconds, which to Josiah seemed like minutes, there was total silence. Such silence, in fact, that even the proverbial pin could have been heard to drop, despite the gentle tick of the clock in the corner.

'Well,' said Bernard hesitantly, 'I really don't know what to say, I'm sure.' His brothers continued to maintain their silence, clearly flabbergasted at Josiah's startling proposition.

'Let me explain,' continued Josiah, eager to keep the upper hand. 'I should, perhaps, expound on the brief details I gave in my letter to you. I own a large estate in the north of the county; it's been in the family for generations and I have been fortunate to build up a tidy and not inconsiderable fortune. I have interests not only in land but also in various manufacturing enterprises, and am always looking to expand into other areas of business. To make headway these days it is often necessary to act swiftly, and that can mean having to lay one's hands immediately on ready cash. Much of my fortune is tied up in land or other assets, and while they are of value they cannot easily or quickly be converted into money. I need to have access to funds at short notice; and where does one turn to at such times? To the banks, of course. And then, I thought, what better than to own one's own bank!

'I have to admit, gentlemen, that I did already know a little about the history of your bank. Your affairs are not entirely a secret, and your present circumstances with regard to your respective ages are well known. And as you said yourself, there are no sons or heirs to pass the business to. I do hope you will forgive me for being somewhat presumptuous, but I did ponder on what might happen to the bank when the sands of time eventually run out, as they must for us all. You see, gentlemen, none of you is in the first flush of youth, and it occurred to me that a generous offer might present you with the opportunity to free yourselves from the worries and responsibilities of the world of banking, and to spend your days at leisure, in the pursuit of whatever pleasures and pastimes take your fancy.'

'Well,' said Bernard after a brief pause, 'there's no doubt that similar thoughts have passed through our minds recently, and the question of inheritance has been concerning us for some time, but with no simple solution. We believe there are some distant cousins in the Newark area descended from a brother of our great-grandfather, but there has been no contact during our lifetime. And our father had two brothers, but they both died young and without issue.'

'And furthermore,' added Josiah, 'I am aware that the bank is a family business, owned in its entirety by the three of you. That would make any sale relatively easy to arrange, should you agree to it. What I have in mind is to make you an offer for the bank outright. That would mean that you would each receive a considerable capital sum which would allow you to enjoy a comfortable and contented retirement, without the day-to-day inconvenience of having to oversee all those niggling little problems and difficulties which invariably arise when managing a financial institution.'

'You certainly make it sound a most attractive proposition,' replied Bernard, 'but if we were to accept we would no longer have a say in the running of the bank. We have always endeavoured to deal fairly, both with our employees, of whom we have a small but dedicated and trustworthy number, and our clients, many of whom have entrusted us with their savings for many years. We would want to see nothing done which would in any way destroy the trust which has existed for so long between us. We are only a small bank, that is true, but we have always acted honourably and we would not want anything to sully the good name and reputation which we have rightly earned. Why, even during the banking crisis in 1825 we survived almost without a scratch because we trusted our customers and they trusted us. There were no scares at the Town and County Bank. Oh no, sir! No panic withdrawal of funds by our clients, unlike some of the other, larger banks in the town, who had invested their clients' funds in risky and, in our view, downright dangerously foolish enterprises. We, I am happy to say, being a little old-fashioned and cautious, weathered the storm with equanimity.'

'Exactly, gentlemen, I couldn't have put it better myself!' exclaimed Josiah, with conviction. 'Yours is exactly the sort of small, long-established and well-run banking institution I have been looking for.

And you have no worries vis-à-vis your staff and your customers. They would all continue to be treated in the same fair and honourable manner which they have enjoyed during your long and admirable stewardship. Of that, you have my word.'

Throughout their discussion, Josiah had managed (with some difficulty, as he privately admitted to himself later) to maintain an air of sincere and well-meaning respectability, of worthy intentions and a genuine desire to preserve the continuing good name and prosperity of the bank.

'I think, sir,' said Bernard, 'you will need to allow my brothers and myself some time to consider your offer. We would not want to rush into any agreement without careful consideration, and of course, we are not yet aware of exactly what sum you might be offering for the business.'

'Of course, I would not have expected anything less. I have had my solicitor draw up a proposal which I would like to leave with you for your perusal,' and reaching into his briefcase, Josiah took out a large document neatly tied in pink ribbon. 'Take as long as you see fit to consider it, and if there are any items you need to discuss further please contact my solicitor. I have to return home tomorrow but he has full authority to act on my behalf. If you decide to proceed, I will have him prepare a contract for the sale and we can then bring the matter to a conclusion.

'There is, however, one condition I must insist on. Whilst I would be taking full control of the bank, I do wish to remain completely anonymous. I have no desire to get involved in the day-to-day running of the business, and my intention would be to appoint a representative to oversee the management of the bank, in conjunction with your existing members of staff. Naturally, I would be consulted from time to time when major decisions need to be taken, but to all intents and purposes the bank would continue to operate as it has for so long, with no change of name. In other words, I wish the sale to be kept confidential, a private matter between ourselves.'

His business concluded, Josiah shook hands with the brothers and left. But instead of returning straight home he took a short detour to Plumptre Square and The Town Arms, where he spoke discreetly to the landlord.

'Very well, sir, leave it to me, I'll arrange it and make sure he gets the message,' said the landlord, as he gratefully pocketed the silver coin Josiah had pressed into his palm.

The following morning, dressed in the shabbiest of clothes, Josiah crept out through the rear entrance to his town house and hurried along once more to The Town Arms. It was early and the pub was almost empty. Going straight to the same room he had occupied for some days before Christmas, he entered, where he found a man sitting in the chair smoking a pipe.

'You got my message then, Mr Giles?'

'I did. It sounded urgent.'

'It is. I have another job for you, and you'll be well paid.'

'What is it this time? More spying, roughing somebody up, sinking a narrow boat or two?'

'No, nothing as dangerous as that. This one's easy. I want you to arrange for a rumour to be spread. You know the railway building that's going on? The main navvy camp is up near Bulwell. I want news to get around that it's the Irish navvies there who are responsible for the cholera outbreak. There's a lot of Irish living down in Narrow Marsh and that's where most of the deaths have occured. I'm sure some of those navvies will have been visiting their fellow countrymen, and we all know how quickly the disease spreads. I want them to become the scapegoats. The locals in Bulwell won't stand for it if they think the navvies are to blame. If you do your job right, that navvy camp will be deserted in no time.'

'That won't help the railway get built, will it?'

'Precisely, Mr Giles, precisely! Now, do we have a deal?'

'We have a deal. You know my terms.'

The two men shook hands and Josiah left. Returning to Castle Gate, he changed out of his shabby clothes and, satisfied with everything he had achieved during the last few days, he set off north to his country retreat.

Two weeks later news arrived from his solicitor that, subject to one or two minor details and a slight increase in the purchase price, his offer for the bank had been accepted. Another week and the contract had been drawn up and signed by both parties. His satisfaction at the conclusion of his latest acquisition was enhanced even further when, the next day, a letter arrived from Peter saying that he expected to be back in England before the month was out, and that the moment the ship docked he would come directly to visit him.

The letter must have been severely delayed en route, for it was only four days later when, as dusk was rapidly falling, a dusty figure, on an equally dishevelled and exhausted-looking horse, was seen riding wearily down the long drive towards the house. As the figure approached, Josiah could see he was dressed in army uniform, and went to the door himself to greet his visitor.

An hour later, Peter having bathed and changed, the two men sat talking over supper.

'You look as if you've had a tiring journey,' said Josiah.

'Indeed. We docked at Holyhead two days ago, early in the morning, so it's taken the best part of three days to get here. Mr Telford's new highway to London is excellent, but once I left it at Oswestry and headed across country I found the roads to be in a very poor state for most of the way. Not as bad as the bog roads in Ireland, but poor all the same. And of course, I wasn't able to change horses. Anyway, here I am. So, what exactly is it that's "come up" that requires our urgent attention?'

'I don't suppose you've been able to keep up-to-date with goings-on over here, other than national news, but there's been a set back with the building of the railway in Nottingham, with which your brother-in-law is so intimately involved. I've not been idle while you've been away and I've been making it my business to find out everything I can about William Daniels and his financial involvement with the railway. He has a lot of money tied up in it; if the railway fails, he could go down with it too, and I know exactly how we can manipulate matters to that end. These circumstances could give us the best chance we've had to see to it that he suffers. It was reported recently that they've hit some unexpected geological problems which are causing the contractors all sorts of difficulties; and then some of the navvies left for better paid work elsewhere, so the whole project is being delayed. And since I wrote to you there's been a public outcry against the navvies, who are being blamed for the cholera outbreak.' And Josiah proceeded to tell Peter about the recent epidemic in Nottingham.

'And why do people think they caused it?'

'Well, they're Irish, most of them. Many of their kith and kin are living in Narrow Marsh where there have been numerous cases, and where the first death occurred. You must know all about the Irish, Peter, having been over there, and the disgusting way they live. So it's not surprising that the navvies are being held responsible. People always need a scapegoat when something bad happens and it's usually foreigners who get the blame whatever the circumstances. So when a rumour started circulating that it was them who had brought the cholera over from Ireland and spread it down in Narrow Marsh, it wasn't long before some of the locals up near the navvy camp at Bulwell started to take the law into their own hands. Those navvies might be a tough lot, but when a mob is determined, especially a Nottingham mob, it can take some stopping. The fact is, whatever the truth, the majority of them have just packed up their shovels and hightailed it out of town. Gone off to find work elsewhere, and who can blame them?'

'But how did these rumours start? And was there any truth in them?'

'Since when did rumours ever have anything to do with the truth? It only takes someone convincing enough to start talking in a pub, and suddenly an allegation becomes hard fact. And the fact is that people believed it. Within hours of the rumour starting an angry mob had descended on the navvy camp. There was a real pitched battle, according to reports, and the constables had to send for the military. But by the time they arrived it was all over. A lot of broken bones and bloody noses; nothing worse. But the navvies got the message. There's not many left up there now and construction work on the railway has almost ceased.'

Peter, who had been observing Josiah carefully, could tell that something was amusing him. He knew Josiah of old, and his scheming ways. 'Well, Josiah, everything seems to have fallen into place very conveniently. If I didn't know you better, I might say a little too conveniently. I assume it was you who spread those rumours.'

'Oh, come on Peter, you know me better than that! You don't think I'd venture into half a dozen backstreet alehouses in Bulwell and spend all night chatting to a bunch of common colliers, ironworkers and stocking makers, not to mention their tiresome womenfolk, do you?'

'Not you personally, of course. But I'd wager you arranged someone to do it for you. Who was it?'

'Do you remember a man called Bill Giles who I mentioned to you some years ago, in fact in this very house on the day we arrived back here from Van Diemen's Land? We were discussing Daniels then, and I told you about him. Not a nice man to know, but of use if you ever want a job doing, the sort of job you wouldn't want to advertise for. Well, Giles has been very useful to me over the years. As long as he gets his money, you get the job done, no questions asked and no secrets revealed.'

'I see. So the navvies have gone and work on the railway has stopped. But how is that going to help us?'

'Daniels has a lot of money invested in the railway. The way things are going at the moment the directors are going to have to find a lot more to get the project started again. One of the contractors is on the verge of bankruptcy so a replacement will have to be found, and he'll demand a bigger fee, what with the problems the others have encountered. And he'll have to pay more for labour. Whichever way you look at it, it's going to cost money and all the directors are going to have to find it, including Daniels.'

'But he does have a business which I believe is doing quite well. How do we know he can't find the money from there?'

'I've had my spies out. He's doing all right, but he doesn't have a lot of ready cash and most of his money is tied up. There's no way he can raise money from his business other than borrowing against it. And where will he go to borrow money?'

'The banks, I would expect.'

'Quite so, which is where I come in.'

Peter looked puzzled. 'I don't follow you.'

'He'll be looking for money quickly on the best possible terms. Imagine that he found a bank willing to lend it to him at a relatively attractive rate of interest and with minimum collateral.'

'And where's he going to find that sort of offer?'

'From me.'

Peter looked at Josiah in astonishment. 'From you? He'd never borrow money from you, even if you offered it at nil per cent interest. He'd smell a rat straight away.'

'No, not from me directly, but from my bank. Oh, I forgot to tell you. I've just bought a bank.'

Peter never ceased to be amazed at some of the ideas Josiah came up with, but this latest revelation rendered him speechless.

'What's the matter, Peter? Lost for words? I think it's time to explain everything. Here, have another drink while I put you in the picture,' and he leaned over and topped up Peter's glass. 'When I read about the problems that had arisen with the railway building, an idea came to me. I knew that Daniels is heavily involved and that if things go wrong the directors will have to find more capital. Then along came the cholera outbreak; that was a bonus and I was able to use that to advantage in the way I've described. I'm sure the next step will be that Daniels will have to take out a loan. It occurred to me that if he borrowed the money from my bank, that would put me in a very powerful position, powerful enough to ruin him.

'Have you heard of the Town and County Bank? No? Well, it's a small family-run affair, very safe, very cautious, and for years has been owned entirely by three ageing brothers. It's not a joint stock company so there are no other shareholders to worry about. The three brothers have no offspring or other near relatives to pass the bank to when they die, and I managed to persuade them that the time had come to sell up and enjoy the proceeds on whatever takes their fancy. I made them a decent offer, and the sale documents have just been signed. I made certain, however, that I remain anonymous, so even the chief clerk and other members of the staff are not aware of the identity of the new owner. The bank will continue to operate exactly as before, and I have already appointed an old business acquaintance of mine, Mr Caleb Morley, to act as manager, to oversee the running of the establishment and consult me regarding important decisions. He's very experienced in financial affairs, but more importantly he owes me a favour, ever since I managed to help him avoid a charge of fraud some years ago. I know too much about his past financial dealings for him to dare to cross me, and he knows that. But best of all, he possesses the most natural charm and persuasive manner any man was ever blessed with. In fact, that's what got him into trouble.

'As soon as we hear that Daniels is looking for extra capital, I'll have Caleb approach him and make him an offer he can't refuse. Once he's taken the bait, we simply wait awhile until it's all been invested in the railway, and then, out of the blue, the bank will demand the return of its loan. Caleb will ensure that the terms are such as to allow us to do that. The result for Daniels will be devastating. He'll not be able to recoup anything from the railway, not until it starts operating and making a profit. He'll have no alternative but to sell his business. He'll not like that, but if he doesn't sell it, the bank will simply seize it to cover the debt. One way or the other, he'll be in my grasp, Peter. He'll be totally in my power. Then I'll crush him. And he'll be back where he belongs, in the gutter.'

Peter sat pondering for a few moments before replying. 'But it seems an awful lot of trouble to go to, just to get even. Surely there are more simple ways.'

'I'm sure there are many ways we could think of to achieve the same end, but not wholly within the law. This way appeals to me. It's quite legal, and with my past that's something I have to be wary of. But apart from anything else, owning the bank is, in itself, a shrewd move. It opens up other sorts of opportunities to make money. This particular bank has always been extremely cautious, and I'm convinced I can increase its profitability by taking more adventurous investment decisions. I have some other ideas of my own which will need money, and I now have my very own source of supply. What could be better?'

'Well, that's true enough. In fact, I had a long conversation with one of my fellow officers while we were on the boat coming over from Ireland. His father has an estate over in Shropshire, not far from Shrewsbury. He owns a sugar plantation in the West Indies and has recently invested heavily in cotton in America. He's also considering mining enterprises in South America, which he reckons could be worth an absolute fortune.'

'Exactly, Peter, that's just the sort of thing I'm talking about. You'll have to put me in touch with this fellow and I'll arrange to visit him. I've heard there are vast quantities of raw materials waiting to be exploited in South America. If there really is money to be made and if he's looking for investors, perhaps I should get involved.

'But to get back to the subject in question. As I said, I've had my spies out, and work has virtually come to a stop on the railway. Something must happen quickly, or they'll be sunk. We just need to keep our ears and eyes open, and when the time's right, we'll act. What I'd like you to do, Peter, is find out as much as you can. You have the family connection and I'm sure your parents will have heard something. Any messages can be left at my town house and if I'm not there I'll ensure they get sent to me up here. As soon as we know he's looking for money, we'll move.'

'I'll do whatever I can. I'll go over to Nottingham in a couple of days and I expect to stay there for a fortnight at least, so I should be able to find something out. But there is one thing that does worry me. I feel just the same way as you do about Daniels, but any harm done to him is going to affect Abigail too and I wouldn't want to see her suffer; after all, she is my sister.'

'I wouldn't worry about Abigail. She can look after herself, you know that as well as I do. And in any case, your mother and father would never see her suffer, or her children. If the worst came to the worst and Daniels did lose everything, they'd find her a home. And they might come to realise what a fool he is after all. You never know, Abigail herself might even agree with them.'

'You may be right. Let's hope so,' said Peter, but without any real conviction.

Two days later, having rested and recovered from his long journey from Holyhead and even longer spell of duty in Ireland, Peter saddled his horse and headed south to Nottingham and his parents' house on High Pavement. Three hours later, unbeknown to Peter, Josiah took the same road. His first call was at The Town Arms, where he left a message with the landlord, asking Bill Giles to meet him there the next morning at ten o'clock. Josiah had no doubt that Peter would be able to find out about William's financial arrangements regarding the railway, but there were other matters that he needed to see to himself, matters of such sensitivity and seriousness that he simply could not afford to let Peter know about.

And so, at ten the next morning, Josiah entered the almost empty pub and found his man, as usual, sitting amidst a haze of tobacco smoke.

'This is getting to be a habit. I hope you've no complaints about my work,' said Giles.

'Not at all. You did well last time. You or whoever it was that started those rumours about the navvies. But I might have a proper job for you soon; I'll let you know if and when. But this time it's serious. If you get caught, you could hang.'

'That'll put the price up,' replied Giles, showing no emotion. 'What is it? Murder?'

'I don't think that will be necessary, unless things went terribly wrong. I might need you to take charge of a couple of kids for a while. Temporarily separate them from their parents. The problem is, it won't be with their agreement.'

'Kidnapping, you mean. Why not just come out and say it?'

'It's not a word I like to use. But yes, that's what I'm talking about.'

'And who are they, these kids?'

'I think it best that we leave those sorts of questions unasked and unanswered for the time being. It might not come to it, but if it does, I need to know that I can rely on you.'

'You know the score. Everything has a price. This won't come cheap though. I'd need to use someone reliable, and they're hard to find.'

'As long as we understand each other. Now, I must go, but I'll get you another pint first, and we can forget this conversation ever took place. Agreed?'

'Conversation? What conversation?'

'Good man, Giles, good man.'

CHAPTER FIFTEEN

—

NOTTINGHAM 1832

'Gentlemen, we have a problem!' The gentlemen in question were the Board of Directors of the Nottingham and Leen Valley Railway Company and the man who spoke was the Chairman, Mr Christopher Aldridge. They were seated around a large oval table in a private room at The White Lion Hotel. At any other such meeting they would have expected to be wined and dined at the company's expense. But not today. Apart from a couple of jugs of ale and some glasses, the table was bare; about as bare as the coffers in the company's bank account.

Outside, a chill autumn breeze was blowing, scattering the falling leaves, and rattling the window panes. The atmosphere inside was almost as chilly. William, as a member of the board, was present and was seated next to Gilbert Wells, his friend and business colleague and one of the men responsible for the original idea to construct the railway.

Mr Aldridge continued. 'You are all, I am sure, aware of the problems we have encountered over the last few months, but for the record I intend to summarise briefly the current position regarding construction. Building of the line began in December 1830 with three separate contractors. No difficulties were anticipated and indeed all was going well until early this year when some complications arose at the northern end of the line relating to the extremely boggy nature of the ground. At the same time, some of the navvies left for higher paid work elsewhere. We all know that the number of railway schemes throughout the kingdom has increased in the last year and competition for labour is growing. And then we have had the cholera outbreak. I do not, and never have, believed that the navvies were responsible for spreading this, but nevertheless many of the inhabitants of the town did believe it, the result being the riots and threats made against the workforce. This has only exacerbated the situation and the northern contract has now stopped. I can tell you that yesterday the contractor formally notified the company that he is unable to fulfil the terms of his contract, and has now filed for bankruptcy.'

At the mention of the word 'bankruptcy' a gentle murmur went round the table and the long faces and worried looks of those present spelled out more than words could say.

'I note the anxiety on your faces,' continued Mr Aldridge, 'but I would urge you not to despair. Fate has dealt us some blows but all is not lost. Most of us have experienced problems in our lifetimes and none of us would have achieved what we have were we unable to rise above such obstacles. Setbacks we may have had, but we are hopeful of a resolution before long. Yesterday I received a report from Mr Reynolds, the surveyor, who has kindly re-examined the northern part of the route with a view to recommending a solution. He has recently returned from the North West where he inspected the railway that opened two years ago between Liverpool and Manchester, where a similar, but more extensive problem was encountered at Chat Moss. Having seen the solution used there, and having spoken at length with the engineer of that line, he has recommended a similar solution which he is confident will rectify the problem. Not only that, but our other two contractors have jointly agreed to take over the northern contract and find sufficient men to restart the work. Such is the good news.

'There is, however, a down side, which I expect will not come as a surprise to any of you. We need to find extra capital. In fact, a very great deal more; and quickly, if we are to complete the line without undue delay. You are, I am sure, aware that we are unable to acquire further capital through the issue of additional shares without first seeking an amendment to the Act, an expensive and time consuming procedure, and the only alternative is for the company to raise the money through the issue of bonds. I am confident that once the line is finished the profits forthcoming will enable us to repay such loans within a relatively modest period of time. And a profitable company will, of course, increase the value of such bonds which may then be traded at a premium. The whole process could be completed much more easily if the company were able to raise this money without seeking outside support. I am therefore asking each of you to agree to contribute.'

'And exactly how much does the company need?' asked one of the assembled group.

'All in all, we need to raise about fifty thousand pounds. If each of us can see fit to contribute five thousand, we can give instructions for work to restart. Until the money is forthcoming, however, I regret things will remain as they are. To put it bluntly: if we cannot find the money, the scheme is dead, the shares will be worthless and we will all have lost everything.'

There then commenced a general discussion amongst the members of the board. William said little, preferring to listen to the others. He was, with a couple of exceptions, the only self-made man present and whatever wealth he possessed he had achieved through hard work. Some of those around the table were men who had come into the world already surrounded by riches, and who had been able to prosper without any real effort. Most of them, he reckoned, could comfortably afford the sum mentioned, but he knew that to contribute himself he would have to borrow the money, for he simply did not have that amount readily available. After further discussion, and the asking of numerous questions, Mr Aldridge rose to his feet once more.

'I would suggest that you all return to your homes and give consideration to what I have said. I would, however, request that you let me have your decision within two weeks at the latest. If we cannot raise sufficient capital ourselves, we will have to look elsewhere and that will take time. And time, gentlemen, is the one thing we do not have. I look forward, then, to receiving your communications at the company's office shortly.'

And with that, the meeting was brought to a close. After the others had left, William and Gilbert stayed behind, and over another glass of ale discussed the day's proceedings.

'Well, Gilbert, I knew there were problems, but fifty thousand! It's an awful lot of money to be found.'

'True enough. But then these schemes don't come cheap. There were always bound to be some risks in such a venture, we all knew that at the outset. But I'm certain it will turn out all right in the end, and I have always maintained that we have to look to the future. Once this line is completed and has proved itself, I'm sure there'll be calls to extend it further south, and that can only add to its profitability. But as Christopher said, we have to find the extra capital. What about you, William? Will you be able to put more money in?'

'I certainly don't have that sort of money on hand; nothing like. Most of the profits from the canal business have been ploughed back in, buying new boats and other equipment. At least I don't owe anything; I've no outstanding debts and I own everything I possess, but I'll have to borrow money to put into the railway.'

'You don't have to. If you can't afford it or don't want to risk it you're under no obligation.'

'I know, but think how it would look. I expect all the others will be investing. If I don't, they'd think it was because I've no confidence in the scheme.'

'Anyhow, I expect you'll want to discuss it with Abigail. I guess she'll have something to say on the matter.'

And that is precisely what William did. That evening he related to her everything that had been discussed at the meeting. Abigail was nothing if not shrewd. Her father had been, and still was, a man of business, and she understood the implications of risk taking and that sometimes one had to borrow money to prosper.

'I could always ask father whether he could lend you the money, although I would rather we stand on our own two feet.'

'I agree. He was very generous to me when we were married. Without his money I would never have been able to buy the canal business. No, I'll find the money myself, somehow.'

'At least let me talk to father about it. You remember I told you I'm going to see them tomorrow. Peter's back home for a few weeks and I haven't seen him yet, so while I'm there I'll speak to father. He does have contacts and he's used to such dealings, so he might be able to offer you some advice.'

The following morning, immediately after breakfast, Abigail took the children and walked up to High Pavement. William had already left on railway business, and Millie went with Abigail as far as St. Peter's Church, then off to the Market Place to buy some provisions. A cool wind still blew, as it had for the past few days. Autumn was coming in early and with a vengeance, thought Abigail. It would be Goose Fair in a fortnight; perhaps they would take the twins to see it this time. As soon as the house was in sight Charles and Catherine ran ahead, racing to be the first there and reach up to grab the large brass doorknocker. By the time Abigail had caught them up, their knocks had been answered and the door was open. Abigail followed them up the steps and into the hall, to be greeted by her mother.

'Your father's had to go out, but he'll be back by midday. Cook's just put some pastries in the oven; she says they'll be ready soon, so we can have them with a cup of tea. Peter's here, but he's not up yet. He was out late last night, meeting some friends in the town. In fact, he hadn't returned when I retired. I expect he'll be paying the price this morning. These young men! I do so worry what he gets up to.'

'Oh, don't fret, mother. He must get into far worse scrapes abroad than ever he does here.'

'I've no doubt you're right, dear, but that's not the point. When he's back home, we expect him to maintain standards. When he's abroad – well, that's a different matter. But enough of Peter; how are you? It seems ages since I last saw you, and how are my lovely grandchildren?'

Mother and daughter sat gossiping while the children played. Soon, cook arrived with a tray of tea and hot pastries fresh from the oven. The aroma must have drifted upstairs, for soon they were joined by Peter, yawning loudly as he entered the room, looking somewhat bedraggled and badly in need of a shave.

'Ah, tea and pastries, just what I need,' he exclaimed, grabbing a plate and pouring himself a cup of the steaming liquid. 'There's something about Nottingham beer that makes a man hungry, especially after a late night session doing the Market Place circuit.'

'Peter! Wherever are your manners?' said Mary, severely. 'Are you blind, as well as drunk? Can't you see your sister's here, and your nieces and nephews? And what in heaven's name is the Market Place circuit?'

'Oh, yes, very sorry Abigail, but I do need this cup of tea. It's good to see you again after all these months. I hope you are well. You certainly look it, and how those children have grown! The Market Place circuit, mother? Well, you start at one end, say near the Malt Cross, and go right the way round, having a pint in every inn and alehouse, till you get back to where you started from. It takes some stamina, I can tell you. Three of them never made it back.'

'Good gracious, Peter, there must be nearly a dozen such establishments round the Market Place!'

'Thirteen, actually, if you include The Nag's Head at the end of Long Row, although the entrance is on High Street, so it probably doesn't count.'

'Peter, I'm ashamed of you. I would expect a man of your position to behave with a little more decorum. Your father won't be impressed! And just who were the others involved in this ridiculous drinking game?'

'Oh, just some of my friends from the old days.'

'Indeed. And if I remember rightly, most of them were good-for-nothings. Came from respectable families, all of them, but no ambition. Lazy, most of them. Wanted for nothing, but not prepared to work. Just what is the world coming to? Why, when your father was your age, he had already acquired his first …'

'Enough, mother, please! Yes, I know how hard father worked to achieve what he has, you've told me before. But just now, I really would like to sit quietly and get rid of this throbbing head. Anyway, I work jolly hard. It's no picnic being responsible for all those men. And if you want to see men really knock the beer back, you should spend an evening with the ranks!'

'I'd rather not, if you don't mind. Of course, Peter, I know you've done very well for yourself but I wish you'd be more careful in choosing your friends. Some of them would do well to take a leaf out of William's book. Look how hard he's worked and what he's achieved. He's built up his canal business and now he's very much involved with this new railway.'

At the mention of William, Peter would normally be expected to take no interest, but on this occasion he suddenly seemed to take note. 'Yes, I'd heard something about that. But isn't it running into difficulties? I thought work had stopped. Isn't that right, Abigail?'

Before Abigail could reply, the door opened and Nicholas entered.

'Ah, there you are dear,' said Mary. 'Abigail's come over with the children, and Peter here is paying the price for his night out with his ne'er-do-well friends. We were just talking about William's involvement with the railway and the problems they're having. That's right, isn't it Abigail?'

'There are some problems, it's true, but nothing that can't be solved.'

'But I heard half the workforce had left, and there's a problem building the line across some boggy ground. I expect it's going to take a lot of money to put all that right,' added Peter.

'Of course it will. But the board had a meeting earlier this week and all the directors are going to put in what's needed to get work started again. They're confident it will be worth it in the long run and that their investments will be returned with interest.'

'Let's hope so,' said Nicholas. 'And just how much extra is needed, if that's not a secret?'

'Well, I wouldn't want such details broadcasting, but within these four walls I can tell you they're looking for five thousand pounds from each of the directors.'

'Five thousand!' exclaimed Nicholas. 'That's a very large sum. How's William going to find that amount? I don't suppose he has that sort of money to hand.'

'No, father, he hasn't. He'll have to borrow it, that's for sure.'

'I might be able to help him myself, but not to that extent.'

'No father! One thing we have agreed is that we wouldn't ask you to lend any of the money. You've been very good to us already in many ways and William insists that he finds it himself. But I did wonder if you could give him any advice, suggest where he might go to borrow such a sum.'

'I think the banks are the only place. I know a lot of men in business but I doubt any of them have that sort of capital available at the moment. Tell him to approach the banks, but to be careful with whom he deals. He needs to satisfy himself that he can trust them and that the interest charged isn't too high.'

Nicholas continued to give Abigail the benefit of his business and financial expertise, advising her as to how William should go about securing the loan. Peter sat silently, not contributing to the debate but carefully taking everything in.

Their discussion over, they all went through to the dining room where the cook had served up lunch, and shortly afterwards Abigail prepared to leave.

'I'll come part of the way with you if you like, Abigail,' offered Peter. 'It must be difficult coping with four youngsters all by yourself; I can give you a hand.'

Abigail was taken aback by Peter's offer. It was unlike him to be so ready to help, especially where the children were concerned, and she knew he had no desire to go to the wharf where he might risk bumping into William.

'I'll just go and get my coat, I won't be a minute.'

Peter ran upstairs to his room and was back downstairs in no time. But it was just long enough for him to scribble a short note addressed to *Josiah Sidmouth, Castle Gate*, seal it and place it in the inside pocket of his coat.

A few minutes later, having said their goodbyes, Abigail and the children left, accompanied by Peter. Spots of rain were falling as they hurried along past Weekday Cross, down Low Pavement into Lister Gate and along Greyfriar Gate, until they reached Canal Street. The entrance to the wharf was a little way along Canal Street to the left.

'I'll leave you here, if that's all right,' suggested Peter.

'Yes, I can easily manage now, it's not far, and thank you for coming with us.' But Abigail knew that Peter really didn't want to come any closer and risk seeing William.

Peter immediately retraced his steps up Greyfriar Gate, but not far. He quickly turned left and cut through Orchard Street, then up Finkhill Street and Walnut Tree Lane until he came to Castle Gate. Turning down Castle Gate, it was only a matter of yards until he reached a mid-terrace Georgian house. He climbed the three steps and knocked hard on the door.

After a short while it was opened by a middle-aged woman who seemed somewhat flustered. She, Peter assumed, was the housekeeper. Having established that Josiah was not at home, Peter took the letter from his pocket and handed it to her, asking her to make sure Josiah received it as soon as possible, to which she concurred, explaining that she was expecting him back within a few days.

Her prediction was accurate, and two days later Josiah arrived looking hot and bothered, as if he had been on a long journey. Where he had been, she knew not, and he was not in the habit of discussing his movements with his housekeeper. But as soon as he had refreshed himself, he opened the letter. It was very short and to the point, and simply read, *William is looking to borrow £5,000. Peter.*

Josiah was not surprised at this news. It was about what he expected and now that he had confirmation he could proceed as he had planned. He needed to speak to Caleb Morley urgently, but in order to maintain his anonymity he preferred to keep away from the bank. So he waited until after six o'clock then put on his coat, and was soon striding across town to an address in Mount East Street, not the most salubrious area, but acceptable enough. He knocked at the door, and before long was admitted by a frail, elderly woman, wearing a woollen shawl, a mobcap and horn-rimmed spectacles.

'You want Caleb? Come in and wait here, I'll go and fetch him,' said the woman in a loud voice, leaving Josiah in no doubt that she was somewhat deaf. She left Josiah standing in the small hallway and vanished into a back room. Presently, Caleb emerged from the same room. He was a man of about forty, of average build, clean-shaven and with a thick head of dark hair, a permanent smile on his face and exuding an air of quiet confidence, bonhomie and complete trustworthiness.

'My dear Josiah, how very good to see you. Do come in. I'll get us a pot of tea. Unless you'd prefer something a little stronger.'

'No, tea will do fine, thank you.' Caleb led Josiah into a cosy and neat front parlour.

'Make yourself comfortable and I'll go and ask mother to make us a brew; the kettle's always on the hob.' He returned a couple of minutes later. 'She shouldn't be too long, although mother is slowing down a bit now, and she's going deaf. The perils of old age, eh! Still, she's a real comfort to me, ever since my dear Emily passed on.'

Once the niceties were over and the tea served, they got down to business. 'There are a couple of things I need to talk to you about, Caleb. Firstly, and most importantly, I have a job for you and I want you to pull out all the stops with this one. You are to offer a bank loan to a man who is in desperate need of a large amount of money, about five thousand pounds I should think.' And Josiah proceeded to explain to Caleb everything he needed to know, but no more. They agreed on what the terms should be and the interest rate offered, sufficiently attractive to make William accept. 'Don't let me down, Caleb. If you succeed there'll be a nice little bonus for you. So turn on the charm and get to work.'

'Trust me, Josiah, trust me. You say this Mr Daniels has an attractive young wife, Abigail. I think perhaps I might try and talk to her first if I can. Get the wife on side, I always say. Achieve that and the battle's half won.'

'Whatever you think, Caleb. I'll leave it to you. But be certain you succeed, that's all. Don't leave it too long, and let me know the outcome; you know how to contact me. Anyway, I must go, there are some other things I need to deal with.'

'I'll see to it first thing tomorrow. But I thought there was something else you wanted to talk about.'

'Oh, yes, thank you, I nearly forgot. I've just returned from visiting a gentleman who lives over in Shropshire. He's very well connected, very wealthy and has extensive interests in a number of far-flung corners of the Empire; India, the West Indies, America and so on. Now he's looking for more capital to expand his investments and get into mining in South America. I was extremely impressed with what he had to say and I've agreed to put some money in. I told him I'll be arranging to have forty thousand pounds transferred to his account. I think it's about time that the Town and County started to get involved in making some *real* money. All the details are here in this envelope. I'll leave you to make the necessary arrangements, Caleb.'

And with that, Josiah departed, leaving a rather bemused Caleb to ponder over the latest instructions from his new employer.

CHAPTER SIXTEEN

—

NOTTINGHAM 1832

The following morning, having breakfasted and put on his best suit of clothes, Caleb set off for the address given to him by Josiah. Despite a biting wind and thin drizzle, there was much activity at the wharf. Two boats were being unloaded and another loaded, with men scuttling back and forth between the canal side and the warehouse, carrying boxes and bales and pushing sack carts and wheelbarrows. Taking care not to become embroiled in all this activity, he stepped up to the front door of the house and, raising his silver-topped walking stick in his left hand, was about to strike the door when it was opened by a young woman.

'Good morning, madam,' said Caleb cheerfully, removing his hat and bowing his head slightly in one easy movement. 'I take it this is the residence of Mr William Daniels.'

'Yes, sir,' said the young woman, 'but I'm afraid he's not at home at the moment.'

'And do I have the pleasure of addressing Mrs Daniels?' The young woman smiled, and Caleb detected a hint of amusement on her face.

'No, sir, I'm Miss Daniels, Millie's my name. William's my brother and I keep house for him. If it's canal business you're here about, you should talk to Benjamin; he's also my brother and looks after the wharf. You'll find him over there in the counting house,' she replied, pointing to a small brick building next to the warehouse.

'I see; a real family business then, Miss Daniels, or may I call you Millie? Such a lovely name I always think. But tell me, Millie, is Mrs Daniels at home? It's not actually canal business I'm here about, more of a personal nature, and I'm sure Mrs Daniels might be able to help me.'

'Yes, sir, she's in. Just step inside and I'll go and fetch her. Who shall I say has called?'

'Oh, I do beg your pardon, how remiss of me. Caleb Morley's the name, representing the Town and County Bank.' Caleb entered and waited in the hall while Millie went upstairs. Shortly, he heard voices and the sound of children laughing and talking, followed by footsteps on the floor above. Then down the stairs came Millie, followed by another woman. Caleb was immediately struck by her beauty. Older than Millie by several years, Caleb guessed her age at perhaps thirty, but still with a fine figure, and flowing golden hair. As she reached the hallway Caleb stepped forward and offered his hand. 'Mrs Daniels, I presume.'

'Yes, sir. Millie says you have some personal matters you wish to discuss. I'm afraid my husband's out on business and won't be back until this evening. Is there anything I can help you with?'

'Quite possibly. Perhaps if I might take just a little of your time and explain the purpose of my visit, you could then let your husband know, and if he's interested in my proposition we could arrange another meeting.'

Intrigued by what Caleb had said, Abigail ushered him into the front parlour and invited him to be seated.

'My name is Caleb Morley and I am the manager of the Town and County Bank. We're situated up on Bridlesmith Gate; you might have seen our premises.' Abigail nodded in affirmation. 'We at the Town and County pride ourselves on keeping au fait with all the goings-on in the area, especially where commerce and finance are concerned.

'We have been following with great interest the progress of the new railway, or perhaps I should say the recent lack of progress of this worthy scheme. I must explain that we at the Town and County are all of a mind that it is an admirable scheme and deserves to be supported to the full, so beneficial do we consider it will be to the town; and we are therefore hopeful that the temporary difficulties will be just that, temporary. Which brings me to the reason for my visit today. We know that your husband is one of the directors - the list of directors is of course public knowledge - but we are also aware that the company is desperately in need of additional funds to restart construction. You might wonder how we know all this, but we do keep our ears to the ground and we understand that each of the directors has been asked to find a sum of money to permit work to restart. I should add that any information which comes to the attention of the bank is treated in the strictest confidence, as is anything I say to you today or to your husband at any future meeting.

'But to get back to the reason for my visit. In view of these developments, it might be that your husband will be seeking a loan. If this is the case, and of course we do not presume to be intimate with his financial affairs, then we would like to make an offer on what we regard as fair and generous terms. We are an old established bank and have always made it our business to assist local enterprises. Other banks might seek to increase their profits with risky speculations, but we prefer less flamboyant and safer investments in schemes we believe have a secure and profitable future. Anyway, Mrs Daniels, I'll not keep you any longer, I suppose you must be very busy. Here's my visiting card and if your husband is interested, perhaps he could call on me at his convenience.'

'Thank you, Mr Morley. As soon as my husband returns I'll convey your offer to him, and if he is interested I'm sure he'll contact you.' Abigail had carefully taken in everything that Caleb had said. She considered him to be pleasant and polite enough, if a little long-winded. What she did not tell him was that at that very moment William was visiting some of the Nottingham banks to try and raise the funds he needed.

William arrived back just after six o'clock, and flopped down into his favourite armchair. 'You know, Abigail, I think that talking to bankers is far more tiring than spending twelve hours shovelling coal out of a narrow boat or working at a stocking frame; and I speak from experience of both.'

'Here you are, William,' said Abigail, handing him a large glass of wine, 'you look as if you need this. Supper will be ready soon, Millie's just preparing it. So, how did you get on?'

'Not too encouraging, I'm afraid. I was kept waiting for over an hour at one of the banks before I could get to speak to the most junior clerk. These bankers seem to live in a world of their own. I got the distinct impression that they are not very keen on lending money, and there was me thinking that was one of their main functions.'

'And did any of them make you an offer?'

'Two of them listened politely and said they would consider it and contact me in the near future. When I asked what they meant by "near future" they were non-committal. One as good as said no; said they had decided not to venture into the world of railways until they were convinced of their usefulness and profitability. Another did make a tentative offer, but the conditions were onerous and the interest they wanted was extortionate. It looks as if I'll have to spend a few more days footslogging. But I've been to all the major banks in the town. I might have to go over to Derby or Leicester and try my luck there.'

'I see. In that case, you might be interested in calling on this gentleman,' and as she spoke, Abigail took from her pocket the visiting card which Caleb had given her.

William took the card, peered at it, turned it over twice then read aloud its short pronouncement: '*Caleb Morley. Manager, Town and County Bank, Bridlesmith Gate, Nottingham*. Where did this come from, Abigail? You've not been following me around have you?' William asked with a smile.

'Far from it. He came to see you. He as good as offered you the money.'

William, with a look of puzzlement on his face, examined the card again as if trying to find some fault with it. 'But I don't understand. Why should he do that? I haven't called there, so how could he know I'm looking for a loan? I know the bank, it's in that ancient building on Bridlesmith Gate. It has a reputation for being a bit staid and old-fashioned and I never thought for a moment that they might be interested, so I didn't bother going in. What exactly did he have to say, this Mr Morley? And what sort of fellow was he?'

'He was very pleasant and seemed genuine enough. He explained that he was aware of what is going on with the railway, the need for more funds, and said the bank was keen to support local enterprises. He also said they would offer fair and generous terms. I told him that if you were interested you would contact him.'

'Well, I suppose there's nothing to lose. I'll call round first thing in the morning and see what he has to say for himself. Now then, is supper ready? I'm starving.'

The following morning William rose early. There were some canal matters he wanted to see to personally before going out, and had even done a couple of hours work before he had his breakfast.

He left the house just before ten o'clock, knowing that the banking houses rarely opened before that hour, and steadily made his way to the Bridlesmith Gate premises of the bank. He pushed open the heavy oak door and found himself in a small hallway with a set of stairs immediately facing him. To his left was another door, on which hung a sign, declaring this to be the Town and County Bank, and inviting visitors to enter. William did just that and found himself in a square, panelled room. Against the far wall, next to a fireplace, was a large desk, behind which sat a clerk, an elderly, balding man, wearing a high-winged collar and dark jacket, who was busily writing in a leather-bound ledger in front of him. A single window, set into a deep wooden frame and fitted with tiny oblong panes of ancient leaded glass, looked out into the street. On the opposite wall were two doors, leading to other parts of the property. As William entered, the clerk looked up from his work and replaced his pen on the ink stand before him.

'Good morning, sir. How can I be of assistance?' William approached, and taking from his pocket the visiting card that Caleb had left, handed it to the clerk.

'I'd like to speak to Mr Morley if he's available. He called to see me yesterday but I was not at home at the time.'

'Please take a seat and I'll go and have a word with him. Who shall I say has called?'

'Mr William Daniels.'

'Thank you, sir. I shan't be a minute.' And the clerk vanished through one of two doors.

A number of leather armchairs were provided for clients, but at this early hour in the world of banking William found himself alone. He made himself comfortable in one of them and looked around him. Apart from the desk and chairs, the room was sparsely furnished. A couple of paintings hanging on the wall over the fireplace, seemingly of some foreign land, were the only items of decoration.

In a little while the clerk returned and asked William to follow him, whereupon he was ushered into another wood-panelled room, the very same room where Josiah had, several weeks previously, made his offer to the Bennett brothers to purchase the bank. Much of the same furniture was there; the large mahogany table, the plush, red leather chairs, the oak sideboard and the tall grandfather clock. But gone were the portraits of the bank's founder and his son.

As he entered, the sole occupant of the room rose from his chair and greeted William heartily with a firm handshake.

'Good morning, Mr Daniels. Please do take a seat. I am sorry I was not able to see you yesterday, but I assume your good lady wife has acquainted you with the reason for my visit.'

'Yes, indeed; but I'm curious to learn how you knew of my need to borrow some money. I have never approached your bank to discuss a loan, and neither am I an existing client of yours.'

Caleb smiled and chuckled to himself as he replied. 'Well, Mr Daniels, I am sorry if I have left you perplexed, and I do apologise for any suspicions you might have of impropriety on our part. Nottingham is certainly a growing town, but the business fraternity is still small enough for us to ensure we know what is going on. We have followed with some interest the development of the railway and we are aware of its current difficulties, which we certainly hope will be only temporary. We do have our contacts in the town, and the decision taken at the recent board meeting to inject additional capital has come to our attention. We understand that some members of the board - and your name was mentioned, in confidence of course - might be seeking a loan. This bank, unlike some others, is fully supportive of the railway and we would be sorry to see it fail, and that is one of the reasons why we are willing to make money available. Naturally we cannot operate on sentiment alone but we happen to consider that the railway will prove to be a successful and profitable venture, and we therefore view any loan to be as safe an investment as one can make at the present time. That, in short, is why I called to see you yesterday. There might be other banks that will approach you, but we don't like to let the grass grow under our feet. Strike whilst the iron's hot, that's always been our motto, Mr Daniels!'

'I see,' said William, somewhat astonished. 'And you're right, I am looking for a loan. Perhaps you could tell me a little more about what exactly you are prepared to offer me.'

Their discussion continued and eventually Caleb got round to asking William what size of loan he was seeking. Of course, he already knew the answer to this, but was able to display an air of genuine ignorance on this point, and seemed not at all put out when the figure of £5,000 was mentioned. In fact, throughout their discussion, William found Caleb to be straightforward and dependable, and had no reason to doubt him or suspect that his intentions were anything other than honest and above board. For the next hour the two men talked at length about the conditions that would attach to such a loan, the interest that would apply, the arrangements for repayment and so on.

At last their meeting came to an end. William promised that he would return with his decision within a day or two after he had had time to consider the matter and talk it over with his wife, and perhaps take further advice. At William's mention of possibly taking further advice, Caleb, for the first time, but only very briefly and barely noticeably, displayed a momentary hint of nervousness. It was so brief, in fact, that he was able to disguise it with a loud cough, and, taking a sip from the glass of water in front of him, declared he must have a frog in his throat.

On leaving the bank, William had other business to attend to in the town and did not arrive home until the evening. As soon as supper was over he told Abigail about his meeting and what had been offered. The deadline which Mr Aldridge had set for making the extra investments was fast approaching. William was eager to finalise matters, but so far had received no other firm offer of a loan from any other bank. Ideally, he would have liked to have taken professional advice and Abigail mentioned her Uncle George, a man of great experience in business and financial affairs. But he was over at Newark and the time it would take to go and visit him was really more than William could afford. He was extremely busy, not only with the railway but also with his own business, and so he made a decision. He would accept the terms offered and take the loan. The next morning, he returned and informed Caleb of this. He in turn promised to have the agreement drawn up and ready to sign by the following week, and the two men shook hands on the deal.

A week later William returned to the bank to sign the agreement, the clerk acting as witness. There were two copies to be signed, one for the bank and one for himself. Each copy consisted of two pages and they all signed at the bottom of the second page. But after they had finished signing, a rather unfortunate incident occurred, which at the time William thought nothing more of. Caleb went to pick up the copies from the desk, but as he did so he accidentally knocked over an ink stand, completely covering the first page of one of the copies with black ink.

'Oh, bother!' said Caleb, a tone of severe annoyance in his voice. 'What a nuisance! I'm so sorry about that, Mr Daniels. I'll have to get a replacement written up. If you don't mind, I'll hang on to them so we can copy all the details. Don't worry though, it'll only take a day or so and as soon as the job's done I'll have your copy brought round to your premises.'

William gave the incident no further thought, and the next day a messenger from the bank delivered the document. William was busy at the time, dealing with a claim from one of his most important customers in respect of a large consignment of lace which, allegedly, had arrived at its destination in London in a damaged condition. And so, without even looking at the document, William simply placed it for safe keeping in his bureau.

Following his meeting with Caleb, William had gone directly to the railway company's office and advised Mr Aldridge that he had now arranged a loan, and that the sum of £5,000 would shortly be transferred from the Town and County Bank to the railway company's account.

Two weeks after that another board meeting was held at The White Lion, where Mr Aldridge was happy to announce that the required amount had now been raised and the contractors instructed to recommence work at the earliest possible date. The mood was far more positive than at their previous meeting, and the confidence of the directors was boosted even more when, by the end of November, work was once again in full swing.

Soon after, the directors spent a day inspecting the whole route and were both satisfied and encouraged with what they saw. Hundreds of men were now toiling to make up for lost time, and even the short days and cold winter weather seemed to have no effect on the visible progress they were making. And all talk of the navvies being responsible for the cholera outbreak had now ceased as the epidemic finally came to an end.

Work carried on throughout the winter and the faster the men worked the more they earned. Had it not been for the insistence of the church authorities that there should be no work done on Christmas Day, many of them would have worked that day as normal. Instead, this enforced holiday merely helped to boost the profits of the numerous pubs and inns in the vicinity of the navvy camps, as the workforce descended en masse, seemingly determined to spend as much of their wages as time would permit.

Meanwhile, in the Daniels's household the Christmas celebrations were of a slightly more sober nature, not that there was any shortage of food and drink. After attending the morning service at St. Mary's, the house became the venue for a large family gathering. William's parents, along with his grandmother and sisters Sarah and Elizabeth came over from Chilwell, and they were joined by Samuel, Edward and Maria. It was not often that the whole family got together, and everyone took the opportunity to swap gossip and find out just what everyone else had been up to.

'So, Sarah,' said William to his sister, who in a few days time would celebrate her twenty-first birthday, 'twenty-one and still an old maid! We all thought you'd be married off by now. Whatever happened to that young carpenter you were courting? I thought you had high hopes there.'

'Oh, William, don't tease,' said Sarah. 'You mean Adam. As soon as he's saved up enough money we'll get married, but he's working so hard at the moment and often has to go away. He works for Mr Pearson over in Chilwell. He has a lot of land there, mostly set out as orchards and nurseries and he builds his own greenhouses. Well, they're so good that they're now getting orders from all over the place. Adam makes the frames for the greenhouses then he has to go and erect them. He can sometimes be away for several weeks at a time, him and the glaziers. And there's one glazier in particular I could mention, he's called Harry, and Elizabeth here has taken a real shine to him.' And it was now the turn of Elizabeth, just eighteen, to be the focus of attention.

'I think,' said Edward, after a while, 'we'll have to have a joint wedding ceremony and get them all hitched at the same time; save a lot of bother. Then there's Benjamin and Millie here. They're both courting too, I believe.'

'But what about you Edward? And you Samuel?' asked Abigail.

'Well, speaking for myself,' replied Samuel, 'I'm quite happy as I am. I get along well enough without a wife to nag me, and I never go short of female company. The other night for example, I was in The Bottle and Glass in Brewhouse Yard, when in walked this lass, lovely little thing she was, a lace trimmer I found out later, so I went up to her and …'

'Yes, thank you, Samuel,' said his mother, firmly, 'I don't think we want to hear any more of that particular story if you don't mind. It's about time you settled down; you too, Edward,' she added, turning to her brother.

Many were the subjects discussed and debated that day. They all reflected on the events of the past year and came to the conclusion that overall it hadn't been a bad one. James and Margaret were nicely settled in over at Chilwell and Samuel and Edward now had steady jobs; the Reform Bill had, at long last, become law; William's canal business was thriving, and the problems with the railway seemed to have been overcome. So, as the old year came to an end, William felt a deep sense of satisfaction and contentment.

And then, at the end of January, just when everything was looking so rosy, the letter arrived.

CHAPTER SEVENTEEN

—

NOTTINGHAM 1833

It was only a thin document, but official-looking all the same and no expense had been spared in using the highest quality paper. It was sealed with wax on which was stamped the initials T&CB, the letters intricately entwined within a simple heraldic device. It was addressed to Mr William Daniels and had been delivered to the wharf house one Tuesday morning towards the end of the month. William was out at the time, but returned shortly after midday. He had just sat down to eat the lunch that Millie had prepared when Abigail came in.

'There's a letter here for you, William. Very formal-looking it is too,' said Abigail, handing it to William across the table. William took it and turned it over, scrutinising it carefully.

'T&CB. Who can this be from?' he asked. The design on the seal looked familiar, but he couldn't immediately recall where he had seen it before. He took a knife and proceeded to cut the seal. All was revealed as he opened it, whereupon he read the heading, *Town and County Bank*. The document consisted merely of one sheet of paper, which William laid out in front of him on the table and began to read. Abigail had just left the room to see to one of the twins, and when she returned she could tell immediately from the look on William's face that something was wrong.

'What's the matter, William? What is it?'

'It must be a mistake.'

'What must?'

'This,' he replied, pointing to the document before him.

'Who is it from? What does it say?'

William handed her the letter. 'Here, Abigail, you'd better read it for yourself.'

Abigail took the letter, sat down and began to read. It was from the Town and County Bank, Bridlesmith Gate, Nottingham, dated 22nd January 1833 and addressed to Mr William Daniels, The Wharf, Canal Street, Nottingham. It was written using black ink, in a fine, clear copperplate hand. Abigail read on:

Sir

I write in relation to the loan agreement dated 25th October 1832 between the Town and County Bank on the first part, and Mr William Daniels on the second part. This is to inform you that, in accordance with the terms of the loan, we hereby give notice that we shall require you to repay to the said bank the sum of £5,000 with immediate effect. We shall therefore be obliged to receive from you the aforesaid sum, to be paid at the above premises no later than one calendar month from the date of this communication, viz, by 22nd February 1833.

I remain, sir, your obedient servant

Caleb Morley
Manager

'Whatever can it mean, William? I don't understand.'

'Neither do I, Abigail. As far as I'm concerned the terms were quite clear. It was always the case that the full amount would be repaid within five years, earlier should I choose, with interest being charged at the agreed rate, calculated daily and paid quarterly. I certainly don't recall any mention of the likelihood of early repayment being enforced.'

'Perhaps it is a mistake. But what will you do? You can't repay it; we just don't have that sort of money to hand.'

William sat quietly for a little while, deep in thought, before replying. 'I think I'll go and have a word with Robert and see what he says. I'll take my copy of the agreement so he can look through it. I'm no lawyer, Abigail, but I did discuss the arrangements most carefully with Mr Morley and I'm quite sure there was nothing in the terms which would allow the bank to make such a demand, unless of course I continually failed to pay the interest. But there's only been one quarter day since I took out the loan, and I paid up promptly. As soon as I've finished lunch I'll walk up to Friar Lane and see if Robert's available.'

Abigail could tell that William was anxious. He rushed through the rest of his lunch, then, taking his copy of the agreement from the bureau, along with the letter from the bank, he placed them into an inside pocket of his coat, said a quick goodbye and set off. It didn't take him long to reach the premises of Robert Kent, his solicitor, where he was greeted by a young clerk.

'I'm afraid Mr Kent is busy just at the moment, sir; he has a client with him. But he'll be able to see you once she's gone. Would you like to wait?'

'Yes, it's rather important. I don't mind waiting.'

It was another hour before Robert was free, but to William it seemed all day and that gave him plenty of time to think. He was not, generally, one to worry. He had experienced lean times enough during his life; times when he'd gone cold and hungry; had been falsely accused of a capital offence and forced to flee the country; he had slept in hedge bottoms and draughty barns, and been compelled to defend himself against bullies and thugs. None of these things had worried him, but he was worried now. What if the bank was in the right and he did have to repay the money? Just how was he going to afford it? He couldn't get it back from the railway company, not now. He might have to sell the canal business along with the house, then how would he make a living? All these thoughts, and more, swept through his mind. Had he been wrong in taking out the loan? Perhaps he should have taken further advice. Perhaps he should have come and discussed it with Robert. But he had been in a hurry, was under a great deal of pressure and wanted to get the matter finalised. Just then his thoughts were abruptly cut short by the clerk.

'Mr Kent is available now, sir, if you'd like to come this way.' William followed him up a flight of stairs and was shown into Robert's office.

'Good afternoon, William,' said Robert, stepping forward to shake his hand, and offering him a chair. 'How nice to see you again. I do hope you and Abigail are well, and not forgetting the children, of course. They must be growing up fast now, I expect.'

'Yes, thank you Robert, they are indeed,' replied William, as he sat down. But Robert could tell from William's tone and demeanour that he had something on his mind, something which caused him to be uncommonly vague and distant, not the usual cheerful and outgoing William he had always known.

'What can I do for you, William? I hope you don't mind me saying so, but you look a little worried.'

'Yes, Robert, I'm sorry to say I am.'

It took about twenty minutes for William to explain the background to the situation in which he now found himself; his involvement with the railway and the difficulties that had arisen; the decision of the directors to find the extra capital required and the circumstances under which William had taken out the loan. Once all this had been told, William produced the letter he had received from the bank, along with his copy of the agreement.

Robert picked up the letter first. 'I have had some dealings with this bank from time to time,' he explained, 'and I've always found them very fair and straightforward. I do know that back in twenty-five, when some other banks went under, they were sitting pretty. They hadn't invested in any wild schemes and they always maintained a good liquidity ratio, not that their investors felt under pressure to withdraw their savings. Now, let's have a look at what you've brought along.'

Robert quickly read the letter, then, putting it to one side, took the agreement out of its envelope, where it had remained since William had received it, and spread it out on his desk. Carefully he scrutinised it, saying little as he did so, other than the occasional *mmm* or *oh*. After several minutes, he sat back in his chair and looked up. He took a deep breath, then just as deeply exhaled.

'I think, William, you might have a problem.' These were just the words William feared, but before he could reply, Robert continued. 'Most of it is straightforward enough, the usual stuff about the length of the loan, when it must finally be repaid in full, the interest rate agreed, and the dates when it must be paid etc. But it's the final clause which I'm concerned about, this one,' and picking up the document he turned to the second page and began to quote: *'The bank reserves the right, in the event of any special or unusual circumstances which might arise, to reclaim the loan in full. In such circumstances, and upon written notice being given, the loan shall be repaid in full within one calendar month. Failure to do so will render the borrower liable to forfeit property or other chattels as the lender may see fit, to the full value of the loan.* In other words, William, they can demand their money back at any time, and if you can't pay, they'll claim whatever you have to its value. In your case, that could be your house and business.'

'Let me see,' said William apprehensively, leaning over the desk. 'I read the agreement most carefully before signing it and I certainly don't remember that being one of the clauses. If I had seen it, I would have queried it, or come and sought your advice. But can they do this? And it does refer here to special circumstances. Just what are the special circumstances which could make them want their money back?'

'That, William, is the nub of it. It doesn't define what those circumstances are, nor does it say who decides if they apply. The way this is worded, it virtually gives the bank carte blanche to do as it likes. I wish you had let me see this document before signing it.'

'Well, so do I, but as I said, I'm positive that clause wasn't there when I signed it. Let me have another look at it.' William gazed at the document again, shaking his head in disbelief as he read it. 'I don't understand. I discussed the whole affair at length with Caleb Morley and no mention was ever made that they might suddenly demand their money back. And even after the agreement had been drawn up, I read it carefully before signing.'

'I assume you went to the bank to sign it. What other witnesses were there?'

'Apart from Caleb, just one of his clerks. Look, that's his signature, Andrew Torr, just below Caleb's and above mine.'

Once again, Robert scrutinised the document. 'If what you're saying is correct, William, then there's only one possibility, but it doesn't really bear consideration, particularly not where this bank is concerned.'

'And what's that?'

'Look here,' said Robert, pointing to the second page, 'the final clause, the one you don't remember seeing before, see how it finishes half way down the page, and below are the three signatures. Caleb signed first, then his clerk, then you, but look at the space between the penultimate clause and Caleb's signature. There's enough room there to have inserted that last clause *after* you all signed. I'm not saying that's what happened, and I can't explain how it could have been done without your knowledge. But if you're adamant that the last clause wasn't there, then that's the only explanation I can come up with. Can you think of any way they could have managed it?'

'None at all,' replied William. 'Caleb seemed completely trustworthy when I spoke to him. Abigail thought the same too. He came to the house to see me but I was out, and he spoke to Abigail. She agreed he seemed genuine.'

'You mean *he* approached *you* about the loan? I assumed you'd gone to the bank.'

'No. I had visited several banks but was having no luck, and then, out of the blue, Caleb turned up and said he'd heard I was after a loan. In fact, he came to the house the very day I was out visiting the other banks. I must admit, it all came as a bit of a surprise, but I went to see him the next day. We had a long discussion and eventually he made me this offer. It did seem very generous, and the interest rate is certainly attractive.'

'A bit too attractive if you ask me,' said Robert.

'What are you hinting at, Robert? Are you saying I might have been duped? But why? And what could their motive be? Remember those other incidents I told you about, the damaged boats, the resurrectionists, and the body my men found in the canal. And now this! I'm becoming more convinced than ever that someone *is* out to ruin me. But if the bank has acted as you suggest, surely there must be something we can do?'

'Unlikely, I'm afraid. They would simply say you had accepted all the conditions. There's absolutely nothing in the document itself which indicates any trickery. It's a sorry business, William, and I just don't know how I can help you. The only other way might be to challenge their special reasons for demanding the money back, but again, the way it's been written I don't think you'd have any chance of winning a court case. Everything is on their side. After all, you signed the agreement in front of two witnesses and took it away. And they'll have their own copy. You did sign two copies, I take it?'

'Yes. But I didn't take my copy with me straight away. It was brought round to the house the next day. They had to hang on to it to make another copy after the ink had been spilt, and …' William suddenly stopped talking, and thought for a moment or two before continuing. 'Of course! *That's* how they must have done it. Now I understand! I didn't think anything of it at the time. I just assumed it was a genuine accident. Then Caleb said he needed to keep my copy to make another one, and …'

'Hold on a minute,' interrupted Robert, 'you've lost me completely. What's all this about spilt ink and another copy?'

William then related to Robert the sequence of events when he went to sign the agreement; how Caleb had spilt ink on the first page of one of the copies after they'd been signed, and his request to keep them so the clerk could make a new copy.

'That must be the answer, Robert. After I'd left the bank, all they needed to do was make a new copy of the front page, the one the ink had been spilt on, and then insert this new clause in the space above our signatures on the second page. But that's fraud, pure and simple. It can only mean that the whole thing was planned. Why would they want to do that? I've never had any dealings with that bank, and you say they have a good reputation.'

'They always have, in my experience. The problem is, though, it would be extremely difficult to *prove* any wrong doing on their part. It would merely be your word against theirs, and they have two witnesses who you can be certain would swear you're in the wrong. *I* believe you, William, but would anyone else? Especially in view of the bank's standing in the community. Look, William, I know all this is very worrying, but my advice is to assume the worst and that the loan has to be repaid. I suggest you see if there is any way you can raise the money. The last thing you want is for the bank to take your home and business. But try not to worry. I know it's easy to say, but you've been through worse than this before and come out on top. And one final thing. Don't reply to the bank's letter. Say nothing to them just yet; you've got a month before they want the money. I'll have a word with some colleagues and see if I can find out anything more about the bank.'

'Well, thank you for your help, Robert. And I'll also make some discreet enquiries myself to see what I can discover about this Caleb Morley; he seems to be at the heart of the matter.'

William returned home and he and Abigail spent the whole evening discussing what to do next, but could come up with no obvious solution. They didn't have the money themselves, and did not wish to ask Abigail's father for help.

'You could go and see Uncle George,' suggested Abigail. 'I don't mean to ask him for money, just for advice. He's a wise old owl; he made his own way in business, just like you. It can't do any harm in talking to him. He might think of something.'

'You're right, Abigail. Yes, I will. I'll take the gig and go first thing tomorrow morning. If I set off early I can be there and back in the day; everything else will just have to wait. Benjamin can look after things here. And I'll tell you one thing, Abigail. I know I've been swindled even though I can't yet prove it. But I will find out who's behind it, and when I do, my God, I'll make them pay.'

William rarely slept late. He was always up early and could usually be found busying himself around the wharf, often before his workmen arrived. But even by his standards he was up very early the next morning. That night he slept fitfully. The events of the day were going round and round in his mind and he began to think of what might become of them all. He tossed and turned for hours and when eventually he did manage to drift off into sleep it was only to be troubled by nightmares. He dreamt that he was back living in Narrow Marsh in a one room hovel, a room with no furniture. He, Abigail and the children were dressed in rags, lying on bare boards, miserable, cold and hungry. All of a sudden, the door opened and there stood a man with a plate of bread, holding it out, offering it to him. But when he tried to reach out for it he couldn't move, try as he might. It was as though his feet were nailed to the floor. And then the man went, slamming the door behind him, only to return again and again, each time with a bigger plate, piled higher with more food; and each time he was unable to get to the door. The children were crying out in hunger, but Abigail lay motionless, her eyes closed tightly. The children were trying to shake her awake but still she did not move. And then, as William began to realise that she was never going to wake again, he suddenly sat bolt upright in bed, sweating and breathing hard. He looked to his side, and heaved a sigh of relief, seeing Abigail lying there, silently sleeping. He lay without moving for a few more minutes then decided that there was no point in trying to get to sleep again. His mind was in a whirl and he was desperate to act.

He got out of bed, picked up his clothes from a chair and quietly slipped downstairs, dressed and went outside to the stables. It was pitch dark and flakes of snow were beginning to fall from the starless night sky. He chose his strongest horse and harnessed it to the gig, throwing in a couple of bags of oats. He went back into the house, and scribbled a brief note on a scrap of paper, telling Abigail that he had gone to Newark and hoped to be back later that day. Taking some bread and cheese from the pantry and a bottle of cold tea, he put on his warmest coat, a thick scarf and a broad brimmed hat and set off. The snow was now falling thick and fast, and William was thankful that he had bought a gig with a hood fitted. Not that it gave much protection. The wind was coming from the east and blew the snow directly into his face. But he didn't care. He had to get to Newark, see George and seek his assistance.

There were few people around at such an early hour, just some lace girls scurrying along quickly and quietly to the factories, shawls drawn tightly over their heads and around their shoulders. As he rattled along through the near deserted streets, the clatter of the horse's hooves on the cobbles echoed eerily from the tall and silent buildings.

Soon he was leaving the town and passing the grey gloomy fortress of the lunatic asylum at Sneinton. He was almost at Lowdham before dawn began to break, a thin, watery light gradually forcing its way through the scudding clouds. At Southwell he stopped by a horse trough in the shadows of the minster where his horse gratefully quenched its thirst and hungrily devoured a bag of oats, whilst William, sheltering as best as he could, ate his own breakfast. By the time they had finished, the small town was beginning to stir, and before long they were on their way again. Leaving by the Newark road, there soon came into view the union workhouse. William had read about it when it had been erected several years before, but this was the first time he had seen it. He was overwhelmed by its sheer size and magnificence, and its dominating presence dwarfed the other farms and cottages in the surrounding fields. A stranger, not aware of its purpose, might easily mistake it for the mansion of a wealthy landowner. How ironic, thought William, that its inhabitants were the poorest of the poor, and just how grim and forbidding must be the lives of those unfortunate and wretched individuals forced to go knocking on its door.

It was almost fully light as the town of Newark came into view. The snow had now eased somewhat, and as he crossed the river bridge by the ruined castle, a clock began to strike the hour of nine. William turned down a side lane and soon reached George's residence, one of a terrace of tall and imposing Georgian houses in a quiet street not far from his wharf by the river. He climbed down from the gig and shook the snow from his coat as best he could. As he approached the door memories came flooding back of when he had first arrived here as a boy of seventeen to come and work for George. This was where he had learned his skills as a boatman, and he would always be grateful to George for taking him in and giving him work when he might otherwise have starved in Nottingham.

He knocked firmly on the door and in a moment or two it was opened by Alice, Abigail's aunt. She stared at the figure standing on the doorstep, but what with the long coat he was wearing, the scarf wound around his neck and the broad-brimmed hat pulled down tightly to protect his face, she was having difficulty recognising him. William, realising her dilemma, removed his hat.

'Good morning, Alice, how are you? It's me, William.'

'William! Well I never. I didn't recognise you, all wrapped up like that. You'd better come in.' William brushed his coat again to remove the remaining snow and shook his hat vigorously, then followed Alice into the hallway.

'George, we have a visitor,' she shouted. 'But what brings you here, William, and so early on such a foul day?' And then something suddenly dawned on her. 'Oh dear! What's happened? What's wrong? It's not Abigail is it? Or one of the children? Do tell me they've not come to any harm.'

'No, Alice, we're all in the best of health. There's no need to upset yourself. I'm here to see George on an urgent business matter.'

At that moment George appeared from the dining room.

'William, my boy! This is a surprise, a surprise indeed. But you look half-starved, come in and warm yourself up. There's a good fire in the dining room.'

'Yes, do go on in,' said Alice. 'And I'm so relieved that you are all well. We were just finishing our breakfast when we heard the knock on the door. I'll go and tell cook to make some more tea and I'm sure you could do with something to eat. Have you had anything today?'

'Just some bread and cheese. I stopped at Southwell for a bite to eat, but more for the horse's sake than mine. I set off just after five this morning and apart from that one stop have ridden hard all the way. But the snow's slowed me down. Even with the hood up on the gig it's been driving straight into my face.'

'I can see that,' said George. 'You sit down there. I'll go and ask the maid to run down to the yard and get one of the stable lads to come up and fetch the horse and gig. He can give the horse some food and put it in the stable out of the snow. I take it you're not planning to set off in the next hour or so?'

'No, but I told Abigail I hoped to be back today.'

William removed his coat and scarf, and, after hanging them to dry on a hook at the side of the fireplace, he seated himself by the fire, stretching out his legs into the hearth. The numbness in his hands and legs soon began to disappear as the warmth returned to his bones. Alice returned shortly with a welcoming plate of ham and eggs and a pot of steaming tea. William had almost finished eating when George came back into the room.

'So, William, do tell us the reason for your visit. It must be something important to bring you here at this hour on such a day.'

For the next hour or so, William explained everything that had happened; his involvement with the railway, the difficulties that had arisen and the need for extra capital; the loan that he had been offered and then the sudden letter, demanding its repayment; his visit to Robert Kent and their suspicions that the bank seemed to be trying to defraud him.

'I can tell you, George, that letter came as a real shock. I know there's something underhand going on but I can't prove it. And if I don't repay the loan in full within a month, they'll be within their rights to take the house and wharf. It was Abigail's idea that I come to see you but we're not asking for money, just advice. She thought you might have some ideas or suggestions. Unless we can come up with something soon, I think we're sunk.'

George had listened carefully as William related these recent events, only interrupting once or twice to clarify some minor detail. After William had finished his narrative, George sat pondering for a few minutes before replying. He, like William, was a self-made man. The son of generations of farm labourers, he had made his own way in the world. He had never fancied a life toiling in the fields like his forefathers, and at the age of ten had started working for a ferryman on the Trent. When he was twelve, tired of simply crossing the river from one bank to the other all day long, and yearning for pastures new, he had secured a position with a boatman operating barges down the river from the Humber; and by the age of twenty-one he had bought his first boat and set up in business in a small way by himself, renting part of a wharf in Newark. Seven years later, having expanded his business and made his first £1,000, he had married Alice Hubbard, the eldest daughter of a wealthy Newark seed merchant. And it was her younger sister, Mary, who had married Nicholas Brown of Nottingham, Abigail's parents. From the day he married Alice, George's business went from strength to strength. Helped by some capital that his father-in-law invested, he purchased the wharf outright. As the towns along the Trent grew and the demand for transport increased, his wealth multiplied to a level which his farm labouring ancestors could only have dreamt about. At last, George spoke.

'You said it was the Town and County Bank which made the loan. I do recollect, some years ago, dealing with that bank. I was never a customer of theirs but I had occasion to go to their premises to settle an account for a barge I had purchased from one of their clients. I think you know, William, that I have an excellent memory for people, and I do remember meeting one of the proprietors. When he found I was from Newark, he told me that his family were originally from these parts. I can't just bring his name to mind, but I'm certain it wasn't Caleb Morley.'

'Bennett. That was his name, Bennett,' said Alice, casually.

George gazed at his wife in amazement. 'Well, Alice, sometimes you never cease to astound me. However do you know that?'

'You're not the only one with a memory for people, George. There were three brothers, Bernard, Bartholomew and Benedict. The family was originally from Newark and it was their grandfather, I believe, who founded the bank in Nottingham about a hundred years ago. Father had some business dealings with the Bennetts and I do remember the three brothers coming over once with their parents to visit us, when I was quite young. Father always said they were all as dull as ditchwater, but at least you could rely on them to treat you fairly. So your experience with the bank, William, does seem somewhat to contradict what father said. But of course, that was a long time ago. Things might have changed since then.'

'From what you've told us,' continued George, 'this fellow Morley seems to be at the centre of things. I wonder if the proprietors know what's going on? I think we ought to talk to them. How would you like me to come back to Nottingham with you, William? I could go to the bank on some pretext or other and see if I could meet one of the Bennett brothers. They'd never know that I was in any way connected with you, and if there is something funny going on it would be far easier for me to find out than if you went to see them. Alice, dear, you wouldn't mind if I left you by yourself for a couple of days, would you?'

'No, George, you go. There have been plenty of times in the past when you've gone off on the boats for days on end, so it wouldn't be the first time. In any case, we need to help William and Abigail in any way we can.'

And so it was agreed. George would return with William and stay for a few days. He had no qualms in being away from the wharf, especially as he had an excellent and reliable manager in whom he was happy to put his trust.

Straight after lunch George packed a small bag with a change of clothes, and after saying goodbye to Alice, he and William walked down to the wharf. While the stable lad got the horse and gig ready, George had a quick chat with his manager to let him know that he'd be away for a day or two.

Soon they were on their way. The snow had now ceased, the sun was shining, and with the wind behind them the journey back to Nottingham was most agreeable. They took their time, stopping again at Southwell for a warming glass of rum and hot water at The Saracen's Head, and by the time they reached Nottingham it was dark.

'Well, this is a pleasant surprise,' said Abigail, as George followed William into the house. 'We haven't seen you for ages. I do hope both you and Aunt Alice are keeping well.'

'As well as can be expected for a couple of our age! But more importantly, how are we going to get you two out of this mess?'

'Oh, I don't know. It really has upset us. I'm worried sick that we might lose everything. And after William has worked so hard to build up the business.'

'Now, Abigail, don't you worry yourself. William and I have had a long talk and I'm going to go to the bank and see what I can find out. Your Aunt Alice surprised us both when she suddenly announced that she knew something about the bank's owners and that they were known to her father. I was unaware of any of that, but it should give me an excuse for calling to see them.

'However, I want you to know, Abigail, that whatever happens, your aunt and I would never see you come to any harm. You know that we both think a lot of you, and you can rest assured that we'll not allow this affair to ruin you. And you're quite right, William has worked extremely hard to get where he is and I for one am proud of what he's achieved, especially as it was me that gave him his first job in the canal trade. So I intend to do everything I can to try and help you. But that's for tomorrow. Right now, I'm sure I can smell cooking. Is dinner ready?'

CHAPTER EIGHTEEN

—

NOTTINGHAM 1833

William slept soundly that night. He felt better in his mind now that he had spoken to George and had been reassured that he would try and help him, and, exhausted by his long day and tiring journey, he soon fell into a deep sleep. The nightmares of the previous night were gone and he awoke refreshed and ready to face whatever the day would bring.

After breakfast, George read once more both the loan agreement and the letter that William had received, then, placing them carefully in his pocket, he set off for Bridlesmith Gate. On entering the bank he was greeted by the same clerk whom William had described.

'Good morning, sir, and how might I be of assistance?'

'And a good morning to you too,' replied George. 'My name is George Jackson and I'd like to speak to one of the Bennett brothers if I may. It doesn't really matter which one.' The clerk eyed George with a slightly puzzled look on his face and hesitated for a moment before replying.

'I'm awfully sorry, sir, but I'm afraid the Bennett brothers no longer have any connection with the bank.' It was now George's turn to appear puzzled. This was not something he had considered as a possibility, but in an instant he realized that it might account for the behaviour of the bank in relation to William's loan.

'I can see if Mr Morley is available if it's important; he's the new manager,' continued the clerk.

'No, that won't be necessary. It was actually a personal matter that I've come about. The Bennetts are old family friends but it's been many years since we last met. I happen to be visiting Nottingham this week, so I thought I'd call on them and renew acquaintances. You couldn't possibly let me know where I might be able to contact any of them could you?'

The clerk looked over his spectacles at George and, deciding that he seemed genuine enough, concluded that no harm could come from being co-operative.

'It's not our usual practice to give out such information, but I think I can trust you, and in any case you would probably not have much difficulty in finding out soon enough if you were to ask around. They're quite a well-known family hereabouts. They all live together in the same house they've occupied all their lives. You'll find it near the top of Derby Road, not far from the barracks.' And the clerk proceeded to give George the directions. He, in return, thanked the clerk, bade him good morning and set off. It was a relatively short walk, albeit mainly uphill, and twenty minutes later George found himself standing in the porch of a neat, square, whitewashed villa set back from the road and standing proudly in its own grounds. He tugged on the bell pull and almost immediately the door was opened by a maid in uniform.

'Good morning,' said George, smiling. 'Would it be convenient to speak to one of the Bennett brothers?'

'Which one would you like to speak to? I'm afraid only Bernard's at home at the moment.'

'Well, in that case, perhaps I might speak to Mr Bernard Bennett,' suggested George, trying hard to keep a straight face.

'Come inside and sit down there,' replied the maid, pointing to a chair inside the hall. 'I'll go and ask him if he'll see you. Who shall I say it is?'

'George Jackson, from Newark, although I doubt the name will mean much to him.' The maid left without saying anything more, but in a few minutes a door opened and out stepped a small, sprightly man whom George judged to be about his own age, clean-shaven and with a full head of white hair.

'Mr Bernard Bennett I presume,' said George, stepping forward and offering his hand.

'Indeed I am,' replied Bernard, shaking his hand. 'And I understand you are Mr George Jackson from Newark. How can I help you?'

'I certainly hope you can. It's rather a long story. If you could spare me a little of your time, I'd be obliged.'

'I'm intrigued. And time is the one thing I now have much more of, since we gave up the business. My two brothers are out at the moment but will be returning for lunch in about an hour, so if you'd like to follow me into the drawing room, it's almost time for sherry and Madeira cake. An old family tradition, you know.'

George followed Bernard into a comfortable and expensively furnished room where he was offered a seat. A decanter of sherry stood on a sideboard alongside a plate of Madeira cake. Bernard poured two glasses and handed one to George, along with a slice of the cake. George then began by explaining that his wife's family, the Hubbards, had known the Bennetts and that, as a young girl, Alice remembered meeting Bernard and his two brothers when they came to Newark with their parents to visit her father.

'You say your wife's name was Alice Hubbard,' said Bernard. 'Now you come to mention it I do recollect a Hubbard family, and I think I also remember Alice. She was younger than we were, if I recall, but my memory is not as good as it was, I'm afraid. Now, Mr Jackson, do tell me how I can be of assistance.'

'Well, the reason I'm here, Mr Bennett, is that I'm hoping you might be able to shed some light on a rather disturbing set of events concerning a relative of mine, Mr William Daniels. He is married to my wife's niece Abigail. They live here in Nottingham and William runs a very successful carrying business from a wharf down on the canal. He has recently had some dealings with the Town and County Bank, which have come to a very distressing conclusion. I went along there this morning, hoping to talk to one of the proprietors, only to be told that you no longer had any connection with the bank.'

'That's correct. Our family owned the bank since it was founded by my grandfather in 1740, but we sold it some months ago. But please continue.'

George proceeded to relate to Bernard the details of the bank loan and the subsequent demand for its return, and then handed to him the agreement and the letter for him to read. When he had finished, George told Bernard about the incident with the spilt ink, and how William and his solicitor suspected that there had been a deliberate attempt to defraud William by inserting the additional clause.

Bernard read the all-important clause again, then, laying the documents down, shook his head. 'We would never have included such a condition in my day. Of course, we would always ensure that we had security against a loan, and there would be appropriate steps we could take should a client fail to pay the interest due. But to demand the return of a loan in full, at such short notice and without reason is something we would never have done. It just wasn't our way of doing business. And it doesn't make sense. So long as the interest is being paid, how could such a move possibly benefit the bank? Unless they are so short of money that they need it back urgently.'

'That had occurred to me too,' said George, 'but tell me, who is this fellow Caleb Morley? If we are right in our suspicions, he would seem to be implicated. And what about the clerk who also signed the document?'

'I'm afraid I have no idea who Caleb Morley is. He wasn't employed by us so he must have been taken on since the bank was sold. But the clerk, Andrew Torr, I can say without hesitation is as honest as the day is long. He started working for the bank when he was just a boy and he must have been with us for nigh on fifty years now. *I* say us. Of course, it's not our bank any longer but I still think of it as ours. I would hate to see its good name tarnished.'

'So who owns it now?' asked George. There was no immediate reply. Instead, Bernard looked down at the floor, and then sighed.

'I regret I'm not at liberty to say. When we sold the bank we promised we wouldn't make it known who the new owner was. He was adamant about that, insisting that he remain anonymous. We've always stuck to our agreements and I couldn't go back on my word.'

'I understand. But if this Caleb is playing fast and loose, perhaps his employer should be told; unless he's also involved. I can tell you, Mr Bennett, that over the past few years a number of incidents have occurred which could have put William's business in jeopardy, and he's convinced that someone has been trying to ruin him. And now this! It's all too much of a coincidence. If we only knew who was behind it we might be able to do something.'

'Well, I'd like to help you, but I'm not sure what I can do. I suppose we could go and talk to Andrew Torr and ask him if he knows anything about it. We can call and see him this evening if you wish. He'll be home by about six o'clock and I know he rarely goes out at night.'

George was prepared to try anything to get to the bottom of the affair, so they agreed to meet by the Malt Cross in the Market Place at seven o'clock. George thanked Bernard for his help then went straight back to the wharf, but William was out. Abigail was keen to hear what progress he had made but he said he would prefer to wait until after he had returned from a further meeting planned for that night.

At seven o'clock he met Bernard as arranged and he led the way up Sheep Lane, along Parliament Street, then through a narrow alley to a small row of cottages. Bernard knocked at the door of the end cottage and they were soon admitted by the clerk whom George had met that morning at the bank. Bernard made the necessary introductions before broaching the subject they had come to discuss.

'Now, Andrew, this is a rather delicate affair, but we're hoping you might be able to throw some light on a matter concerning the bank. We will understand if you'd rather not comment, but anything you are able to tell us would be in the strictest confidence. We suspect something untoward might be going on concerning Mr Jackson's nephew. Mr Jackson will tell you briefly what it's about.'

As soon as George had finished talking, Andrew put his head into his hands as if in despair.

'Oh, Mr Bennett, you wouldn't believe how much has changed since you sold the bank. I'm being asked to do things I would never have contemplated before, not necessarily against the law but which seem underhand. I don't like the way the bank's being run and I'm seriously thinking of handing in my notice. Yes, I do know about the loan but I didn't know it had been called in. Mr Morley never mentioned that to me. And I clearly remember the incident when the ink was spilt, but that was the last I knew of it. Normally, I prepare such documents, but on this occasion Mr Morley was insistent that he did them himself. I thought that rather odd as it's always been a clerk's job to write up contracts and the like, but I've learned not to argue with him. And as to some of the investments he's been making recently! I've had to deal with the paperwork and you would be horrified at the amount of money the bank has been pouring into what I would consider very risky enterprises - mining in South America, that's the latest. I take quite an interest in such matters, as you know, Mr Bennett, and some of the companies the bank's been investing in seem to me to be nothing more than money making schemes. I doubt they have any intention of actually undertaking any mining; they're just after investors' money, and once they've got their hands on it they'll simply disappear.'

'That must be very disturbing for anyone who has money with the bank,' said George. 'If things are as you say, they could lose everything. But tell me, Mr Torr, have you ever met the new owner of the bank?'

'Never. Only Mr Morley ever deals with him. But there was one particular man who came into the bank several weeks ago. He arrived with Mr Morley and they both went straight through to his office. He seemed to have an air of authority about him and I wondered if that might be him.'

'Can you describe him?' asked George.

'I only saw him briefly. Aged about fifty I would guess, a bit portly and seemed almost aristocratic. I only heard him say a word or two and he sounded well spoken. And I think I heard Mr Morley refer to him as Josiah.'

On hearing the name Josiah, George looked at Bernard, and he could tell that the name meant something to him, too.

'Well, Andrew,' said Bernard as he and George got ready to leave, 'thank you for your help. I'm so sorry about the way things are going for you at the bank. If you do decide to leave, you come and see me. I still have a lot of contacts and I'm sure there are many other banks that would be willing to take on an experienced clerk like you.'

George and Bernard stepped out into the cold and retraced their steps along Parliament Street and down into the Market Place.

'Let me buy you a sherry,' said George all of a sudden. 'You've been so helpful it's the least I can do, and it'll help warm you up on such a cold night.'

Before Bernard could say no, George grabbed him by the arm and steered him into The Talbot, which they were passing. They found a quiet seat in a corner and George soon returned with a large glass of sherry and a pint of ale for himself.

'I couldn't help but observe,' said George, 'that when Mr Torr was telling us about the visitor to the bank, and mentioned the name Josiah, you looked as if you might have recognised the man he was describing. I know that I did and I suspect I know who he is. And if I am right, it could mean a great deal of trouble for my nephew. The person I'm thinking of is a dangerous man to cross. He's also extremely wealthy, which means he can wield a lot of power. He can be most charming and amiable when he chooses to be, but he's utterly ruthless. If I were to tell you that he spent nearly five years in Van Diemen's Land for two serious crimes, including the attempted murder of my niece, you will perhaps begin to understand the sort of individual he is.'

Bernard was on the point of replying, but George continued. 'I'm not asking you to betray a trust, because I know you promised not to reveal who purchased the bank. So I'm going to write a name on this piece of paper,' and, taking out a small notebook, he tore out a page and with the stub of a pencil wrote on it, then folded the paper in half and handed it to Bernard. 'You don't have to say a word. I'm just going outside for a minute or two. Have a look at the name I've written there. If you're still here when I get back, I'll know I was wrong. But if you're not here, I'll know my worst suspicions have been confirmed. But your conscience can remain clear, Mr Bennett.'

George got up and went out into the back yard of the pub. Bernard opened the piece of paper and read the name written on it, then screwed it up, put it in his pocket, and knocked back the last of his sherry. A few minutes later George returned; but of Bernard there was no sign. George went to the bar and ordered another pint then sat down quietly by himself. He took a good half hour to drink it and whilst doing so he considered his next move. Slowly he formulated a plan of action, one which had its risks but which he was confident would succeed. At last, satisfied with his day's work, he left the pub and walked down to the wharf. William had now returned home and he and Abigail were anxiously waiting to hear what George had been able to discover.

'Well, although I say it myself, I'm rather pleased with what I've achieved today. But I'm afraid I'm going to have to keep you in the dark for a little while. I've seen a number of people and found out quite a lot, but there are one or two more things I need to arrange, so you'll just have to be patient and trust me for the moment; all will be revealed shortly. In the meantime I want you both to stop worrying. You have another three weeks before the loan is due to be repaid and your old Uncle George is pulling the strings now. And do you know, I'm quite enjoying it. But you might have to put up with me for a bit longer.'

'You may stop as long as you wish,' said Abigail, 'you know we like having you to stay.'

'Thank you, Abigail, but I think your aunt will have something to say if I'm not back soon. And there are some matters I need to see to in Newark as well as here in Nottingham.'

The next morning George went out again, once more to the bank on Bridlesmith Gate. He got there just as it was opening and was able to have a quiet word with the clerk.

'Good morning Mr Torr. I hope you are well today.'

'Mr Jackson, this is a surprise. I'm as well as can be expected. How can I help you?'

'Could you arrange for me to see Mr Morley as soon as possible? Don't say anything to him about our meeting last night. Just tell him that I called in to discuss opening an account and depositing a very large sum of money with the bank. He doesn't know me, but under the circumstances, I've no doubt he'll be more than happy to talk to me.'

'Of course. He'll be in later this morning but he'll be busy until lunchtime. You could come back this afternoon, about three o'clock. I think you should be able to see him then.'

George spent the rest of the day down at the canal side, visiting some of the other traders there whom he had known for many years. He did think of calling to see Abigail's parents, but decided that he would leave that visit for another time. He preferred to keep his present visit as low-key as possible, and the fewer people who knew he was here the better.

At three o'clock sharp he presented himself once more at the bank and was shown into Mr Morley's office. After the usual formalities, George explained that he had a large sum of money which he wished to invest with a view to achieving a better return than he was currently enjoying.

'I've been in business for many years, over at Newark, but I also have contacts here in Nottingham. I heard a little whisper from one of them that this bank has recently changed hands and that you're now making some excellent investments worldwide. I applaud that sort of enterprising spirit and I'd like to be a part of it. I'll come straight to the point, Mr Morley. I have ten thousand to invest, and want to place it where it can work for me. Now, are you interested? It's currently in my bank at Newark, but if you'll agree to open an account for me here, I'll have a bankers draft sent to you without delay. I'll be back in Newark in a couple of days and I'll make it my first job once I'm there.'

It didn't take Caleb very long to accept. Ten thousand would certainly come in very handy at the moment. Josiah had recently sunk almost all the bank's liquid assets into a diamond mining enterprise in Brazil, and whilst it might bring handsome returns in the future it had left the bank very short. Sometimes Caleb worried what would happen should there be any sudden large demands for cash withdrawals.

George stayed one more night with William and Abigail and the next morning set off for Newark. One of George's colleagues at the wharves had a boat heading down the Trent that day and he had arranged for George to be dropped off at Newark on the way. But before leaving he had one last word with William.

'I'll need to return to Nottingham in a few weeks. Your loan is due to be repaid on the 22nd February. I'd like you to come over in the gig and collect me on the twentieth and bring that brother of yours with you, Samuel. He's a big strapping lad if I remember rightly. I'll have something quite valuable with me and I'd feel safer if we had another pair of hands.'

William looked mystified. 'Yes, I'll do that. But what's going on George? I wish you'd tell me what you've been up to. And the loan? What am I to do about that?'

'Nothing, William, absolutely nothing. Don't think any more about it. You'll not hear anything from the bank, not before the twenty-second, that's for certain. You'll just have to trust me, William.'

CHAPTER NINETEEN

—

NEWARK 1833

George Jackson was a wealthy man; a very wealthy man. Not only had his business prospered greatly over the years, but his wife, Alice, had inherited a considerable sum after both her parents had died, an inheritance which had been split between her and her sister Mary. He and his wife had far more than they would ever need to live a life of complete leisure and luxury, had they so chosen. But George was not a man for luxuries and neither was Alice. And despite having a manager to look after his business, George was never happier than when he was down at his wharf, keeping an eye on what was happening, chatting to his workmen and customers, and listening to all the gossip and news which the boatmen always had an abundance of. Sometimes George worried about all this wealth and what would happen to it when he and Alice had passed on. They had never been blessed with children of their own, so had to decide whom to leave their money, property and business to.

And so, a few years earlier, they had drawn up their wills. The business was to be left to William, their house to Abigail, and the rest of their fortune was to be split between Peter, Abigail and her four children. Not that they had told any of them what their intentions were. But then, right out of the blue, a serious problem had arisen which could affect the life of his beloved niece and her family.

Two days previously he had been sitting in The Talbot in Nottingham's Market Place drinking a pint of ale, trying to work out the answer to this problem. And he had come up with a solution, but knew that he would have to risk a great deal of money in order to succeed. At first, that had concerned him. But then, when he reckoned up what he was really worth, he realised that it didn't matter. Were he to lose all the money he would need to pull off his plan, he knew he could afford it; not that he intended to lose even a single shilling. And how he looked forward to carrying out his plan! The pleasure he would get from succeeding would be worth every last penny.

And so, following a hearty breakfast, it was with a bright and cheerful disposition that he put on his best coat and told Alice that he had some important business to conduct at the bank, and that he would be back by midday. George had used the same bank in Newark for many years and counted the manager, Victor Blower, not only as a trusted business colleague but also as one of his friends. He didn't need to make an appointment to see Victor. So long as he hadn't got another client with him, he would always find time for a chat with George.

He walked up the road from his house and cut through a narrow lane leading into the wide expanse of the Market Square. It was market day and all was hustle and bustle. Picking his way carefully through the crowds, he crossed to the far side of the square where the bank stood, tall and proud at the corner of a narrow street. George went straight in, where he was greeted by one of the clerks, and five minutes later he found himself seated in the manager's office.

'Good to see you again, George,' said Victor, opening a cupboard door in his large leather-topped desk and taking out a decanter of whisky and two glasses. 'The usual?'

'That seems an excellent idea, especially on such a cold morning. Thank you, Victor. And you'd better pour yourself a large one. You might need it when you hear what I have to say.'

'That sounds ominous. Nothing untoward I hope.'

'No. I just need some money, a rather large amount.'

'Well, it's never been a problem in the past.'

'I've never asked you for fifteen thousand pounds in the past.'

Victor almost choked on his whisky. 'You did say fifteen thousand?'

'I did.'

'I thought you did. That's an awful lot of money, George, if you don't mind my saying so.'

'I told you it was. You'd better have another whisky. But it's not quite as bad as it might seem. It's a rather long and complicated story and I can't explain it right now, but I will tell you all about it later. In about a month's time. And by then, I expect to have put most of it back.'

'I see. And how would you like it? I know you have sufficient funds in your account, but I'm afraid we don't hold that amount of cash here.'

'I only need five thousand in cash. A mixture of notes and coins will suffice, but I won't need that just yet. I'll come and collect it on the twentieth of next month if that's convenient. The other ten thousand can be by a banker's draft, made payable to the Town and County Bank.'

'Very well, George. I'll have it prepared. If you call in tomorrow it'll be ready for you. The Town and County Bank, you say. That's a Nottingham bank isn't it? I hope you're not deserting us after all these years!'

'Not at all, Victor. I'm just helping out a relative who needs a bit of financial assistance, but as I said, I'll tell you about it later. I think you'll find it all rather interesting.' George and Victor continued to chat for while, and then George left, leaving the rather bewildered bank manager to finish his whisky.

The next day George called to pick up the banker's draft, and, taking it back home, he sat down at his desk and penned a short letter, addressed to Mr Caleb Morley at the Town and County Bank, Bridlesmith Gate, Nottingham.

Sir

In consequence of our recent discussion, I have pleasure in enclosing a banker's draft in the sum of £10,000 drawn in favour of the Town and County Bank. I will be obliged if you will credit this to my account, and forward me your receipt in respect of the same. By a good stroke of fortune, a very large windfall, expected to be in the region of £5,000 is about to come my way and I have decided that I wish to add this to my investment with your bank. In connection with this matter I shall be in Nottingham on 21st of next month and trust you will do me the favour of receiving me that morning at eleven o'clock, when I shall bring the additional funds with me. It is likely to be in cash, but

I assume that this will not inconvenience you.

I remain, sir, faithfully yours

George Jackson

When Caleb Morley received this letter he could barely conceal his delight. Ten thousand to hand and another five thousand to follow! Josiah would be overjoyed when he eventually got to hear of it.

The following week, George received his receipt from Caleb, along with his assurance that he would be at the bank as requested and looked forward to meeting him again.

Three weeks later, just before noon on the morning of the 20th February, a knock came at his door, and George opened it and greeted William and Samuel. They were, of course, expected, and Alice had asked her cook to prepare an early lunch for three hungry men prior to their journey to Nottingham. This they devoured ravenously, and once they had finished, George and his two companions climbed into William's gig. Alice stood on the doorstep and waved them goodbye.

'Take care, George. Give my love to Abigail and the children.'

'I will. And don't worry, Alice; I've got these two lads to look after me. I expect I'll be back within three or four days.'

But before heading out of Newark, they made a short detour to the bank. Samuel stayed with the gig while George and William went inside. A few minutes later, they emerged, carrying between them a metal box about two feet long and half as wide and deep. This they lifted onto the gig, and placed under the seat.

'It should be safe enough there,' said George, 'but you guard it with your life, Samuel.'

'Why, what's in it?'

'Money, Samuel. More money than you've ever seen in your life.'

'What's it for?'

'William asked me that when we collected it. You'll both have to wait till tomorrow when all will be revealed. For now, you must be patient and trust me. And don't let it out of your sight. Fortunately, I don't think we have any highwaymen in these parts!'

With three big men and a heavy box, they didn't race to get back, and stopped a couple of times to give the horse a rest and a drink of water. It was dark by the time they turned out of Canal Street and through the gates of the wharf. Once the horse had been fed and stabled and the metal box safely hidden away, the three of them joined Abigail for supper.

'Come on, George,' said William, 'tell us what's going on. You can't keep us in the dark any longer. We know that box has money in it, you've already said that; but what's it for? Is it anything to do with my loan? That's due to be repaid in a couple of days.'

'In a way, yes. But it's not quite as straightforward as that. Tomorrow morning all four of us are going up to the Town and County Bank to see Mr Caleb Morley. He's expecting me at eleven, but not William or Abigail, and of course, he's never met Samuel. But he's going to be in for a big surprise when we all turn up.'

'You want me to come with you?' asked Samuel.

'Of course I do, Samuel. I guess you're just as curious as William and Abigail, and in any case I want you to help us guard that heavy box. And if things should turn nasty your presence will be a great help.'

'So you saw Caleb Morley when you were last over here,' said William. 'What did you find out? Is it him that's trying to defraud me out of my money? And did you get to see the bank's owner?'

'A lot of questions, William, a lot of questions. I don't blame you for asking, but you'll have to be patient, just till tomorrow morning when everything will become clear.'

Despite their persistent efforts it was plain that George was not going to reveal anything further, and then he declared that he was tired and was going to bed.

'I'm off too,' said Samuel, 'but I'll be back down here by ten o' clock in the morning.'

The next day dawned bright but cold. Samuel arrived earlier than he said, eager to get going. The gig was brought round and when they were ready the box was carried out from the house and they all climbed aboard. They soon reached the bank, and as they drew up outside, George spoke. 'Once we're in there, leave the talking to me. Don't say anything unless I ask you to.'

Samuel got out first and tethered the horse to a post, then helped William with the box. They all followed George into the bank. 'Good morning Mr Torr, I'm here to see Mr Morley. He is expecting me.'

The clerk looked quizzically over the top of his glasses at the other three who accompanied George. William, he recognised, but not the man helping him carry a metal box, nor the woman with them. 'I'll just check that Mr Morley's free. Please wait there a moment.' A few seconds later he returned. 'Please come this way.'

George went in first, and, much to the surprise of the clerk, the others followed him. But for Caleb Morley it was an even bigger surprise. He was expecting George, but no one else, and as soon as he saw William he became nervous. Caleb knew that William's loan was due to be repaid the following day and was confident the deadline would pass without payment. So why was he here now? And more to the point why was he here with George? As Caleb dithered, George took control of the situation.

'Just put the box down there on the floor, lads, and come and take a seat. Abigail, you sit next to me,' said George manoeuvring chairs to form a semicircle facing Caleb's desk.

'Well, I'm very pleased to meet you all,' said Caleb uneasily and without an iota of conviction in his voice. 'I have to say, Mr Jackson, this is a turn up for the books. I certainly didn't anticipate a delegation, but I'm sure you have a good reason for bringing your friends along.'

'Not just friends, Mr Morley, but relatives. Not blood relatives, but near enough for me to take a keen interest in their wellbeing. Abigail here is my niece, the daughter of my wife's sister, and this is her husband Mr William Daniels. But of course, you've already met both of them. And this is Samuel, William's brother. A big strong lad is our Samuel. He kindly agreed to come along and help carry this heavy box.'

'I see,' replied Caleb, eyeing the metal box. If it contained what he thought it did, then he could understand why it would take two men to carry it. 'Now, Mr Jackson, are we to get down to business? I take it you are quite happy to discuss matters with everyone present?' Caleb was perplexed. Why, he wondered, should George's decision to make an additional investment into his account concern anyone else, relatives or not?

'Most definitely, Mr Morley. In fact, since what we have to say concerns them, I was *insistent* that they came along. So, first things first. You are, of course, aware of the loan which the bank so kindly made available to William. Not only made available, but was most determined that he should accept. Indeed it was you who sought him out to make him that offer. And then, within a couple of months, lo and behold, he received a letter demanding the repayment of the loan,' and reaching into an inside pocket of his jacket, George withdrew both the letter and the agreement and placed them on the desk before him. 'I'm sure you'll recognise them both. After all, they are in your own handwriting.'

Caleb glanced down at the documents but said nothing, as George continued.

'Why the bank should demand repayment so soon is a matter which I will return to shortly, but since you are determined to be repaid we'll not disappoint you, so here it is. Lads, the box please, there's plenty of room on the desk.' William and Samuel lifted the box onto the desk and George, taking a brass key from his pocket, unlocked the lid and lifted it up. The box was full to the brim; a mixture of bank notes and coins. 'Trust me, Mr Morley; it's all there, five thousand pounds to the last farthing. You may count it if you wish, we don't mind, we've got all day. But one thing we do insist on is your receipt. Here's William's copy of the agreement; if you will kindly endorse it at the bottom that it has now been repaid in full, and sign and date it, that will suffice. Oh, and please take care not to spill any ink on it this time!'

Caleb knew when he was beaten. Taking up a pen, with a somewhat shaky hand he endorsed and signed the document as requested and pushed it back towards George.

'Thank you, Mr Morley. Well, that's the first item dealt with. There you are William,' said George, handing the document to him. 'Take care of that, it might be needed later.

'And now to the next item. I know you were expecting me here today to make an additional investment into my account. Unfortunately, there's been a change of plan. I'm afraid something's "come up" as they say, and far from putting more money in, I find it necessary to take some out. How was it you put it in your letter to William? Ah, yes, I recall: *in the event of any special or unusual circumstances which might arise, to reclaim the loan in full.* Well, I'm afraid that some special and unusual circumstances have now arisen which make it necessary for me to withdraw my money. Actually, I only require five thousand pounds today, so if you will kindly fetch it up from your vaults, we'll take it with us. The other five thousand remaining in my account I shall need within a week's time.'

Caleb's face was a picture. William had been watching him carefully but he couldn't work out whether it was anger or fear that had gradually been spreading across it, as George taunted him relentlessly. Either way, he was no longer the confident, friendly, sincere individual who had been so keen to persuade him to accept the bank's offer of the £5000 he needed.

'I'm very sorry, Mr Jackson,' said Caleb, trying desperately to assert his authority, 'but I'm afraid that won't be possible. We just can't make that sort of repayment at the drop of a hat. We require notice for such a large withdrawal. In any case, the bank simply doesn't retain that amount of cash on the premises.'

'*Really?*' replied George.

'Yes, really,' declared Caleb, firmly. 'Very few banks keep that amount on hand.'

'Well, that's strange. Because unless my eyes deceive me, there appears to be five thousand pounds sitting on your desk and staring us all in the face! So I tell you what, Mr Morley, I'll take this box and its contents away with me, and that's the whole matter settled without any fuss. You won't even have to go down into your vaults,' and taking the key from his pocket he closed the lid and locked it once more. 'William, Samuel, please remove my money from Mr Morley's desk. Now, Mr Morley, unlike you, I do like to keep things above board, so here is my receipt for the five thousand I've withdrawn today; and there's my written confirmation that I wish to close my account with the Town and County Bank. My instructions are quite clear. You are to send a draft direct to my bank in Newark. All the details are there. And one last thing, Mr Morley; if the five thousand pounds isn't lodged with my bank within the week, I shall instruct my solicitor to commence an action for its recovery. Of course, the writ won't be served on you personally, as you are only an employee, but I doubt that your employer will be very happy at this turn of events when you explain things to him, now will he? I understand that Sir Josiah Sidmouth can turn very nasty when things don't go his way.'

At the mention of his name, Abigail gasped loudly. But William, who so far had said not a word, remained perfectly calm; and then he spoke. 'So he *was* behind it. I might have guessed. And I suppose he got you to do his dirty work for him. Whose idea was it to add that extra clause without my knowing?'

'I really don't know what you're talking about,' stuttered Caleb.

'Come now, Mr Morley,' mocked George, 'don't try and wriggle out of it. You added that extra clause after the document had been signed, and it's in your handwriting. You were good enough to send me a sample of it when you wrote to me recently. And we have a witness who will testify to the fact. Attempted fraud I'd call it. That could put you behind bars for a very long time, or send you to where your partner-in-crime recently returned from. I suspect this whole affair was engineered with one aim in mind - to try and ruin William. I expect you thought he'd be unable to repay the loan and have to sell his business and home. Well, you've got your money back now and much good may it do you, although from what I hear you've been sinking most of it deep into South American diamond mines. Let's hope they find some. If not, I'm afraid the Town and County could be in Queer Street. So, don't try any more funny business and just make sure that my five thousand gets back to me next week, or I go straight to the authorities. And a good day to you sir!'

William and Samuel took the box, and the four of them left without saying anything further. They climbed into the gig and were just about to set off when William got out again.

'Just wait there, I won't be long,' and in an instant he had re-entered the bank. He walked straight past the startled clerk, through the door and back into Caleb Morley's Office. As he walked in, Caleb was sitting at his desk, his head cradled in his hands, but on seeing William enter, he immediately stood up.

'What are you doing? You can't just walk in here unannounced. What do you want?' William walked round to Caleb's side of the desk, and as he did so he picked up his silver-topped walking cane from a coat stand. Then, grabbing him tightly by his throat so that he could barely breathe, he lifted him bodily from the floor, and pushed him hard against the wall.

'If you ever come near me or my family again, or do anything to harm any of us, I'll take this fancy walking stick of yours and shove it where the sun don't shine.' He waited a few seconds more, then released his grip on Caleb, who dropped to his feet, red-faced, choking, and gasping for breath. Then, taking the walking stick in his right hand, William placed it under Caleb's chin and raised his head until their eyes met. 'And you tell Sidmouth when you see him that the same applies to him too, except that in his case it won't be a silver-topped cane, it'll be a red-hot poker. And you can also tell him that from now on I'll be keeping an eye out for him. He doesn't frighten me; and don't you forget, we have enough evidence to have both of you locked up for the rest of your lives.' Then, placing the stick on the desk, William quietly left the bank.

'What have you been doing, William?' asked Abigail as he climbed back beside her.

'Oh, I just needed to have a quiet word with Mr Morley; nothing to worry about. Now, I suggest we get this money safely back home, and have a drink to celebrate an excellent morning's work.'

Half an hour later, seated in the living room, Abigail raised her glass. 'To Uncle George,' she said, and then gave him a big hug. 'Without your help we'd never have got out of this mess.'

'And to your good fortune, and to that of the railway too,' responded George. And they all raised their glasses and joined in the toasts.

'But I'm a bit confused,' said Samuel, 'with all this money going backwards and forwards; surely George, you're out of pocket.'

'No, not at all. I'm still owed five thousand, the balance of the ten thousand I put into the Town and County some weeks ago; but William has now repaid the loan he had from the bank.'

'Yes, but that was repaid with the five thousand we brought over from your bank at Newark. So you've repaid that. And what about the five thousand William put into the railway. That's still there, so where has that come from?'

'You're right, Samuel, it is a bit confusing,' replied William. 'It means that George has actually put money into the railway, not me, so I owe George five thousand, and I shall make sure he gets it back, with interest.'

'Now, William, that's something I can talk to you about later. I always maintained the railway would be a sound investment and I've no doubt that in time it will pay a handsome dividend, so I'm in no hurry to have it back. And I regard it as a far safer investment than South American diamond mines. The main thing is, you and Abigail are no longer under any threat from the bank, and we've also got to the bottom of who was behind it. The only danger now might come from Sidmouth himself.'

'Oh, I wouldn't worry about him', said William. 'I had words with Morley before we left; that's why I went back into the bank. I think we've heard the last of Sidmouth.'

'Well, I hope you're right,' added Samuel, 'but I wouldn't bank on it. You know what he's like and he won't be at all happy about what's happened today. I'd like to be a fly on the wall when Morley gives him the news. If you want me to sort him out, William, I will. I've got some good mates and between us we could really put the wind up him.'

'Thanks, Samuel, but I think it might be better to leave things as they are just for now. I'm pretty certain they won't try anything more, not after what I told Morley.'

'Why, what did you say to him?'

'Let's just say I made it clear exactly what would happen to him and Sidmouth if ever they crossed my path again, and I know he didn't like what he heard. I think he got the message.'

'Let's hope so,' said George. 'But now I need to make plans to get myself and this box back home. How do you two lads fancy another trip over to Newark?'

CHAPTER TWENTY

—

NOTTINGHAM 1833

Caleb Morley had never seen any man so angry. Josiah Sidmouth was apoplectic with rage to the point at which Caleb began to fear for his own safety.

'And just how did they find out about me?' bellowed Josiah, thumping the table violently. 'Someone must have told them. If I find out who it was I'll kill him. It wasn't you was it? Or that miserable clerk?'

'No of course not, and the clerk doesn't know you anyway.'

'But they found out somehow, didn't they? And why didn't you let me know that it was George Jackson who was investing large amounts of money in the bank? I know him of old, he's Abigail Daniels's uncle. If I'd known it was him I'd have smelled a rat straight away.'

'Well, how was I to know? In any case, you haven't been to the bank in weeks, and I had no reason to be suspicious. I thought you'd be pleased to have such a wealthy new client.'

'And then you allowed him to repay Daniels's debt. What were you thinking of?'

'Josiah, there was nothing I could do. He brought the money back, all five thousand of it. How could I possibly have refused to accept it?'

'And if that wasn't bad enough, you immediately gave it straight back to him! You know we require notice for that sort of withdrawal. Whatever were you doing, letting him take it away?'

Caleb was now becoming angry himself. 'It's all very well you saying that, but you weren't there. I was outnumbered three to one, four to one if you include the woman. That William's a bit handy, as I found out; but his brother! You wouldn't want to get the wrong side of him, believe me. In any case, even if I had been able to hang on to the five thousand, they've got our number all right. They know exactly what happened with that document. They've only to go to the authorities and we could end up in gaol.'

'*We?* You mean *you*, I think, Caleb. I had nothing to do with it. It was you who wrote it.'

'You knew exactly what was happening, Josiah, so don't try and blame me. I tell you, if I go down, I'll take you with me. Anyway, with a bit of luck it needn't go any further. As long as Jackson gets his other five thousand back within the week, that'll be the end of the matter.'

'You know we don't have that amount of money in the bank at the moment, Caleb.'

'But it's a bankers draft we'll be sending, not cash.'

'Maybe, but you know what our situation is.'

'Only too well. But it was you who insisted on buying South American mining shares. That's what's left us with virtually no cash in hand.'

'Where I invest the bank's money is my affair and I'll put it where I choose. It's my bank, my money.'

'Actually, Josiah, it belongs to our clients. Let's hope they don't all want it back at the same time or we really will be in a mess. And if what I read in the Journal last week is right, I would start to get a bit worried.'

For the first time since Caleb arrived at Josiah's house that morning, Josiah was lost for words. But only momentarily.

'I haven't seen the Journal. What was it saying?'

'There was an article about South American mining enterprises. It reckoned that some of the ventures are worthless, that many of the mines don't even exist and that the companies were merely set up to get hold of investors' money, and now the proprietors have vanished along with the cash. It also claimed that many of the mines that are in production are not nearly as profitable as was predicted.'

'Did it say which companies were involved? Did it give any names?'

'No. It merely suggested that anyone with money invested would be prudent to find out just where they stood. And it made no mention of any banks investing there.'

'Well, you leave that to me. I'll make some enquiries. In the meantime don't do anything about repaying that five thousand. Jackson can whistle for his money as far as I'm concerned. Let him sweat for a while.'

'But you know what will happen. I told you what he said.'

'Threats, Caleb, just idle threats. He'll get his money back, when it suits me, but I'm not going to be dictated to by some jumped-up bargeman, especially a relative of William Daniels! And as long as I own the Town and County Bank I'll decide who gets repaid, and when. In any case, if what the Journal says is true, he might have to wait a bit longer.'

Had Josiah been aware that his housekeeper, the redoubtable Mrs Barton, was listening at the keyhole, lured there by the row that was going on within, not only would he have kept his voice down but he would certainly have threatened her with the dire consequences that would ensue should she breathe a word of anything she had heard. He might even have sacked her on the spot. But unfortunately for Josiah, he was oblivious to the presence of the eavesdropper on the other side of the door.

Now, Mrs Barton liked to keep up-to-date with all the local gossip and tittle-tattle. And she equally felt it her duty to share with her many friends and acquaintances any little snippets of information which she became privy to and considered that the rest of Nottingham should also be made cognisant of.

And so, as soon as Caleb had left and Josiah had also hurriedly departed, saying he would not be back until much later that evening, she put on her best coat and hat, and taking her umbrella from the stand in the hallway marched off purposefully in the direction of the Market Place, where, it being market day, she knew there were sure to be many willing recipients eager to hear her latest bulletin.

But the problem with Mrs Barton was, that while she had an insatiable appetite for news and a God-given talent for overhearing private conversations, her understanding of financial matters was about on a par with her ability to keep a secret. One of her other traits was a tendency to exaggerate. And so, within no time at all, news was spreading around Nottingham that the Town and County Bank had no money left in its safe, that every last penny had been sent to miners in South America who had run off with it and spent it on liquor and loose women, and that anybody with money in the bank would never see any of it again. And whilst these wild rumours might have contained a smidgen of truth, the result was entirely predictable. As the rumours spread, the gravity of the situation magnified, until those who actually had money deposited there began to panic. The bank was forced to issue a statement, which the newspapers were happy to print, declaring that there was no truth in the rumours and that their clients had nothing to fear.

Nevertheless, when panic begins, otherwise sane people behave irrationally, and very soon queues began to form outside the bank as depositors sought to withdraw their funds. The consequences were inevitable and before long the bank did run out of money, and Mrs Barton's predictions became self-fulfilling.

'There you are, I told you as much!' she boasted to one of her closest friends the day after the town constables were forced to send for help from troops at the barracks, when an angry mob threatened to break into the bank. And Mrs Barton's esteem amongst her acquaintances rose to an all-time high.

In Newark, George went to see his solicitor. He had waited a week for the return of his £5,000; in fact he had waited a further two weeks whilst his own bank tried, without success, to contact the Town and County to enquire about the return of Mr Jackson's money. But his solicitor was confident that he would be able to secure the return of his client's funds, especially since the bank was in the sole ownership of a very rich man who had ample assets to his name.

Meanwhile, that very rich man had himself been busy. He had been away from Nottingham for several days whilst he made a visit to Shropshire to discuss his recent investment of £40,000 in South American mining enterprises. He returned to Nottingham feeling extremely angry and frustrated, having learned that his investments had now been reduced to less than a tenth of their original value. His worst fears had been realised, and his displeasure was all the greater when he arrived home to find waiting for him a letter from a Newark solicitor demanding the immediate settlement of an outstanding debt for his client, Mr George Jackson, and threatening action if he did not respond by return. Such a communication would not normally have bothered him, but he knew that unless this was dealt with swiftly, other, more serious allegations regarding an incident of fraud might come to light. And the last thing he wanted was to be charged again with any sort of criminal offence.

He was in a quandary, and he knew it. He had risked much of his own money, along with most of the bank's, and it had now all but gone. He needed to raise money quickly but was reluctant to sell any of his estate in the north of the county, particularly since the rents from his tenant farmers generated a sizeable annual income.

There was only one thing for it, and much as he hated what he was about to do, he decided he had no choice. He therefore replied to the Newark solicitor, advising him that owing to an unfortunate, but hopefully temporary cash flow problem, he was unable to meet his demand, but suggested that the debt be quickly settled by the offer of his town house in Nottingham, a handsome early-Georgian property standing in a prime position with a large garden and adjacent plot of land. But knowing that its value alone might not match the debt, and not wishing to prolong the affair, he agreed to include all its furniture, much of which was of the finest quality and of considerable value. It was, therefore, with a feeling of relief, but equally one of bitter regret, when he soon received acceptance of his offer.

But Josiah Sidmouth was not a man to admit defeat easily. So, whilst the transfer of the property was being arranged, he was already making plans to recoup its value. He reckoned that if a house and its contents were worth £5,000, then surely a man and his wife would pay a similar sum for the return of their children. Especially if they had a rich uncle who could afford it.

CHAPTER TWENTY-ONE

—

NOTTINGHAM 1833

At long last the cold winds of winter gave way to the warm breezes of spring. In the meadows the crocuses had forced their way up through a blanket of green and trees were bursting forth with early blossom. Abigail stood at the window, peering out onto the wharf. She loved this time of the year, but missed having a garden of her own. The canal side was not an ideal place for the children to play, but she was thrilled in the knowledge that all that was about to change. For her Uncle George and Aunt Alice had recently made a special journey to see her and William, and had offered them the house they had recently acquired in Castle Gate. When they explained how it had come into their possession and who its previous owner had been, she and William were at first reluctant to accept it. But George soon persuaded them to change their minds. He told them that they had no use of it themselves and neither did they need the money they could make by selling it.

They also took them into their confidence and revealed that they had made them both the principal beneficiaries of their wills, so why not take the house now and enjoy the use of it? And Abigail had to admit that it made sense, especially as she had just informed William that she was pregnant with their fifth child. A house in a fashionable part of the town, away from the noise, smells and dangers of the canal side and with its own large garden would be ideal for a growing family. It was only a five minute walk from the wharf, and in any case Benjamin had now all but taken over the running of the business as William needed to devote most of his time to the railway. And since Benjamin was soon to be married, it was agreed that he should remain at the wharf house with his new bride, and Millie would move with the family to Castle Gate.

Preparations for the move were already well in hand, and for over a week Abigail and Millie had been busy packing things away into tea chests. Most of the furniture, however, was to be left at the wharf house, as a wedding present for Benjamin, since the new house was beautifully furnished with many valuable antique pieces.

William, meanwhile, was fully occupied dealing with matters relating to the railway. There were so many things to be done in readiness for its opening which, if all went to plan, would be in a few months time. Construction had been moving at a fast pace recently, once the problems of the previous year had been overcome. The formation for the line was now virtually complete, with all the cuttings and embankments, bridges and culverts almost ready, and the laying of sleepers and rails had already begun at some locations. At the southern end of the line, the transhipment wharf with the canal was now finished. This was situated on the west of the town, towards Lenton, and just outside the town boundary. A new side cut to the canal had been made, where boats could load and unload, with adjacent rail sidings and warehouses and cranes to tranship goods between wagons and boats.

While all this was going on, William and Gilbert had left on another trip to the North East to visit Mr Stephenson's locomotive works at Newcastle. They had already placed an order for four locomotives and wished to view the progress and arrange shipping of these. It was the intention to move them by boat from Tyneside to the Humber, then down the Trent to Nottingham and on to the new wharf at Lenton. But because of their size, they were to be transported in parts and reassembled on arrival. Mr Stephenson had agreed to send two of his engineers to oversee this part of the work.

William had been gone for two days, and Abigail and Millie had almost finished their packing. It was a glorious spring morning, so Abigail suggested to Millie that they should reward themselves with a day off.

'I promised to call and see mother and father this week,' said Abigail. 'They're keen to hear all about the new house, so I think I'll go up there today. Why don't you take the children down to the river? It's such a lovely day, you could take some food and have a picnic and I'll come and join you later. Stay near to the bridge and I'm sure to find you.'

Millie didn't need any persuading, and within the hour had prepared enough food and drink for them all and packed it into a small hamper. While she set off towards the meadows with four very excited children, Abigail walked up to her parents' house. She spent an hour or two there before leaving, then strolled along past St. Mary's, down Hollow Stone and through Plumptre Square onto the London Road. As she walked towards the river, she was in the very best of spirits. The worry over William's loan had now disappeared, they would soon be moving into a fine new house and there was the prospect of a new baby and a wedding to look forward to. A boat passed by on the adjacent canal, low down in the water, fully laden with coal. She recognised it as one of William's, bound no doubt for the Grantham Canal and the Duke of Rutland's wharf serving Belvoir Castle.

Before long she reached the ancient stone bridge over the river, where she left the road and walked down onto the meadow by the water's edge. Groups of people were sitting on the grass, enjoying the sunshine; children were playing and men and boys were fishing. At first she could not see Millie or the children so continued to walk along, but shortly she spotted, lying on the ground, the picnic hamper that Millie had taken with her. Her heart began to pound. Where were they all? Had something happened? And then, suddenly, she heard Millie calling her name, and turned to see her and the twins, close by one of the arches of the bridge. She breathed a sigh of relief, but within seconds her heart was pounding once more as Millie started shouting and waving her arms frantically. And Abigail knew, instinctively, that something was wrong. Quickly she ran back towards the bridge until she reached a breathless and tearful Millie. She was holding the twins, one in each hand; but of Charles and Catherine there was no sign.

'Millie, whatever's the matter? What's happened?'

'Oh, Abigail,' she sobbed hysterically, 'it's Charles and Catherine. I can't find them. I don't know where they are. I think I've lost them.'

'What do you mean? I don't understand. Weren't they with you?'

It took a few moments for Millie to compose herself before she was able to continue. 'We were all sitting on the grass over there, and we'd had something to eat. Then Charles and Catherine said they wanted to play down at the water's edge. I told them to be careful and not to go too near the water and not to wander off. I was keeping an eye on them, but then the twins both started to play up, you know what they're like, and Simon knocked a bottle of water all over Sophia. I was just seeing to them and when I'd finished I looked up but I couldn't see Charles and Catherine anywhere. I shouted their names, then took the twins and started to look for them. I've been right along the bank as far as the canal lock but there's no sign of them. And the lockkeeper said he hadn't seen them either. Oh, Abigail, what are we going to do? I fear they might have gone into the river, and look how fast it's running.'

Although it was a fine sunny day, the river was deeper than usual and running very fast. There had been much rain over the past week and all the swollen tributaries for miles upstream had caused the river to rise. On hearing Millie's news, Abigail sunk to the ground, a sudden feeling of panic and dread gripping her heart. Half an hour before, she had been full of the joys of spring, with not a care in the world. But now she feared that her two eldest children had gone forever and that she would never see them again. The commotion soon brought some of the other bystanders to enquire what the matter was, and two small search parties were quickly arranged, one going one way along the bank, one the other. Someone said they would go and search along the road as they might have wandered up there.

Abigail, now beside herself with worry, ran up and down the bank, crying out desperately for her children. Millie kept hold of the twins, not daring to let them out of her sight, lest they too should come to harm. But it was all to no avail. No trace could be found of Charles and Catherine. A fisherman, sitting close to the bridge, said he had seen a boy and a girl walking up the bank towards the road, but they'd been in the company of a man and a woman and he hadn't taken much notice.

After a while, Millie persuaded Abigail they should return home. They had searched everywhere and there was no sign of either child. Abigail was reluctant to leave, but eventually she agreed to go, knowing there was little more she could now do. They gathered up the picnic hamper and slowly and sadly walked back to the town. All Abigail wanted now was to have William by her side. But she knew he would not be back from Newcastle for another day or two. It was Millie who made the suggestion, and insisted that Abigail and the twins go straight to her parent's house and spend the night there. She knew that Abigail needed to have her family around her, and she promised to come up and let her know the minute William got back.

That night was the longest Abigail could remember. She barely slept. All she could do was ask herself, over and over again, why hadn't she gone with Millie and the children to the river. If she hadn't visited her parents, none of this would have happened. If only she had done that, her two precious children would still be alive. The thought of them being washed down the river to a cold and watery grave was more than she could bear. In time, she assumed, their bodies would be found, but that could be weeks away and she feared that she might never be able to give them a proper burial. Only as the dawn began to break did she finally drift off into sleep, the sheer exhaustion at last taking its toll.

It was almost midday when she was woken by the twins tugging at the bedclothes and asking for her. She picked them up and laid them on the bed beside her, hugging them closely, terrified of letting them out of her sight. The poor mites, she thought. They were totally unaware of the tragedy that had struck and had no idea that they would never see their brother and sister again. She got out of the bed and put on a dressing gown. As she came down the stairs she could hear voices in the parlour and as she entered she found Millie talking to her mother.

'Oh, Abigail, how are you this morning? You look so tired. And it's all my fault, I know it is. If only I'd taken better care of them this would never have happened. Benjamin's been down to the river and he's put the word out amongst all the boatmen to keep a good look out. He thinks it's just possible that they might still be found. He says they could have been washed downstream but then managed to get out onto the bank.'

Abigail sank into a chair, a look of torment and utter hopelessness on her face. 'I hope you're right, Millie, but I doubt it. The river was running so fast that only the strongest swimmer could have survived in it, but Charles and Catherine could barely swim. I fear the worst. But don't blame yourself Millie. It's my fault. I should have come with you. I should never have expected you to look after all the children by yourself. Oh, I wish William were here.'

'When are you expecting him?' asked Mary.

'I don't know. He might be back today, or tomorrow, or the next day. It all depends on how quickly they get their business done.'

'Well, that's settled then, Abigail. You and the twins must remain here. Millie will come and let you know when William returns.'

Abigail didn't reply. She was deep in thought and seemed oblivious to everything around her.

'You'd better get off home now,' said Mary, quietly, to Millie. 'I'll look after her. Just keep us informed if anything happens.'

Millie got up to leave and Mary showed her to the door.

'I will. And the moment William gets back I'll send him over. Oh, I've just remembered, this came today,' and Millie took out an envelope from her coat pocket and handed it to Mary. 'Benjamin found it pushed under the door this morning when he got up, so whoever brought it must have done so very early.'

Millie left and Mary went back into the parlour. The envelope was addressed to Mr & Mrs Daniels, but Mary didn't want to bother Abigail, so she put it on the mantelpiece and went off to see about lunch.

Nicholas had been out since early morning and didn't return until about six o'clock. 'Is there any news, Mary?' he asked as he entered the parlour, where his wife was sitting on a settee, telling the twins a story.

'I'm afraid not. Millie called this morning to see Abigail, but she didn't get up till nearly midday. She's having a sleep right now. Dinner's almost ready but I won't wake her; she can have something later if she wants.'

Mary and Nicholas finished their dinner and Mary put the twins to bed. Nicholas was sitting reading the newspaper and Mary had just come down the stairs when a loud knock came at the door. Nicholas got up to answer it, but by the time he got there Mary had already opened it, and William rushed in, looking drawn and haggard.

'William, my dear, you look exhausted. Come in and sit down.'

'I need to see Abigail first. Where is she?'

'She's upstairs, but she's asleep. I think it might be better if you don't wake her just yet. Go and sit by the fire, and I'll bring you a drink. And have you had anything to eat?'

'No, I only got back home half an hour ago. Gilbert and I left York at six this morning and we've barely eaten since then. Millie's just told me what's happened. I can't believe it. It's terrible. Abigail loved those two so much; I don't know how she's going to cope.'

'Well, I'll get cook to bring you some food and then we'll see if Abigail's awake. I've put the twins to bed. They've asked once or twice where Charles and Catherine are and we said they've had to go away for a little while. We didn't know what else to say to them but sooner or later they'll have to be told. And I'm sure it will be better coming from you and Abigail.'

Despite the fact he was hungry, William could only pick at the food on his plate. More important things were on his mind. He took a drink of beer then stood up. 'I must go and see if Abigail is awake yet,' he said.

'I had a look while you were eating and she was still asleep. Don't you think you'd better wait a little longer?'

'All right. But not too long. I need to speak to her.'

'Of course, William, but you're welcome to stay here the night if you want. Oh, by the way, Millie brought this up,' said Mary, taking the envelope from the mantelpiece and handing it to William. 'I don't know what it is, but she said it was delivered very early this morning.' William looked at the envelope and turned it over.

'I don't recognise the writing,' he said, picking up a knife from the table and cutting open the seal. He took out the single sheet of folded paper and opened it. As he read the short message scribbled thereon his heart missed a beat. He didn't know whether to cry out in joy or in despair, but once the implication of what it said had sunk in, he chose the former. 'They're alive,' he screamed. 'They're still alive,' and, throwing the paper on the table, he leapt up and ran out of the door and up the stairs, shouting as he went, 'Abigail, it's all right, they're still alive.'

Nicholas picked up the piece of paper. It contained a short message, written in black ink in a scribbled, almost childlike hand.

'My God, Mary, listen to this,' and he read aloud the chilling message: *You can have your children back, but it will cost you £5,000. If you agree, hang a white cloth from the top window of your house overlooking*

Canal Street tonight. We'll let you know where to take the money. If you don't, you'll not see them again. It's blackmail, Mary, blackmail and kidnapping,' he exclaimed as he passed the letter over for Mary to read herself. As he did so, they heard footsteps coming down the stairs and William and Abigail came in.

'Here it is,' said William, taking the note from Mary and handing it to Abigail. She took it, and quickly read what William had already told her. Mary glanced at her daughter, who a few hours ago looked as if she had the weight of the world on her shoulders and would never smile again. But what a difference now! How awful, though, that it should take such a dreadful threat against her children to make her happy again.

'Thank God they're safe,' cried Abigail. 'But what are we to do, William? We don't have five thousand pounds. Who's doing this? And why? And how did they get hold of the children?'

'I have my suspicions who might be behind it. But for now we'll have to do as they say; we have no choice. We'll hang the cloth out the window, then at least we'll find out when and where they want the money. As long as we go along with their demands, the children will be safe. But I'll not let whoever it is get away with it. I promise you, Abigail, we'll get the children back, and I'll track down those responsible. And heaven help them when I get hold of them!'

Their plans to stay overnight were now abandoned, and before long William, Abigail and the twins were back home, giving Millie and Benjamin the news. Samuel was also there, having called round to see how Abigail was, and whether William had got back from his visit up north.

'I could keep watch all night if you want,' volunteered Samuel. 'Someone will have to come round to see if you've hung the cloth out the window; and then they'll have to deliver another note about the money.'

'Thanks Samuel,' said William, 'but many people walk along Canal Street and you'd have a hard job identifying the kidnappers. And you can be sure they'll try and get the ransom demand to us without being seen. In any case, it could be days before that happens.'

'I expect you're right. But surely you're not just going to hand over the money without a fight. We ought to try and find out who's behind it and teach them a lesson they won't forget.'

'Don't worry Samuel; that's exactly what I plan to do. But in any case, we haven't got five thousand pounds. And there's not much we can do till we hear from them again. As soon as we do, then we'll work out our next move.'

'Well, let me know the minute you hear anything. Whatever you decide, you can rely on me to help you.'

As Samuel walked back home, thinking about the kidnapping made him furious. William, he knew, would always take a more measured approach. He always preferred to act within the law, although he was never reluctant to face threats head on and stand up and fight for himself and his family when circumstances required it. But Samuel was all for direct action. Sometimes, he thought, you had to take the law into your own hands. So far as he was concerned there could only be one person behind all this, and that was Sidmouth, the man who'd tried to ruin William with the bank loan.

But Samuel knew that Sidmouth would never sully his own hands, and that he'd have someone doing his dirty work for him. And then he remembered that man Giles. He was the one responsible for the other incidents involving William - Bullivant had told him so. Perhaps, he thought, it was time to pay Giles a visit and see what he had to say for himself. Better if he didn't involve William, though. And by the time he reached his lodgings his mind was made up.

'Edward,' he shouted as he walked in, 'come on, put your coat on, we're off to The Kings Head. We've got work to do!'

CHAPTER TWENTY-TWO

—

NOTTINGHAM 1833

By the time they turned the corner from Garners Hill into Narrow Marsh, Samuel had brought Edward up-to-date with the latest news of the kidnapping and ransom demand. 'I'll lay money on it that Sidmouth's behind it and that Giles is mixed up with it too. Remember what Bullivant told us the night we roughed him up a bit, that Giles is a vicious man with some powerful friends. What we need to do is get hold of Bullivant again and make him tell us where Giles hangs out. Then we'll go and have a word with him. I meant to do that before, but never got round to it.'

'But don't forget what Bullivant said about him. Told us nobody ever crosses him and gets away with it, and advised us to keep well away from him.'

'I know. But Giles doesn't scare me. And if he is mixed up with kidnapping Charles and Catherine and threatening to kill them, then it's him that needs to watch his back!'

They soon reached The King's Head, Bullivant's home from home, ordered a couple of pints and seated themselves in a corner of a back bar. It was an hour and two pints later when Samuel suddenly interrupted Edward as he was talking. 'There he is, he's just gone past the door; he must have been in the front bar.' Samuel and Edward quickly got up and went out into the corridor that led to the other rooms and the rear door of the pub. They went out the back into a small cobbled yard. It was getting dark, but there was enough light to see. At the far end of the yard on the left was a brick privy. 'He can't have gone home yet, it's too early for him. He must be in there,' whispered Samuel. Sure enough, after a while he came out, swaying slightly as he buttoned up his trousers. 'You keep watch out here Edward, and don't let anyone into the shit house. Leave this to me. It won't take long.' Samuel walked towards Bullivant who, hearing footsteps, looked up, peering through the gloom. But before he was able to recognise the figure that approached, Samuel had grabbed him by the scruff of his neck, wheeled him round and pushed him back through the open door of the privy. It was small, with barely enough room for one occupant, let alone two, and the one tiny dirt-encrusted window afforded a bare minimum of light. The stench was overpowering. The tub was three-quarters full; perhaps the night-soil men hadn't been round for a number of days.

'Remember me, do you Mr Bullivant?' He looked up at Samuel and squinted. For a few seconds he was in the dark, then suddenly a spark of recognition came back to him.

'Oh, it's you. What do you want?'

'Information, that's all. Just a bit of information. And the sooner you give it, the sooner you can get back to your beer.'

'I told you all you wanted to know before. I ain't got nowt else to say.'

'You'd better have. There's only one question - where can I find Giles?'

'What do you want him for?'

'None of your business. Just tell me where I can find him.'

'You don't want to mix with him; I told you that last time.'

'You're beginning to annoy me. Now, unless you want a close look at the contents of this tub, you'd better start talking.' But even before Bullivant had time to consider the options, Samuel grabbed him by the collar and forced his head down until it vanished into the black gaping hole, his nose almost making contact with the evil-smelling effluent. Bullivant cried out to be released, but Samuel left him there for a bit longer before pulling him out again, spluttering and coughing and gasping for air.

'All right, all right, but for God's sake don't tell him I told you or I'm a dead man. The Town Arms, Plumptre Square. The landlord there's a mate of his. He can get a message to him.'

Samuel released his grip on Bullivant and he staggered off back towards the door of the pub.

'Come on, Edward,' said Samuel, 'no time like the present. I fancy a pint in The Town Arms. Not been there in years!'

It was only a matter of minutes walk away and soon they found themselves supping a pint in the tap room.

'What now?' asked Edward.

'As soon as the landlord's free I'll have a quiet word with him; see if I can find out something about Giles and where we might track him down. We'll have to box clever, though. The good thing is I've not been in here for ages and I don't recognise the landlord, so hopefully he won't know who I am.'

They sat and waited, patiently, until the landlord had stopped serving. Samuel went up to the bar, and leaned over.

'Same again is it?' asked the landlord.

'No, it's just a bit of information I'm after,' he replied in deliberately hushed tones. 'I'm trying to get hold of Bill Giles. I've an important message for him and I was told I can find him in here.'

The landlord viewed Samuel suspiciously. 'Who are you? I don't know you. What do you want with him?'

'Ah, that's something I can't say. I've been entrusted with an important message for him and I'm under strict instructions only to speak to Mr Giles personally. All I need to know is where I can find him.'

'And I'm under strict instructions never to give his address to strangers. But if you want to see him, come back tomorrow evening at about five o'clock and I'll make sure he's here. But don't go wasting his time, mind. He's a busy man and he don't like being messed about. Who shall I say called?'

'Just say a friend of a friend. And make sure he does turn up. Tell him his life depends on it.'

Samuel and Edward downed their beer and left.

'So what now?' asked Edward. 'We can't just confront him in the bar and ask him what he knows about the kidnapping. I bet he'll have some mates with him, just in case of trouble.'

'No, we'll follow him, see where he goes and get him alone. Then we'll make him talk.'

'But we don't know what he looks like. We can hardly ask the landlord to point him out.'

'No need to. We don't know what he looks like but Benjamin does.

Remember when he followed Bullivant that day when he brought those bodies to the wharf to send to London. He saw Giles with Bullivant and said he'd never forget his face. We'll bring him along with us. We won't go in the pub, just hang about outside until he comes out.'

The plan was set. Benjamin was put in the picture, and the next evening the three of them went down to Plumptre Square.

'What's in there?' asked Benjamin, pointing to a leather bag slung over Samuel's shoulder.

'Just a few things I thought might come in handy. Best to be prepared I always think.'

They waited out of sight in an alley on the opposite side of the road. Several men went in and out of the pub, but still nobody who Benjamin recognised. Then, about thirty minutes after the time they said they'd be there, the door opened and a man stepped out. He had the look of someone who was mightily annoyed.

'That's him!' whispered Benjamin, 'without a doubt; I'm certain of it.'

'Right,' said Samuel, 'you get off home, Benjamin. We don't want you getting involved, especially with your wedding coming up! You come with me, Edward and we'll see where he goes.'

They followed him the full length of Narrow Marsh, down Sussex Street into Leen Side, and along Canal Street, keeping just enough distance so as not to arouse his suspicions. They passed the back of William's house, and, as they did so, Samuel noticed that their quarry briefly glanced up at the window where the white cloth had been hung. Just before the entrance to the waterworks, Giles turned up Finkhill Street then left into Mortimer Street. There were fewer people about here, and Samuel and Edward had to drop back somewhat to avoid being seen. They turned into Mortimer Street just in time to see him going into a house at the far end on the right-hand side. Samuel stopped, and said to Edward, 'Let's just wait here for a while and see if he comes out again.' They didn't have long to wait and after about ten minutes he emerged once more and continued to the end of Mortimer Street and onto Castle Road.

'Quick,' said Samuel, 'we don't want to lose him.' And running up the street they turned the corner just in time to see him cross the road and head towards Brewhouse Yard, a notorious meeting place for criminals of every kind. 'Right, Edward, this could be our chance. Just follow me and do exactly as I say.'

Small groups of men and women were loitering outside The Hanging Gate and The Trip to Jerusalem, but, much to Samuel's relief, Giles passed by both pubs and continued on into the yard, between the rows of houses and cottages on either side. High above was the towering sandstone rock upon which stood the now blackened empty shell of Nottingham Castle. The rock itself contained numerous caves and passages, excavated hundreds of years ago from the soft rock. Much of Nottingham was built on sandstone, and many such caves had been dug over the centuries, especially where houses had been built up against outcrops of the rock. Most were used for storage, others for workshops and some even afforded cheap and simple living quarters. At least one passage led from ground level, near to where they now stood, right up and into the castle grounds, believed to have been used as a secret entrance to the old medieval castle in centuries past when it had been a royal retreat. Samuel knew these caves. He had spent many hours in his youth playing here and exploring them, and he knew that many now stood empty and unused.

'Now's our chance,' whispered Samuel to Edward, and he opened the flap of the leather bag and drew out a long steel object. For a brief second, a glint of light reflected off it, and Edward saw it to be a long-bladed knife. Samuel had quickened his pace and they were now only a matter of yards from their man.

'Bill Giles?' asked Samuel, assertively. The man stopped abruptly and slowly turned round. His action had clearly given him away. 'Bill Giles?' repeated Samuel.

'Who wants to know?' he replied in a gruff and gravelly voice. By now, Samuel had approached and was within touching distance of him. Quick as a flash, and before he could move, Samuel placed his left arm firmly round Giles's shoulders, as if greeting an old friend, but with his right hand brought the razor-sharp edge of the blade up against his throat.

'Now, if you want to live, do exactly as I say. Just carry on walking forward slowly. I'll be right behind you with this knife at your back.

One murmur and you're dead.'

Giles did as he was told. They walked to the far end of the yard, past the last cottage and round the base of the castle rock. Just beyond lay the entrance to one of the caves. Samuel manoeuvred Giles in, the point of the knife still in the small of his back. The visibility inside the cave was no more than a few yards, and for a moment or two they all struggled to see until gradually their eyes adjusted to the dim light.

'There's some candles and a tinder box in the bag,' said Samuel, handing it to Edward. 'Light one up so we can see what we're doing. And there's a length of rope. We'll need that too.'

The candle was lit and they were now able to see much more clearly. The cave widened out, and at the far end a narrow tunnel could be seen, vanishing deep into the heart of the rock. Samuel steered Giles further into the tunnel, which continued for some distance, forming a passageway leading to other caves on both sides. Samuel selected one of these, where he knew they could neither be seen nor heard from anyone on the outside. On one wall, above a ledge cut out of the rock, were some rusty iron hooks, indicating that this cave had probably been used as a store room in years gone by.

'Sit him down there, Edward, and tie him up to those hooks, good and tight.' Edward took the rope from the bag, and in no time at all Giles was trussed up like a Christmas Goose. Samuel took the candle and held it close to Giles's face. Benjamin had described him as an evil-looking sod. He wasn't wrong, thought Samuel. He was a man of about fifty, of medium height, well-built, clean-shaven and with close-cropped hair. His nose had clearly been broken and his cauliflower ears suggested that he might have been a fighter in his younger days. There were at least three visible scars on his face and his lips bore a permanent sneer. But it was his piercing eyes, ice-cold and steel-grey that, more than anything, suggested he was a man you would not want to cross.

But evil as he might be, Samuel was not impressed. He could look after himself and was not easily intimidated. And his anger at what had happened to his niece and nephew made him even more determined.

'You still haven't answered my question. Are you Bill Giles?'

'What if I am? What's it to you?'

'Just answer the question.'

'Who I am is no concern of yours. But I never forget a face. And once I get out of here you'll soon find out what I'm capable of. You're going to have to watch your back everywhere you go.'

Considering that he was trussed up and outnumbered two to one, the man showed a remarkable degree of arrogant self-confidence. But he was beginning to annoy Samuel, who decided it was time to get tough. Picking up the knife, he placed its point a hair's breadth away from Giles's left eyeball.

'And what makes you think you're going to get out of here? From now on, I ask the questions and you answer them, unless you want me to cut your eyes out. And don't think I won't.' Then, just to prove he meant business, Samuel placed the knife above Giles's right eyebrow, and slowly drew it across his forehead until little trickles of blood began to drip down his face. For the first time, the man seemed somewhat apprehensive. The realisation that Samuel wasn't bluffing had apparently sunk in.

'All right, so what if I am Bill Giles? What do you want with me?'

'I want to know what's happened to my niece and nephew. They were kidnapped a few days ago and now someone's demanding five thousand pounds for their lives. And I think you're involved.'

'Don't know what you're talking about. Nothing to do with me.'

'Oh, I think it is, Mr Giles, just like the bodies you tried to send down to London by canal; just like the men you tried to implicate with the burning of the silk mill at Beeston. I know for a fact you were mixed up with those incidents. Then there was the old man, Walter Blundy, found drowned in the canal. I bet you had a hand in that too. And all these things had one thing in common; they were aimed at harming my brother, William Daniels. And I don't like it when people upset my family. You thought you could get away with it, but you reckoned without me. You probably didn't even know I existed. Probably thought William was a bit of a soft touch. Well, now you've met his younger brother. And I'm no soft touch. I know all about your reputation. A lot of people are terrified of you, but I'm not.

'So, Giles, you're going to tell me everything I want to know, and if you don't, you'll never be seen again; at least not alive. I believe there's still a demand in the hospitals for fresh corpses for dissection, and I'd bet you'd make a fine specimen. How ironic that would be, especially after your own involvement with the body snatchers! Or perhaps you might happen to fall into the canal one dark night, just like Walter Blundy. I'm sure that could be arranged. On the other hand, we could just leave you here to rot. It could be years before anyone found your body. So start talking. Where are the children? And don't lie. You won't be going anywhere until they're back home safe and sound.'

Giles knew he was in an impossible situation. He realised that Samuel posed a serious threat, and he had no desire to lose his own life just to protect the man who was paying him.

'You'll find them in Mortimer Street, house with a dark green door on the left just round the corner from Castle Road.'

'Well, you'd better start praying no harm has come to them. Edward, you go straight round to William's and give him the news, but don't go into too much detail about how we found out. I'll explain all that later. I suggest you take a couple of constables with you to Mortimer Street. Once the children are safe, come back here, and then, Mr Giles, we might think about letting you go. Although there's just one more thing we need you to tell us. Who was it put you up to this? We know all about you and how you get paid to do other people's dirty work. So, just who's been paying you?'

'I've told you all I'm going to. You know where the kids are. That's all I'm saying.'

'Really? I think we'll see about that. Edward, you get off to William's. I want to have a quiet word with our friend here, see if I can't loosen his tongue.'

What happened next, Samuel never revealed to anyone, not even to Edward. But suffice it to say that it didn't take him long to persuade Giles to reveal that it was Josiah Sidmouth who had paid him to arrange the kidnapping, and that he was also behind the other incidents designed to harm William.

Within the hour Edward had given the news to William, and along with the constables they made their way to the house on Mortimer Street. Dusk was beginning to fall as they banged on the door, which was opened by a severe and mean-looking woman. She was soon joined by an equally stern-looking man who had been heard, as he approached the door, demanding to know what all the noise was about. But once he saw the two constables on the doorstep his demeanour changed and he went strangely quiet. The constables did not wait for an invitation but marched straight into the house. It was a dank, miserable place, poorly furnished and smelling of damp and decay. A dim oil lamp stood on a table in the living room. When questioned, the couple, a Mr and Mrs Cutts, denied all knowledge of the affair. William produced the ransom demand he had received and showed it to them. Mrs Cutts stood firm in her denial, but William detected a look of panic on the man's face. They were still pleading their innocence as a search of the premises began. The house was three storeys high but narrow, with two rooms on each floor. It didn't take them long to search all the rooms, but of the children there was no sign. Every cupboard was opened, every bed looked under, but to no avail. The constables were on the verge of going, believing that they were on a wild-goose chase, but Edward was not satisfied. He had been there when Giles had spilt the beans and had no doubt that he was telling the truth. The mood Samuel had been in, he doubted that Giles would have risked making the story up.

'They must be here somewhere,' Edward said. 'Come along, William, we'll have another look.' They went up the stairs to the top floor and worked their way downwards, re-examining every room, but could find no place where two children might have been hidden. The back room on the ground floor was a small scullery and up against the rear wall stood a tall double cupboard. This had already been searched, but Edward opened the two full length doors again. There were two rows of shelves, one on each side, stretching from top to bottom. The right-hand side was full with pots and pans, bottles and jars, the other side completely empty. But again there was no way that a baby, let alone two children, could be hidden in there.

'I'm very sorry, Mr Daniels,' said one of the constables, 'but there's nothing more we can do. You've searched the premises yourselves from top to bottom and you must agree there's no sign of your children. We must assume you've been given some wrong information.'

Reluctantly, they all left the house, and the door was slammed shut behind them. The constables set off down the street back towards the town centre while William and Edward walked round the corner into

Castle Road.

'Are you sure we've been to the right house, Edward?'

'Positive. The house with the green door, the one we saw Giles go in. And the way your Samuel was threatening him he wouldn't dare not tell us the truth. He made it quite clear to Giles what would happen if we didn't get Charles and Catherine back safely. Threatened to leave him there to rot, and he can't escape from that cave, not the way I tied him up ...' Suddenly, Edward stopped in mid-sentence. 'That's it! Of course, a *cave!* Follow me, William, I think I know where they are.' And turning round, he ran back into Mortimer Street. 'Quick, William, you go after those constables, they can't have got very far. I'll stop here and make sure Cutts and his wife don't get away with the children. If I'm right, they'll be making plans right now to move them.'

William did as Edward told him and in a few minutes was back with the constables.

'So what's this all about?' one of them asked.

'I think I know where the children might be hidden,' replied Edward. 'You remember that cupboard in the scullery. Didn't you think it odd the way the shelves on one side were all full but those on the other side completely empty? And didn't you notice how unusually clean the empty shelves were compared with everything else in the house? Not only that, but when we looked in there I thought I could feel a draught coming from behind. Now it's dawned on me. These houses back onto an outcrop of sandstone. I'll bet a lot of them have got storage caves dug out the rock.'

Edward didn't wait for the constables to act, but knocked loudly on the door. There was no response. He knocked again, thumping the door until it visibly shook on its hinges. They waited. Nothing. For a third time he laid into the door. It would have been impossible for anyone inside not to have heard the incessant hammering.

'They must still be in there. Surely they can't have escaped,' said Edward, as he turned the handle. The door was locked but he didn't wait for the constables' permission, and with all the power he could muster he aimed his boot at the door just below the handle. There was a deafening crack as the timber around the lock gave way, and the door burst open. Edward was first in, and headed directly for the scullery followed closely by William, whilst the constables searched the upstairs rooms yet again. Edward went straight to the cupboard and opened the doors. Everything was exactly as it had been. He leaned over and tapped on the rear panel of the cupboard.

'Hear that, William? It's hollow,' and picking up an empty stone jar from one of the shelves, he thrust it at the thin wooden panel, which immediately split, leaving a gaping hole. 'There, look. What did I tell you?'

Behind the cupboard, instead of a wall, was the opening into a dark recess. The rear panel was hinged and formed a door. William opened this secret door, revealing the entrance to a cave. Edward ran back into the sitting room and picked up the oil lamp which still burned on the table. The constables had now returned, having found no trace of life upstairs, and the four men entered the cave. It was fairly small and showed signs of having been used as a store room, but was now empty. In one corner some steps led downwards. They started to descend these and, as they did so, they heard the distinct banging of a door, the sound clearly coming from below them. Edward, lamp in hand, led the way down the steps, which turned a corner and opened out into another cave. As they entered it, Edward swung the lamp round to illuminate every nook and cranny. This cave was much larger than the one above, and in the centre a thick pillar of sandstone, about four feet in diameter, had been left to support the roof. Around this pillar a ledge, or seat, had been left when the cave had been excavated, and other similar seats were cut into the rock around the sides of the cave. William had seen this same layout in other caves in the town, some attached to pubs and known to have been used for cock fighting. Some, it was reckoned, still were.

In a far corner of the cave was a solid wooden door. 'They must have escaped through there,' said one of the constables. 'We'll go and have a look.'

Edward continued to swing the lamp and, as he did so, William suddenly noticed something jutting out behind the pillar. Grabbing the lamp from Edward he went round to see what it was.

'Edward, look, they're here!' William cried, ecstatically. 'Charles and Catherine. We've found them!' The two children were lying on the ledge, and it was Catherine's legs that William had seen. They were lying head-to-head, silent and still. Edward looked down as William picked Catherine up and cradled her in his arms. He feared the worst, for neither child made a sound. He was certain they were dead. Edward went to pick up Charles, and as he did so he felt a faint breath against his cheek.

'He's breathing, William. He's still alive! Look, Catherine's the same. They're not dead, they must have been drugged.'

At that moment the constables returned, both relieved and delighted at the sight that met their eyes. 'Thank God they're safe,' said one of them. 'You'd better get them back home. We'll sort things out here. That door leads to a yard at the back of Castle Terrace. They can't have got far though. Leave it to us. We'll put out a hue and cry. We'll soon find them.'

William didn't need telling twice. 'Right, Edward, let's get these two back home as quickly as we can, and I'll send for a doctor.'

As he and Edward hurried back to the wharf house, all he could think of was that his children were safe. He couldn't wait to see Abigail and tell her the good news. As soon as he opened the door she came running to meet them. Her joy was overwhelming. A few days before she was convinced that Charles and Catherine were both dead. Then came the news that they were alive, but would die unless the ransom was paid. And now here they were, safely back home. But they were still unconscious. William sent Benjamin to fetch the doctor and Abigail put the children to bed. They were still waiting for the doctor when Samuel turned up. Edward took him quietly on one side and quickly explained what had happened.

'What about Giles?' asked Edward. 'What have you done with him?'

'Oh, he'll not be going far,' replied Samuel. 'I thought it might do him good to have a bit of time to himself to think things over. We'll go back and release him later. Or maybe we won't. Or perhaps we should wait until the Cutts have been caught and see if they implicate him. Then we can let the authorities deal with him.'

A little while later the doctor arrived and examined the children. 'They don't appear to have suffered any serious harm,' he said reassuringly. 'They're just in a very deep sleep. You were right, they have been drugged; laudanum I expect. But it's nothing that a good night's rest won't cure. I'll call back tomorrow to see how they are.'

By the following morning Charles and Catherine had almost recovered from the effects of the concoctions given to them by the Cutts. They could remember little of their time imprisoned in the house on Mortimer Street, and it appeared they had been kept drugged for most of the time, presumably to keep them quiet. They did, however, remember being approached by a man and a woman down by the river, who were very friendly and gave them some gingerbread, and told them that they had a strange animal in a cage. They said they had brought it back from a foreign land, and it was now in their carriage which was up on the bridge, and if they came straight away they could have a look at it. Full of curiosity, they had gone along with them. They recalled climbing up into the carriage, but after that could remember little more.

Later that day came the news that Mr and Mrs Cutts had been arrested. Enquiries with neighbours revealed they had a daughter in Bulwell whom they sometimes visited. At first she denied having seen her parents for over a month, but persistent questioning and the threat of dire consequences soon made her change her story. She admitted they had come to see her the day before, in a state of great agitation, but could not explain why. She said they had then gone to visit some friends nearby; and it was here that they were apprehended. When they realised the game was up, the Cutts were only too ready to name names and try and lay the blame elsewhere, and that of Bill Giles figured prominently in their defence.

'What are we going to do about Giles?' asked Edward. 'We can't just leave him there for ever.'

'I expect the authorities will be out looking for him right now,' replied Samuel. 'Perhaps we should give them a hand. I think, Edward, it's time we took Mr Giles for a walk!'

There were some quizzical looks from bystanders that evening at the sight of a dishevelled-looking individual, his hands tied behind his back and a rope around his neck, being led by two young men through the streets of Nottingham towards the Town Hall. And the constable on duty was most surprised, but also very appreciative, when he was informed that this was the man now wanted in connection with the kidnapping.

The news of the incident soon spread throughout the town, even before the weekly newspapers were able to carry reports. But one of the last men to hear of the affair was the very man responsible for having instigated it.

News did not travel fast to his country estate near Retford, and it was not until he received his copy of the Nottingham Journal the following week that Josiah Sidmouth learned of the arrest of a Mr and Mrs Cutts and a Mr Bill Giles, all of whom were now languishing in prison awaiting trial on a charge of abduction and kidnap. But their fate did not concern him. What did concern him was whether his part in the crime would be revealed. He was as ignorant of Mr and Mrs Cutts as they were of him. Giles had obviously recruited them to carry out the kidnap, so he was the only one who could pose a threat. But he had known Giles for some time, and, despite his reputation, Josiah believed him to be a man who knew when to keep his mouth shut. Revealing Josiah's part in the affair would not save him, and he had been well paid to do the job. Kidnapping was rarely a capital offence and a gaol term was the most likely outcome. But Josiah needed to be quite certain, and so, despite Giles's present incarceration, he managed to get a message to him promising him another £25 for his silence. What Josiah did not know, of course, was that there were others who did know of his involvement, and could prove to be far more harmful to him than the forces of the law.

The trial was due to begin four weeks later. But by a bizarre coincidence, Mr and Mrs Cutts, who had been kept in separate cells, were both found dead a week before the trial could start. An immediate inquest was held and in both cases death was found to be due to arsenic poisoning, with a verdict that both had taken their own lives. It was never satisfactorily explained how they came to be in possession of the poison, and their only two visitors, their daughter and a friend, vehemently denied supplying it. The authorities seemed reluctant to pursue the matter further, with the result that when Giles eventually did appear in the dock, the principal witnesses for the prosecution were now lying cold in their grave. So, for the want of evidence, the case was dismissed and Giles went free.

There were, of course, two others who could have come forward to give evidence of Giles's guilt, but Samuel and Edward preferred to do things their own way, and they knew who was ultimately responsible for the kidnapping. William and Abigail were, naturally, incensed that the man responsible had walked free, and could not understand why Samuel seemed so unconcerned.

'Don't worry about Giles,' he said to them when news arrived of his release. 'He'll not bother you anymore, believe me.'

'And how can you be so certain?' queried William.

'Some things are better left unsaid. You'll just have to trust me; I think it's better that you don't know.'

Later that night, over supper, Abigail and William were discussing recent events.

'What do you think Samuel meant when he said that some things are better left unsaid and that it's better we don't know?'

William pondered for a few moments before replying. 'I've known Samuel since he was a baby. He's got into some real scrapes in his time and I don't expect he'll ever change. He does like to do things his own way, but one thing's absolutely clear in my mind - his heart's in the right place. We're lucky to have him on our side. He promised us Giles won't bother us anymore and I trust him. So perhaps we should just accept what he said and leave things at that. I know he'll be as good as his word.'

And indeed he was, because just as William and Abigail were finishing their supper, in a quiet part of the town Samuel was having a few choice words with Bill Giles. He wasn't used to being told what to do by anyone, but by the time Samuel had finished with him he was under no illusion that he had met his match. A month later, when Samuel made some discreet enquiries, he learned that Giles had moved to London. And as far as is known, he was never seen in Nottingham again.

CHAPTER TWENTY-THREE

—

NOTTINGHAM 1833

Two weeks later William and Abigail moved to their new home. Charles and Catherine had fully recovered from their ordeal with no visible signs of harm, but were now far more wary of strangers. Shortly after their move, Mary and Nicholas called round to see how they had settled in. William was out on railway business, the line being almost ready, and last minute arrangements were being made for the planned opening. Abigail and Millie were busy tidying up after the move while the children were happily playing in the garden.

It was strange for Nicholas, seeing his daughter living in a house he knew so well, for he had often been here when Josiah, once a good friend and business partner, had owned it. But that was before the incident involving Abigail which had led to the final rift between the two men. How ironic, thought Nicholas, that had Josiah been successful in winning Abigail's hand, she would already have been the mistress of this very house. But would she have been happy? And what sort of husband would he have made? His subsequent behaviour hardly boded well. And then Nicholas began to ponder how often the course of one's life can be affected by the merest chance meeting. Abigail was now married to a man whom Nicholas admired for his devotion to his family, a man born to poverty but who, through sheer hard work and determination, had become a successful businessman. Yet at one time he had sought to have him arrested for the arson of one of his properties. But if William had not chanced to pass by his house one Christmas morning just as Abigail stepped out the door, they might never have met.

'Nicholas, you haven't heard a word I've said! Are you going deaf?' asked Mary, somewhat irritated.

'Oh, I'm sorry my dear. I was miles away.'

'I was just telling Abigail that we're expecting Peter back next week on leave. He'll be astonished when he hears everything that's happened since he was last here. Mind you, that was over a year ago.'

'And when he does get back,' said Abigail, 'I intend to let him know in no uncertain terms just what his old friend Josiah has been up to.'

'But you can't be certain, dear. We don't know for sure he was behind the kidnapping.'

'Mother, I do sometimes think you are a little naive. It's not just the kidnapping. We know it was Josiah who tried to bankrupt us with his phoney loan, and then there were all those other little incidents over the years.'

'I know, dear. I'm not trying to defend him, but he's never been charged and brought to trial for any of those offences.'

'Which proves just how devious he is in not getting caught! But there's no doubt in my mind, or in William's. You should have heard what Samuel told us about that man Giles. I know Samuel can be a little unconventional in his methods and he won't say exactly what took place between them, but it seemed to work and Giles eventually admitted to him that Josiah *was* behind it all.'

'That's as maybe, but don't be too hard on Peter. He's not to blame for anything Josiah might have done. In any case, I don't expect he's even spoken to Josiah for years, what with him being overseas so much.'

'I wouldn't put money on it, mother!'

Abigail's words were well founded. Of course, they were given in jest, for she knew that her mother never had been a gambler. But had she been, and had she put money on her son not having been in contact with Josiah, she would have lost. In fact, as Mary (who, unlike her husband, had never previously visited Josiah's former residence) was enthusiastically inspecting each and every room of her daughter's new home, her son had just arrived back at the headquarters of his regiment, following a long posting to the Indian subcontinent. And as soon as he had landed in England, Peter had written to Josiah at his ancestral home to tell him of his intended visit.

A few days later he had set off towards Nottinghamshire. But it was not to his parents' home that he headed first, but to the north of the county, and as dusk was falling Peter found himself riding down the long driveway towards the imposing mansion, just as he had done over a year before. But this time there was no Josiah to greet him. He tugged hard at the bell pull, and eventually the door was opened by the butler.

Peter soon established that Josiah was away on family business, but was expected back home sometime within the next day or so. He was in a quandary. He wanted to see him before he went to Nottingham, to find out what had transpired since their last meeting and the outcome of the plan to lend William the money. Should he go back to Nottingham now then come back in a couple of days? He was tired after his long ride, it was getting late, and if he did so he would only have to return north again.

However, the butler knew Peter from his previous visits and agreed that he could stay until Josiah returned. Following a meal, which the cook kindly provided for him, Peter decided to have an early night. This was the first time he had slept in a comfortable bed for over three months, the first time, in fact, since he had been royally and intimately entertained by the daughter of a lesser Indian prince who believed he had everything to gain by being on friendly terms with the British. Had the prince become aware of the extent to which his daughter had enthusiastically sought to cement the entente, then diplomatic relations might have become somewhat strained. Fortunately for his daughter, and even more so for Peter, he had remained in blissful ignorance of the liaison.

The next morning Peter did not rise until late. He had some lunch and then, it being a warm sunny day, decided to have a stroll round the estate. The parkland extended for a considerable distance in all directions and it was an hour or two before he arrived back at the house. Having some time to while away before dinner, he went into the library to see what he might find to amuse himself. Most of the books were old tomes on subjects such as philosophy, ancient history and religion and were of little interest to him. He could not believe that they were really to Josiah's taste either and assumed they must have been acquired by an earlier ancestor. Unable to find anything that really interested him, he sat down in a comfortable armchair against the window, affording a fine view of the terrace and gardens. To one side of the chair was a small table, upon which lay a newspaper. He picked it up and found it to be a two-week old copy of the Nottingham Journal. He turned the pages, glancing randomly at the closely packed columns of news, both national and local, when his attention was suddenly drawn to an item that had been marked with a small cross in the margin. And then he noticed the name 'Bill Giles' which seemed to jump out from the mass of tiny print. At the top of the column was the heading *Abduction Case Dismissed*. Peter recalled Josiah telling him about a man by the name of Bill Giles, and intrigued, he read in full the report that followed:

At the Town Hall on Wednesday last, the case against Mr Bill Giles on a charge of child abduction was dismissed by Mr Justice Bridgewater for want of evidence. Readers may recall the detailed report that appeared in our issue of 26th April of the abduction and imprisonment of the two elder children, a boy and a girl, of Mr William Daniels a canal carrier and wharfinger of Nottingham. The children had gone missing whilst in the company of an aunt and their two younger siblings close to the river at Trent Bridge, and it was at first thought that the unfortunate children had been swept away by the currents, the river at that time being considerably swollen. However, Mr Daniels subsequently received a note demanding the sum of £5,000 for their safe return. Acting on information received, the children's father, accompanied by his uncle, went to an address in Mortimer Street, where the children were found concealed in a cave at the rear of the house, having been plied with a solution of laudanum. The occupants of the property, a Mr and Mrs Cutts, were soon traced to the house of a neighbour of their daughter at Bulwell, and were promptly arrested. They quickly admitted the offence, but stated in their defence that they had been paid to carry out the abduction by a Mr Bill Giles, who had also made certain threats against them should they refuse. He too was subsequently delivered up to the constables, but denied any part in the affair. The trial of the three accused was set for 22nd May, but a week earlier, both Mr and Mrs Cutts, who were detained in separate cells at the House of Correction, were found dead from the effects of arsenic poisoning, the assumption being made that this was the result of suicide. As the two deceased were the only witnesses against Mr Giles, Mr Justice Bridgewater said that he had no alternative but to dismiss the case and release the accused.

Peter could barely believe what he had read. It must be his niece and nephew who had been abducted, for he wasn't aware of another canal carrier named William Daniels. He read the article again, to satisfy himself of the details. And then, an awful possibility began to dawn on him. Could Josiah have been behind these events? Peter knew full well of his obsession with seeking vengeance against William. He himself had even helped him with his plan to try and ruin William financially, but having been abroad for so long he had no idea what the outcome had been. This was one of the reasons why he had come to see Josiah before going back to Nottingham, to find out what had happened. But nothing had ever been mentioned about harming the children.

Peter had also observed over the last few years just how much Josiah's resolve had hardened and that he appeared even more bitter than ever, to the point at which he had become completely obsessed with his desire for revenge. This one aim seemed to have taken over his life. But would he really go to the extent of abducting two young children and threatening their lives? Peter decided he had to know.

But he had to wait another day, for it was not until late the following afternoon that Josiah eventually arrived back. The two men, old friends for many years, greeted each other cordially enough, although Peter sensed that Josiah appeared somewhat distant, as if he had something on his mind.

'Well, this is a surprise, Peter. I didn't expect you. I had no idea you were home on leave.'

'We only got back from India last week. As soon as I landed I sent you a letter to say I'd be coming to visit, but it must have arrived after you'd left.'

'Yes, I've been up north visiting some distant relatives; family matters. But how about you? You must tell me what you've been up to.'

Over dinner the two men talked at length and Peter gave a full account of his travels and adventures since their last meeting. But the one subject he wanted to hear about had so far not been raised. He waited, hoping that Josiah would bring it up, but he didn't. Peter decided he had waited long enough.

'What happened with your loan to Daniels? Did everything work out as you planned?' he asked, but he could tell from Josiah's expression what the answer was going to be.

'There was nothing wrong with the planning. It would have worked perfectly if it hadn't been for that interfering old jumped-up boatman from Newark, George Jackson,' he replied, forgetting it was Peter's uncle he was insulting. 'If he hadn't come galloping to the rescue, Daniels would have been finished by now.'

Although he seemed reluctant to discuss the affair, Peter was determined to find out just what had occurred. At last, after much persuasion, Josiah gave a blow-by-blow account of what had transpired.

'And there you have it. Daniels is still in business, and to add insult to injury he's now living in luxury in my house on Castle Gate.'

'So, what do you intend to do now? You were adamant you were going to ruin him. Surely you're not going to let the whole thing drop, especially not now he's got your house?'

For the first time since they had become acquainted, Josiah detected a hint of sarcasm in Peter's tone. 'Oh, I'll destroy Daniels, one way or another, have no fears about that. I've plenty of other ideas.'

'You've not tried anything else then?'

Josiah hesitated for a moment before replying. 'Why do you ask? I've told you I've plenty of other ideas. It's just a matter of waiting for the right opportunity.'

'Well, it seems somebody else has also taken a dislike to him. I've just been reading an item in your Nottingham Journal about the kidnapping of two of his children, my niece and nephew. Fortunately, they were rescued before any harm came to them. But that man Bill Giles was involved. What was it you said about him? Oh yes, I remember – "not a pleasant chap, but if ever you need something underhand to be done, he's the man to arrange it … never gets his own hands dirty but has plenty of others to do his work for him … as long as he gets his money you get the job done, no questions asked and no secrets revealed …"'

Peter looked Josiah directly in the eye. 'Tell me honestly, Josiah, were you behind it? You know I have no time for Daniels, but it was my own sister's children who were abducted. I could never condone that.'

'Come now, Peter, you don't really believe that I would do such a thing, do you?' replied Josiah, dismissively.

'I really don't know what to believe anymore, Josiah. It's strange that this should take place so soon after your other plan failed. And that man Giles was involved, too. Very well, Josiah, look me in the eye and tell me you *weren't* involved.' Peter could tell that Josiah was becoming irritated. He'd seen him like this once or twice before, but now he was also on the defensive.

'I'm sorry, Peter. I've said all I intend to say on the subject, and as far as I'm concerned the matter's at an end. And if that's all our friendship means to you, then I suggest you leave.'

Peter realised he was wasting his time, and whilst Josiah had not actually denied being the instigator of the abduction, Peter believed he now had the answer to his question.

Early the following morning he rose, saddled his horse and set off for Nottingham. He arrived back at his parents' home about midday. They were overjoyed to see him after such a long absence, and after lunch they all settled down to swap stories and bring each other up-to-date with their latest news. Of course, Nicholas and Mary had much to relate about the sensational events concerning Abigail and William, not only the recent abduction of Charles and Catherine but the previous attempt to bankrupt them. But Peter did not reveal what he already knew, and even whom he suspected might be the ringleader. And as soon as Abigail heard that Peter had arrived back, she called to see him.

It was a rather strained meeting. She was pleased that her brother had returned home once more, safe and sound, after a long spell overseas. But there was much she wanted to talk to him about, and was determined to find out how much he knew. And so, having spent a little time discussing the usual trivialities, and at last finding herself alone with Peter, she broached the subject.

'I expect mother and father have already told you about our own adventures since you were last here.'

'Yes,' said Peter somewhat sheepishly. 'It must have been dreadful for you all. I do hope that's an end to your troubles.'

'Did you know we've moved into Josiah's house in Castle Gate? And the circumstances under which we came to be living there? And do you know whom I believe was behind the abduction? Have mother and father told you that, too?'

'Well, they did mention that you thought Josiah was involved.'

'Thought! No, Peter, we don't *think*, we *know!* The man's mad. He even purchased a bank so he could lend William the money he needed for the railway. Then he tried to ruin us by suddenly demanding it back at short notice, thinking he could force us to sell the business, our livelihood. Fortunately, Uncle George came to our rescue. Not only that, but he was able to turn the tables on Josiah, and it was *his* business that went down. That's how we came into possession of his house. I know Josiah of old, and that would really have upset him. Which is why he planned the children's abduction. Of course, he managed to avoid being charged with any offence, but Samuel is adamant that Josiah was behind it. It was Samuel and Edward who tracked down that man Giles, and he confessed all to Samuel. Don't ask me how he managed to elicit that bit of information from him, but I believe him. I know you've been friends with Josiah for years, and I know what you think about William. You've never made any secret of it, ever since we eloped and you and Josiah came to hunt us down. It's obvious Josiah's been out to ruin William. He must have talked to you about it, so, Peter, what do you have to say for yourself? Just how much do you know? You are my brother and I really don't want to fall out with you, but you must tell me the truth.'

For what seemed like an age, Peter said nothing. Abigail could tell that her comments had hit a raw nerve and made him think. But at last, after taking a deep breath, he spoke.

'I knew that Josiah wanted to avenge himself for what had happened. He blamed William for his being transported. It hurt his pride and he was determined to get even. I knew about his plan to try and ruin William's business, but I told him I was uneasy because it would affect you and the children. But Josiah convinced me that mother and father would never see you suffer, that it was William he really wanted to harm. But I had already gone overseas before he put that plan into action. If I had still been here I might have been able to stop him. And as for the abduction, I had no knowledge of that at all. I was thousands of miles away at the time. In fact, I'll tell you something I haven't told mother and father. I was at Josiah's earlier this week. I called to see him before coming here. He was away when I arrived, but before he returned I found a newspaper with an account of the abduction and the trial that collapsed after the death of two of the accused. You have to believe me, Abigail, I swear I knew nothing about it. If I had, I would have done everything I could to stop him. I challenged him to deny he had anything to do with it, but I couldn't get a straight answer from him. I think Josiah was responsible. Anyway, we ended up disagreeing and he as good as threw me out. I left first thing yesterday morning without speaking to him again. When you said he's mad, you were right. I have noticed, over the years, how much more bitter he has become. I don't think I shall ever see him again.'

Abigail realised that it had been hard for Peter to own up to what he knew. But she was relieved that he had, at last, been honest with her. She felt that a great weight had been lifted from her shoulders, but not, she suspected, as heavy as the one lifted from Peter's. She had managed to rid herself of Josiah's unwanted attentions years ago. Then her father had seen sense and severed all his business connections with him. And now, at long last, Peter had seen the truth.

Before returning to his regiment and a posting to Canada, Peter went to visit Abigail and the children in their new home. She was happy that he had called, but was sorry that William was out that morning. She hoped that now Peter had come to see Josiah in his true colours he might, after all, get to know and like William. Ah well, she thought, as he left, that will have to wait till next time.

CHAPTER TWENTY-FOUR

—

NOTTINGHAM 1833

At the railway company offices in the town there was a great deal of excitement. News had been received that a large seagoing barge, containing the components for the four locomotives ordered by the company, had just left the Humber and was now heading down the Trent. It was expected to arrive at Nottingham within a few days, where the contents were to be transhipped to narrower barges for the short journey along the canal and through the town to the new railway wharf at Lenton, and preparations were at once put in hand to have men and machinery ready to unload them the minute they arrived. Engineers were travelling with the locomotives to oversee their reassembly, and the plan was to have at least two of them ready as soon as possible, for the company was keen to open the line and start earning money. If all went according to plan, the railway would be open for traffic by the end of September, to be preceded by a grand opening ceremony to which the most important local public figures and entrepreneurs would be invited.

The line itself was now complete, and all the rails had been laid. A firm of wagon builders had been busy at the southern end of the line, using one of the warehouses there as a temporary factory. Timber had been arriving by canal for a number of months, along with sets of iron wheels, axles and frames from the ironworks at Butterley. The new mine at Hucknall had been in production for several weeks and a large amount of coal was already stockpiled, waiting to be sent down to Nottingham, then onwards by canal. And many of the manufacturers along the route had already pledged to use the railway once it opened.

It had not, initially, been the intention to convey passengers over the railway, as the company believed that freight would be by far the most profitable cargo on what they anticipated would be a very busy line. But having noted the success of passenger trains on the Liverpool and Manchester Railway, the directors had had second thoughts, and so they ordered the construction of three passenger carriages which could be attached to goods trains, when it was considered worthwhile. These would also be available for the directors' periodic inspections of the line, but more immediately were to be used on the opening day by some of the more important local dignitaries, such as the Lord Mayor and members of the town council. The other invited guests were to be accommodated in open goods wagons which would be suitably furnished for the occasion.

For the opening ceremony the company had decided to run a special train hauled by two of the locomotives, carrying the invited party from Nottingham to the northern terminus at Linby, then back to Hucknall, where twenty fully laden coal wagons would be attached and the complete train would then return to Nottingham. This inaugural train was to be greeted on its return by the town band, and, following the usual speeches, a large banquet would be held, using one of the warehouses as a dining hall. Meanwhile, all the navvies and other workmen who had been involved with the line's construction were to enjoy a hog roast and free ale, served on land adjoining the canal.

The progress of the new railway had attracted much interest, which intensified now that the project was nearing its completion. And when news got around that the barge conveying the locomotives was approaching Nottingham, a crowd soon gathered by the river to watch them being transhipped into four canal boats for the last leg of their journey.

Most residents of the town had never seen a steam locomotive, and hordes of curious onlookers began to gather each day at the new railway wharf at Lenton, to try and catch a glimpse of these extraordinary machines taking shape.

The two engineers sent to oversee their construction were skilled craftsmen, Mark, the senior man, and Luke, his junior, always referred to by their workmates back home as the 'two apostles'. With the help of some locally hired hands, and by working long hours, the first engine was reassembled and ready for testing in less than three weeks. The boiler was filled with water and a fire lit in the firebox. As the spectators watched with mounting anticipation, and the company directors with some trepidation, the water slowly began to heat up until little wisps of steam began to appear from its chimney. The least concerned men present were Mark and Luke who, satisfied that everything was in order and knowing it would be a while before sufficient pressure was available to move the engine, had retired to take some refreshments and have a deserved rest.

Eventually, as the steam pressure rose, the engine slowly began to come to life, like some mythical dragon waking from a long sleep, and the noise of gently hissing steam could be heard. The engineers diligently examined every component, raising the steam pressure to seek out any minor leaks or faulty connections in the labyrinth of pipes and valves, at times disappearing underneath the engine to search out any signs of escaping steam. At last, satisfied that all was in order, they signalled their intention to set it in motion.

The engine was standing at the end of a siding close to the canal, about a hundred yards from the point where it joined the main line. Climbing onto the footplate, Mark pushed a large lever forward, then, taking another in his hand pulled it hard towards him. For a few moments, as everyone held their breath, nothing happened. Then, to the accompaniment of a great roar of escaping steam, the two pistons, one on either side, slowly and smoothly began to move, causing the wheels to turn and the engine to move forward, steadily increasing in speed.

A mighty cry went up from the crowd as the engine trundled along the track; hats were thrown into the air and everyone began to cheer. Little boys, held aloft on their fathers' shoulders, gazed in awe at the sight before them. This was a scene they would relate to their own children and grandchildren in years to come. And there were old men present, too, one of them born even before the time when Bonnie Prince Charlie had marched south from Scotland to try and take the English throne, until he had been turned back at Derby. What wonders had these old men lived to witness! Then someone started to sing 'for he's a jolly good fellow' and all the crowd joined in as Mark and Luke, to their utter delight, stood up on the footplate, doffed their peaked caps and took a bow.

The test was a complete success and work started at once on the second engine. So confident were the directors that it too would be completed in time, that they confirmed that the formal opening day for the Nottingham and Leen Valley Railway would be on Friday 27th September. The local newspapers carried detailed reports of the testing of the engine, and announced the arrangements for the opening ceremony. And the directors, pleased at the way things had progressed, and relieved that, at long last, their plans were about to become a reality, held a small celebratory dinner at The White Lion Hotel.

But in the north of the county, a man, embittered and alone, sat in his library reading these reports and made a mental note of the opening date, 27th September. He remembered that date very well. How could he possibly forget it? He recalled a previous celebration he had attended in Nottingham on that very same date many years before, a dinner party to celebrate the eighteenth birthday of Abigail Daniels, or Abigail Brown as she was then. That should have been the day when she agreed to marry him. Instead, she had humiliated him in front of the entire gathering and rejected him in favour of William Daniels. And he vowed to himself that this time he would give her a birthday present she would remember for the rest of her life.

CHAPTER TWENTY-FIVE

—

NOTTINGHAM 1833

The day of the opening dawned bright with a slight breeze. The previous few days had been hectic for everyone connected with the railway, with last minute arrangements being made to ensure everything went smoothly. The company had been recruiting employees for many weeks and William had taken on the task of organising the training of these men for their various positions. Most of the work was new, certainly for the recruits, and even William had only limited experience of the knowledge and skills required in the operation of a steam railway. So the company had arranged for Ralph Armstrong to come down from Newcastle and oversee the necessary training. It was Ralph who had conducted William and Gilbert on their tour around Tyneside when they had first gone to inspect the railways already operating there. Ralph had a lifetime's experience, both in mining and the working of colliery railways and was an authority on all aspects of these industries. A better man could not have been found to help them. The only problem was that at first most of the recruits could barely understand a word he said. But they soon got used to his Geordie accent, and by the opening day, the company was satisfied that Ralph had achieved everything he had been asked to do.

The second engine had been completed in good time, and Ralph, along with Mark and Luke, had spent many days training the drivers and firemen. A number of test runs had been made over the line, not only for the purposes of tuition, but also to check and finely tune the engines and ensure that the track and other engineering features were sound. These test runs soon began to attract large crowds of people, and some of them, unaccustomed to the dangers that the engines could pose, climbed over the fences to get a closer look and wandered along the track, oblivious to the risks they were taking. Some of the more youthful and adventurous individuals even tried to race the engines, both on foot and on horseback.

William rose early on the morning of the twenty-seventh. There was much to be done that day, and the directors had agreed they would all meet at the railway wharf at seven o'clock sharp. But before he left home William took a few minutes to wish Abigail a very happy birthday. Along with all the other directors' wives, Abigail had been invited to the opening ceremony and banquet, but as the baby was due shortly she had not yet made up her mind whether to attend, but had already decided not to travel on the inaugural train.

'I'll see how I feel later,' she told William before he set off. 'I might get along for the banquet. I know it doesn't start till about three o'clock, so if I'm not too tired I'll join you. But if I'm not there, don't worry. I'll be quite all right and Millie's here should I need anything. I do hope everything goes well, and make sure you enjoy every minute of today. You've worked so hard to make this happen; it deserves to succeed.'

'Thanks, Abigail. Oh, by the way, I've arranged for Samuel and Edward to go to the navvies' hog roast this afternoon. I know they weren't involved with the railway construction but they both said they fancied joining in, and after everything they've done for us recently it was the least I could do. Anyway, I asked them to call here on their way, so they can bring you along if you decide to come. Benjamin will also join them if he's not too busy.'

William kissed Abigail goodbye and set off in his gig for the short drive to Lenton. Ralph, Mark and Luke had already been there for several hours, having arrived early to get up steam and make last minute checks of the engines, whilst half a dozen boys were busy with oily rags giving them a final polish. Both had been painted in a deep shade of green, lined out in crimson and yellow, with all the brass fittings polished to a mirror-like finish. The train was already positioned next to a temporary platform, and consisted of the three passenger coaches and five open goods wagons, each of which had been specially fitted with seats and cushions, and an awning in case of rain. In all there were seats for a hundred and fifty. The train was not due to depart until eleven o'clock, but many of the guests had begun to arrive much earlier, eager not to miss any of the excitement of this momentous and unique occasion. The whole wharf area was bedecked with flags, streamers and bunting, and the caterers were hard at work setting up the temporary dining hall in the warehouse, arranging tables and chairs, and laying out cutlery, crockery and wine glasses.

The directors were soon busy greeting their guests, showing them around and answering their many questions, until at a quarter to eleven the chairman requested that all the ladies and gentlemen should now take their seats on the train. The two engines had already been attached at the front, and at eleven o'clock precisely, to the sound of a postillion's horn, the train slowly began to move forward, out of the terminus and onto the main line. The wharf area had been cordoned off to prevent spectators encroaching onto the site, but nothing was going to stop the townsfolk from witnessing this auspicious event. On each side of the line, men, women and children stood and watched, cheering as the train made its triumphal way northwards. It was soon out into the country and gathering speed, and as it passed through Basford and Bulwell it seemed that all work must have stopped for the day, so large were the crowds. Just north of Hucknall it passed the new colliery, where in a siding stood the string of loaded coal wagons that would be attached to the train on its return. But, as it passed by, none of the colliers who had assembled to view the spectacle, and certainly nobody on the train, noticed a figure that crept out from behind a hut and quickly climbed into one of the loaded wagons.

After a journey of about an hour the train arrived at the northern terminus of the line at Linby. The two engines were uncoupled and run to the other end of the train, and, after taking on water, were ready to set off on the return journey.

Before long the train was again approaching Hucknall, where it came to a stand alongside the colliery. The engines were uncoupled, and proceeded to shunt the coal wagons from the colliery siding and attach them to the front of the train. As soon as they were ready they set off once more. The passengers were now at the rear of the train, and, as it went round the various curves, they were able to look forward and see the whole line of wagons snaking round the bends, the engines effortlessly drawing the whole procession onwards, steam and smoke billowing from their chimneys, whilst the rhythmical exhaust beat from the pistons and the regular *clunk clunk* of the wheels passing over the rail joints added an almost musical accompaniment to the whole exhilarating experience.

As the train continued on its way, the crowds seemed to have grown, as even more people turned out, determined not to miss this historic occasion. Eventually, it slowed down as it reached its destination, and at a walking pace turned into the railway wharf, whereupon the town band struck up with a resounding rendition of 'See The Conquering Hero Comes'. Once the train had come to a stand the guests began to alight, and were immediately ushered into the warehouse, suitably festooned with bunting, and decked out with large vases of flowers. Four long tables had been set out, each heaving with plates of tempting and mouthwatering dishes, and bottles of vintage wine. Once the guests were seated, the chairman of the company requested silence, and, after a short speech extolling the virtues of the enterprise, proposed a toast to the success of the railway. More speeches followed, from the mayor and other dignitaries, each expressing their confidence in the contribution the railway would make to the town's prosperity, after which the feast began in earnest, the diners being entertained by the band as it played a selection of popular melodies.

An hour or so later, the drained wine bottles and empty plates bore witness that the banquet had been enjoyed by all. Gradually, the guests began to disperse, and a succession of carriages pulled up alongside the warehouse to take them back to their homes.

In the adjacent field, however, a real shindig was still in full swing. Hundreds of navvies and other railway employees were having the time of their lives, with ample supplies of roast pork and beef and an endless stream of beer. Abigail had not turned up for the banquet, which didn't surprise William, considering her present condition, so he decided to walk over and see if he could find Samuel and Edward, to ask how she was when they had called for her.

As he walked towards the field, he passed the train of coal wagons brought down from Hucknall. This had been a day of celebration but work had to go on, and now the banquet was over one of the engines had started to shunt the wagons into sidings alongside the canal, ready for the coal to be transhipped into waiting boats. William soon found

Samuel and Edward, along with Benjamin, and the three of them were having a rare old time.

'Follow me,' he said 'and you can have a look at how things work. They've just started shunting the wagons, and if you want I'll have a word with the driver; I'm sure he'll let you join him on the footplate.'

'You go on ahead, Samuel,' said Edward. 'Me and Benjamin will just finish our drinks, then we'll join you.' Samuel followed William, who went and spoke to the driver.

'Come on, Samuel, climb up and you can see what it's like to ride on a railway engine. I'll leave you to it, though, as I must get back to the warehouse. There are one or two things I need to sort out before I go home.'

William started to walk back to the warehouse, and was just passing the line of wagons when suddenly, without warning, a voice from behind spoke his name. He instantly remembered this voice from the past. It had been a long time, but there was no doubt in his mind to whom it belonged. William turned round and saw the man climbing down from one of the wagons. He was dressed in scruffy clothes, covered in coal dust, as were his face and hands, but William knew him all the same. This was not how Josiah Sidmouth normally looked, but nothing could disguise those features. Josiah was now standing facing William, no more than nine or ten yards away, and in each hand he held a pistol. William recognised them straight away for what they were: duelling pistols.

It had been many years since the two men had confronted each other. Fifteen to be precise. To the very day, in fact. William looked at Josiah, and whilst he had aged, there was no disguising the same old arrogance and look of pure hatred on his face. It only took an instant for William to guess Josiah's intentions and the danger he now faced, and he knew he had to try and play for time.

'What do you want?' asked William.

'Isn't that obvious, Daniels? You know exactly what I want, what I wanted, but you took her from me. I've waited fifteen years for this moment and now you're going to pay for what you've done to me. It's Abigail's birthday today, isn't it? Well, I'm going to leave her with a present she'll never forget.' Slowly, he raised his right hand and pointed the pistol directly at William.

For a split second he froze, waiting for the flash of powder as the trigger was pulled. Then, in an attempt to avoid the shot, he threw himself to the ground, hoping to crawl beneath one of the wagons for cover. But he was too late, for as he did so he heard the crack of the pistol, and felt a sudden stinging sensation in his left thigh. The ball had found its mark, but not the one Josiah was aiming for. William instinctively put his hand to his leg and felt warm blood flowing from the wound. He was in such pain that he was barely able to move, but knew he had to try and get under the wagon for protection, when suddenly, with a jolt, it began to roll forward. William waited helplessly, expecting at any second to hear the second pistol shot, but instead, there came the cry of a familiar voice.

'Put it down, Sidmouth, drop that pistol, or God help me I'll crush your skull like a rotten apple.' William looked up, and to his sheer joy and relief he saw the reassuring figure of Samuel. He was holding a long-handled coal hammer which he swung menacingly from side-to-side. From his position high up on the footplate of the engine, Samuel had seen Josiah pointing the pistol at William. As fast as he could, he had leapt down, grabbing the hammer as he went, and rushed to protect his brother. Slowly, Samuel moved to place himself between Josiah and William.

'You don't know me, do you Sidmouth? But I know all about you. Your man Giles told me everything. You thought he'd keep his mouth shut, but he squealed like a stuck pig when I got to work on him. I told him I wasn't going to stand by and do nothing when he threatened my family, and now I'm telling you.'

'So you're Samuel Daniels. Your reputation goes before you. You might have put one over Giles, but you don't frighten me. You're a nobody, a Narrow Marsh gaolbird. Think you can protect your brother? Well, just look at him now, grovelling down there in the dirt where he belongs. I'll finish him off first, then I'll deal with you.'

'Gaolbird, eh? I suppose it takes one to know one. But for all your money and your fancy ways, you're nothing but a loser, Sidmouth. You lost Abigail; you lost your house; you even lost your bank. And now you could be about to lose your life,' taunted Samuel. 'All you've got left is one shot, and there's two of us. So drop your pistol. I've told you once, nobody threatens my family and gets away with it.'

But Josiah was beyond listening to reason. Samuel's gibes had only served to make him even angrier. He raised his second pistol, trying to get a clear sight of William and take aim. Samuel, realising the danger, hurled the coal hammer at Josiah then lunged himself straight at him. The hammer struck a glancing blow on Josiah's right arm, but he managed to hold on to the loaded pistol in his left hand.

William looked up to see the two of them grappling and wrestling with each other. Alongside, the wagons continued to trundle past. Samuel, determined to disarm Josiah, and using all his strength, threw him to one side but as he did so, there came a crack as the second pistol was fired. Samuel slumped to the ground, and Josiah, unable to regain his balance, stumbled towards the tracks. The wagons had already been uncoupled from each other and were moving separately. With a curse on his lips, Josiah then fell between two of them. He disappeared from sight and after a brief pause, there followed a bloodcurdling scream. Then the screaming stopped, but the wagons moved on. William looked round, and the grisly sight that met his eyes was something that would haunt him for years. For when Josiah had fallen, it had been across, and not between the rails. The cast iron wheels under the weight of five tons of coal had sliced through his soft flesh like a hot knife through butter, leaving his torn and twisted body scattered across the tracks.

Samuel lay motionless where he had fallen. He had taken the full force of the shot at close range and blood was gushing freely from a hole in his chest. William managed to drag himself to his brother's side and put an arm under his head to raise it off the ground.

'Samuel, speak to me. It's me, William.' Samuel slowly opened his eyes and looked up.

'Did I stop him William? I told him I wouldn't let him harm you. Are you safe?'

'Yes, Samuel, you stopped him. For ever. He'll never harm anyone again.'

'I'm glad about that. I told him, nobody threatens my family and gets away with it.' And as he spoke these words, Samuel's eyes closed again, for the last time.

William was still cradling Samuel in his arms when Edward and Benjamin appeared. They had come looking for Samuel and had heard the shots, but were devastated at the shocking sight which met their eyes. Poor Samuel, lying there, devoid of life. Ten minutes earlier he had been living it up with the rest of them, the life and soul of the party. And never had they seen William so utterly distraught. It was with the greatest difficulty that they persuaded him he must get to a doctor before he lost any more blood. The gig was brought round and William was helped in. Benjamin then took down one of the large decorative flags and he and Edward wrapped Samuel's body in it and placed it alongside William in the gig, and quickly they made their way back to William's house.

An hour later William was being examined by the doctor, who removed the ball lodged in his thigh and bandaged the wound. 'You'll be fine, no lasting damage done. But you'll have to rest for some time. See to it that he does, Mrs Daniels! He'll need the dressing changing every few days. Have you someone who can help you? You really shouldn't be straining yourself right now, not in your condition.'

'We'll manage,' replied Abigail, quietly. After the doctor had left, she sat with William by his bedside trying to comfort him as tears silently fell down his face. She had never seen him so distressed, and although she too had been badly affected by the tragic events of that fateful afternoon, she knew she had to be strong and supportive. 'What's happened is a dreadful tragedy,' said Abigail, softly, 'but I'm sure Samuel didn't suffer. You know he always looked up to you, and looked out for you. And he saved your life. If it hadn't have been for him, I believe Josiah would have killed you. We'll all miss Samuel terribly. I know I will, but he wouldn't want you to be so sad. He'd want you to remember all the good times you had.'

'You're right, Abigail, we'll all miss him terribly. And things won't ever be the same again, not without Samuel around. We did have some good times in the past. But we had some lean times too, especially when we were kids living in Narrow Marsh. And we're rid of Josiah now. He can't ever be a threat to us again and it's Samuel we have to thank for that. I remember the very last words he said: *"nobody threatens my family and gets away with it"*. He was true to his word, he always was. He saved my life. If we have a boy, Abigail, I think we should name him after the uncle he'll never get to know.'

The funeral took place three days later at St. Mary's Church and was attended by a large congregation of family and friends. The doctor had advised William against leaving the house too soon, but nothing could have stopped him saying goodbye to his brother. After the funeral, the mourners went to The Durham Ox, where Edward had arranged for the wake to be held. It was one of Samuel's favourite haunts, a place where he had spent so many happy hours, and everyone present drank to his memory and reminisced about him with great affection.

And then, just a week after Samuel had been buried, it was Abigail's turn to grieve, when her mother and father received a letter from the Colonel of The South Gloucestershire Regiment, informing them that their son, Lieutenant Peter Brown, had died from wounds received defending settlers from a rebel attack whilst on duty in Canada, and had been buried with the usual military honours.

'They say things come in threes,' said Abigail. 'I haven't shed a tear for Josiah, but now we've both lost a brother. I know Peter and I had our differences, but his death has come as an awful shock. And I do so wish you and Peter had been able to make things up. It was Josiah who was responsible for the rift between you, but Peter had at last come to realise what he was really like. I think the two of you could have become friends, but it's too late now. Oh dear, William, I'll be glad when this year's over.'

It was now William's turn to support his wife. He held her in his arms as she sobbed gently. 'Don't cry, Abigail, remember what you told me. Just think of the good times. I agree, though, I'll be glad to see the back of this year, too. So much achieved, yet so much tragedy. But we should both try and look on the bright side now. There's Benjamin's wedding soon, and then, God willing, there'll be a christening to look forward to as well.'

With everything that had been going on, Benjamin and his bride-to-be, Rachel, had agreed to delay their wedding. Then, in mid-November, Abigail gave birth. And it was a boy. And she and William were both secretly thrilled about it.

'Look,' said William when he first set eyes on his new son, 'he's got

Samuel's nose and chin, just like his granddad.'

'Yes he has,' said Abigail, cradling the new baby in her arms. 'And if he has Samuel's charm and determination he won't go far wrong. Not forgetting your brains, of course, William!'

It was decided to hold a double ceremony, and on the same day in early December, with William acting as best man, Benjamin and Rachel were married and immediately afterwards the new baby was christened. No sooner had Benjamin tied the knot than he was back at the altar, this time as godfather, with Millie as godmother to their new nephew, Samuel Daniels.

There were so many guests invited to the celebrations, that a large room was hired at The White Lion for the combined wedding breakfast and christening feast. Once the guests had finished eating, William, as the best man, rose to make his speech. After toasting the bride and groom, and wishing them all future happiness, he declared that there was something else he wanted to say.

'While we're all here together, I'd like to take this opportunity to say just a few more words. Not too many, I promise you, as I'm still not up to standing for long just at the moment! Twelve years ago I was an exile in France, fearful of returning and facing arrest for a crime I hadn't committed. But thanks to my good old friend John Collins, God rest his soul, and to Abigail of course, I was able to return and clear my name. And now, here we are, twelve years on, and I have everything any man could ever hope for; a loving wife and five healthy children; a magnificent house; a thriving business and a seat on the board of the new railway.

'And so I'd now like to propose a few more toasts. First, to my new son, Samuel; may he live long and grow wise. To George and Alice, who saved us from bankruptcy and made us a gift of our home. To Edward, who came back from France, took Samuel under his wing and became his comrade-in-arms.

'But, most of all, to the one who saved the lives of Charles and Catherine and then mine, and in so doing, selflessly gave his own - Samuel, the best brother a man could ever wish for. So raise your glasses everyone, and God bless you all!'

Before you start *Leen Times*, read …

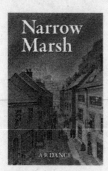

NARROW MARSH

An exciting historical saga set in
Nottingham in the early years of
the 19th century

Nottingham, 1811 - a time of fear and hardship for the town's framework knitters. With low wages and long working hours, desperate men turn to direct action. And when a man is killed, someone has to pay the ultimate price. Young William Daniels witnesses the public execution, and from that day onwards he develops a burning desire for justice and freedom. But his chance encounter with the headstrong daughter of a wealthy factory owner sets in motion a tumultuous chain of events that will change his life forever. Set in early 19th century Nottingham, in an era of bitter social unrest, *Narrow Marsh* is a dramatic story of life, love and hope.

'One of the best novels I have read. The story just flew through my fingers and I couldn't turn the pages fast enough.'
East Midlands Arts

'A highly evocative story of early 19th century high and low life. At its heart, one of England's most notorious slums. Unputdownable.'
John Brunton, journalist and author

'The sense of overriding hope against unrest and misfortune will stay with you long after you finish this rewarding novel.'
Nottinghamshire Today

Narrow Marsh is published by Arundel Books
ISBN 978-0-9558133-0-6

Available from all good book shops, price £6.99
Also available post-free direct from the publisher.
Please send cheques payable to Arundel Books.

Coming soon …

THE WESTBROOK AFFAIR

A R DANCE

Young Joseph Lambert has enjoyed all the childhood privileges befitting the son of a wealthy Yorkshire squire. But when his widowed father is mysteriously killed in a riding accident, his comfortable world is suddenly torn apart. Joseph's elder brother, the dissolute and self-indulgent Miles, inherits the estate and promptly abandons his young brother, leaving him to fend for himself.

Determined to seek his fortune, the thirteen-year-old orphan makes his way to Sheffield where he secures an apprenticeship in a cutlery factory. Seven years later, now an accomplished and skilled craftsman, he marries Hannah and soon a daughter, Eliza, is born.

But barely is Eliza old enough to know her father, when tragedy strikes. Hannah is struggling to support herself and her daughter, when one day an old lady arrives with an astonishing tale to tell.

And slowly, a forgotten family secret begins to unfold.

Set in Yorkshire and Nottinghamshire in the mid-19th century, *The Westbrook Affair* is a gripping story of poverty and wealth, betrayal and greed, and ultimately the search for justice and the truth.

The Westbrook Affair will be published by Arundel Books in 2012